The first romance stories **Stephanie Laurens** read were set against the backdrop of Regency England, and these continue to exert a special attraction for her. As an escape from the dry world of professional science, Stephanie started writing Regency romances, and she is now a *New York Times*, *USA Today* and *Publishers Weekly* bestselling author.

Stephanie lives in a leafy suburb of Melbourne, Australia, with her husband and two daughters, along with two cats, Shakespeare and Marlowe.

Learn more about Stephanie's books from her website at www.stephanielaurens.com

Praise for Stephanie Laurens:

'This sensual tale of lust and seduction in 19th century England will leave you weak at the knees'
Now

'Stephanie Laurens' heroines are marvellous tributes to Georgette Heyer: feisty and strong'
Cathy Kelly

'Sinfully sexy and deliciously irresistible'
Booklist

Mastered by
Love

A Bastion Club Novel

Stephanie
LAURENS

piatkus

PIATKUS

First published in the US in 2009 by Avon Books,
an imprint of HarperCollins Publishers, New York
First published in Great Britain as a paperback original in 2009 by Piatkus
by arrangement with Avon
Reprinted 2009 (twice), 2010 (twice), 2011

A CIP catalogue record for this book
is available from the British Library.

ISBN 978-0-7499-4013-3

Typeset in Baskerville by M Rules
Printed in the UK by CPI Mackays, Chatham ME5 8TD

Papers used by Piatkus are from well-managed forests
and other responsible sources.

MIX
Paper from
responsible sources
FSC® C104740

Piatkus
An imprint of
Little, Brown Book Group
100 Victoria Embankment
London EC4Y 0DY

An Hachette UK Company
www.hachette.co.uk

www.piatkus.co.uk

Mastered by Love

The Bastion Club

"a last bastion against the
matchmakers of the ton"

MEMBERS

#7 ~~Christian Allardyce~~   *Lady*
~~Marquess of Dearne~~   *Letitia*
                              Randall

#2 ~~Anthony Blake,~~   *Alicia*
~~Viscount Torrington~~   *"Carrington"*
                              Pevensey

~~#5 Jocelyn Deverell~~   *Phoebe*
~~Viscount Paignton~~   *Malleson*

#1 THE LADY CHOSEN
#2 A GENTLEMAN'S HONOR
#3 A LADY OF HIS OWN
#4 A FINE PASSION

#3 ~~Charles St. Austell,~~
~~Earl of Lostwithiel~~

*Lady
Penelope
Selborne*

#6 ~~Gervase Tregarth,~~
~~Earl of Crowhurst~~

*Madeline
Gascoigne*

#4 ~~Jack Warnefleet,~~
~~Baron Warnefleet of~~
~~Minchinbury~~

*Lady Clarice
Attwood*

#1 ~~Tristan Wemyss,~~
~~Earl of Trentham~~

*Leonora
Carling*

#5 TO DISTRACTION
#6 BEYOND SEDUCTION
#7 THE EDGE OF DESIRE

Chapter 1

September 1816
Coquetdale, Northumbria

It wasn't supposed to have been like this.

Wrapped in his greatcoat, alone on the box seat of his excellently sprung curricle, Royce Henry Varisey, tenth Duke of Wolverstone, turned the latest in the succession of post-horses he'd raced up the highway from London onto the minor road leading to Sharperton and Harbottle. The gently rounded foothills of the Cheviot Hills gathered him in like a mother's arms; Wolverstone Castle, his childhood home and newly inherited principal estate, lay close by the village of Alwinton, beyond Harbottle.

One of the horses broke stride; Royce checked it, held the pair back until they were in step, then urged them on. They were flagging. His own high-bred blacks had carried him as far as St. Neots on Monday; thereafter he'd had a fresh pair put to every fifty or so miles.

It was now Wednesday morning, and he was a long way from London, once again – after sixteen long years – entering home territory. Ancestral territory. Rothbury and the dark glades of its forest lay behind him; ahead the rolling, largely treeless skirts of the Cheviots, dotted here and there with the inevitable sheep, spread around the even more barren hills themselves, their backbone the border with Scotland beyond.

The hills, and that border, had played a vital role in the evolution of the dukedom. Wolverstone had been created after the Conquest as a marcher lordship to protect England from the depredations of marauding Scots. Successive dukes, popularly known as the Wolves of the North, had for centuries enjoyed the privileges of royalty within their domains.

Many would argue they still did.

Certainly they'd remained a supremely powerful clan, their wealth augmented by their battlefield prowess, and protected by their success in convincing successive sovereigns that such wily, politically powerful ex-kingmakers were best left alone, left to hold the Middle March as they had since first setting their elegantly shod Norman feet on English soil.

Royce studied the terrain with an eye honed by absence. Reminded of his ancestry, he wondered anew if their traditional marcher independence – originally fought for and won, recognized by custom and granted by royal charter, then legally rescinded but never truly taken away, and even less truly given up – hadn't underpinned the rift between his father and him.

His father had belonged to the old school of lordship, one that had included the majority of his peers. According to their creed, loyalty to either country or sovereign was a commodity to be traded and bought, something both Crown and country had to place a suitable price upon before it was granted. More, to dukes and earls of his father's ilk, "country" had an ambiguous meaning; as kings in their own domains, those domains were their primary concern while the realm possessed a more nebulous and distant existence, certainly a lesser claim on their honor.

While Royce would allow that swearing fealty to the present monarchy – mad King George and his dissolute son, the Prince Regent – wasn't an attractive proposition, he held no equivocation over swearing allegiance, and service, to his country – to England.

As the only son of a powerful ducal family and thus barred by long custom from serving in the field, when, at the tender age of twenty-two, he'd been approached to create a network of English spies on foreign soil, he'd leapt at the chance. Not only had it offered the prospect of contributing to Napoleon's defeat, but with his extensive personal and family contacts combined with his inherent ability to inspire and command, the position was tailor-made; from the first it had fitted him like a glove.

But to his father the position had been a disgrace to the name and title, a blot on the family escutcheon; his old-fashioned views had labeled spying as without question dishonorable, even if one were spying on active military enemies. It was a view shared by many senior peers at the time.

Bad enough, but when Royce had refused to decline the commission, his father had organized an ambush. A public one, in White's, at a time of the evening when the club was always crowded. With his cronies at his back, his father had passed public judgment on Royce in strident and excoriating terms.

As his peroration, his father had triumphantly declared that if Royce refused to bow to his edict and instead served in the capacity for which he'd been recruited, then it would be as if he, the ninth duke, had no son.

Even in the white rage his father's attack had provoked, Royce had noted that "as if." He was his father's only legitimate son; no matter how furious, his father would not formally disinherit him. The interdict would, however, banish him from all family lands.

Facing his apoplectic sire over the crimson carpet of the exclusive club, surrounded by an army of fascinated aristocracy, he'd waited, unresponsive, until his father had finished his well-rehearsed speech. He'd waited until the expectant silence surrounding them had grown thick, then he'd uttered three words: *As you wish.*

Then he'd turned and walked from the club, and from that day forth had ceased to be his father's son. From that day he'd been known as Dalziel, a name taken from an obscure branch of his mother's family tree, fitting enough given it was his maternal grandfather – by then dead – who had taught him the creed by which he'd chosen to live. While the Variseys were marcher lords, the Debraighs were no less powerful, but their lands lay in the heart of England and they'd served king and country – principally country – selflessly for centuries. Debraighs had stood as both warriors and statesmen at the right hand of countless monarchs; duty to their people was bred deeply in them.

While deploring the rift with his father, the Debraighs had approved Royce's stance, yet, sensitive even then to the dynamics of power, he'd discouraged their active support. His uncle, the Earl of Catersham, had written, asking if there was anything he could do. Royce had replied in the negative, as he had to his mother's similar query; his fight was with his father and should involve no one else.

That had been his decision, one he'd adhered to throughout the subsequent sixteen years; none of them had expected vanquishing Napoleon to take so long.

But it had.

Through those years he'd recruited the best of his generation of Guards, organized them into a network of secret operatives, and successfully placed them throughout Napoleon's territories. Their success had become the stuff of legend; those who knew correctly credited his network with saving countless British lives, and contributing directly to Napoleon's downfall.

His success on that stage had been sweet. However, with Napoleon on his way to St. Helena, he'd disbanded his crew, releasing them to their civilian lives. And, as of Monday, he, too, had left his former life – Dalziel's life – behind.

He hadn't, however, expected to assume any title beyond the courtesy one of Marquess of Winchelsea. Hadn't expected to immediately assume control of the dukedom and all it comprised.

His ongoing banishment – he'd never expected his father to back down any more than he himself had – had effectively estranged him from the dukedom's houses, lands, and people, and most especially from the one place that meant most to him – Wolverstone itself. The castle was far more than just a home; the stone walls and battlements held something – some magic – that resonated in his blood, in his heart, in his soul. His father had known that; it had been the same for him.

Despite the passage of sixteen years, as the horses raced on Royce still felt the pull, the visceral tug that only grew stronger as he rattled through Sharperton, drawing ever closer to Wolverstone. He felt faintly surprised that it should be so, that despite the years, the rift, his own less than susceptible temperament, he could still sense . . . home.

That home still meant what it always had.

That it still moved him to his soul.

He hadn't expected that, any more than he'd expected to be returning like this – alone, in a tearing rush, without even his longtime groom, Henry, another Wolverstone outcast, for company through the empty miles.

On Monday, while tidying the last of Dalziel's files from his desk, he'd been planning his return to Wolverstone. He'd imagined driving up from London by easy stages, arriving at the castle fresh and rested – in suitable state to walk into his father's presence . . . and see what came next.

He'd imagined an apology from his father might, just might, have featured in that scene; he'd been curious to see, yet hadn't been holding his breath.

But now he'd never know.

His father had died on Sunday.

Leaving the rift between them – vicious and deep, naturally enough given they were both Variseys – unhealed. Unaddressed. Unlaid to rest.

He hadn't known whether to curse his father or fate for leaving him to cauterize the wound.

Regardless, dealing with his past was no longer the most urgent matter on his plate. Picking up the reins of a far-flung and extensive dukedom after a sixteen-year absence was going to demand all his attention, command all of his abilities to the exclusion of all else. He would succeed – there was neither question nor option in that regard – but how long it would take, and what it would cost him . . . how the devil he was to do it, he didn't know.

It wasn't supposed to have been like this.

His father had been hale and healthy enough for a man in his sixties. He hadn't been ailing; Royce trusted that if he had, someone would have broken his father's prohibition and sent him word. Instead, he'd been blindsided.

In his version of his return, his father and he would have made their peace, their truce, whatever arrangement they would have made, then he would have started refreshing his knowledge of the estate, filling in the gap between when he'd been twenty-one, and last at Wolverstone, to his present thirty-seven.

Instead, his father was gone, leaving him to pick up the reins with a lag of sixteen years in knowledge hanging like a millstone around his neck.

While he had absolute confidence – Varisey confidence – that he would fill his father's shoes more than adequately, he wasn't looking forward to assuming emergency command over unfamiliar troops in terrain that would have shifted in unforeseen ways over the past sixteen years.

His temper, like that of all Variseys, especially the males, was formidable, an emotion that carried the same cutting edge as their broadswords of long ago. He'd learned to control it rather better than his father, to keep it reined, another weapon to be used to conquer and overcome; not even those who knew him well could detect the difference between mild irritation and a killing rage. Not unless he wished them to know. Control of his emotions had long become second nature.

Ever since he'd learned of his father's demise, his temper had been surging, restless, largely unreasoning, violently hungry for some release. Knowing the only release that would satisfy had, courtesy of fickle fate, been denied him forever.

Not having any enemy to lash out at, to exact vengeance from, left him walking a tightrope, his impulses and instincts tightly leashed.

Stony-faced, he swept through Harbottle. A woman walking along the street glanced curiously at him. While he was clearly heading for Wolverstone, there being no other destination along this road to which a gentleman of his ilk might be going, he had numerous male cousins, and they all shared more than a passing resemblance; even if the woman had heard of his father's death, it was unlikely she would realize it was he.

Since Sharperton the road had followed the banks of the Coquet; over the drumming of the horses' hooves, he'd heard the river burbling along its rocky bed. Now the road curved north; a stone bridge spanned the river. The curricle rattled across; he drew a tight breath as he crossed into Wolverstone lands.

Felt that indefinable connection grip and tighten.

Straightening on the seat, stretching the long muscles in his back, he eased the horses' pace, and looked around.

Drank in the familiar sights, each emblazoned in his memory. Most were as he'd expected – exactly as he recalled, only sixteen years older.

A ford lay ahead, spanning the River Alwin; he slowed the horses and let them pick their way across. As the wheels drew free of the water, he flicked the reins and set the pair up the slight rise, the road curving again, this time to the west.

The curricle topped the rise, and he slowed the horses to a walk.

The slate roofs of Alwinton lay directly ahead. Closer, on his left, between the road and the Coquet, sat the gray stone church with its vicarage and three cottages. He barely spared a glance for the church, his gaze drawn past it, across the river to the massive gray stone edifice that rose in majestic splendor beyond.

Wolverstone Castle.

The heavily fortified square Norman keep, added to and rebuilt by successive generations, remained the central and dominant feature, its crenellated battlements rising above the lower roofs of the early Tudor wings, both uniquely doglegged, one running west, then north, the other east, then south. The keep faced north, looking directly up a narrow valley through which Clennell Street, one of the border crossings, descended from the hills. Neither raiders, nor traders, could cross the border by that route without passing under Wolverstone's ever-watchful eyes.

From this distance, he could make out little beyond the main buildings. The castle stood on gently sloping land above the gorge the Coquet had carved west of Alwinton village. The castle's park spread to east, south, and west, the land continuing to rise, eventually becoming hills that sheltered the castle on the south and west. The Cheviots themselves protected the castle from the north winds; only from the east, the direction from which the road approached, was the castle vulnerable to even the elements.

This had always been his first sight of home. Despite all, he felt the connection lock, felt the rising tide of affinity surge.

The reins tugged; he'd let the horses come to a halt. Flicking the ribbons, he set them trotting as he looked about even more keenly.

Fields, fences, crops, and cottages appeared in reasonable order. He went through the village – not much more than a hamlet – at a steady clip. The villagers would recognize him; some might even hail him, but he wasn't yet ready to trade greetings, to accept condolences on his father's death – not yet.

Another stone bridge spanned the deep, narrow gorge through which the river gushed and tumbled. The gorge was the reason no army had even attempted to take Wolverstone; the sole approach was via the stone bridge – easily defended. Because of the hills on all other sides, it was impossible to position mangonels or any type of siege engine anywhere that wasn't well within a decent archer's range from the battlements.

Royce swept over the bridge, the clatter of the horses' hooves drowned beneath the tumultuous roar of the waters rushing, turbulent and wild, below. Just like his temper. The closer he drew to the castle, to what awaited him there, the more powerful the surge of his emotions grew. The more unsettling and distracting.

The more hungry, vengeful, and demanding.

The huge wrought-iron gates lay ahead, set wide as they always were; the depiction of a snarling wolf's head in the center of each matched the bronze statues atop the stone columns from which the gates hung.

With a flick of the reins, he sent the horses racing through. As if sensing the end of their journey, they leaned into the harness; trees flashed past, massive ancient oaks bordering the lawns that rolled away on either side. He barely noticed, his attention – all his senses – locked on the building towering before him.

It was as massive and as anchored in the soil as the oaks. It had stood for so many centuries it had become part of the landscape.

He slowed the horses as they neared the forecourt, drinking in the gray stone, the heavy lintels, the deeply recessed windows, diamond paned and leaded, set into the thick walls. The front door lay within a high stone arch; it had originally been a portcullis, not a door, the front hall beyond, with its arched ceiling, originally a tunnel leading into the inner bailey. The front façade, three stories high, had been formed from the castle's inner bailey wall; the outer bailey wall had been dismantled long ago, while the keep itself lay deeper within the house.

Letting the horses walk along the façade, Royce gave himself the moment, let emotion reign for just that while. Yet the indescribable joy of being home again was deeply shadowed, caught up, tangled, in a web of darker feelings; being this close to his father – to where his father should have been, but no longer was – only whetted the already razor-sharp edge of his restless, unforgiving anger.

Irrational anger – anger with no object. Yet he still felt it.

Dragging in a breath, filling his lungs with the cool, crisp air, he set his jaw and sent the horses trotting on around the house.

As he rounded the north wing and the stables came into view, he reminded himself that he would find no convenient opponent at the castle with whom he could loose his temper, with whom he could release the deep, abiding anger.

Resigned himself to another night of a splitting head and no sleep.

His father was gone.

It wasn't supposed to have been like this.

Ten minutes later, he strode into the house via a side door, the one he'd always used. The few minutes in the stables hadn't helped his temper; the head stableman, Milbourne, hailed from long ago, and had offered his condolences and welcomed him back.

He'd acknowledged the well-meant words with a curt nod, left the post-horses to Milbourne's care, then remembered and paused to tell him that Henry – Milbourne's nephew – would be arriving shortly with Royce's own pair. He'd wanted to ask who else of the long-ago staff were still there, but hadn't; Milbourne had looked too understanding, leaving him feeling . . . exposed.

Not a feeling he liked.

His greatcoat swirling about his booted calves, he headed for the west stairs. Pulling off his driving gloves, he stuffed them into a pocket, then took the shallow steps three at a time.

He'd spent the last forty-eight hours alone, had just arrived – and now needed to be alone again, to absorb and in some way subdue the unexpectedly intense feelings returning like this had stirred. He needed to quiet his restless temper and leash it more firmly.

The first floor gallery lay ahead. He took the last stairs in a rush, stepped into the gallery, swung left toward the west tower – and collided with a woman.

He heard her gasp.

Sensed her stumbling and caught her – closed his hands about her shoulders and steadied her. Held her.

Even before he looked into her face, he didn't want to let her go.

His gaze locked on her eyes, wide and flaring, rich brown with gold flecks, framed by lush brown lashes. Her long hair was lustrous wheat-gold silk, wound and anchored high on her head. Her skin was creamy perfection, her nose patrician straight, her face heart-shaped, her chin neatly rounded. Itemizing those features in a glance, his gaze fixed on her lips. Rose-petal pink, parted in shocked surprise, the lower lushly tempting, the urge to crush them beneath his was nearly overpowering.

She'd taken him unawares; he hadn't had the slightest inkling she'd been there, gliding along, the thick runner muffling her footsteps. He'd patently shocked her; her wide eyes and parted lips said she hadn't heard him on the stairs, either – he'd probably been moving silently, as he habitually did.

She'd staggered back; an inch separated his hard body from her much softer one. He knew it was soft, had felt her ripe figure imprinted down the front of him, seared on his senses in that instant of fleeting contact.

On a rational level he wondered how a lady of her type came to be wandering these halls, while on a more primitive plane he battled the urge to sweep her up, carry her into his room, and ease the sudden, shockingly intense ache in his groin – and distract his temper in the only possible way, one he hadn't even dreamed would be available.

That more primitive side of him saw it as only right that this female – whoever she was – should be walking just there, at just that time, and was just the right female to render him that singular service.

Anger, even rage, could convert into lust; he was familiar with the transformation, yet never had it struck with such speed or strength. Never before had the result threatened his control.

The consuming lust he felt for her in that instant was so intense it shocked even him.

Enough to have him slapping the urge down, clenching his jaw, tightening his grip, and bodily setting her aside.

He had to force his hands to release her.

"My apologies." His voice was close to a growl. With a curt nod in her direction, without again meeting her eyes, he strode on, swiftly putting distance between them.

Behind him he heard the hiss of an indrawn breath, heard the rustle of skirts as she swung and stared.

"Royce! Dalziel – whatever you call yourself these days – stop!"

He kept walking.

"Damn it, I am not going to – *refuse to* – scurry after you!"

He halted. Head rising, he considered the list of those who would dare address him in such words, in such a tone.

The list wasn't long.

Slowly, he half turned and looked back at the lady, who patently didn't know in what danger she stood. Scurry after him? She should be fleeing in the opposite direction. But . . .

Long-ago recollection finally connected with present fact. Those rich autumn eyes were the key. He frowned. "Minerva?"

Those fabulous eyes were no longer wide, but narrowed in irritation; her lush lips had compressed to a grim line.

"Indeed." She hesitated, then, clasping her hands before her, lifted her chin. "I gather you aren't aware of it, but I'm chatelaine here."

Contrary to Minerva's expectation, the information did not produce any softening in the stony face regarding her. No easing of the rigid line of his lips, no gleam of recognition in his dark eyes – no suggestion that he'd realized she was someone he needed to help him, even though, at last, he'd placed her: Minerva Miranda Chesterton, his mother's childhood friend's orphaned daughter. Subsequently his mother's amanuensis, companion, and confidante, more recently the same to his father, although that was something he most likely didn't know.

Of the pair of them, she knew precisely who she was, what she was, and what she had to do. He, in contrast, was probably uncertain of the first, even more uncertain of the second, and almost certainly had no clue as to the third.

That, however, she'd been prepared for. What she wasn't prepared for, what she hadn't foreseen, was the huge problem that now faced her. All six-plus feet of it, larger and infinitely more powerful in life than even her fanciful imagination had painted him.

His stylish greatcoat hung from shoulders that were broader and heavier than she recalled, but she'd last seen him when he'd been twenty-two. He was a touch taller, too, and there was a hardness in him that hadn't been there before, investing the austere planes of his face, his chiseled features, the rock-hard body that had nearly sent her flying.

Had sent her flying, more than physically.

His face was as she remembered it, yet not; gone was any hint of civilized guise. Broad forehead above striking slashes of black brows that tilted faintly, diabolically, upward at the outer ends, a blade of a nose, thin mobile lips guaranteed to dangerously fascinate any female, and well-set eyes of such a deep dark brown they were usually unreadable. The long black lashes that fringed those eyes had always made her envious.

His hair was still solidly sable, the thick locks fashionably cropped to fall in waves about his well-shaped head. His clothes, too, were fashionably elegant, restrained, understated, and expensive. Even though he'd been traveling hard, all but racing for two days, his cravat was a subtle work of art, and beneath the dust, his Hessians gleamed.

Regardless, no amount of fashion could screen his innate masculinity, could dim the dangerous aura any female with eyes could detect. The passing years had honed and polished him, revealing rather than concealing the sleekly powerful, infinitely predatory male he was.

If anything, that reality seemed enhanced.

He continued to stand twenty feet away, frowning as he studied her, making no move to come closer, giving her witless, swooning, drooling senses even more time to slaver over him.

She'd thought she'd outgrown her infatuation with him. Sixteen years of separation should surely have seen it dead.

Apparently not.

Her mission, as she viewed it, had just become immeasurably more complicated. If he learned of her ridiculous susceptibility – perhaps excusable in a girl of thirteen, but

13

hideously embarrassing in a mature lady of twenty-nine – he'd use the knowledge, ruthlessly, to stop her from pressuring him into doing anything he didn't wish to do. At that moment, the only positive aspect to the situation was that she'd been able to disguise her reaction to him as understandable surprise.

Henceforth she would need to continue to hide that reaction from him.

Simple . . . was one thing that wasn't going to be.

Variseys as a breed were difficult, but she'd been surrounded by them from the age of six, and had learned how to manage them. All except *this* Varisey . . . oh, this was not good. Unfortunately not one, but two deathbed promises bound her to her path.

She cleared her throat, tried hard to clear her head of the disconcerting distraction of her still jangling senses. "I didn't expect you so early, but I'm glad you made such good time." Head high, eyes locked on his face, she walked forward. "There's a huge number of decisions to be made –"

He shifted, turning away, then restlessly turned back to her. "I daresay, but at present, I need to wash off the dust." His eyes – dark, fathomless, his gaze impossibly sharp – scanned her face. "I take it you're in charge?"

"Yes. And –"

He swung away, was off again, his long legs carrying him swiftly around the gallery. "I'll come and find you in an hour."

"Very well. But your room's not that way."

He halted. Once again stood facing away for the space of three heartbeats, then, slowly, he turned.

Again she felt the dark weight of his gaze, this time pinning her more definitely. This time, rather than converse over the yawning gap that once again separated them, a gap she now would have preferred to maintain, he walked, stalked, slowly back to her.

He kept walking until no more than a foot remained between them, which left him towering over her. Physical intimidation was second nature to male Variseys; they learned it from the cradle. She would have liked to say the ploy had no effect, and in truth it didn't have the effect he intended. The effect was something quite other, and more intense and powerful than she'd ever dreamed. Inside she quaked, trembled; outwardly she held his gaze and calmly waited.

First round.

He lowered his head slightly so he could look directly into her face. "The keep hasn't rotated in all the centuries since it was built." His voice had lowered, too, but his diction had lost nothing of its lethal edge. If anything that had sharpened. "Which means the west tower lies around the gallery."

She met his dark gaze, knew better than to nod. With Variseys one never conceded the slightest point; they were the sort that, if one surrendered an inch, took the whole county. "The west tower lies that way, but your room is no longer there."

Tension rippled through him; the muscle in the side of his jaw tightened. His voice, when he spoke, had lowered to a warning growl. "Where are my things?"

"In the ducal apartments." In the central part of the keep, facing south; she didn't bother telling him what he already knew.

She stepped back, just far enough to wave him to join her as, greatly daring, she turned her back on him and started strolling farther into the keep. "You're the duke now, and those are your rooms. The staff have slaved to have everything in readiness there, and the west tower room has been converted into a guest chamber. And before you ask" – she heard him reluctantly follow her, his longer legs closing the distance in a few strides – "*everything* that was in the west tower room is now in the duke's rooms – including, I might add, all your armillary spheres. I had to move every single one myself – the maids and even the footmen refuse to touch them for fear they'll fall apart in their hands."

He'd amassed an exquisite collection of the astrological spheres within spheres; she hoped mention of them would encourage him to accept the necessary relocation.

After a moment of pacing silently beside her, he said, "My sisters?"

"Your father passed away on Sunday, a little before noon. I dispatched the messenger to you immediately, but I wasn't sure what you wished, so I held back from informing your sisters for twenty-four hours." She glanced at him. "You were the farthest away, but we needed you here first. I expect they'll arrive tomorrow."

He glanced at her, met her eyes. "Thank you. I appreciate the chance to find my feet before having to deal with them."

Which, of course, was why she'd done it. "I sent a letter with the messenger to you for Collier, Collier, and Whitticombe."

"I sent it on with a covering letter from me, asking them to attend me here, with the will, at the earliest opportunity."

"Which means they'll arrive tomorrow, too. Late afternoon, most likely."

"Indeed."

They turned a corner into a short hall just as a footman closed the massive oak door at the end. The footman saw them, bowed low, then retreated.

"Jeffers will have brought up your bags. If you need anything else —"

"I'll ring. Who's the butler here these days?"

She'd always wondered if he'd had anyone in the household feeding him information; obviously not. "Retford the younger — old Retford's nephew. He was the underbutler before."

He nodded. "I remember him."

The door to the duke's apartments neared. Clinging to her chatelaine's glamour, she halted beside it. "I'll join you in the study in an hour."

He looked at her. "Is the study in the same place?"

"It hasn't moved."

"That's something, I suppose."

She inclined her head, was about to turn away when she noticed that, although his hand had closed about the door-knob, he hadn't turned it.

He was standing staring at the door.

16

"If it makes any difference, it's been over a decade since your father used this room."

That got her a frowning look. "Which room did he use?"

"He moved to the east tower room. It's remained untouched since he died."

"When did he move there?" He looked at the door before him. "Out of here."

It wasn't her place to hide the truth. "Sixteen years ago." In case he failed to make the connection, she added, "When he returned from London after banishing you."

He frowned, as if the information made no sense.

Which made her wonder, but she held her tongue. She waited, but he asked no more.

Brusquely he nodded in dismissal, turned the knob, and opened the door. "I'll see you in the study in an hour."

With a serene inclination of her head, she turned and walked away.

And felt his dark gaze on her back, felt it slide down from her shoulders to her hips, eventually to her legs. Managed to hold back her inner shiver until she was out of his acutely observant sight.

Then she picked up her pace, walking swiftly and determinedly toward her own domain – the duchess's morning room; she had an hour to find armor sufficiently thick to protect her against the unexpected impact of the tenth Duke of Wolverstone.

Royce halted just inside the duke's apartments; shutting the door, he looked around.

Decades had passed since he'd last seen the room, but little had changed. The upholstery was new, but the furniture was the same, all heavy polished oak, glowing with a rich, golden patina, the edges rounded by age. He circled the sitting room, running his fingers over the polished tops of sideboards and the curved backs of chairs, then went into the bedroom – large and spacious with a glorious view south over the gardens and lake to the distant hills.

He was standing before the wide window drinking in that view when a tap on the outer door had him turning. He raised his voice. "Come."

The footman he'd seen earlier appeared in the doorway from the sitting room carrying a huge china urn. "Hot water, Your Grace."

He nodded, then watched as the man crossed the room and went through the doorway into the dressing room and bathing chamber.

He'd turned back to the window when the footman reappeared. "Your pardon, Your Grace, but would you like me to unpack your things?"

"No." Royce looked at the man. He was average in everything – height, build, age, coloring. "There's not enough to bother with . . . Jeffers, is that right?"

"Indeed, Your Grace. I was the late duke's footman."

Royce wasn't sure he'd need a personal footman, but nodded. "My man, Trevor, will be arriving shortly – most likely tomorrow. He's a Londoner, but he's been with me for a long time. Although he has been here before, he'll need help to remember his way."

"I'll be happy to keep an eye out for him and assist in whatever way I can, Your Grace."

"Good." Royce turned back to the window. "You may go."

When he heard the outer door click shut, he quit the window and headed for the dressing room. He stripped, then washed; drying himself with the linen towel left ready on the washstand, he tried to think. He should be making mental lists of all he had to do, juggling the order in which to do them . . . but all he seemed able to do was feel.

His brain seemed obsessed with the inconsequential, with matters that were not of immediate importance. Such as why his father had moved out of the duke's apartments immediately after their confrontation.

The act smacked of abdication, yet . . . he couldn't see how such a proposition could mesh with reality; it didn't match his mental picture of his father.

His bag contained a complete set of fresh clothes – shirt, cravat, waistcoat, coat, trousers, stockings, shoes. He donned them, and immediately felt better able to deal with the challenges that waited beyond the door.

Before returning through the bedroom to the sitting room, he glanced around, assessing the amenities.

Minerva – his chatelaine – had been right. Not only were these rooms appropriate given he was now the duke, the atmosphere felt right – and he had a sneaking suspicion his old room wouldn't have suited him, fitted him, anymore. He certainly appreciated the greater space, and the views.

Walking into the bedroom, his gaze fell on the bed. He felt certain he would appreciate that, too. The massive oak four-poster supporting a decadently thick mattress and silk covers, piled high with thick pillows, dominated the large room. It faced the window; the view would always be restful, yet interesting.

At present, however, restful yet interesting couldn't sate his need; as his gaze returned to the crimson-and-gold silk-brocade bedspread, took in the crimson silk sheets, his mind supplied a vision of his chatelaine reclining there.

Naked.

He considered the vision, deliberately indulged; his imagination was more than up to the task.

As unlooked-for developments went, his chatelaine took the prize. Little Minerva was no longer so little, yet . . .

Being his mother's protégée, and thus under his father's protection, too, would normally have placed her off-limits to him, except that both his father and mother were now dead, and she was still there, in his household, an established spinster of his class, and she was . . . what? Twenty-nine?

Within their circles, by anyone's assessment she was now fair game, *except* . . . while he'd developed an immediate and intense lust for her, she'd shown no sign whatever that she returned his interest; she'd appeared coolly, calmly unaffected throughout.

If she'd reacted to him as he had to her, she would have

been in there now – more or less as he was imagining her, boneless and drowsy, a smile of satiation curving her lush lips as she lay sprawled, naked and utterly ravished, on his bed.

And he would be feeling a great deal better than he was. Sexual indulgence was the only distraction capable of taking the violent edge from his temper, capable of dulling it, dampening it, draining it.

Given his temper was so restlessly aroused, and desperately seeking an outlet, he wasn't surprised it had immediately fixed on the first attractive woman to cross his path, transmuting in a heartbeat to a driving lustful passion. What he was surprised by was the intensity, the incredible clarity with which his every sense, every fiber of his being, had locked on her.

Possessively and absolutely.

His arrogance knew few bounds, yet all the ladies who'd ever caught his eye . . . he'd always caught theirs first. That he wanted Minerva while she didn't want him had thrown him off-balance.

Unfortunately, her disinterest and his consequent unsettled state hadn't dampened his desire for her in the least.

He'd simply have to grin and bear it – continue to rein his temper in, denying it the release it sought, while putting as great a distance between him and her as possible. She might be his chatelaine, but once he learned who his steward, his agent, and the various others who were responsible for overseeing his interests were, he would be able to curtail his contact with her.

He glanced at the clock on the mantelpiece. Forty minutes had passed. Time to go to the study and settle in before she arrived to speak with him. He would need a few minutes to grow accustomed to occupying the chair behind his father's desk.

Walking into the sitting room, he looked up – and saw his armillary spheres lined up along the mantelpiece opposite, the mirror behind creating the perfect showcase. The sight drew him across the room. Scanning the collection, fingers idly stroking long-forgotten friends, he halted before one, his fingers stilling on a gold-plated curve as memories of his father presenting it to him on his eighteenth birthday slid through his mind.

After a moment, he shook free of the recollection and continued on, studying each sphere with its interlocking, polished metal curves . . .

The maids and even the footmen refuse to touch them for fear they'll fall apart in their hands.

Halting, he looked closer, but he'd been right. Each sphere hadn't just been dusted; every single one had been lovingly polished.

He glanced back along the line of spheres, then he turned and walked to the door.

Chapter 2

Armor of the sort she needed wasn't easy to find. Glancing at the clock in the duchess's morning room, Minerva told herself she'd simply have to manage. It was just over an hour since she'd left Royce; she couldn't hide forever.

Sighing, she stood, smoothing down her dull black skirts. She'd be wearing her mourning gowns for the next three months; luckily the color suited her well enough.

A small piece of reassurance to cling to.

Picking up the documents she'd prepared, she headed for the door. Royce should be in the study and settled by now; she stepped into the corridor, hoping she'd given him enough time. Courtesy of her infatuation and consequent close observation of him whenever they'd been in the same place – which covered all the time he'd spent at Wolverstone or in the London house from the age of fourteen, when she'd joined the household as a six-year-old and on setting eyes on him had been instantly smitten, to when he'd reached twenty-two – she knew him much better than he could possibly guess. And she'd known his father even better; the matters they had to discuss, the decisions Royce had to make that day and over those following, would not be easy, not without emotional cost.

She'd been in London with his mother at the time of the confrontation in White's; they'd heard enough reports to have a fairly clear idea of what had, beneath the words, really happened. Given Royce's puzzlement on hearing when his father had moved out of the ducal apartments, she wasn't at all sure he – Royce – had as clear a vision of that long-ago debacle as she. Aside from all else, he would have been in a shocking temper – nay, fury – at the time. While his intellect was formidable and his powers of observation normally disconcertingly acute, when in the grip of a Varisey rage she suspected his higher faculties didn't work all that well.

His father's certainly hadn't, as that long-ago day had proved.

Regardless, it was time to beard the lion in his den. Or in this case, prod the new wolf in his study.

The corridors of the huge house were often quiet, but today the staff crept even more silently; not even distant sounds disturbed the pall.

She walked calmly on through the unnatural stillness.

She'd spent the last hour assuring herself that her eruption of unwelcome awareness had been due to shock – because he'd come upon her unawares and nearly mown her down. That her reaction was due solely to the *unexpectedness* of feeling his hard hands curl over her shoulders – and then he'd lifted her, literally off her feet, and set her aside.

And then he'd walked on.

That was the key point she had to remember – that all she'd felt was in her head. As long as it stayed there, and he remained unaware of it, all would be well. Just because her long-ago – as she'd thought long-dead – infatuation had chosen this thoroughly inconvenient moment to surge back to life, didn't mean she had to indulge it. Twenty-nine was too old for infatuations. She was, absolutely and undeniably, too wise to obsess over a gentleman, let alone a nobleman – and she well knew the distinction – like him.

If he ever guessed her susceptibility, he would use it ruthlessly for his own ends, and then she and her mission would be in very deep trouble.

The study door appeared ahead, Jeffers standing dutifully

alongside; eyeing the closed panel, she wasn't overly surprised to feel a certain wariness building. The truth was . . . if she'd considered herself free to do as she pleased, instead of acting as Royce's dutiful chatelaine and easing him into his new role, she would be spending the afternoon penning letters to her friends around the country inquiring if it would be convenient for her to visit. But she couldn't leave yet – wasn't free to flee yet.

She'd made a vow – two vows actually, but they were the same vow so it was really only one. First to his mother when she'd died three years ago, and she'd made the same vow last Sunday to his father. She found it interesting – indeed, revealing – that two people who hadn't shared much over the last twenty years should have had the same dying wish. Both had asked her to see Royce settled and properly established as the next Duke of Wolverstone. What they'd meant by "properly established" was, given the subject, plain enough; they'd wanted her to ensure that he was fully informed of all aspects of the dukedom, and that he understood and put in place all that was required to secure his position.

So on top of all else, she would need to see him wed.

That event would mark the end of her debt to the Variseys. She knew how much she owed them, how beholden to them she was. She'd been a six-year-old stray – no pauper, and as wellborn as they, but with no relatives to watch over her, and no claim on them – yet with negligent grace they'd taken her in, made her one of the family in all but name, included her in a way she'd had no right to expect. They hadn't done it expecting anything from her in return – which was one reason she was determined to carry out the late duke's and duchess's last wishes to the letter.

But once Royce's bride was established as his duchess and was able to take over the reins she currently managed, her role here would end.

What she did next, what she would make of her life, was a prospect that, until last Sunday night, she'd spent no time dwelling on. She still had no idea what she would do when her time at Wolverstone came to a close, but she had more than sufficient funds to keep herself in the luxury to which, thanks to the Variseys, she was now accustomed, and there was a whole world beyond Coquetdale and London to explore. There were all sorts of exciting prospects to consider, but that was for later.

Right now she had a wolf – quite possibly bruised and inclined to be savage – to deal with.

Halting before the study door, she inclined her head to Jeffers, tapped once, and went in.

Royce was sitting behind the huge oak desk. The desktop was unnaturally neat and clear, devoid of the usual papers and documents commensurate with it being the administrative heart of a massive estate. Long-fingered hands, palms flat, on the desk, he glanced up as she entered; for a fleeting instant she thought he looked . . . lost.

Shutting the door, she glanced at the document uppermost in her hand as she walked across the rug – and spoke before he could. "You need to approve this." Halting before the desk, she held out the sheet. "It's a notice for the *Gazette*. We also have to inform the palace and the Lords."

Expression impassive, he looked at her, then lifted one hand and took the notice. While he read it, she sat in one of the chairs before the desk, settled her skirts, then arranged her prepared sheets in her lap.

He shifted and she looked up – watched as he reached for a pen, glanced at the nib, flipped open the ink pot, dipped, then applied the pen to her notice, slowly and deliberately crossing out one word.

After blotting it, he inspected the result, then reached across the desk and handed it back to her. "With that correction, that will do for the news sheets."

He'd crossed out the word "beloved" in the phrase "beloved father of." She suppressed the impulse to raise her brows; she should have anticipated that. Variseys, as she'd been told often enough and had seen demonstrated for decades, did not love. They might be seething cauldrons of emotion in all other respects, but not one of them had ever laid claim to love. She nodded. "Very well."

Putting that sheet at the bottom of her pile, she lifted the next, looked up – and saw him regarding her enigmatically. "What?"

"You're not 'Your Grace'-ing me."

"I didn't 'Your Grace' your father, either." She hesitated, then added, "And you wouldn't like it if I did."

The result was an almost inhuman purr, a sound that slid across her senses. "Do you know me that well, then?"

"That well, yes." Even though her heart was now in her throat, she kept firm control over her voice, her tone. She held out the next sheet. "Now, for the Lords." She had to keep him focused and not let him stray into disconcerting diversions; it was a tactic Variseys used to distract, and then filch the reins.

After a pregnant moment, he reached out and took the sheet. They thrashed out a notification for the Lords, and an acceptably worded communication for the palace.

While they worked, she was aware of him watching her, his dark gaze sharp, as if he were studying her – minutely.

She steadfastly ignored the effect on her senses – prayed it would wane soon. It had to, or she'd go mad.

Or she'd slip and he'd notice, and then she'd die of embarrassment.

"Now, assuming your sisters arrive tomorrow, and the people from Collier, etcetera, as well, given we expect your aunts and uncles to arrive on Friday morning, then if you're agreeable, we could have the will read on Friday, and that would be one thing out of the way." Looking up from tidying her documents, she arched a brow at him.

He'd slumped back, outwardly relaxed in the large admiral's chair; he regarded her impassively for several long moments, then said, "We could – if I was agreeable – have the funeral on Friday."

"No, we couldn't."

Both his brows slowly rose. "No?" There was a wealth, a positive surfeit of intimidation packed into the single, softly uttered word. In this case, on multiple counts, it was misplaced.

"No." She met his gaze, held it. "Think back to your mother's funeral – how many attended?"

His stillness was absolute; his gaze didn't shift from hers. After another long silence, he said, "I can't remember." His tone was even, but she detected a roughness, a slight weakness; he honestly couldn't recall, quite possibly didn't like thinking of that difficult day.

With him banished from his father's lands, but the church and graveyard at Alwinton enclosed within Wolverstone's boundaries, he'd literally driven around his father's edict; his groom had driven his curricle to the church's lych-gate, and he'd stepped directly onto hallowed ground.

Neither he nor his father had spoken to anyone – let alone exchanged so much as a glance – through the long service and the subsequent burial. That he couldn't remember how many had been in the church testified that he hadn't been looking around, unaffected; his normally extremely observant faculties hadn't been functioning.

Calmly, she recited, "There were over two hundred counting only family and members of the ton. For your father, that number will be more like three hundred. There'll be representatives of the king, and Parliament, quite aside from family and friends – let alone all those who will make a point of coming all the way up here simply to register their connection, however tenuous, with the dukedom."

He pulled a face, then in an explosion of movement sat up. "How soon can it be arranged?"

Relief slid through her veins. "The notice of death will run in the *Gazette* on Friday. Tomorrow, once your sisters are here to consult, we should send off a notice about the funeral – that will then run in the Saturday editions. Realistically, given so many will be coming from the south, the earliest we could hold the funeral would be the following Friday."

He nodded, reluctant but accepting. "Friday, then." He hesitated, then asked, "Where's the body being kept?"

"In the icehouse, as usual." She knew better than to suggest he should view his father's body; he either would of his own accord, or wouldn't. It would be better if he did, but there were some areas into which, with him, she wasn't prepared to stray; it was simply too dangerous.

Royce watched as she shuffled through the papers in her lap – eyed her hair, lustrous and gleaming. Wondered how it would look draped over her very white skin when said skin was bare and flushed with passion.

He shifted in the chair. He desperately needed distraction. He was about to ask for a list of staff – she was so damned efficient he would wager his sanity she would have one in her pile – when heavy footsteps approached the door. An instant later, it opened, admitting a majestic butler.

The butler's gaze fixed on him. Framed in the doorway, he bowed low. "Your Grace." Straightening, he bowed more shallowly to Minerva, who rose to her feet. "Ma'am."

Refocusing on Royce, who, as Minerva was standing, rose, too, the stately personage intoned, "I am Retford, Your Grace. I am the butler here. On behalf of the staff, I wish to convey our condolences on the death of your father, and extend our welcome to you on your return."

Royce inclined his head. "Thank you, Retford. I believe I recall you as underbutler. Your uncle always had you polishing the silver."

Retford perceptibly thawed. "Indeed, Your Grace." He glanced again at Minerva. "You wished me to inform you when luncheon was ready, ma'am."

Royce noted the meaningful look the pair exchanged before his chatelaine said, "Indeed, Retford. Thank you. We'll be down directly."

Retford bowed to them both, then with another "Your Grace," withdrew.

Still standing, Royce caught Minerva's eye. "Why are we going down directly?"

She blinked her eyes wide. "I was sure you'd be hungry." When he remained unmoving, patently waiting, her lips lifted fractionally. "And you need to allow the staff to formally greet you."

28

He summoned a not-entirely-feigned expression of horror. "Not the whole damned lot of them?"

She nodded and turned to the door. "Every last one. Names and positions – you know the drill. This is a ducal residence, after all." She watched as he came around the desk. "And if you're not hungry now, I can guarantee you'll be in dire need of sustenance by the time we're finished."

Moving past her, he opened the door, held it. "You're going to enjoy this, aren't you? Seeing me floundering."

As he followed her into the corridor, she shook her head. "You won't flounder – I'm your chatelaine. I'm not allowed to let you flounder at such moments – that's my job."

"I see." He quelled an urge to take her arm; she clearly didn't expect him to – she was already walking briskly toward the main stairs. Sinking his hands in his trouser pockets, he fixed his gaze on the floor before their feet. "So how, exactly, do you propose to do your job?"

By whispering in his ear.

She remained immediately on his left all the way down the long line of eager staff, murmuring their names and positions as he nodded to each one.

He could have done without the distraction. The temptation. The all but constant taunting, however unintentional, of his less civilized self.

The housekeeper, Mrs. Cranshaw – Cranny as he'd always called her – blushed rosily when he smiled and called her by that long-ago nickname. Other than Retford and Milbourne, there were no others who hailed from the last time he'd been there.

They finally reached the end of the long line. After the last scullery maid had blushed and bobbed, Retford, who had followed behind them radiating approval as much as a butler of his station ever did, stepped forward and bowed them into the smaller dining salon.

Royce would have gone to his customary chair halfway down the table, but Retford swept to the large carver at its head and held it . . . he smoothly continued up the table and sat in his father's place.

Now his – a fact he was going to have to get used to.

Jeffers sat Minerva on his left; from her and Jeffers's behavior, that was her customary position.

He remembered his need to create distance between them, remembered his question about the staff, but she'd left her papers upstairs.

Luckily, as soon as the platters had been set before them and the majority of footmen withdrew, she asked, "One thing we – Retford, Milbourne, Cranny, and I – need to know is what staff you have, and which household you wish them attached to."

A safe, sensible question. "I have a valet – Trevor. He was with me before."

Staring ahead, she narrowed her eyes. "He's younger than you, slightly tubby – at least he was."

A reasonable if brief description of Trevor.

She glanced at Retford, standing back on Royce's right; the butler nodded, indicating that he, too, remembered Trevor. "That's fortuitous, as I doubt Walter, your father's valet, would suit. However, that leaves us with the question of what to do with Walter – he won't want to leave Wolverstone, or the family's service."

"Leave that to me." Royce had long ago learned to value experience. "I have an idea for a position that might suit him."

"Oh?" She looked her question, but when he didn't reply, but instead served himself from a platter of cold meats, she frowned, then asked, "Is Henry still your groom?"

He nodded. "I've already spoken with Milbourne – Henry should arrive tomorrow. He'll remain my personal groom. The only other to join the household here will be Handley." He met Minerva's gaze. "My secretary."

He'd wondered how she would take that news. Somewhat to his surprise, she beamed. "Excellent. That will absolve me of dealing with your correspondence."

"Indeed." A good first step in edging her out of his daily orbit. "Who dealt with my father's correspondence?"

"I did. But there are so many communications crossing a duke's desk, and so much I have to attend to as chatelaine, if we'd entertained more, there would have been problems. As it was, things often didn't get dealt with as expeditiously as I would have liked."

He was relieved she truly was prepared to let his correspondence pass out of her hands. "I'll tell Handley to check with you if he has any questions."

She nodded, absorbed with peeling a fig. He watched her take the first bite, saw her lips glisten – quickly looked down at the apple he was coring.

When next he glanced up, she was staring across the table, frowning in an abstracted way. As if sensing his gaze, she asked, still without looking at him, "Is there anyone else we should expect to accommodate?"

It took a moment for him to catch her meaning; it was the word "accommodate" that finally impinged, confirmed by the faint blush tinting her cheeks. "No." Just to ensure she – and Retford, too – were quite clear on the point, he stated, "I don't have a mistress. At present."

He'd tacked on the "at present" to make sure they believed him. Rapidly canvassing the possible eventualities, he added, "And unless I inform you otherwise, you should act on the assumption that that situation remains unchanged."

Mistresses, for him, constituted a certain danger, something he'd learned before he'd reached twenty. Because he'd been heir to one of the wealthiest dukedoms, his mistresses – due to his tastes, inevitably drawn from the ton – had shown a marked tendency to develop unrealistic ideas.

His declaration had tweaked Minerva's curiosity, but she merely nodded, still not meeting his eyes. She finished her fig, and laid down her fruit knife.

He pushed back from the table. "I need a list of the stewards and agents for each of the various properties."

She rose as Jeffers drew out her chair. "I have a list prepared – I left it on my desk. I'll bring it to the study."

"Where is your lair?"

31

She glanced at him as they headed for the stairs. "The duchess's morning room."

He didn't say anything, but walked by her side up the stairs and into the keep, to the room that, centuries ago, had been a solar. Its oriel window looked out over the rose garden to the south and west of the keep.

Following her into the room, he halted just over the threshold. While she went to a bureau against one wall, he scanned the room, searching for some sense of his mother. He saw the tapestry cushions she'd loved to make idly cast on the sofas, but other than that the room held few lingering hints of her. It was light, airy, distinctly feminine, with two vases of fresh flowers scenting the air.

Minerva turned and walked toward him, perusing a number of lists. She was so alive, so anchored in the here and now, he doubted any ghosts could linger near.

She looked up, saw him; a frown formed in her eyes. She glanced at the twin sofas, the only place they might sit, then faced him. "We'll do better going over these in the study."

She was uncomfortable having him in her domain. But she was right; the study was the more appropriate setting. Even more to the point, it had a desk behind which he could hide the worst of his reaction to her.

Stepping aside, he waved her through the door. He trailed her around the gallery, but finding his gaze transfixed by her subtly swaying hips, he lengthened his stride to walk alongside her.

Once they were ensconced in the study – once more firmly in their roles of duke and chatelaine – he went through her list of his stewards and agents, extracting every detail he deemed useful – in addition to the names and positions, physical descriptions and her personal opinion of each man. At first she balked at voicing the latter, but when he insisted proved his point by providing a comprehensive and astute character study for each incumbent.

His memories of her from long ago weren't all that detailed; what he had was an impression of a no-nonsense female uninclined to histrionics or flights of fancy, a girl with her feet firmly planted on the ground. His mother had trusted her implicitly, and from all he was learning, so had his sire.

And his father had never trusted easily, no more than he.

By the time they reached the end of her lists, he was convinced that he, too, could trust her. Implicitly. Which was a huge relief. Even keeping her at a physical distance, he would need her help to get through the next days, possibly weeks. Possibly even months. Knowing that her loyalties lay firmly with the dukedom – and thus with him as the duke – was reassuring.

Almost as if he could trust her to protect his back.

Which was a distinctly odd notion for a man like him to have of a woman. Especially a lady like her.

Unknowingly underscoring his conclusion, having regathered her scattered papers, leaving those he'd appropriated, she hesitated. When he caught her eye and arched a brow, she said, "Your father's man of business is Collier – not the same Collier as Collier, Collier, and Whitticombe, but their cousin."

He could now read her tone. "Whom you don't trust."

"Not so much don't trust as have no confidence that he knows all that much about managing money. Heaven knows, I don't, but I've seen the returns on the dukedom's investments, and they don't impress. I get significantly better returns on my funds, which are handled by another firm."

He nodded. "I have my own man of business – Montague, in the city. He does get impressive returns. I'll instruct him to contact Collier and go through the books, then assume control."

She smiled. "Excellent." She shifted, looked at the lists before him. "If you don't need me for anything else . . .?"

He wished he didn't, but he had to know, and she was the only one he could ask. He focused on the pen in his hand – his father's. "How did my father die?"

She stilled. He didn't look up, but waited; he sensed she was ordering her thoughts. Then she said, "He had a seizure. He was perfectly well earlier – we met over breakfast – then he went into the library as he always did on Sunday mornings to read the news sheets. We don't know when he was struck down, but when he didn't ring for his elevenses, as he invariably did, the cook sent Jeffers to check. Jeffers found him lying on the floor behind his desk. He'd tried to reach the bellpull, but had collapsed."

She paused, then went on, "Retford summoned me. I stayed with your father while they sent for the doctor and made a stretcher to carry him to his room. But he didn't last that long."

Royce glanced up. Her gaze was far away, unfocused. "You were with him when he died?"

She nodded.

He looked down, turned the pen in his fingers. "Did he say anything?"

"He was unconscious until quite close to the end. Then he stirred, and asked for you."

"Me?" He looked up. "Not my sisters?"

"No – he'd forgotten. He thought you were here, at Wolverstone. I had to tell him you weren't." She refocused on him. "He passed away quite peacefully – if he had been in pain, it was before we found him."

He nodded, not quite meeting her eyes. "Thank you." After a moment, he asked, "Have you told the others?"

She knew to whom he was referring – his father's illegitimate children.

"The girls are on one or other of the estates, so I sent letters out yesterday. Other than O'Loughlin, to whom I sent word, the males are out of reach – I'll pen letters once we know the bequests, and you can sign them." She looked at him. "Or Handley could do it, if you wish."

"No. I'd appreciate it if you would handle that. You know them – Handley doesn't. But leave O'Loughlin to me. I don't want to start mysteriously losing sheep."

She rose. "He wouldn't, would he?"

"He would, if nothing else to gain my attention. I'll deal with him."

"Very well. If there's nothing more you need from me, I'll start planning the funeral, so once your sisters arrive we can proceed without delay."

He nodded curtly. "Please God."

He heard a soft chuckle as she glided to the door. Then she left, and he could, at last, focus on picking up the dukedom's reins.

He spent the next two hours going over her lists and the notes he'd made, then penning letters – short, to-the-point scrawls; he was already missing Handley.

Jeffers proved invaluable, knowing the fastest route to fly his communications to each of his holdings; it appeared he needed a personal footman after all. Through Jeffers he arranged to meet with Wolverstone's steward, Falwell, and Kelso, the agent, the following morning; both lived in Harbottle, so had to be summoned.

After that . . . once Jeffers had left with the last of his missives, Royce found himself standing at the window behind the desk, looking north toward the Cheviots and the border. The gorge through which the Coquet ran was visible here and there through the trees. A race had been cut into the steep bank some way north of the castle, channeling water to the castle mill; only the mill's slate roof was visible from the study. After the mill, the race widened into an ornamental stream, a series of pools and ponds slowing the pummeling torrent until it flowed peacefully into the large manmade lake south of the castle.

Royce followed the line of the stream, his gaze fixing on the last pool before the view was cut off by the castle's north wing. In his mind, he continued along the banks, to where the stream reached the lake, then farther around the western bank . . . to where the icehouse stood back from the shore in a grove of sheltering willows.

He stood for a while more, feeling rather than thinking. Then accepting the inevitable, he turned and walked to the door. Stepping out, he looked at Jeffers. "I'm going for a walk. If Miss Chesterton looks for me, tell her I'll see her at dinner."

"Yes, Your Grace."

He turned and started walking. He supposed he'd get used to

the form of address, yet . . . it wasn't supposed to have been like this.

The evening, blissfully quiet though it was, felt like the lull before a storm; after dinner, sitting in the library watching Minerva embroider, Royce could sense the pressures building.

Viewing the body laid out in the icehouse hadn't changed anything. His father had aged, yet was recognizably the same man who'd banished him – his only son – for sixteen years, the same man from whom he'd inherited name, title and estate, his height and ruthless temperament, and not much else. Yet temper, temperament, made the man; looking down on his father's no longer animate face, harsh featured even in death, he'd wondered how different they truly were. His father had been a ruthless despot; at heart, so was he.

Sunk in the large armchair angled before the hearth wherein a small fire burned incongruously bright, he sipped the fine malt whisky Retford had poured him, and pretended that the ancient, luxurious yet comfortable surroundings had relaxed him.

Even if he hadn't sensed storms on his horizon, having his chatelaine in the same room guaranteed he wouldn't – couldn't – relax.

His eyes seemed incapable of shifting for any length of time away from her; his gaze again drawn to her as she sat on the chaise, eyes on her needlework, the firelight gilding her upswept hair and casting a rosy sheen over her cheeks, he wondered anew at the oddity – the inconvenient fact – that she wasn't attracted to him, that he apparently didn't impinge on her awareness while he – every sense he possessed – was increasingly fixated on her.

The arrogance of the thought occurred to him, yet in his case was nothing more than the truth. Most ladies found him attractive; he usually simply took his pick of those offering, crooked his finger, and that lady was his for however long he wanted her.

He wanted his chatelaine with an intensity that surprised him, yet her disinterest precluded him from having her. He'd never pursued a woman, actively seduced a woman, in his life, and at his age didn't intend to start.

After dressing for dinner – mentally thanking Trevor who had foreseen the necessity – he'd gone to the drawing room armed with a catechism designed to distract them both. She'd been happy to oblige, filling in the minutes before Retford had summoned them to the dining room, then continuing through the meal, reminding him of the local families, both ton and gentry, casting her net as far as Alnwick and the Percys, before segueing into describing the changes in local society – who were now the principal opinion makers, which families had faded into obscurity.

Not that much had changed; with minor adjustments, his previous view of this part of the world still prevailed.

Then Retford had drawn the covers and she'd risen, intending to leave him to a solitary glass of port. He'd opted instead to follow her to the library and the whisky his father had kept there.

Prolonging the torture of being in her presence, yet he hadn't wanted to be alone.

When he'd commented on her using the library instead of the drawing room, she'd told him that after his mother's death, his father had preferred her to sit with him there . . . suddenly recalling it was he, not his father, walking beside her, she'd halted. Before she could ask if he'd rather she repaired to the drawing room, he'd said he had further questions and waved her on.

On reaching the library, they'd sat; while Retford had fetched the whisky, he'd asked about the London house. That topic hadn't taken long to exhaust; other than having to rethink his notion of having his butler Hamilton take over as butler there, all else was as he'd supposed.

A strangely comfortable silence had ensued; she was, it seemed, one of those rare females who didn't need to fill every silence with chatter.

Then again, she'd spent the last three years' evenings sitting with his father; hardly surprising she'd grown used to long silences.

Unfortunately, while the silence normally would have suited him, tonight it left him prey to increasingly illicit thoughts of her; those currently prevailing involved stripping her slowly of her weeds, unwrapping her curves, her graceful limbs, and investigating her hollows.

All of which seemed guiltily wrong, almost dishonorable.

He inwardly frowned at her – a picture of ladylike decorum as, entirely oblivious of the pain she was causing him, needle flashing she worked on a piece of the same sort of embroidery his mother had favored, petit point he thought it was called. Technically, her living unchaperoned under his roof might be termed scandalous, yet given her position and how long she'd resided there . . . "How long have you been chatelaine here?"

She glanced up, then returned to her work. "Eleven years. I took on the duties when I turned eighteen, but neither your mother nor your father would consent to me to being titled chatelaine, not until I turned twenty-five and they finally accepted I wouldn't wed."

"They'd expected you to marry." So had he. "Why didn't you?"

She glanced up, flashed a light smile. "Not for want of offers, but no suitor offered anything I valued enough to grant him my hand – enough to change the life I had."

"So you're satisfied being Wolverstone's chatelaine?"

Unsurprised by the bald question, Minerva shrugged. She would willingly answer any question he asked – anything to disrupt the effect that him sitting there, at his languid, long-legged ease in a sprawl that was so quintessentially masculine – broad shoulders against the high back of the chair, forearms resting along the padded arms, the long fingers of one hand cradling a cut-crystal tumbler, powerful thighs spread apart – was having on her benighted senses. Her nerves were so taut his presence made them flicker and twang like violin strings. "I won't be chatelaine forever – once you marry, your duchess will take up the reins, and then I plan to travel."

"Travel? Where to?"

Somewhere a long way from him. She studied the rose she must have just embroidered; she couldn't remember doing it. "Egypt, perhaps."

"Egypt?" He didn't sound impressed by her choice. "Why there?"

"Pyramids."

The darkly brooding look he'd had before he'd asked when she'd become chatelaine returned. "From all I've heard, the area around the pyramids is rife with Berber tribesmen, barbarians who wouldn't hesitate to kidnap a lady. You can't go there."

She imagined informing him that she'd long had a dream of being kidnapped by a barbarian, tossed over his shoulder, and carted into his tent, there to be dropped on a silk-draped pallet and thoroughly ravished – of course he'd been the barbarian in question – and then pointing out that he had no authority over where she went. Instead, she settled for a response he'd like even less. Smiling gently, she looked back at her work. "We'll see."

No, they wouldn't. She wasn't going anywhere near Egypt, or any other country seething with danger. Royce toyed with lecturing her that his parents hadn't raised her to have her throw her life away on some misguided adventure . . . but with his temper so uncertain, and her response guaranteed to only escalate the tension, he kept his lips shut and swallowed the words.

To his intense relief, she slipped her needle into her work, then rolled the piece up and placed it into a tapestry bag that apparently lived beneath one end of the chaise. Leaning down, she tucked the bag back into position, then straightened and looked at him. "I'm going to retire." She rose. "Don't stir – I'll see you tomorrow. Good night."

He managed a growled "good night" in reply. His eyes followed her to the door – while he fought to remain in the chair and let her go. Her idea about Egypt hadn't helped, stirring something primitive – even more primitive – within him. Sexual hunger was a tangible ache as the door shut softly behind her.

Her room would be in the keep, somewhere not far from his new rooms; despite the ever-increasing temptation, he wasn't going there.

She was his chatelaine, and he needed her.

Until he was solidly established as duke, the reins firmly in his hands, she was his best, most well-informed, reliable, and trustworthy source of information. He would avoid her as much as possible – Falwell and Kelso would help with that – but he would still need to see her, speak with her, on a daily basis.

He'd see her at meals, too; this was her home after all.

Both his parents had been committed to raising her; he had every intention of honoring that commitment even though they were gone. Although not formally a ward of the dukedom, she stood in much the same position . . . perhaps he could cast himself as *in loco parentis*?

That would excuse the protectiveness he felt – that he knew he would continue to feel.

Regardless, he would have to bear with her being always around, until, as she'd pointed out, he married.

That was something else he would have to arrange.

Marriage for him, as for all dukes of Wolverstone, indeed, for all Variseys, would be a cold-bloodedly negotiated affair. His parents' and sisters' marriages had been that, and had worked as such alliances were meant to; the men took lovers whenever they wished, and once heirs were produced, the women did the same, and the unions remained stable and their estates prospered.

His marriage would follow that course. Neither he nor any Varisey was likely to indulge in the recent fashion for love matches, not least because, as was recognized by all who knew them, Variseys, as a breed, did not love.

Not within marriage, and not, as far as anyone knew, in any other capacity, either.

Of course, once he was wed, he'd be free to take a mistress, a long-term one, one he could keep by his side . . .

The thought rewoke all the fantasies he'd spent the last hour trying to suppress.

With a disgusted grunt, he drained the amber liquid in his glass, then set it down, rose, adjusted his trousers, and headed off to his empty bed.

Chapter 3

At nine the next morning, Royce sat at the head of the table in the breakfast parlor, and, alone, broke his fast. He'd slept better than he'd expected – deeply, if not dreamlessly – and his dreams hadn't been of his past, but rather fantasies that would never come to be.

All had featured his chatelaine.

If not always entirely naked, then at least less than clothed.

He'd woken to discover Trevor crossing the bedroom, ferrying hot water to the bathing chamber beyond. The keep had been built in an era when keeping doors to a minimum had been a wise defense; clearly knocking a door between the corridor and his dressing room and bathing chamber was an urgent necessity. He'd made a mental note to tell his chatelaine.

He'd wondered if she would ask why.

While he'd lain back and waited for the inevitable effect of his last dream to fade, he'd rehearsed various answers.

He'd walked into the breakfast parlor with a keen sense of anticipation, disappointingly doused when, despite the late hour, she hadn't been there.

Perhaps she was one of those females who breakfasted on tea and toast in her room.

Curbing his misplaced curiosity about his chatelaine's

habits, he'd sat and allowed Retford to serve him, determinedly suppressing a query as to her whereabouts.

He was working his way through a plate of ham and sausages when the object of his obsession swept in – gowned in a gold velvet riding habit worn over a black silk blouse with a black ribbon tied above one elbow and a black riding hat perched atop her golden head.

Wisps of hair had escaped her chignon, creating a fine nimbus beneath the hat. Her cheeks glowed with sheer vitality.

She saw him and smiled, halting and briskly tugging off her gloves. A crop was tucked under one arm. "Two demon-bred black horses have arrived in the stables with Henry. I recognized him, amazingly enough. The entire stable staff are milling about, fighting to lend a hand to get your beasts settled." She arched a brow at him. "How many more horses should we expect?"

He chewed slowly, then swallowed. She enjoyed riding, he recalled; there was a taut litheness to her form as she stood poised just inside the door, as if her body were still thrumming to the beat of hooves, as if the energy stirred by the ride still coursed her veins.

The sight of her stirred him to an uncomfortable degree.

What had she asked? He raised his eyes to hers. "None."

"None?" She stared at him. "What did you ride in London? A hired hack?"

Her tone colored the last words as utterly unthinkable – which they were.

"The only activities one can indulge in on horseback in the capital don't, in my book, qualify as riding."

She wrinkled her nose. "That's true." She studied him for a moment.

He returned his attention to his plate. She was debating whether to tell him something; he'd already learned what that particular, assessing look meant.

"So you've no horse of your own. Well, except old Conqueror."

He looked up. "He's still alive?" Conqueror had been his

42

horse at the time he'd been banished, a powerful gray stallion just two years old.

She nodded. "No one else could ride him, so he was put to stud. He's more gray than ever now, but he still plods around with his mares." Again she hesitated, then made up her mind. "There's one of Conqueror's offspring, another stallion. Sword's three years old now, but while he's broken to the bit, he refuses to be ridden – well, not for long." She met his eyes. "You might like to try."

With a brilliant smile – she knew she'd just delivered a challenge he wouldn't be able to resist – she swung around and left the room.

Leaving him thinking – yet again – of another ride he wouldn't mind attempting.

"So, Falwell, there's nothing urgently requiring attention on the estate?" Royce addressed the question to his steward, who after wrinkling his brow and dourly pondering, eventually nodded.

"I would say, Your Grace, that while there might be the usual minor details to be attended to here and there, there is nothing outstanding that leaps to mind as necessary to be done in the next few months." Falwell was sixty if he was a day; a quietly spoken, rather colorless individual, he bobbed his head all but constantly – making Royce wonder if he'd developed the habit in response to his sire's blustering aggression.

Seeming to always agree, even if he didn't.

Both steward and agent had responded to his summons, and were seated before the study desk while he attempted what was rapidly becoming a hostile interrogation. Not that they were hostile, but he was feeling increasingly so.

Suppressing his incipient frown, he attempted to tease some better understanding from them. "It'll be winter in a few months, and then we won't be able to attend to anything of a structural nature until March, or more likely April." He found it difficult to believe that among all the buildings and out-buildings, nothing needed repairing. He turned his gaze on his agent. "And what of the holdings? Kelso?"

The agent was of similar vintage to Falwell, but a much harder, leaner, grizzled man. He was, however, equally dour.

"Nothing urgent that needs castle intervention, Y'r Grace."

They'd used the phrase "castle intervention" several times, apparently meaning assistance from the ducal coffers. But they were talking of barns, fences, and cottages on his lands that belonged to the estate and were provided to tenant farmers in exchange for their labor and the major portion of the crops. Royce allowed his frown to show. "What about situations that *don't* require 'castle intervention'? Are there any repairs or work of any kind urgently needed there?" His tone had grown more precise, his diction more clipped.

They exchanged glances – almost as if the question had confused them. He was getting a very bad feeling here. His father had been old-fashioned in a blanket sense, the quintessential marcher lord of yore; he had a growing suspicion he was about to step into a briar patch of old ways he was going to find it difficult to live within.

Not without being constantly pricked.

"Well," Kelso eventually said, "there's the matter of the cottages up Usway Burn, but your father was clear that that was for the tenants to fix. And if they didn't fix things by next spring, he was of a mind to demolish the cottages and plow the area under for more corn, corn prices being what they are."

"Actually," Falwell took up the tale, "your late father would have, indeed should have, reclaimed the land for corn this summer – both Kelso and I advised it. But I fear" – Falwell shook his head, primly condescending – "Miss Chesterton intervened. Her ideas are really *not* to be recommended – if the estate were to constantly step in in such matters we'd be forever fixing every little thing – but I believe your late father felt . . . constrained, given Miss Chesterton's position, to at least give the appearance of considering her views."

Kelso snorted. "Fond of her, he was. Only time in all the years I served him that he didn't do what was best for the estate."

"Your late father had a sound grasp of what was due the

estate, and the tenants' obligations in that regard." Falwell smiled thinly. "I'm sure you won't wish to deviate from that successful, and indeed traditional, path."

Royce eyed the pair of them – and was perfectly sure he needed more information, and – damn it! – he'd need to consult his chatelaine to get it. "I can assure you that any decisions I make will be guided by what is best for the estate. As for these cottages" – he glanced from one man to the other – "I take it that's the only outstanding situation of that ilk?"

"As far as I'm aware, Y'r Grace." Kelso paused, then added, "If there are other matters requiring attention, they've yet to be brought to my notice."

Royce fought not to narrow his eyes; Kelso knew, or at least suspected, that there were other repairs or rectification needed, but the estate people weren't bringing them to him. He pushed back from the desk. "I won't be making any decisions until I've had time to acquaint myself with the details."

He rose; both men quickly came to their feet. "I'll send word when next I wish to see you."

There was enough steel in his tone to have both men murmur in acquiescence, bow low, and, without protest, head for the door, even though Falwell had earlier informed him that his father had met with them on the first Monday of every month. For Royce's money, that was far too infrequently. His father might not have needed more frequent meetings, but information was something he couldn't function, hated trying to function, without.

He stood staring at the door long after the pairs' retreating footsteps had faded. He'd hoped they would provide a bulwark between him and his chatelaine in all matters pertaining to the estate, yet after speaking with them for an hour, he wasn't prepared to accept their views as being the full story on any subject. Certainly not on the Usway Burn cottages.

He wondered what Minerva's views were – and why his father, who'd never doted on another in his life, much less changed his behavior to appease someone, had seen fit to, because of her ideas, stay his hand.

He'd have to ask her.

Seeing his plan to keep her at a distance crumble to dust, he couldn't hold back a growl. Swinging around the desk, he headed for the door. Jerking it open, he stepped out, startling Jeffers, who snapped to attention.

"If anyone should ask, I've gone riding."

"Yes, Your Grace."

Before eliciting his chatelaine's advice about the cottages, he'd test her advice about the horse.

She'd been right.

Incontestably right. Thundering over the gently rolling landscape, letting the gray stallion have his head, he felt the air rush past his face, felt an exhilaration he'd missed shooting down his veins, sensed all around him the hills and fields of home racing past at a madman's pace – and blessed her insightfulness.

His father had been an excellent horseman, but had never had the patience for a mount with a mind of its own. He, on the other hand, enjoyed the challenge of making a compact with a horse, persuading it that it was in its best interests to carry him – so that together they could fly before the wind.

Sword was now his. He would carry him whenever and wherever he wished simply for a chance to run like this. Without restriction, without restraint, flying over fences, leaping rocks and burns, careening between the hills on their way to the breeding fields.

On leaving the study, he'd stridden straight for the stables and asked Milbourne for the stallion. On hearing he intended to ride the recalcitrant beast, Milbourne and Henry had accompanied him to the paddock at the rear of the castle's holding fields. They'd watched him work the stallion, patient yet demanding; the pair had grinned delightedly when Sword had finally trotted all around the paddock with Royce on his back, then Royce had put the horse at the barred gate and sailed over to their cheers.

As he'd told Minerva, he hadn't kept a horse in London.

When he'd visited friends in the country, he'd ridden mounts they'd provided, but none had been of the ilk of Sword – a heavy hunter fully up to his weight, strong, solid, yet fleet of foot. His thighs gripping the stallion's wide barrel, he rode primarily with hands and knees, the reins lying lax, there only if needed.

Despite his lack of experience, Sword had all but instantly picked up Royce's directions, almost certainly because Royce was strong enough to impress them on him clearly. But that took focused strength and concentration, an awareness of the horse and its inclination that few riders possessed; by the time the breeding fields came into view, Royce was no longer surprised that not even Milbourne had been able to ride the stallion.

Grasping the reins, he let Sword feel the bit, slowing him by degrees, until they were trotting.

He wanted to see Conqueror; he didn't know why. He wasn't a sentimental man, yet the memories stirred through riding his old mount's son had driven him there. Standing in his stirrups, he scanned the wide field, then heard a distant but soft trumpet; Sword answered with a snort and picked up his pace.

A group of horses emerged from a fold in the land, trotting, then galloping toward the fence.

Conqueror was in the lead. Much the same size as his son, yet heavier with age, the big gray slowed, ears flicking back and forth as he eyed Royce.

Halting Sword by the fence, Royce leaned over and held out his hand, a dried apple on his palm. "Here, boy."

Conqueror whinnied and came forward, lipped the apple from Royce's palm, chewed, then leaned over the rail and – ignoring his son – butted Royce.

He grinned, patting the great head. "Remember me, do you?"

Conqueror shook his head, mane dancing, then he noticed Sword's interest in the mares who'd followed him to the fence.

With a thunderous snort, Conqueror moved forward, pushing the mares away, herding them back.

Put in his place – second to Conqueror's harem – Royce sat and watched the small herd move away.

Settling back in the saddle, he patted Sword's sleek neck, then looked around. They were high on the rise of Castle Hill, north of the castle; looking down the valley, he could see the massive bulk of his home bathed in bright sunlight. It was barely noon.

Turning, he traced the valley northward, picking out the brown track of Clennell Street as it wound its way up through the hills. Temptation whispered.

He hadn't made any appointments for the afternoon.

The restlessness that had plagued him even from before he'd learned of his father's death, brought on, he suspected, by having to end Dalziel's reign while having no alternative life organized and waiting, then compounded by being thrust unprepared into the ducal harness, still roiled and churned inside, rising up at odd moments to distract and taunt him.

To unexpectedly undermine his natural Varisey confidence, and leave him uncertain.

Not a feeling he'd ever liked, and, at thirty-seven, one that irked. Mightily.

He glanced at Sword, then flicked the reins. "We've time enough to escape."

Urging the gray forward, he set course for the border and Scotland beyond.

He'd said he'd deal with O'Loughlin.

Royce found the farmhouse easily enough – the hills didn't change – but what had changed was the farmhouse itself. When last he'd seen it, it had been little more than a crofter's cottage with a lean-to barn alongside. Extended and refashioned, long and low, faced with rough-cut stone, thick timbers and with good slate on the roof, the house – now definitely a farmhouse – appeared warm and quietly prosperous, nestling back against a protecting rise, with a new, good-sized barn to one side.

A low stone wall circled the yard; as Royce walked the tiring Sword through the opening, a dog started barking.

Sword shifted, skittered.

The dog was chained inside the open barn door.

Drawing rein, Royce halted and sat patiently waiting for his calm, his lack of reaction, to sink in; once Sword had noticed and quieted, he dismounted.

Just as the farmhouse door opened and a mountain of a man strode out.

Royce met his half brother's blue eyes; other than their height and the width of their shoulders, the only physical resemblance lay in the set of their eyes, nose, and chin. Hamish's brown curls were starting to gray, but otherwise he seemed in his usual rude health. Royce smiled and stepped forward, holding out his hand. "Hamish."

His hand was engulfed, and then so was he, hauled into one of his half brother's bear hugs.

"Ro!" Hamish released him with a cuff to the back that – if he hadn't been expecting it – would have made Royce stagger. Grabbing his shoulders, Hamish searched his face. "Regardless of the reason, it's damned good to have you back."

"It's good to be back." Hamish released him and Royce glanced at the hills, at the view across their peaks to Windy Gyle. "I knew I missed it – I hadn't realized by how much."

"Och, well, you're back now, even if it took the old bastard dying to do it."

"The old bastard" was Hamish's way of referring to their father, not an insult, but a term of affection.

Royce's lips twisted. "Yes, well, he's gone, which is one reason I'm here. There are things –"

"To talk about – but after you've come in an' met Molly and the bairns." Hamish glanced at the barn, then pointed at a small face peeking out. "Hoi – Dickon! Come and see to this horse . . ." Hamish glanced at Sword, shifting nervously at the end of the rein.

Royce smiled. "I think I'd better help Dickon."

Hamish trailed alongside as Royce led Sword to the barn. "Isn't this the stallion that wouldn't let the old bastard ride him?"

"So I've heard. I didn't have a horse, so now he's mine."

"Aye, well, you always had the right touch with the head-strong ones."

Royce smiled at the boy waiting by the barn door; Hamish's blue eyes stared back at him. "This isn't one I've met before."

"Nah." Halting beside the lad, Hamish ruffled his hair. "This one came while you were away." He looked down at the boy, who was regarding Royce with wide eyes. "This here's the new duke, lad – you call him Wolverstone."

The boy's eyes switched to his father. "Not 'the old bastard'?"

Royce laughed. "No – but if there's no one else about but family, you can call me Uncle Ro."

While Royce and Dickon settled Sword in an empty stall, Hamish leaned on the wall and brought Royce up to date with the O'Loughlins. When Royce had last been at Wolverstone, Hamish, two years older than he, had had two young "bairns"; through the occasional letters they'd exchanged, Royce knew Hamish was now the proud father of four, Dickon at ten being the third.

Leaving the barn, they crossed the yard and entered the house; both Hamish and Royce had to duck beneath the low lintel.

"Hi, Moll!" Hamish led the way into a large parlor. "Come see who's here."

A short, rotund woman – more rotund than Royce remembered her – came bustling in from the kitchen beyond, wiping her hands on her apron. Bright blue eyes were set in a sweet round face beneath a shock of coppery red curls. "Really, Hamish, as if that's any way to summon me. Anyone would think you were a heathen –" Her eyes lit on Royce and she halted. Then she shrieked – making both men wince – and flung herself at Royce.

He caught her, laughed as she hugged him wildly.

"Royce, Royce!" She tried to shake him, an impossibility for her, then looked up into his face, beaming delightedly. "It's so *good* to see you back."

His own smile widened. "It's good to be back, Moll." He

was increasingly realizing how true that was, how deep within him the feeling of coming home reached. Touched. "You're looking as fetching as ever. And you've expanded the family since last I was here."

"Och, aye." Molly sent a mock-glare Hamish's way. "Himself got busy, you might say." Face softening, she looked at Royce. "You'll stay to lunch, won't you?"

He did. There was thick soup, mutton stew, and bread, followed by cheese and ale. He sat at the long table in the warm kitchen, redolent with succulent aromas and filled with constant babble, and marveled at Hamish's children.

Heather, the eldest, a buxom seventeen, had been a tiny tot when he'd last seen her, while Robert, sixteen and bidding fair to be as large as Hamish, had been a babe in arms, with Molly barely recovered from the birthing. Dickon was next in age, then came Georgia, who at seven looked very like Molly and seemed equally feisty.

As they'd taken their seats, the four had regarded him with wide eyes, as if drinking him in with their confident candid gazes – a combination of Hamish's shrewdness and Molly's openheartedness – then Molly had set the soup on the table and their attention had shifted; they'd thereafter blithely treated him as family, as "Uncle Ro."

Listening to their chatter, to Robert reporting to Hamish on the sheep in some field, and Heather telling Molly about a chicken gone broody, Royce couldn't help but register how comfortable he felt with them. In contrast, he'd be hard-pressed to name his legitimate sisters' offspring.

When his father had banished him from all Wolverstone domains and banned all communication with him, his sisters had fallen in with his father's wishes. Even though all three had been married and mistresses of their own establishments, they'd made no move to stay in touch, not even by letter. If they had, he would have at least corresponded, because he'd always known this day would come – when he was the head of the family, and in charge of the dukedom's coffers, on which his sisters still drew, and, through them, their children did, too.

Like everyone else, his sisters had assumed the situation wouldn't last long. Certainly not for sixteen years.

He'd kept a list of his nephews and nieces culled from birth notices in the *Gazette*, but in the rush had left it in London; he hoped Handley would remember it.

"But when did you get to the castle?" Molly fixed her bright gaze on him.

"Yesterday morning."

"Aye, well, I'm sure Miss Chesterton will have everything in hand."

He noted Molly's approval. "You know her?"

"She comes up here to discuss things with Hamish now and then. Always takes tea with us – she's a proper lady in every way. I imagine she'll have everything running smoothly as usual." Molly fixed her eyes on his face. "Have you decided when the funeral will be?"

"Friday next week." He glanced at Hamish. "Given the ton's inevitable interest, that was the earliest." He paused, then asked, "Will you come?"

"Moll and I will come to the church." Hamish exchanged a glance with Molly, who nodded, then he looked at Royce and grinned. "But you'll have to manage on your own at the wake."

Royce sighed. "I had hoped presenting them with a Scottish giant might distract them. Now I'll have to think of something else."

"Nah – I should think you yourself, the prodigal son returned, will be distraction enough."

"That," Royce said, "was my point."

Hamish chortled and they let the matter slide; Royce steered the conversation to local farming conditions and the upcoming harvest. Hamish had his pride, something Royce respected; his half brother had never set foot inside the castle.

As he'd expected, on the subject of farming he got more pertinent information from Hamish than from his own steward and agent; the farms in the area were scraping by, but were not exactly thriving.

Hamish himself was faring rather better. He held his lands freehold; his mother had been the only daughter of a freeholder. She'd married later in life, and Hamish had been her only child. He'd inherited the farm from her, and with the stipend his father had settled on him, had had the capital to expand and improve his stock; he was now a well-established sheep farmer.

At the end of the meal, Royce thanked Molly, bussed her cheek, then, following Hamish, snagged an apple from the bowl on the dresser, and they took their talk outside.

They sat on the stone wall, feet dangling, and looked across the hills. "Your stipend continues to your death, but you knew that." Royce took a bite of his apple; it crunched sharply.

"Aye." Hamish settled beside him. "So how did he die?"

"Minerva Chesterton was with him." Royce related what she'd told him.

"Have you managed to contact all the others?"

"Minerva's written to the girls – they're all on one or other of the estates. That's eleven of the fifteen." His father had sired fifteen illegitimate children on maids, tavern wenches, farm and village lasses; for some reason he'd always drawn his lovers from the local lower orders. "The other three men are in the navy – I'll write to them. Not that his death materially changes anything."

"Aye, still, they'll need to know." Hamish eyed him for a moment, then asked, "So, are you going to be like him?"

Tossing away his apple core, Royce slanted him a narrow-eyed glance. "In what way?"

Unabashed, Hamish grinned. "In exactly the way you thought I meant. Are you going to have every farmer in the region locking up his daughters?"

Royce snorted. "Definitely not my style."

"Aye, well." Hamish tugged at one earlobe. "Never was mine, either." For a moment they dwelled on their sire's sexual proclivities, then Hamish went on, "It was almost as if he saw himself as one of the old marcher lords, royal perquisites and all. Within his domains, he saw, he wanted, he took – not, as I heard it, that any of the lasses resisted all that much. M' mother certainly didn't. Told me she never regretted it – her time with him."

Royce smiled. "She was talking about you, you daft beggar. If she hadn't spent that time with him, she wouldn't have had you."

"P'rhaps. But even in her last years, she used to get a wistful look in her eye whenever she spoke of him."

Another moment passed, then Royce said, "At least he looked after them."

Hamish nodded.

They sat for a time, drinking in the ever-changing views, the play of light over the hills and valleys, the shifting hues as the sun edged to the west, then Hamish stirred and looked at Royce. "So, will you be mostly at the castle, then, or will London and the sassenach ladies lure you south?"

"No. In that respect I'll be following in his footsteps. I'll live at the castle except when duty to the estate, family or the Lords calls me south." He frowned. "Speaking of living here, what have you heard of the castle's agent, Kelso, or the steward, Falwell?"

Hamish shrugged. "They've been your father's eyes and ears for decades. Both are . . . well, not quite local anymore. They live in Harbottle, not on the estate, which causes some difficulty. Both were born on the estate, but moved to the town years ago, and for some reason your father didn't object – suspect he thought they'd still know the land. Not something you forget all that easily, after all."

"No, but things, conditions, change. Attitudes change, too."

"Och, well, you'll not get those two changing anything in a hurry. Right set in their ways – which I always supposed was why they suited the old bastard so well. Right set in his ways, he was."

"Indeed." After a moment of reflecting on his sire's resistance to change, and how deep that had gone, Royce admitted, "I might have to replace them – retire them – both, but I won't know until I've had a chance to get out and about and assess matters for myself."

"If it's information on the estate you need, your chatelaine can fill you in. Minerva's the one everyone goes to if there's a problem. Most have grown weary – in fact, *wary* – of going to Falwell or Kelso. Like as not, if they make a complaint, either nothing gets done, or the wrong thing – something worse that wasn't intended – happens."

Royce leveled a direct look at Hamish. "That doesn't sound good."

It was a question, one Hamish understood. "Aye, well, you'd written that you'd be giving up that commission of yours, and I knew you'd come home – didn't think there was any need to write and tell you how things were not going quite so well. I knew you'd see it once you got back, and Minerva Chesterton was doing well enough holding the fort." He shrugged his massive shoulders; they both looked south, over the peaks toward Wolverstone. "It might be not the done thing for me to say this, but perhaps it's as well that he's gone. Now you've got the reins, and it's more than time for a new broom."

Royce would have smiled at the mixed metaphor, but what they were discussing was too serious. He stared in the direction in which his responsibilities, growing weightier by the hour, lay, then he slid from the wall. "I should go."

Hamish paced alongside as he went to the barn and saddled Sword, then swung up to the saddle and walked the big gray into the yard.

Halting, he held out his hand.

Hamish clasped it. "We'll see you Friday at the church. If you get caught having to make a decision about something on the estate, you can rely on Minerva Chesterton's opinion. People trust her, and respect her judgment – whatever she advises will be accepted by your tenants and workers."

Royce nodded; inwardly he grimaced. "That's what I thought."

What he'd feared.

He saluted, then flicked the reins, and set Sword for Clennell Street and Wolverstone.

Home.

He'd torn himself away from the peace of the hills . . . only to discover when he rode into the castle stables that his sisters – all three of them, together with their husbands – had arrived.

Jaw set, he stalked toward the house; his sisters could wait – he needed to see Minerva.

Hamish's confirmation that she was, indeed, the current champion of the estate's well-being left him with little choice. He was going to have to rely on her, spend hours gleaning everything he could about the estate from her, ride out with her so she could show him what was going on – in short, spend far more time with her than he wished.

Than was wise.

Entering the house by the side door, he heard a commotion ahead, filling the cavernous front hall, and steeled himself. Felt his temper ratchet up another notch.

His elder sisters, Margaret, Countess of Orkney, and Aurelia, Countess of Morpeth, had agreed, implicitly if not explicitly, with his father over his erstwhile occupation; they'd supported his banishment. But he'd never got on well with either of them; at best he tolerated them, and they ignored him.

He was, always had been, much closer to his younger sister, Susannah, Viscountess Darby. She hadn't agreed or disagreed with his banishment; no one had asked her, no one would have listened to her, so she'd wisely kept her mouth shut. He hadn't been surprised about that. What had surprised, even hurt a trifle, was that she'd never sought to contact him over the past sixteen years.

Then again, Susannah was fickle; he'd known that even when they'd been much younger.

Nearing the hall, he changed his stride, letting his boot heels strike the floor. The instant he stepped onto the marble tiles of the hall, his footsteps rang out, effectively silencing the clamor.

Silks swooshed as his sisters whirled to face him. They looked like birds of prey in their weeds, their veils thrown back over their dark hair.

He paused, studying them with an impersonal curiosity. They'd aged; Margaret was forty-two, a tall, commanding dark-haired despot with lines starting to score her cheeks and brow. Aurelia, forty-one, was shorter, fairer, brown-haired, and from the set of her lips looked to have grown even more severely disapproving with the years. Susannah . . . had made a better fist of growing older; she was thirty-three, four years younger than Royce, but her dark hair was up in a confection of curls, and her gown, although regulation black, was stylishly fashionable. From a distance, she might pass for an adult daughter of either of her elder sisters.

Imagining how well that thought would go down, he looked back at the older two, and realized they were struggling with the fraught question of how to address him now he was the duke, and no longer simply their younger brother.

Margaret drew in a huge breath, breasts rising portentously, then swept forward. "There you are, Royce!" Her chiding tone made it clear he should have been dutifully awaiting their arrival. She raised a hand as she neared – intending to grip his arm and shake it, as had been her habit when trying to make him do something. "I –"

She broke off – because he'd caught her eye. Breath strangling in her throat, she halted, hand in the air, faintly shocked.

Aurelia bobbed a curtsy – a perfunctory one not nearly deep enough – and came forward more cautiously. "A dreadful business. It's been a very great shock."

No "How are you?" No "How have you been these last sixteen years?"

"Of course, it's been a shock." Susannah strolled up. She met his eyes."And I daresay it was an even bigger shock for you, all things considered." Reaching him, she smiled, stretched up, and kissed his cheek. "Welcome home."

That, at least, had been genuine. He nodded to her. "Thank you."

57

From the corner of his eye, he saw the other two exchange an irritated glance. He scanned the sea of footmen sorting through the piles of boxes and trunks, preparing to cart them upstairs, saw Retford look his way, but he was searching for Minerva.

He found her in the center of the melee, talking to his brothers-in-law. She met his eyes; the men turned, saw him looking their way, and came to greet him.

With an easy smile, Peter, Earl of Orkney, held out his hand. "Royce. It's good to see you again."

Stepping forward, he grasped Peter's hand, responding equally smoothly, then stepped still farther from his sisters to shake hands with David, Aurelia's husband, and lastly to exchange a pleasant greeting with Hubert, Viscount Darby – wondering, as he always did when faced with Hubert, why Susannah had married the faintly bumbling, ineffably good-natured fop. It could only have been for his fortune. That, and his willingness to allow Susannah to do whatever she pleased.

His maneuvering had brought him to Minerva's side. He caught her eye. "I take it everyone's rooms are organized?"

"Yes." She glanced at Retford, who nodded. "Everything's in hand."

"Excellent." He looked at his brothers-in-law. "If you'll excuse us, my chatelaine and I have estate business to attend to."

He nodded to them; they inclined their heads in reply, turning away.

But before he could turn and head up the stairs, Margaret stepped forward. "But we've only just got here!"

He met her gaze. "Indeed. No doubt you'll need to rest and refresh yourselves. I'll see you at dinner."

With that, he turned and climbed the stairs, ignoring Margaret's gasp of outrage. An instant later, he heard Minerva's slippers pattering up behind him and slowed; one glance at her face as she drew level was enough to tell him she disapproved of his brusqueness.

Wisely, she said nothing.

But on reaching the gallery, she halted a footman heading downstairs. "Tell Retford to offer afternoon tea to the ladies, and the gentlemen, too, if they wish, in the drawing room. Or if the gentlemen prefer, there are spirits in the library."

"Yes, ma'am." With a bow, the footman hurried on.

She turned to him, eyes narrow, lips compressed. "Your sisters are going to be trying enough as it is – you don't need to goad them."

"*Me?* Goad *them?*"

"I know they're irritating, but they always are. You used to be much better at ignoring them."

He reached the study door and opened it. "That was before I was Wolverstone."

Minerva frowned as she followed him into the study, leaving it to Jeffers, who'd trailed behind them upstairs, to close the door. "I suppose that's true. Margaret will undoubtedly try to manage you."

Dropping into the chair behind the desk, he flashed her a smile that was all teeth. "She's welcome to try. She won't succeed."

She sank into her usual chair. "I suspect she's guessed that."

"One can only hope." He fixed her with a gaze that, despite its distractingly rich darkness, was surprisingly sharp. "Tell me about the cottages up Usway Burn."

"Ah – your meeting with Falwell and Kelso. Did they tell you the cottages should be demolished?"

When he nodded, she drew breath, then hesitated.

His lips thinned. "Minerva, I don't need you to be polite, or politic, and certainly not self-effacing. I need you to tell me the truth, your conclusions, including your suspicions – and most especially your thoughts on how the estate people feel and think." He hesitated, then went on, "I've already realized I can't rely on Falwell or Kelso. I plan to retire them – pension them off with thanks – as soon as I can find suitable replacements."

She exhaled. "That's . . . welcome news. Even your father had realized their advice wasn't getting him the results he wanted."

"I assume that's why he held off doing as they suggested over these cottages?" When she nodded, he ordered, "Tell me – from the beginning."

"I'm not sure when the problems started – more than three years ago, at least. I didn't start working alongside your father until after your mother died, so my knowledge starts from then." She drew breath. "I suspect Kelso, backed by Falwell, had decided, more than three years ago, that old Macgregor and his sons – they hold the Usway Burn farm and live in the cottages – were more trouble than they're worth, and that letting the cottages fall down, then plowing them under, thus increasing the acreage, then letting that land to other tenants to farm, was a preferable option to repairing the cottages."

"You disagree." No question; he steepled his fingers before his face, his dark eyes never moving from hers.

She nodded. "The Macgregors have farmed that land since before the Conquest – as far as I can make out, literally. Evicting them will cause a lot of disquiet on the estate – along the lines of, if it could happen to them, who's safe? That's not something we need in these already uncertain times. In addition, the issues aren't as straightforward as Falwell makes out. Under the tenancy agreement, repair of damage from the wear and tear of use falls to the tenant, but structural work, repairs to the fabric needed to offset the effects of time and weather – that's arguably the responsibility of the estate.

"*However*, in one respect Falwell and Kelso are correct – the estate can't be seen to be repairing the first sort of damage, wear and tear. That would land us with requests from every tenant for the same consideration – but with the state the Usway Burn cottages are now in, you can't repair the fabric without simultaneously repairing the wear and tear."

"So what do you suggest?"

"The Macgregors and Kelso don't get on, never have, hence the present situation. But the Macgregors, if approached correctly, are neither unreasonable nor intractable. The situation, as it is now, is that the cottages urgently need wholesale repair, and the Macgregors want to keep farming that land. I'd

60

suggest a compromise – some system whereby both the estate and the Macgregors contribute to the outcome, and subsequently reap the benefits."

He studied her in silence. She waited, not the least discomfited by his scrutiny. Rather more distracted by the allure that didn't decrease even when, as with his sisters, he was being difficult. She'd always found the underlying danger in him fascinating – the sense of dealing with some being who was not, quite, safe. Not domesticated, nowhere near as civilized as he appeared.

The real him lurked beneath his elegant exterior – there in his eyes, in the set of his lips, in the disguised strength in his long-fingered hands.

"Correct me if I err" – his voice was a low, hypnotic purr – "but any such collaborative effort would step beyond the bounds of what I recall are the tenancy agreements used at Wolverstone."

She dragged in air past the constriction banding her lungs. "The agreements would need to be renegotiated and redrawn. Frankly, they need to be, to better reflect the realities of today."

"Did my father agree?"

She wished she could lie. "No. He was, as you know, very set in his ways. More, he was inimical to change." After a moment, she added, "That was why he put off making any decision about the cottages. He knew that evicting the Macgregors and pulling down the cottages was the wrong thing to do, but he couldn't bring himself to resolve the issue by altering tradition."

One black brow quirked. "The tradition in question underpins the estate's financial viability."

"Which would only be strengthened by getting more equitable agreements in place, ones which encourage tenants to invest in their holdings, to make improvements themselves, rather than leaving everything to the landowner – which on large estates like Wolverstone usually means nothing gets done, and land and buildings slowly decay, as in this instance."

Another silence ensued, then he looked down.

Absentmindedly tapped one long finger on the blotter. "This is not a decision to be lightly made."

She hesitated, then said, "No, but it must be made soon."

Without raising his head, he glanced up at her. "You stopped my father from making a decision, didn't you?"

Holding his dark gaze, she debated what to say . . . but he knew the truth; his tone said as much. "I made sure he remembered the predictable outcomes of agreeing with Falwell and Kelso."

Both his brows rose, leaving her wondering whether he'd been as sure as his tone had suggested, or whether she'd been led to reveal something he hadn't known.

He looked down at his hand, fingers now spread on the blotter. "I'll need to see these cottages —"

A tap on the door interrupted him. He frowned and looked up. "Come."

Retford entered. "Your Grace, Mr. Collier, from Collier, Collier, and Whitticombe, has arrived. He's awaiting your pleasure in the hall. He wished me to inform you he was entirely at your service."

Royce inwardly grimaced. He glanced at his chatelaine, who was revealing unexpected depths of strength and determination. She'd been able to, not manipulate, but influence his father . . . which left him uneasy. Not that he imagined she'd acted from any but the purest of motives; her arguments were driven by her views of what was best for Wolverstone and its people. But the fact she'd prevailed against his father's blustering, often bullying will – no matter how else he'd aged, that wouldn't have changed – combined with his own continuing, indeed escalating obsession with her, all compounded by his need to rely on her, to keep her near and interact with her daily . . .

His sisters, by comparison, were a minor irritation.

Minerva was . . . a serious problem.

Especially as everything she said, everything she urged, everything she was, appealed to him – not the cold, calm, calculating, and risk-averse duke, but the other side of him – the side that rode young stallions just broken to the saddle over hill and dale at a madman's pace.

The side that was neither cold, nor risk-averse.

He didn't know what to do with her, how he could safely manage her.

He glanced at the clock on a bureau by the wall, then looked at Retford. "Show Collier up."

Retford bowed and withdrew.

Royce looked at Minerva. "It's nearly time to dress for dinner. I'll see Collier, and arrange for him to read the will after dinner. If you can organize with Jeffers to show him to a room, and to have him fed . . .?"

"Yes, of course." She rose, met his gaze as he came to his feet. "I'll see you at dinner."

She turned and walked to the door; Royce watched while she opened it, then went out, then he exhaled and sank back into his chair.

Dinner was consumed in a civil but restrained atmosphere. Margaret and Aurelia had decided to be careful; both avoided subjects likely to irritate him, and, in the main, held their tongues.

Susannah made up for their silence by relating a number of the latest on-dits, censored in deference to their father's death. Nevertheless, she added a welcome touch of liveliness to which his brothers-in-law responded with easy good humor.

They dined in the family dining room. Although much smaller than the one in the main dining salon, the table still sat fourteen; with only eight of them spread along the board, there remained plenty of space between each place, further assisting Royce's hold on his temper.

The meal, the first he'd shared with his sisters for sixteen years, passed better than he'd hoped. As the covers were drawn, he announced that the reading of the will would take place in the library.

Margaret frowned. "The drawing room would be more convenient."

63

He raised his brows, set his napkin beside his plate. "If you wish you may repair to the drawing room. I, however, am going to the library."

She compressed her lips, but rose and followed.

Collier, a neat individual in his late fifties, bespectacled, brushed, and burnished, was waiting, a trifle nervous, but once they'd settled on the chaise and chairs, he cleared his throat, and started to read. His diction was clear and precise enough for everyone to hear as he read through clause after clause.

There were no surprises. The dukedom in its entirety, entailed and private property and all invested funds, was left to Royce; aside from minor bequests and annuities, some new, others already in place, it was his to do with as he pleased.

Margaret and Aurelia sat silently throughout. Their handsome annuities were confirmed, but not increased; Minerva doubted they'd expected anything else.

When Collier finished, and had asked if there were any questions, and received none, she rose from the straight-backed chair she'd occupied and asked Margaret if she would like to repair to the drawing room for tea.

Margaret thought, then shook her head. "No, thank you, dear. I think I'll retire . . ." She glanced at Aurelia. "Perhaps Aurelia and I could have tea in my room?"

Aurelia nodded. "What with the travel and this sad business, I'm greatly fatigued."

"Yes, of course. I'll have them send up a tray." Minerva turned to Susannah.

Who smiled lightly. "I believe I'll retire, too, but I don't want tea." She paused as her elder sisters rose, then, arm in arm, passed on their way to the door, then she turned back to Minerva. "When are the rest of the family arriving?"

"Your aunts and uncles are expected tomorrow, and the rest will no doubt follow."

"Good. If I'm to be trapped here with Margaret and Aurelia, I'm going to need company." Susannah glanced around, then sighed. "I'm off. I'll see you tomorrow."

Minerva spoke to Hubert, who asked for a tisane to be sent

to his room, then retreated. Peter and David had helped themselves to whisky from the tantalus, while Royce was talking with Collier by the desk. Leaving them all to their own devices, she left to order the tea tray and the tisane.

That done, she headed back to the library.

Peter and David passed her in the corridor; they exchanged good nights and continued on.

She hesitated outside the library door. She hadn't seen Collier leave. She doubted Royce needed rescuing, yet she needed to ascertain if he required anything further from her that night. Turning the knob, she opened the door and stepped quietly inside.

The glow from the desk lamps and those by the chaise didn't reach as far as the door. She halted in the shadows. Royce was still speaking with Collier, both standing in the space between the big desk and the window behind it, looking out at the night as they conversed.

She drew nearer, quietly, not wishing to intrude.

And heard Royce ask Collier for his opinion on the leasing arrangements for tied cottages.

"The foundation of the nation, Your Grace. All the great estates rely on the system – it's been proven for generations, and is, legally speaking, solid and dependable."

"I have a situation," Royce said, "where it's been suggested that some modification of the traditional form of lease might prove beneficial to all concerned."

"Don't be tempted, Your Grace. There's much talk these days of altering traditional ways, but that's a dangerous, potentially destructive road."

"So your considered advice would be to leave matters as they are, and adhere to the standard, age-old form?"

Minerva stepped sideways into the shadows some way behind Royce's back. She wanted to hear this, preferably without calling attention to her presence.

"Indeed, Your Grace. If I may make so bold" – Collier puffed out his chest – "you could not do better than to follow your late father's lead in all such matters. He was a stickler for

65

the legal straight and narrow, and preserved and grew the dukedom significantly over his tenure. He was shrewd and wise, and never one for tampering with what worked well. My counsel would be that whenever any such questions arise, your best tack would be to ask yourself what your sire would have done, and do precisely that. Model yourself upon him, and all will go well – it's what he would have wished."

Hands clasped behind his back, Royce inclined his head. "Thank you for your advice, Collier. I believe you've already been given a room – if you encounter any difficulty relocating it, do ask one of the footmen."

"Indeed, Your Grace." Collier bowed low. "I wish you a good night."

Royce nodded. He waited until Collier had closed the door behind him, before saying, "You heard?"

He knew she was there, behind him in the shadows. He'd known the instant she'd walked into the room.

"Yes, I heard."

"And?" He made no move to turn from the window and the view of the dark night outside.

Drifting closer to the desk, Minerva drew a tight breath, then stated, "He's wrong."

"Oh?"

"Your father didn't wish you to be like him."

He stilled, but didn't turn around. After a moment, he asked, voice quiet, yet intense, "What do you mean?"

"In his last moments, when I was with him here, in the library, he gave me a message for you. I've been waiting for the right moment to tell you, so you would understand what he meant."

"Tell me now." A harsh demand.

"He said: 'Tell Royce not to make the same mistakes I made.'"

A long silence ensued, then he asked, voice soft, quietly deadly, "And what, in your opinion, am I to understand by that?"

She swallowed. "He was speaking in the most general terms.

The widest and broadest terms. He knew he was dying, and that was the one thing he felt he had to say to you."

"And you believe he wished me to use that as a guide in dealing with the cottages?"

"I can't say that – that's for you to decide, to interpret. I can only tell you what he said that day."

She waited. His fingers had clenched, each hand gripping the other tightly. Even from where she stood, she could feel the dangerous energy of his temper, eddies swirling and lashing, a tempest coalescing around him.

She felt an insane urge to go closer, to raise a hand and lay it on his arm, on muscles that would be tight and tensed, more iron than steel beneath her palm. To try, if she could, to soothe, to drain some of that restless energy, to bring him some release, some peace, some surcease.

"Leave me." His tone was flat, almost grating.

Even though he couldn't see, she inclined her head, then turned and walked – calmly, steadily – to the door.

Her hand was on the knob when he asked, "Is that all he said?"

She glanced back. He hadn't moved from his stance before the window. "That was all he told me to tell you. 'Tell Royce not to make the same mistakes I made.' Those, exactly those, were his last words."

When he said nothing more, she opened the door, went out, and shut it behind her.

Chapter 4

Royce strode into the breakfast parlor early the next morning, and trapped his chatelaine just as she finished her tea.

Eyes widening, fixed on him, she lowered her cup; without taking her gaze from him, she set it back on its saucer.

Her instincts were excellent. He raked her with his gaze. "Good – you're dressed for riding." Retford had told him she would be when he'd breakfasted even earlier. "You can show me these cottages."

She raised her brows, considered him for a moment, then nodded. "All right." Dropping her napkin beside her plate, she rose, picked up her riding gloves and crop, and calmly joined him.

Accepting his challenge.

Loins girded, jaw clenched, he suffered while, with her gliding beside him, he stalked to the west courtyard. He'd known his sisters would breakfast in their rooms, while their husbands would come down fashionably later, allowing him to kidnap her without having to deal with any of them.

He'd ordered their horses to be saddled. He led the way out of the house; as they crossed the courtyard toward the stables, he glanced at Minerva as, apparently unperturbed, she walked alongside. He'd steeled himself to deflect any comment about their exchange last night, but she'd yet to make one. To press her point that he didn't have to be like his father in managing the dukedom.

That he should break with tradition and do what he felt was right.

Just as he had sixteen years ago.

Regardless of her silence, her opinion reached him clearly.

He felt as if she were manipulating him.

They reached the stable yard and found Henry holding a dancing Sword while Milbourne waited with her horse, a bay gelding, by the mounting block.

On her way to Milbourne, she glanced at the restless gray. "I see you tamed him."

Taking the reins from Henry, Royce planted one boot in the stirrup and swung his leg over the broad back. "Yes."

Just as he'd like to tame her.

Teeth gritted, he gathered the reins, holding Sword in as he watched her settle in her sidesaddle. Then she nodded her thanks to Milbourne, lifted the reins, and trotted forward.

He met her eyes, tipped his head toward the hills. "Lead the way."

She did, at a pace that took some of the edge from his temper. She was an excellent horsewoman, with an excellent seat. Once he'd convinced himself she wasn't likely to come to grief, he found somewhere else to fix his gaze. She led him over the bridge, then across the fields, jumping low stone walls as they headed north of the village. Sword kept pace easily; he had to rein the gray in to keep him from taking the lead.

But once they reached the track that meandered along the banks of Usway Burn, a tributary of the Coquet, they slowed, letting the horses find their own pace along the rocky and uneven ground. Less experienced than the gelding, Sword seemed content to follow in his wake. The track was barely wide enough for a farm cart; they followed its ruts up into the hills.

The cottages stood halfway along the burn, where the valley widened into reasonable-sized meadows. It was a small but fertile holding. As Royce recalled, it had always been prosperous.

It was one of the few acreages on the estate given over to corn. With the uncertainty in supply of that staple, and the consequent increase in price, he could understand Kelso's and Falwell's push to increase the acreage, but . . . the estate had always grown enough corn to feed its people; that hadn't changed. They didn't need to grow more.

What they did need was to keep farmers like the Macgregors, who knew the soil they tilled, on the estate, working the land.

Three cottages – one large, two smaller – had been built in the lee of a west-facing hill. They splashed across the burn at a rough ford. As they neared the buildings, the door of the largest opened; an old man, bent and weathered, came out. Leaning on a stout walking stick, he watched without expression as Royce drew rein and dismounted.

Kicking free of her stirrups, Minerva slid to the ground; reins in one hand, she saluted the old man. "Good morning, Macgregor. His Grace has come to take a look at the cottages."

Macgregor inclined his head politely to her. As she led her bay to a nearby fence, she reached for Royce's reins, and he handed them over.

He walked forward, halting before Macgregor. Old eyes the color of stormy skies held his gaze with a calmness, a rooted certainty, that only age could bring.

Royce knew his father would have waited, silent and intimidating, for an acknowledgment of his station, then possibly nodded curtly before demanding Macgregor show him the cottages.

He offered his hand. "Macgregor."

The old eyes blinked wide. Macgregor dropped his gaze to Royce's hand; after an instant's hesitation, he shifted his grip on the walking stick's knobbed head, and grasped the proffered hand in a surprisingly strong grip.

Macgregor looked up as their hands parted. "Welcome home, Y'r Grace. And it's right glad I am to see you."

"I remember you – frankly, I'm amazed you're still here."

"Aye, well, some of us grow older than others. And I

remember you, too – used to see you riding wild over yon hills."

"I fear my days of wildness are past."

Macgregor made a sound denoting abject disbelief.

Royce glanced at the buildings. "I understand there's a problem with these cottages."

Minerva found herself trailing the pair, entirely redundant, as Macgregor, famed crustiness in abeyance, showed Royce around, pointing out the gaps in the walls, and where the rafters and roof beams no longer met.

Exiting the larger middle cottage, they were crossing to the smaller one to the left when she heard distant hoofbeats. She halted in the yard. Royce would have heard the horse approaching, but he didn't take his attention from Macgregor; the pair went into the smaller cottage. Raising a hand to shade her eyes, she waited in the yard.

Macgregor's oldest son, Sean, appeared, riding one of their workhorses. He slowed, halted just inside the yard, and dismounted, leaving the traces he'd used as reins dragging. He hurried to Minerva. "The rest of the lads and me are working the upper fields. We saw you come riding in." He looked at the smaller cottage. "Is that the new duke in there with Da?"

"Yes, but –" Before she could assure him that his father and his duke were managing perfectly well, Royce led the way out of the tiny cottage, ducking low to miss the lintel. He glanced back as Macgregor followed, then came on.

"This is Sean Macgregor, Macgregor's oldest son. Sean, Wolverstone." Minerva hid a grin at Sean's astonishment when Royce nodded and, apparently without thought, offered his hand.

After a stunned instant, Sean quickly gripped it and shook.

Releasing him, Royce turned to the last cottage. "I should look at them all while I'm here."

"Aye." Macgregor stumped past him. "Come along, then. Not much different to the others, but there's a crooked corner in this one."

He beckoned Royce to follow, and he did.

Sean stood, mouth a-cock, and watched as Royce ducked

through the cottage door in his father's wake. After a moment, he said, "He's really looking."

"Indeed. And when he comes out, I suspect he'll want to discuss what can be done." Minerva looked at Sean. "Can you speak for your brothers?"

He shifted his gaze to her face, nodded. "Aye."

"In that case, I suggest we wait here."

Her prophecy proved correct. When Royce emerged from the dimness of the third cottage, his lips were set in a determined line. He met her gaze, then turned to Macgregor, who had followed him into the mild sunshine. "Let's talk."

They – Royce, Minerva, Macgregor, and Sean – sat at the deal table in the big cottage and thrashed out an arrangement that satisfied them all. While not condoning Kelso's and Falwell's tack, Royce made it clear that the precedent that would be set if the cottages were repaired under the current lease was not one he would countenance; instead, he offered to refashion the lease. It took them an hour to agree on the basic principles; deciding how to get the work done took mere minutes.

Somewhat to her surprise, Royce took charge. "Your lads need to give their time to the harvest first. Once that's in, they can help with the building. You" – he looked at Macgregor – "will supervise. It'll be up to you to make sure the work is done as it should be. I'll come up with Hancock" – he glanced at Minerva – "I assume he's still the castle builder?" When she nodded, he went on, "I'll bring him here, and show him what we need done. We have less than three months before the first snow – I want all three cottages leveled and three new ones completed before winter sets in."

Macgregor blinked; Sean still looked stunned.

When they left the cottage, Minerva was beaming. So, too, were Macgregor and Sean. Royce, in contrast, had his inscrutable mask on.

She hurried to get her horse, Rangonel. There was a convenient log by the fence for a mounting block; scrambling into her saddle, she settled her skirts.

After shaking hands with the Macgregors, Royce cast her a

glance, then retrieved Sword and mounted. She urged Rangonel alongside as he turned down the track.

At the last, she waved to the Macgregors. Still beaming, they waved back. Facing forward, she glanced at Royce. "Am I allowed to say I'm impressed?"

He grunted.

Smiling, she followed him back to the castle.

"*Damn it!*" With the sounds of a London evening – the rattle of wheels, the clop of hooves, the raucous cries of jarveys as they tacked down fashionable Jermyn Street – filling his ears, he read the short note again, then reached for the brandy his man had fortuitously just set on the table by his elbow.

He took a long swallow, read the note again, then tossed it on the table. "The duke's dead. I'll have to go north to attend his funeral."

There was no help for it; if he didn't appear, his absence would be noted. But he was far from thrilled by the prospect. Until that moment, his survival plan had revolved around total and complete avoidance, but a ducal funeral in the family eradicated that option.

The duke was dead. More to the point, his nemesis was now the tenth Duke of Wolverstone.

It would have happened sometime, but why the hell *now*? Royce had barely shaken the dust of Whitehall from his elegantly shod heels – he certainly wouldn't have forgotten the one traitor he'd failed to bring to justice.

He swore, let his head fall back against the chair. He'd always assumed time – the simple passage of it – would be his salvation. That it would dull Royce's memories, his drive, distract him with other things.

Then again . . .

Straightening, he took another sip of brandy. Perhaps having a dukedom to manage – one unexpectedly thrust upon him immediately following an exile of sixteen years – was precisely the distraction Royce needed to drag and hold his attention from his past.

Royce had always had power; his inheriting the title changed little in that regard.

Perhaps this really was for the best?

Time, as ever, would tell, but, unexpectedly, that time was here.

He thought, considered; in the end he had no choice.

"Smith! Pack my bags. I have to go to Wolverstone."

In the breakfast parlor the following morning, Royce was enjoying his second cup of coffee and idly scanning the latest news sheet when Margaret and Aurelia walked in.

They were gowned, coiffed. With vague smiles in his direction, they headed for the sideboard.

He glanced at the clock on the mantelpiece, confirming it was early, not precisely the crack of dawn, yet for them . . .

His cynicism grew as they came to the table, plates in hand. He was at the head of the table; leaving one place empty to either side of him, Margaret sat on his left, Aurelia on his right.

He took another sip of coffee, and kept his attention on the news sheet, certain he'd learn what they wanted sooner rather than later.

His father's four sisters and their husbands, and his mother's brothers and their wives, together with various cousins, had started arriving yesterday; the influx would continue for several days. And once the family was in residence, the connections and friends invited to stay at the castle for the funeral would start to roll in; his staff would be busy for the next week.

Luckily, the keep itself was reserved for immediate family; not even his paternal aunts had rooms in the central wing. This breakfast parlor, too, on the ground floor of the keep, was family only, giving him a modicum of privacy, an area of relative calm in the center of the storm.

Margaret and Aurelia sipped their tea and nibbled slices of dry toast. They chatted about their children, their intention presumably to inform him of the existence of his nephews and nieces. He studiously kept his gaze on the news sheet. Eventually his sisters accepted that, after sixteen years of not knowing, he was unlikely to develop an interest in that direction overnight.

Even without looking, he sensed the glance they exchanged, heard Margaret draw in one of her portentous breaths.

His chatelaine breezed in. "Good morning, Margaret, Aurelia." Her tone suggested she was surprised to find them down so early.

Her entrance threw his sisters off-balance; they murmured good mornings, then fell silent.

With his eyes, he tracked Minerva to the sideboard, taking in her plain green gown. Trevor had reported that on Saturday mornings she eschewed riding in favor of taking a turn about the gardens with the head gardener in tow.

Royce returned his gaze to the news sheet, ignoring the part of him that whispered, "A pity." He wasn't entirely pleased with her; it was just as well that when he rode out shortly, he wouldn't come upon her riding his hills and dales, so he wouldn't be able to join her, her and him alone, private in the wild.

Such an encounter would do nothing to ease his all but constant pain.

As Minerva took her seat farther down the board, Margaret cleared her throat and turned to him. "We'd wondered, Royce, whether you had any particular thoughts about a lady who might fill the position of your duchess."

He held still for an instant, then lowered the news sheet, looked first at Margaret, then at Aurelia. He'd never gaped in his life, but . . . "Our father isn't even in the ground, and you're talking about my wedding?"

He glanced at his chatelaine. She had her head down, her gaze fixed on her plate.

"You'll have to think of the matter sooner rather than later." Margaret set down her fork. "The ton isn't going to let the most eligible duke in England simply" – she gestured – "be!"

"The ton won't have any choice. I have no immediate plans to marry."

Aurelia leaned closer. "But Royce –"

"If you'll excuse me" – he stood, tossing the news sheet and his napkin on the table – "I'm going riding." His tone made it clear there was no question involved.

He strode down the table, glanced at Minerva as he went past.

He halted; when she looked up, he caught her autumn eyes. His own narrow, he pointed at her. "I'll see you in the study when I get back."

When he'd ridden far enough, hard enough, to get the tempest of anger and lust roiling through him under control.

Striding out, he headed for the stables.

By lunchtime on Sunday he was ready to throttle his elder sisters, his aunts, and his aunts-by-marriage, all of whom had, it seemed, not a thought with which to occupy their heads other than who – which lady – would be most suitable as his bride.

As the next Duchess of Wolverstone.

He'd breakfasted at dawn to avoid them. Now, in the wake of the ruthlessly cutting comments he'd made the previous night, silencing all such talk about the dinner table, they'd conceived the happy notion of discussing ladies, who all just happened to be young, well-bred, and eligible, comparing their attributes, weighing their fortunes and connections, apparently in the misguided belief that by omitting the words "Royce," "marriage," and "duchess" from their comments, they would avoid baiting his temper.

He was very, very close to losing it – and inching ever closer by the second.

What were they thinking? Minerva couldn't conceive what Margaret, Aurelia, and Royce's aunts hoped to achieve – other than a blistering set-down which looked set to be delivered in a thunderous roar at any minute.

If one were possessed of half a brain, one did not provoke male Variseys. Not beyond the point where they grew totally silent, and their faces set like stone, and – the final warning – their fingers tightened on whatever they were holding until their knuckles went white.

76

Royce's right hand was clenched about his knife so tightly all four knuckles gleamed.

She had to do something – not that his female relatives deserved saving. If it were up to her, she'd let him savage them, but . . . she had two deathbed vows to honor, which meant she had to see him wed – and his misbegotten relatives were turning the subject of his marriage into one he was on the very brink of declaring unmentionable in his hearing.

He could do that – and would – and would expect and insist and ensure he was obeyed.

Which would make her task all the harder.

They seemed to have forgotten who he was – that he was Wolverstone.

She glanced around; she needed help to derail the conversation.

There wasn't much help to be had. Most of the men had escaped, taking guns and dogs and heading out for some early shooting. Susannah was there; seated on Royce's right, she was wisely holding her tongue and not contributing to her brother's ire in any way.

Unfortunately, she was too far from Minerva's position halfway down the board to be easily enlisted; Minerva couldn't catch her eye.

The only other potential conspirator was Hubert, seated opposite Minerva. She had no high opinion of Hubert's intelligence, but she was desperate. Leaning forward, she caught his eye. "Did you say you'd seen Princess Charlotte and Prince Leopold in London?"

The princess was the darling of England; her recent marriage to Prince Leopold was the only topic Minerva could think of that might trump the subject of Royce's bride. She'd imbued her question with every ounce of breathless interest she could muster – and was rewarded with instant silence.

Every head swung to the middle of the table, every female pair of eyes followed her gaze to Hubert.

He stared at her, eyes showing the surprise of a startled

77

rabbit. Silently she willed him to reply in the affirmative; he blinked, then smiled. "I did, as a matter of fact."

"Where?" He was lying – she could see he was – but he was willing to dance to her tune.

"In Bond Street."

"At one of the jewelers?"

Slowly, he nodded. "Aspreys."

Royce's aunt Emma, seated next to Minerva, leaned forward. "Did you see what they were looking at?"

"They spent quite a bit of time looking at brooches. I saw the attendant bring out a tray – on it were –"

Minerva sat back, a vacuous smile on her face, and let Hubert run on. He was well-launched, and with a wife like Susannah, his knowledge of the jewelry to be found in Aspreys was extensive.

All attention had swung to him.

Leaving Royce to finish his meal without further aggravation; he needed no encouragement to apply himself to the task.

Hubert had only just passed on to the necklaces the royal couple had supposedly examined when Royce pushed away his plate, waved Retford's offer of the fruit bowl aside, dropped his napkin beside his plate, and stood.

The movement broke Hubert's spell. All attention swung to Royce.

He didn't bother to smile. "If you'll excuse me, ladies, I have a dukedom to run." He started striding down the room on his way to the door. Over the heads, he nodded to Hubert. "Do carry on."

Drawing level, his gaze pinned Minerva. "I'll see you in the study when you're free."

She was free now. As Royce strode from the room, she patted her lips, edged back her chair, waited for the footman to draw it out for her. She smiled at Hubert as she stood. "I know I'll regret not hearing the rest of your news – it's like a fairy tale."

He grinned. "Never mind. There's not much more to tell."

She swallowed a laugh, fought to look suitably disappointed as she hurried from the room in Royce's wake.

He'd already disappeared up the stairs; she climbed them, then walked quickly to the study, wondering which part of the estate he'd choose to interrogate her on today.

Since their visit to Usway Burn on Friday, he'd had her sitting before his desk for a few hours each day, telling him about the estate's tenant farms and the families who held them. He didn't ask about profits, crops, or yields, none of the things Kelso or Falwell were responsible for, but about the farms themselves, the land, the farmers and their wives, their children. Who interacted with whom, the human dynamics of the estate; that was what he questioned her on.

When she'd passed on his father's dying message, she hadn't known whether he'd actually had it in him to be different; Variseys tended to breed true, and along with their other principal traits, their stubbornness was legendary.

That was why she hadn't delivered the message immediately. She'd wanted Royce to see and know what his father had meant, rather than just hear the words. Words out of context were too easy to dismiss, to forget, to ignore.

But now he'd heard them, absorbed them, and made the effort, responded to the need, and scripted a new way forward with the Macgregors. She was too wise to comment, not even to encourage; he'd waited for her to say something, but she'd stepped back and left him to define his own way.

With skill and luck, one could steer Variseys; one couldn't lead them.

Jeffers was on duty outside the study. He opened the door and she walked in.

Royce was pacing back and forth before the window behind the desk, looking out at his lands, his every stride invested with the lethal grace of a caged jungle cat, muscles sleekly taut, shifting beneath the fine weave of his coat and his thigh-hugging buckskin breeches.

She simply stood, unable to look away; instinct wouldn't allow her to take her eyes from such a predatory sight.

And looking was no hardship.

She could sense his whipping temper, knew he could lash

out, yet was utterly sure he would never hurt her. Or any woman. Yet the turbulent emotions seething within him, swirling in powerful currents all around him, would have most women, most men, edging away.

Not her. She was attracted to the energy, to the wild and compelling power that was so intrinsic a part of him.

Her dangerous secret.

She waited. The door had closed; he knew she was there. When he gave no sign, she advanced and sat in the chair.

Abruptly, he halted. He hauled in a huge breath, then swung around, and dropped into his chair. "The farm at Linshields. Who holds it these days – is it still the Carews?"

"Yes, but I think you probably remember Carew senior. It's his son who runs the farm now."

He kept her talking for the next hour, pressing her, questions flying at a cracking pace.

Royce tried to keep his mind wholly focused on business – on the information he drew from her – yet her answers flowed so freely he had time to truly listen, not just to what she was saying but to her voice, the timbre, the faint huskiness, the rise and fall of emotions as she let them color her words.

She had no reticence, no shields, not on this subject, not any longer. He didn't need to watch for hints of prevarication, or of reserve.

So his wider senses had time to dwell on the rise and fall of her breasts, the way one errant curl fell across her forehead, time to note the gold flecks that came alive in her eyes when she smiled over some recounted incident.

Eventually, his questions ended, died. His temper dissipated, he sat back in his chair. Physically relaxed, inwardly brooding. His gaze on her.

"I didn't thank you for saving me at luncheon."

Minerva smiled. "Hubert was a surprise. And it was your relatives we saved, not you."

He grimaced, reached out to reposition a pencil that had rolled across the blotter. "They're right in that I will need to marry, but I can't see why they're so intent on pushing the subject at this time." He glanced at her, a question in his eyes.

"I've no idea why, either. I'd expected them to leave that topic for at least a few months, mourning and all. Although I suppose no eyebrows would be raised if you became betrothed within the year."

The fingers of one hand tapping the blotter, his gaze sharpened. "I'm not of a mind to let them dictate, or even dabble in, my future. It might, therefore, be wise to get some idea of the potential . . . candidates."

She hesitated, then asked, "What style of candidate are you thinking of?"

He gave her a look that said she knew better than to ask. "The usual style – a typical Varisey bride. How does it go? Suitable breeding, position, connections and fortune, passable beauty, intelligence optional." He frowned. "Did I forget anything?"

She fought to keep her lips straight. "No. That's more or less the full description."

No matter that he might differ from his father in managing people and the estate, he wouldn't differ in his requirements of a bride. The tradition of Varisey marriages predated the dukedom by untold generations, and, even more telling, suited their temperament.

She saw no reason to disagree with his assessment. The new fashion of love matches within the nobility had little to offer the Variseys. They did not love. She'd spent more than twenty years among them, and had never seen any evidence to the contrary. It was simply the way they were; love had been bred out of them centuries ago – if it had ever been in their mix at all. "If you wish, I could make a list of the candidates your relatives – and no doubt the grandes dames who come up for the funeral – mention."

He nodded. "Their gossip may as well be useful for something. Add anything relevant you know, or hear from reliable sources." He met her eyes. "And, no doubt, you'll add your opinion, as well."

She smiled sweetly. "No, I won't. As far as I'm concerned, choosing your bride is entirely your affair. I won't be living with her."

He gave her another of his bland, you-should-know-better looks. "Neither will I."

She inclined her head, acknowledging that fact. "Regardless, your bride is not a subject on which I would seek to influence you."

"I don't suppose you'd like to promulgate that view to my sisters?"

"Sadly, I must decline – it would be a waste of breath."

He grunted.

"If there's nothing else, I should go and see who else has arrived. Cranny, bless her, needs to know how many will sit down to dine."

When he nodded, she rose and headed for the door. Reaching it, she glanced back, and saw him sprawled in his chair, that brooding look on his face. "If you have time, you might like to look at the tithing from the smaller crofts. At present, it's stated as an absolute amount, but a percentage of profit might suit everyone better."

He arched a brow. "Another radical notion?"

She shrugged and opened the door. "Just a suggestion."

So here he was at Wolverstone, under his nemesis's roof. His very large roof, in this far distant corner of Northumberland, which was a point, he now realized, that worked in his favor.

The estate was so very far from London that many of the visitors, especially those who were family, would stay for a time; the castle was so huge it could accommodate a small army. So there was, and would continue to be, plenty of cover; he would be safe enough.

He stood at the window of the pleasant room he'd been given in the east wing, looking down on the castle gardens, beautifully presented and bursting with colorful life in the last gasp of the short northern summer.

He had an appreciation for beautiful things, an eye that had guided him in amassing an exquisite collection of the most priceless items the French had had to offer. In exchange he'd given them information, information that, whenever he'd been able, had run directly counter to Royce's commission.

Whenever possible, he'd tried to harm Royce – not directly, but through the men he'd commanded.

From all he'd been able to glean, he'd failed, dismally. Just as he'd failed, over the years, over all the times he'd been held up against Royce, measured against his glorious cousin and found wanting. By his father, his uncle, most of all by his grandfather.

His lips curled; his handsome features distorted in a snarl.

Worst of all, Royce had seized his prize, his carefully hoarded treasure. He'd stolen it from him, denying him even that. For all his years of serving the French, he'd received pre-cisely nothing – not even the satisfaction of knowing he'd caused Royce pain.

In the world of men, and all through the ton, Royce was a celebrated success. And now Royce was Wolverstone to boot.

While he . . . was an unimportant sprig on a family tree.

It shouldn't be so.

Dragging in a breath, he slowly exhaled, willing his features back into the handsome mask he showed the world. Turning, he looked around the room.

His eye fell on a small bowl sitting on the mantelpiece. Not Sevres, but Chinese, quite delicate.

He walked across the room, picked up the bowl, felt its light-ness, examined its beauty.

Then he opened his fingers and let it fall.

It smashed to smithereens on the floor.

By late Wednesday afternoon, all the family were in residence, and the first of the guests invited to stay at the castle had begun to arrive.

Royce had been instructed by his chatelaine to be on hand to greet the more important; summoned by Jeffers, he gritted his teeth and descended to the hall to welcome the Duchess of St. Ives, Lady Horatia Cynster, and Lord George Cynster.

Although St. Ives's estates lay in the south, the two dukedoms shared a similar history, and the families had supported each other through the centuries.

"Royce!" Her Grace, Helena, Duchess of St. Ives – or the Dowager Duchess, as he'd heard she preferred to style herself – spotted him. She glided to meet him as he stepped off the stairs. "*Mon ami*, such a sad time."

He took her hand, bowed, and brushed a kiss over her knuckles – only to have her swear in French, tug him lower, stretch up on her toes, and press a kiss first to one cheek, then to the other. He permitted it, then straightened, smiled. "Welcome to Wolverstone, Your Grace. You grow lovelier with the years."

Huge, pale green eyes looked up at him. "Yes, I do." She smiled, a glorious expression that lit her whole face, then she let her gaze skate appreciatively down him. "And you . . ." She muttered something in colloquial French he didn't catch, then reverted to English to say, "We had expected to have you return to our salons – instead, you are now here, and no doubt plan to hide yourself away." She wagged a delicate finger at him. "It will not do. You are older than my recalcitrant son, and must marry soon."

She turned to include the lady beside her. "Horatia – tell him he must let us help him choose his bride *tout de suite*."

"And he'll pay as much attention to me as he will you." Lady Horatia Cynster, tall, dark-haired, and commanding, smiled at him. "Condolences, Royce – or should I say Wolverstone?" She gave him her hand, and like Helena, pulled him nearer to touch cheeks. "Regardless of what you might wish, your father's funeral is going to focus even more attention on your urgent need of a bride."

"Let the poor boy find his feet." Lord George Cynster, Horatia's husband, offered Royce his hand. After a firm hand-shake, he shooed his wife and sister-in-law away. "There's Minerva looking harassed trying to sort out your boxes – you might help her, or you might end with each other's gowns."

The mention of gowns had both grandes dames' attention

shifting. As they moved to where Minerva stood surrounded by a bewildering array of boxes and trunks, George sighed. "They mean well, but it's only fair to warn you you're in for a time of it."

Royce raised his brows. "St. Ives didn't come up with you?"

"He's following in his curricle. Given what you just experienced, you can understand why he'd take rain, sleet, and even snow over spending days in the same carriage as his mother."

Royce laughed. "True." Beyond the open doors, he saw a procession of three carriages draw up. "If you'll excuse me, some others have arrived."

"Of course, m'boy." George clapped him on the back. "Escape while you can."

Royce did, going out through the massive doors propped open in welcome and down the shallow steps to where the three carriages were disgorging their passengers and baggage amid a chaos of footmen and grooms.

A pretty blond in a fashionable pelisse was directing a footman to take care of her boxes, unaware of Royce's approach. "Alice – welcome."

Alice Carlisle, Viscountess Middlethorpe, turned, wide-eyed. "Royce!" She embraced him, tugging him down to plant a kiss on his cheek. "What an unexpected event – and before you'd even returned."

Gerald, her husband, heir to the earldom of Fyfe, stepped down from the carriage, Alice's shawl in one hand. "Royce." He held out his other hand. "Commiserations, old man."

The others had heard, and quickly gathered, offering condolences along with strong hands, or scented cheeks and warm embraces – Miles Ffolliot, Baron Sedgewick, heir to the earldom of Wrexham, and his wife, Eleanor, and the Honorable Rupert Trelawny, heir to the Marquess of Riddlesdale, and his wife, Rose.

They were Royce's closest friends; the three men had been at Eton with him, and the four had remained close through the subsequent years. Throughout his self-imposed social exile, theirs had been the only events – dinners, select soirees – that he'd attended. Over the last decade, he'd first encountered each of his many lovers at one or other of these three ladies' houses, a fact of which he was sure they were aware.

These six made up his inner circle, the people he trusted, those he'd known the longest. There were others – the members of the Bastion Club and now their wives – whom he would likewise trust with his life, but these three couples were the people he shared closest connection with; they were of his circle, and understood the pressures he faced, his temperament, understood him.

Minerva was one he could now add to that circle; she, too, understood him. Unfortunately, as he was reminded every time he saw her, he needed to keep her at a distance.

With Miles, Rupert, and Gerald there, he felt much more . . . himself. Much more certain of who he really was, what he really was. Of what was important to him.

For the next several minutes, he let himself slide into the usual cacophony that resulted whenever all three couples and he were together. He led them inside and introduced them to his chatelaine, relieved when it became obvious that Minerva, and Alice, Eleanor, and Rose, would get on. He would ensure that his three friends were entertained, but given the way the next days looked set to go, he was planning on avoiding all gatherings of ladies; knowing Minerva would watch over his friends' wives meant their entertainment would likewise be assured, and their stay at Wolverstone as comfortable as circumstances permitted.

He was about to accompany them up the main stairs when the rattle of carriage wheels had him glancing into the forecourt. Slowing, a carriage rolled into view, then halted; he recognized the crest on its door.

He nudged Miles's arm. "Do you remember the billiard room?"

Miles, Gerald, and Rupert had visited before, long ago. Miles arched a brow. "You can't imagine I'd forget the place of so many of your defeats?"

"Your memory's faulty – they were your defeats." Royce saw

Gerald and Rupert looking down at him, questions in their eyes. "I'll meet you there once you've settled in. Some others have arrived who I need to greet."

With nods and waves, the men followed their wives up the stairs. Royce turned back into the front hall. More guests were arriving; Minerva had her hands full. The hall was continually awash with trunks and boxes even though a company of footmen were constantly ferrying loads upstairs.

Leaving them to it, Royce walked outside. He'd last seen the couple descending from the latest carriage mere weeks ago; he'd missed their wedding, deliberately, but he'd known they would come north to support him.

The lady turned and saw him. He held out a hand. "Letitia."

"Royce." Lady Letitia Allardyce, Marchioness of Dearne, took his hand and stretched up to kiss his cheek; she was tall enough to do so without tugging him down. "The news was a shock."

She stepped back while he exchanged greetings with her husband, Christian, one of his ex-colleagues, a man of similar propensities as he, one who had dealt in secrets, violence, and death in their country's defense.

The three turned toward the castle steps, the men flanking Letitia. She looked into Royce's face. "You weren't expecting to have the dukedom thrust upon you like this. How's your temper holding up?"

She was one of the few who would dare ask him that. He slanted her an unencouraging look.

She grinned and patted his arm. "If you want any advice on restraining temper, just ask the expert."

He shook his head. "Your temper's dramatic. Mine's . . . not."

His temper was destructive, and much more powerful.

"Yes, well." She fixed her gaze on the door, fast drawing near. "I know this isn't something you want to hear, but the next days are going to be much worse than you imagine. You'll learn why soon enough, if you haven't already. And for what it's worth, my advice, dear Royce, is to grit your teeth and rein-force the reins on your temper, because they're about to be tested as never before."

Expressionless, he stared at her.

She smiled brightly back. "Shall we go in?"

Minerva saw the trio enter, and walked over to greet the newcomers. She and Letitia knew each other well, which, she realized, surprised Royce. She hadn't met Dearne before, but approved of his presence, and especially his statement that he was there in part representing Royce's closest ex-colleagues from his years in Whitehall.

He added to Royce, "The others asked us to convey their regards."

Royce nodded in acknowledgment; despite his perpetual mask, she sensed he was . . . touched. That he appreciated the support.

She'd already assigned rooms to all those expected; handing Letitia and Dearne over to Retford to magisterially guide upstairs, she watched them ascend. Felt Royce's gaze on her face. "I know Letitia from all the years I spent with your mother in London."

He gave an almost imperceptible nod; that was what he'd wanted to know.

She'd met Miles, Rupert, and Gerald when they'd visited years ago, had met them and their wives in more recent times, too, although only in passing at ton entertainments. She'd been intrigued to learn – relieved to learn – that they'd stood by Royce over the years. She'd often wondered just how alone he'd been. Not completely, thank heaven, yet she was starting to suspect, his friends aside, that he wasn't as socially adept as he was going to need to be.

The next days were going to be a strain on him, in more ways than she thought he realized.

Turning from the stairs, she surveyed the hall, still a bustling hive of activity. At least there were no guests waiting to be greeted; for the moment, she and Royce were alone amid the sea of luggage.

"You should know," she murmured, "that there's something afoot regarding your wedding. I haven't yet learned exactly what – and your friends' wives don't know, either, but they'll keep their ears open. I'm sure Letitia will." She glanced at his face. "If I hear anything definite, I'll let you know."

His lips twisted in a partially suppressed grimace. "Letitia warned me that something I wouldn't like was coming – she didn't specify what. It sounded as if she, too, wasn't entirely sure."

Minerva nodded. "I'll speak with her later. Perhaps, together, we can work it out."

Another carriage rolled to a halt beyond the steps; she cast him a glance, then went out to greet his guests.

Late that evening, on returning to his rooms after soundly thrashing Miles at billiards, Royce stripped off his coat and tossed it to Trevor. "I want you to keep your ears open on the subject of my marriage."

Trevor raised his brows, then took his waistcoat from him.

"Specifically" – Royce gave his attention to unraveling his cravat – "my bride." He met Trevor's gaze in the mirror above the tallboy. "See what you can learn – tonight if possible."

"Naturally, Your Grace." Trevor grinned. "I'll bring the pertinent information with your shaving water in the morning."

The next day was the day before the funeral. Royce spent the morning riding with his friends; on returning to the stables, he stopped to speak with Milbourne while the others went ahead. A few minutes later, he followed them back into the castle, seizing the moment alone to review the scant information Trevor had relayed that morning.

The grandes dames were fixated on the necessity of him marrying and getting an heir. What neither Trevor nor his chatelaine, whom he'd seen over breakfast, had as yet ascertained was why there was such intensity, well beyond the merely prurient, almost an air of urgency behind the older ladies' stance.

Something definitely was afoot; his instincts, honed by years of military plotting, ducking, and weaving, were more than pricking.

He strode into the front hall, the necessity of gathering better intelligence high in his mind.

"Good morning, Wolverstone."

The commanding female tones jerked him out of his thoughts. His gaze met a pair of striking hazel eyes. It took him an instant to place them – a fact the lady noted with something akin to exasperation.

"Lady Augusta." He went forward, took the hand she offered him, half bowed.

To the gentleman beside her, he offered his hand. "My lord."

The Marquess of Huntly smiled benignly. "It's been a long time, Royce. Sad that we have to meet again in such circumstances."

"Indeed." Lady Augusta, Marchioness of Huntly, one of the most influential ladies of the ton, eyed him measuringly. "But circumstances aside, we'll need to talk, my lad, about your bride. You must marry, and soon – you've been dragging your heels for the past decade, but now the time has come, and you'll have to choose."

"We're here to bury my father." Royce's accent made the statement a none-too-subtle rebuke.

Lady Augusta snorted. "Indeed." She jabbed a finger at his chest. "Which is precisely my point. No mourning for you – in the circumstances the ton will excuse you, and gladly."

"Lady Augusta!" Minerva hurried down the main stairs, all but tripping in her haste to rescue them all. "We were expecting you yesterday and wondered what had happened."

"Hubert happened, or rather Westminster called, and he was delayed, so we set out rather later than I'd wished." Augusta turned to envelop her in a warm embrace. "And how are you, child? Managing with the son as well as you did with the father, heh?"

Minerva shot Royce a look, prayed he'd keep his mouth

90

shut. "I'm not sure about that, but do come upstairs, both of you." She linked her arm with Augusta's, then did the same with Hubert on her other side. "Helena and Horatia are already here. They're in the upstairs salon in the west wing."

Chatting easily, she determinedly towed the pair up the stairs. As she turned them along the gallery, she glanced down and saw Royce standing where they'd left him, an expression like a thundercloud on his usually impassive face.

Meeting his eyes, she fleetingly shrugged, brows high; she had yet to learn what was fueling the grandes dames' avid interest in the matter of his bride.

Correctly interpreting her look, Royce watched her guide the pair out of his sight, even more certain that Letitia had been right.

Whatever was coming, he wasn't going to like it.

Chapter 5

That evening, Royce walked into the great drawing room in no good mood; neither he, Minerva, nor Trevor had yet managed to learn exactly what was going on. The large room was crowded, not just with family but also with the elite of the ton, including representatives of the Crown and the Lords, all gathered for the funeral tomorrow, and talking in hushed tones as they waited for the summons to dine.

Halting just over the threshold, Royce surveyed the assembly – and instantly perceived the answer to his most pressing need. The most powerful grande dame of them all, Lady Therese Osbaldestone, was seated between Helena and Horatia on the chaise before the fireplace. She might have been a mere baroness in the company of duchesses, marchionesses, and countesses, yet she wielded more power, political and social, than any other lady of the ton.

More, she was on excellent terms with said duchesses, marchionesses, and countesses; whatever she decreed, they would support. Therein lay much of her power, especially over the male half of society.

Royce had always treated her with respect. Power, the amassing and wielding of it, was something he understood; it was bred in his marrow – something her ladyship appreciated.

She must have arrived while he was out riding.

He walked to the chaise, inclined his head to her companions, then to her. "Lady Osbaldestone."

Intensely black eyes – true obsidian – fixed on his face. She nodded, trying to read him, and failing. "Wolverstone."

It was the first time she'd called him that – the first time he'd felt the weight of the mantle on his shoulders. Taking the hand she offered, he bowed, careful not to overdo the observance; she respected those who knew their place, knew what was due to them.

"My condolences on your father's death. Sadly, it comes to us all, although in his case the timing could have been better."

He inclined his head, declined to rise to the lure.

She uttered a soft "humph." "We need to talk – later."

He acquiesced with a half bow. "Later."

Swallowing his impatience, he moved away, letting those of his relatives and connections he'd thus far avoided have at him. Weathering their greetings and accepting their condolences grated on his nerves; he was relieved when Minerva joined the circle about him and set about distracting those he'd already spoken with, subtly but effectively moving them on.

Then Retford announced that dinner was served. Minerva caught his eye, whispered as she passed close, "Lady Augusta."

He assumed that was who he was to lead in to dinner; he located the marchioness – yet his senses, ensorcelled simply by Minerva passing so close, continued to track her.

She wasn't doing anything to attract his notice. In her weeds, she should have faded into the sea of black surrounding him; instead she – just she – seemed to shine in his awareness. The dull black suited her golden loveliness. With an effort hauling his mind from slaveringly dwelling on the loveliness inside the dull black, he surrendered to duty and strolled to Lady Augusta, while trying to push the lingering, elusive, wantonly feminine scent of his chatelaine from his brain.

The conversations in the drawing room had been muted. Continuing the trend, dinner proved an unexpectedly somber meal, as if everyone had suddenly recalled why they were there – and who no longer was. For the first time since he'd viewed the body, he felt touched by his father's absence, sitting in the great carver where his sire used to sit, looking down the long table, lined by more than sixty others, to Margaret sitting at the other end.

A different perspective, one not previously his.

His gaze tracked back to Minerva, seated toward the table's center, opposite Susannah, and surrounded by his cousins. There were nine male cousins present from both sides of his family, Variseys and Debraighs; given the numbers attending, his younger female cousins weren't expected.

His maternal uncle, the Earl of Catersham, was seated on Margaret's right, while the eldest of his paternal aunts, Winifred, Countess Barraclough, sat on Royce's left. Beyond her sat his heir, Lord Edwin Varisey, the third brother of his grandfather's generation, while on his right, next to Lady Augusta and facing Edwin, was his cousin several times removed, Gordon Varisey, eldest son of the late Cameron Varisey, Edwin's younger brother; after the childless Edwin, Gordon stood next in line for the ducal crown.

Edwin was an ancient fop. Gordon was dark and dour, but underneath a sound man. Neither expected to inherit the dukedom, which was just as well; despite his resistance to discussing the subject with all and sundry, Royce had every intention of marrying and siring an heir to whom he would pass the title. What he failed to comprehend was why he needed the help of the grandes dames to achieve that goal, and why it had to be achieved so urgently.

Luckily, the mood of the dinner, with the ladies in dull black, gray, or deep purple, with no jewels beyond jet and no fans or furbelows, and the gentlemen in black coats, many sporting black cravats, had suppressed all talk of his nuptials. Conversations continued to be low-voiced, constant, yet no one laughed, or smiled other than wistfully; across him, Augusta, Winifred, and Edwin swapped tales of his father, to which he pretended to pay attention.

Then the covers were drawn, and Margaret rose and led the ladies back to the drawing room, leaving the men to enjoy port and brandy in relative peace. Some of the formality eased as gentlemen moved to form groups along the table. Royce's cousins congregated in the center, while the older men gravitated to flank his uncle Catersham at the far end.

His friends came to join him, filling the chairs the ladies and Edwin and Gordon had vacated. Joining them, Devil Cynster, Duke of St. Ives, passing behind his chair, briefly clasped his shoulder. His pale green eyes met Royce's as he glanced up. Devil had lost his father and succeeded to his dukedom when he'd been fifteen. With a nod, Devil moved on, leaving Royce reflecting that at least he was shouldering the burden at a significantly older age; then again, Devil had had his uncle, George, to rely on, and George Cynster was a wise, knowledgeable, and capable man.

Devil took the seat next to Christian, easily sliding into the camaraderie of the group; they all opted for whisky, and sat savoring the smoky liquor, lazily exchanging the latest sporting news, and a few salaciously risqué on-dits.

With his impatience to learn what Lady Osbaldestone would tell him steadily mounting, as soon as it was reasonable he led the gentlemen back to the drawing room. Devil ambled beside him; they stopped shoulder to shoulder just inside the room, letting the other men pass by.

Royce surveyed the gathering; from the glances that came his way, many conversations had reverted to the subject of his bride. "At least no one's expecting you to marry tomorrow."

Devil's black brows rose. "You obviously haven't spoken to my mother on that subject."

"She called you recalcitrant."

"Indeed. And you have to remember she's French, which is the excuse she uses to be as outrageous as she pleases in pursuit of her goal."

"You're hardly in your dotage," Royce returned. Devil was six years younger than he. "And you've a string of acceptable heirs. What's the rush?"

"Precisely my question," Devil purred, his green eyes fixed

on someone in the crowd. Then he slanted a glance at Royce, one brow arching. "Your chatelaine . . .?"

A fist clamped about his heart. The effort not to react – not to snarl and show his teeth – almost stole his breath. He waited a heartbeat, his eyes locked with Devil's, then quietly murmured, "No." After an instant, he added, "I believe she's spoken for."

"Is she?" Devil held his gaze for an instant longer, then he glanced across the room – at Minerva. "Earlier, she just frowned and told me to go away."

"Unlike most ladies, she probably meant it." Royce couldn't stop himself from adding, "If I were you, I'd take her at her word. Heaven knows, I do." He imbued the last words with sufficient masculine long-suffering to have Devil grin once more.

"Ah, well – I won't be here that long."

"Abstinence, they say, is good for the soul."

Devil shot him a look as if asking who he thought he was fooling, then wandered off into the crowd.

Royce watched him go, and muttered to himself, "However, abstinence is hell on the temper." And his was worse that most to begin with.

In search of relief, he located Lady Osbaldestone and would have immediately gone to her side, except for the numerous guests who lined up to waylay him.

Not family, but the ton's elite, including Lord Haworth, representing the Crown, and Lord Hastings, representing the Lords. None were people he could dismiss with just a word, not even a word and a smile; he had to interact, engage in social exchanges all too often layered with multiple meanings . . . he was reaching, had come close to socially stumbling, when Minerva appeared beside him, serenely calm, a stately smile on her lips, and the hints he needed ready on her tongue.

After just a few words, he realized she was an adept in this sphere, and gratefully, if reluctantly, attached himself to her apron strings. The alternative was too damning to permit him to indulge in any pretense.

He needed her. So he had to metaphorically grit his teeth and bear the sexual abrasion of her nearness – it was that or come to social grief, and he'd be damned if he did that. Failure in anything had never been an option, yet this arena was not one in which he'd had any real experience. Yet now he was Wolverstone, people expected him to simply take on the mantle; they seemed to have forgotten the sixteen years he'd spent outside their pale.

For the next half hour, Minerva was his anchor, his guide, his savior.

Courtesy of her vows, she had to be, or, damn him, he'd founder on the social shoals, or come to grief on the jagged rocks of political repartee.

She managed the glib exchanges with half her brain – the other half was entirely consumed by something akin to panic. A frenzied awareness of what would happen if he brushed her shoulder with his arm, if, for some benighted reason, he thought to take her hand. Beneath her smiles, underneath her ready replies, ran an expectation of disaster that clenched her lungs tight, leaving her nearly breathless, every nerve taut, ready to leap with hypersensitive reaction.

At one point, after she'd excused them from a group where the exchanges had looked set to grow too pointed for his – or her – good, he seized the moment of fleeting privacy to lower his head, lower his voice, and ask, "Was my father any good at this?"

Ruthlessly suppressing the effect of the subtle caress of his breath over her ear, she shot him a glance. "Yes, he was."

His lips twisted in a grimace. "So I'm going to have to learn how to manage this, too."

It was the look in his eyes as he glanced around, more than his words, that had her feeling sorry for him; he'd had to take on the business of the dukedom unprepared, and he had made and was making a huge effort in that regard, and succeeding. But this arena of high-level political and social games was one in which he also had to perform, and for that his exile – from the age of twenty-two to thirty-seven – had left him even less well prepared.

"You're Wolverstone now, so yes, you'll have to learn." She had every confidence that, if he applied himself – his incredible intellect, his excellent memory, and his well-honed will – he would succeed. To ensure he accepted the challenge, she added, "And I won't be forever by your side."

He met her gaze at that, his eyes so dark she couldn't read anything in them. Then he nodded and looked ahead as the next wave of guests approached.

The next time they moved on, Royce murmured, "I've been commanded to attend Lady Osbaldestone." Her ladyship was conversing with one of his cousins at the side of the room just ahead of them. "I can manage her if you'll keep the rest at bay. I need to speak with her alone."

Minerva caught his eye. "About this bride business?"

He nodded. "She knows the reason – and once I prostrate myself before her, will take great delight in informing me of it, no doubt."

"In that case, go." She smoothly stepped forward to intercept the next couple seeking an audience with him.

Lady Osbaldestone saw him approaching, and with a few words dismissed his cousin Rohan; hands folded over the head of the cane she didn't really need, she waited before one of the long windows for him to join her.

She arched a brow as he halted before her. "I take it you have, by now, been informed of the need for you to wed with all speed."

"Indeed. In various ways, by a number of your cronies." He fixed his eyes on hers. "What I don't understand is the reason behind the supreme urgency."

She stared at him for a moment, then blinked. She regarded him for an instant more, then murmured, "I suppose, having been in social exile . . . then you were summoned back here before . . ." Lips compressing, she narrowed her eyes. "I suppose it's conceivable that, omniscient though you are rumored to be, you might not have been alerted to the recent developments."

"Obviously not. I will be eternally grateful if you would enlighten me."

She snorted. "You won't be grateful, but clearly someone must. Consider these facts. One, Wolverstone is one of the wealthiest duchies in England. Two, it was created as a marcher lordship. Three, your heir is Edwin, already one step away from senile, and after him, Gordon, who while arguably a legally entitled heir, is nevertheless sufficiently distant to be challenged."

He frowned. "By whom?"

"Indeed." Lady Osbaldestone nodded. "The source of the threat." She held his gaze. "The Crown."

His eyes narrowed. "Prinny?" His voice was flat, his tone disbelieving.

"He's neck-deep in debt, and sinking ever faster. I won't bore you with the details, but I and others have heard from reliable sources close to our dear prince that the search for plunderable funds is on in earnest, and Wolverstone has been mentioned, specifically along the lines of, if anything should, heaven forbid, happen to you, then as matters stand it might be possible to press for the title, and all its entailed wealth, to revert to the Crown in escheat."

He could understand the reasoning, but . . . "There's a significant difference between Prinny, or more likely one of those panderers close to him, making such a suggestion, and it actually being acted upon, even were something to mysteriously happen to me."

Lady Osbaldestone frowned; something like exasperated alarm showed briefly in her eyes. "Don't shrug this off. If you were married, Prinny and his vultures would lose interest and look elsewhere, but while you aren't . . ." She closed a clawlike hand about his arm. "Royce, accidents happen – you of all people know how easily. And there are those around the Regent who are already looking to the day he'll be king, and how he might reward those who can put him in their debt."

When he continued to regard her impassively, she released him and arched a brow. "Did Haworth say anything beyond the expected comments on your father's demise?"

He frowned. "He asked if I had suffered any injury during my service to the Crown."

"I thought you served from behind a desk in Whitehall."

"Not always."

Her brows rose. "Indeed? And who knew that?"

Only Prinny and his closest advisors.

She knew the answer without him saying. She nodded. "Precisely. 'Ware, Wolverstone. That's who you now are, and your duty is clear. You have to marry without delay."

He studied her eyes, her face, for several heartbeats, then inclined his head. "Thank you for telling me."

He turned and walked away.

The actual funeral – the event he and the castle's household had spent the last week and more preparing for, that a good portion of the ton had traveled into Northumbria for – was something of an anticlimax.

Everything went smoothly. Royce had arranged for Hamish and Molly to be given seats at the front of the side chapel, ahead of those reserved for the senior household staff and various local dignitaries. He saw them there, exchanged nods across the church. The nave was filled with the nobility and aristocracy; even using the side aisles, there was barely room enough for all the visitors.

The family spread over the front pews to both sides of the central aisle. Royce stood at the center end of the first pew, conscious of his sisters and their husbands ranged beside him, of his father's sisters and Edwin in the pew across the aisle. Even though the ladies were veiled, there was not a single tear to be found among them; Variseys all, they stood stone-faced, unmoved.

Minerva also wore a fine black veil. She was at the center end of the pew one row back and opposite his. He could see her, watch her, from the corner of his eye. His uncle Catersham and his wife were beside her; his uncle had given Minerva his other arm into the church and up the aisle.

As the service rolled on, he noted that her head remained bowed, that her hand remained clenched tight about a hand-kerchief – putting sharp creases in the limp, damp square of lace-edged linen. His father had been a martinet, an arrogant despot, a tyrant with a lethal temper. Of all those here, she had lived most closely with him, been most frequently exposed to his flaws, yet she was the only one who truly mourned him, the only one whose grief was deeply felt and sincere.

Except, perhaps, for him, but males of his ilk never cried.

As was customary, only the gentlemen attended the burial in the churchyard while a procession of carriages ferried the ladies back to the castle for the wake.

Royce was among the last to arrive back; with Miles beside him, he walked into the drawing room, and found all proceeding as smoothly as the funeral itself. Retford and the staff had all in hand. He looked around for Minerva, and found her arm-in-arm with Letitia, looking out of one window, their heads bent close.

He hesitated, then Lady Augusta beckoned and he went to hear what she wished to say. Whether the grandes dames had issued a directive he didn't know, but not one lady had mentioned marriage, not even any eligible candidate, at least not within his hearing, at any time that day.

Grateful, he circulated, imagining his chatelaine would say he ought to . . . he missed hearing her words, missed having her beside him, subtly, and if he didn't respond not so subtly, steering him.

The wake didn't end so much as dissolve. Some guests, including all those who had to hasten back to political life, had arranged to depart at its close; they left as their carriages were announced. He shook their hands, bade them Godspeed, and watched their coaches dwindle with relief.

Those who intended to remain – a core of the ton including most of the grandes dames as well as many of the family – drifted off in twos and threes, going out to stroll the lawns, or to sit in groups and slowly, gradually, let their customary lives, their usual interests, reclaim them.

After waving the last carriage away, then seeing Minerva step onto the terrace with Letitia and Rupert's Rose, Royce escaped to the billiard room, unsurprised to find his friends, and Christian and Devil, already there.

They played a few sets, but their hearts weren't in it.

As the sun slowly sank, streaking the sky with streamers of red and purple, they lounged in the comfortable chairs about the fireplace, punctuating the silence with the occasional comment about this or that.

It was into that enfolding, lengthening silence that Devil eventually murmured, "About your wedding . . ."

Slumped in a wing chair, Royce slowly turned his head to regard Devil with an unblinking stare.

Devil sighed. "Yes, I know – I'm the last one to talk. But George and Catersham both had to leave – and *both* apparently had been asked to bring the matter to your attention. Both tapped me on the shoulder to stand in their stead. Odd, but there you have it."

Royce glanced at the five men slumped in various poses around him; there wasn't one he wouldn't trust with his life. Letting his head fall back, he fixed his gaze on the ceiling. "Lady Osbaldestone spun me a tale of a hypothetical threat to the title that the grandes dames have taken it into their heads to treat seriously – hence they believe I should marry with all speed."

"Wise money says the threat isn't entirely hypothetical."

It was Christian who spoke; Royce felt a chill touch his spine. Of those present, Christian would best appreciate how Royce would feel about such a threat. He also had the best intelligence of dark deeds plotted in the capital.

Keeping his gaze on the ceiling, Royce asked, "Has anyone else heard anything of this?"

They all had. Each had been waiting for a moment to speak with him privately, not realizing the others had similar warnings to deliver.

Then Devil pulled a letter from his pocket. "I have no idea what's in this. Montague knew I was coming north and asked me to give this to you – into your hand – after the funeral. Specifically after, which seems to be now."

Royce took the letter and broke the seal. The others were silent while he read the two sheets it contained. Reaching the end, he slowly folded the sheets; his gaze on them, he reported, "According to Montague, Prinny and his merry men have been making inquiries over how to effect the return of a marcher lord title and estate in escheat. The good news is that such a maneuver, even if successfully executed, would take a number of years to effect, given the claim would be resisted at every turn, and the escheat challenged in the Lords. And as we all know, Prinny's need is urgent and his vision short-term. However, invoking all due deference, Montague suggests that it would be wise were my nuptials to occur within the next few months, because some of Prinny's men are not so shortsighted as their master."

Lifting his head, Royce looked at Christian. "In your professional opinion, do I stand in any danger of being assassinated to bolster Prinny's coffers?"

Christian grinned. "No. Realistically, for Prinny to claim the estate your death would need to look like an accident, and while you're at Wolverstone, that would be all but impossible to arrange." He met Royce's gaze. "Especially not with you."

Only Christian and the other members of the Bastion Club knew that one of Royce's less well-known roles over the past sixteen years had been as secret executioner for the government; given his particular skills, killing him would not be easy.

Royce nodded. "Very well – so it seems the threat is potentially real, but the degree of urgency is perhaps not as great as the grandes dames think."

"True." Miles caught Royce's eyes. "But that's not going to make all that much difference, is it? Not to the grandes dames."

The day had finally come to an end. Minerva had one last duty to perform before she retired to her bed; she felt wrung out, more emotionally exhausted than she'd expected, yet once everyone else had retired to their rooms, she forced herself to go to the duchess's morning room, retrieve the folio, then walk through the darkened corridors of the keep to the study.

She was reaching for the doorknob when she realized someone was inside. There was no lamplight showing beneath the
door, but the faint line of moonlight was broken by a shadow,
one that moved repetitively back and forth . . .

Royce was there. Pacing again.

Angry.

She looked at the door – and simply knew, as if she could
somehow sense his mood even through the oak panel. She
wondered, felt the weight of the folio in her hand . . . raising
her free hand, she rapped once, then gripped the knob, opened
the door, and went in.

He was a dense, dark shadow before the uncurtained
window. He whirled as she entered. "Leave –"

His gaze struck her. She felt its impact, felt the dark intensity as his eyes locked on her. Realized that, courtesy of the
faint moonlight coming through the window, he could see
her, her movements, her expression, far better than she could
his.

Moving slowly, deliberately, she closed the door behind her.

He'd stilled. "What is it?" His tone was all lethal, cutting
fury, barely leashed.

Cradling the folio in her arms, resisting the urge to clutch it
to her chest, she said, "Lady Osbaldestone told me the reason
the grandes dames believe you need to wed as soon as practi-
cable. She said she'd told you."

He nodded tersely. "She did."

Minerva could sense the depth of the anger he was, temporarily, suppressing; to her, expert in Varisey temper that she
was, it seemed more than the situation should have provoked.
"I know this has to be the last thing you expected to face, to
have forced on you at this time, but . . ." She narrowed her
eyes, trying to see his expression through the wreathing shadows. "You'd expected to marry – most likely in a year's time.
This brings the issue forward, but doesn't materially change all
that much . . . does it?"

Royce watched her trying to understand – to comprehend
his fury. She stood there, not the least afraid when most men he

knew would be edging out of the door – indeed, wouldn't have come in in the first place.

And of all those he considered friend, she was the only one who might understand, probably would understand . . .

"It's not that." He swung back to stare out of the window – at the lands it was his duty to protect. To hold. "Consider this." He heard the harshness in his voice, the bitterness, felt all his pent-up, frustrated anger surge; he gripped the windowsill tightly. "I spent the last sixteen years of my life essentially in exile – a social exile I accepted as necessary so that I could serve the Crown, as the Crown requested, and as the country needed. And now . . . the instant I resign my commission, and unexpectedly inherit the title, I discover I have to marry immediately to protect that title and my estate . . . from the Crown."

He paused, dragged in a huge breath, let it out with "Could it be any more ironic?" He had to move; he paced, then turned, viciously dragged a hand through his hair. "How *dare* they? *How* . . ." Words failed him; he gestured wildly.

"Ungrateful?" she supplied.

"*Yes!*" That was it, the core fueling his fury. He'd served loyally and well, and this was how they repaid him? He halted, stared out again.

Silence descended.

But not the cold, uncaring, empty silence he was used to.

She was there with him; this silence held a warmth, an enfolding comfort he'd never before known.

She hadn't moved; she was a good ten and more feet away, safely separated from him by the bulk of the desk, yet he could still feel her, sense her . . . feel an effect. As if her just being there, listening and understanding, was providing some balm to his excoriated soul.

He waited, but she said nothing, didn't try to make light of what he'd said – didn't make any comment that would provoke him to turn his temper – currently a raging, snarling beast – on her.

She really did know what not to do – and to do. And when.

He was about to tell her to go, leaving him to his now

muted, less anguished thoughts, when she spoke, her tone matter-of-fact.

"Tomorrow I'll start making a list of likely candidates. While the grandes dames are here, and inclined to be helpful, we may as well make use of their knowledge and pick their brains."

It was the sort of comment he might have made, uttered with the same cynical inflection. He inclined his head.

He expected her to leave, but she hesitated . . . He remembered the book she'd held in her hands just as she said, "I came here to leave you this."

Turning his head, he watched her walk forward and lay the book – a folio – on his blotter. Stepping back, she clasped her hands before her. "I thought you should have it."

He frowned; leaving the window, he pushed his chair aside and stood looking down at the black folio. "What is it?" Reaching out, he opened the front cover, then shifted so the moonlight fell on the page revealed. The sheet was inscribed with his full name, and the courtesy title he'd previously used. Turning that page, he found the next covered with sections cut from news sheets, neatly stuck, with dates written beneath in a hand he recognized.

Minerva drew breath, said, "Your mother started it. She used to read the news sheets after your father had finished with them. She collected any piece that mentioned you."

Although the details of his command had been secret, the fact of it hadn't been, and he'd never been backward in claiming recognition for the men who'd served under him. Wellington, in particular, had been assiduous in mentioning the value of the intelligence provided, and the aid rendered, by Dalziel's command; notices of commendations littered the folio's pages.

He turned more leaves. After a moment, he said, "This is your writing."

"I was her amanuensis – I stuck the pieces in and noted the dates."

He did as she'd thought he would, and flipped forward to

where the entries ended. Paused. "This is the notice from the *Gazette* announcing the end of my commission. It ran . . ." His finger tapped the date. "Two weeks ago." He glanced at her. "You continued after my mother died?"

Her eyes had adjusted; she held his gaze. This was the difficult part. "Your father knew." His face turned to stone, but . . . he kept listening. "I think he'd always known, at least for many years. I kept the folio, so I knew when it moved. Someone was leafing through it – not the staff. It always happened late at night. So I kept watch, and saw him. Every now and then he'd go to the morning room very late, and sit and go through it, reading the latest about you."

He looked down, and she went on, "After your mother died, he insisted I kept it up. He'd circle any mention as he went through the news sheets, so I wouldn't miss any relevant article."

A long silence ensued; she was about to step back, and leave him with his parents' memento of his last sixteen years, when he said, his voice low, soft, "He knew I was coming home."

He was still looking down. She couldn't see his face. "Yes. He was . . . waiting." She paused, trying to find the right words. "He didn't know how you would feel, but he . . . wanted to see you. He was . . . eager. I think that's why he got confused, thinking you were here, that you'd already come, because he'd been seeing you here again in his mind."

Her throat closed up. There wasn't anything more she had to say.

She forced herself to murmur, "Tomorrow I'll bring you that list once I've made it."

Turning, she walked to the door, went through without looking back, and left him to his parents' memories.

Royce heard her go, despite the sorrow pouring through him, wished she'd stayed. Yet if she had . . .

She could make her list, but there was only one lady he wanted in his bed.

Reaching out blindly, he found his chair, drew it closer, then sat and stared at the folio. In the quiet darkness, no one could see if he cried.

By eleven the next morning, Minerva had made an excellent start on a list of potential candidates for the position of Duchess of Wolverstone.

Sitting in the duchess's morning room, she wrote down all she'd thus far gleaned of the young ladies and why each in particular had been suggested.

She felt driven, after last night even more so, to see the matter of Royce's wedding dealt with as expeditiously as possible. What she felt for him . . . it was ridiculous – she knew it was – yet her infatuation-obsession was only growing and deepening. The physical manifestations – and the consequent difficulties – were bad enough, but the tightness in her chest, around her heart, the sheer sorrow she'd felt last night, not for his dead father but for him, the nearly overwhelming urge to round his damned desk and lay a hand on his arm, to comfort him – even in the dangerous state he'd been in to recklessly offer comfort . . .

"No, no, no, and *no!*" Lips set, she added the latest name Lady Augusta had suggested to her neat list.

He was a Varisey, and she, better than anyone, knew what that meant.

A tap sounded on the door.

"Come!" She glanced up as Jeffers looked in.

He smiled. "His Grace asked if you could attend him, ma'am. In his study."

She looked down at her list; it was complete to this moment. "Yes." She rose and picked it up. "I'll come right away."

Jeffers accompanied her across the keep and held open the study door. She walked in to find Royce sitting behind his desk, frowning at the uncluttered expanse.

"I spoke with Handley this morning – he said that as far as he knew there were no estate matters pending." He fixed her with an incipient glare. "That can't be right."

Handley, his secretary, had arrived earlier in the week, and to her immense relief had proved to be a thoroughly dependable, extremely efficient, exemplarily loyal man in his early thirties; he'd been a huge help through the preparations and the funeral itself. "Handley's correct." She sat in the chair before the wide desk. "We dealt with all matters likely to arise last week. Given we were going to have so many visitors at the castle, it seemed wise to clear your desk." She looked at the expanse in question. "There's nothing likely to land on it before next week."

She looked at the list in her hand. "Except, of course, for this." She held it out to him.

He hesitated, then, reluctantly, reached out and took it. "What is it?"

"A list of potential candidates for the position you need to fill." She gave him a moment to cast his eyes over the page. "It's only a partial list at present – I haven't had a chance to check with Helena and Horatia yet – but you could start considering these ladies, if there's any one that stands out . . ."

He tossed the list on his blotter. "I don't wish to consider this subject now."

"You're going to have to." She had to get him married so she could escape. "Aside from all else, the grandes dames are staying until Monday, and I have a strong suspicion they expect to hear a declaration from you before they leave."

"They can go to the devil."

"The devil wouldn't have them, as you well know." She dragged in a breath, reached for patience. "Royce, you know you have to decide on your bride. In the next few days. You know why." She let her gaze fall to the list before him. "You need to make a start."

"*Not* today." Royce fixed her with a glare, one powerful enough to have her pressing her lips tight against the words he sensed were on her tongue.

The situation . . . was insupportable. Literally. He felt tense, edgy; his restlessness had developed an undercurrent with which he was familiar – he'd been without a woman too long.

Except he hadn't. That wasn't, exactly, the problem. His

109

problem was sitting across his desk wanting to lecture him about the necessity of choosing some mindless ninnyhammer as his bride. As the lady who would share his bed.

Instead of her.

He needed . . . to get away from her before his temper – or his restlessness, both were equally dangerous – slipped its leash. Before she succeeded in prodding him to that extent. Unfortunately, his friends and their wives had left that morning; he'd wanted to beg them to stay, but hadn't – they all had young families awaiting them at home, and had been eager to get back.

Devil had left, as well, driving himself down the Great North Road. He wished he could have gone, too; they could have raced each other back to London . . . except all he wanted, all he now needed, was here, at Wolverstone.

A good part of what he wanted sat across the desk, waiting to see what he was going to do, ready to counter it, to pressure him into making his choice . . .

He narrowed his eyes on her face. "Why are you so keen to assist the grandes dames in this matter" – he let his voice soften, grow quieter – "even against my wishes?" Eyes locked on hers, he raised his brows. "You're *my* chatelaine, are you not?"

She held his gaze, then fractionally, instinctively, raised her chin. "I'm *Wolverstone's* chatelaine."

He was a master interrogator; he knew when he hit a vein. He considered her for a moment, then evenly said, "I am Wolverstone, a fact you haven't forgotten, so what exactly do you mean?"

Her debating-whether-to-tell-him expression surfaced; he waited, outwardly patient, knowing she'd conclude that she had to.

Eventually, she dragged in a breath. "I made a vow – two vows. Or rather, the same vow twice. Once to your mother before she died, and then before he died, you father asked me for the same promise, which I gave." Her eyes, a medley of autumn browns, held his. "I promised them I'd see you settled and properly established as the tenth Duke of Wolverstone."

Minerva waited to hear his response to that — her unarguable excuse for pressing him to follow the grandes dames' advice and choose a bride forthwith.

From the instant he'd started questioning her, his face — never all that informative — had become impossible to read. His expression was all stone, revealing no hint of his thoughts, much less his feelings.

Abruptly he pushed away from the desk.

Startled, she blinked, surprised when he stood. She got to her feet as he rounded the desk.

"I'm going riding."

The growled words froze her where she stood.

For one instant, his eyes, full of dark fire and unreadable emotion, pinned her, then he stalked past her, flung open the door, and was gone.

Utterly stunned, she stared at the open doorway. And listened to his footsteps, angry and quick, fade away.

Hamish laughed so hard he fell off the wall.

Disgusted, when his half brother continued to chortle, Royce nudged his shoulder with his boot. "If you don't stop, I'll have to get down and thrash you to within an inch of your life."

"Och, aye." Hamish hauled in a breath and wiped tears from his eyes. "You and which sassenach army?"

Royce looked down at him. "We always won."

"True." Hamish struggled to tamp down his mirth. "You won the wars, but not every battle." Staggering to his feet, he wheezed; one hand held to his side, he hoisted himself back up beside Royce.

They both looked out across the hills.

Hamish shook his curly head. "I still keep wanting to laugh — oh, not about *why* you need to bed your bride with all urgency — that's the sort of thing our ancestors went to war over — but the notion of you — *you* — being hounded by these great ladies, all waving lists and wanting you to choose . . . heh, lad, you have to admit it's funny."

"Not from where I sit – and as yet it's only Minerva waving a list." Royce looked at his hands, loosely clasped between his knees. "But that's not the worst of it. Choosing a bride, having a wedding – doing it all *now* – that's merely an irritation. But . . . I'm not sure I can manage the estate, and everything that's bound up in that – the social, the political, the business, the people – without Minerva, but she's not going to stay once I marry."

Hamish frowned. "That would be a loss." A moment passed, then he said, "Nay – I can't see it. She's more Wolverstone than you. She's lived here, what? Twenty years? I can't see her leaving, not unless you want her to."

Royce nodded. "So I thought, but I've since learned better. When I first returned, she told me she wouldn't be my chatelaine forever, that when I married and she could pass the keys to my wife, she'd leave. That sounded reasonable at the time, but since then I've learned how important she is to the estate, how much she contributes to its management even outside the castle, and how vital she is to *me* – I honestly couldn't have survived the last days without her, not socially. I'd have fallen on my face more than once if she hadn't been there, literally by my side, to get me over the hurdles." He'd already explained about the social handicap his exile had saddled him with.

He looked out across the hills toward those that were his. "This morning she told me of the deathbed vows she'd made to my parents – to see me established as duke, which includes seeing me appropriately wed. *They* are what's holding her here. I'd assumed she . . . wasn't averse to being my chatelaine, that if I asked, she would stay."

He'd thought she liked being *his* chatelaine, that she *enjoyed* the challenge he posed to her management skills, but . . . after hearing of her vows, he no longer felt he had any claim at all on her, on her loyalty, her . . . affection.

Given his continued desire for her, and her continued lack of desire for him, the news of those vows had shaken him – and he wasn't accustomed to that sort of shaking. Never had he felt such a hollow, desolate feeling in the pit of his stomach.

"I don't suppose," Hamish suggested, looking toward Wolverstone, too, "that there's an easy way out of this?"

"What easy way?"

"Mayhap Minerva's name could find its way onto your list?"

"Would that it could, but neither she nor anyone else will put it there. This morning's list named six young ladies, all of whom have significant fortunes and hail from the senior noble families in the realm. Minerva's well-bred, but not in that league, and her fortune can't compare. Not that any of that matters to *me*, but it does to society, and therefore to her because of her damned vows." He drew breath, held it. "But aside from all that – and I swear if you laugh at this I *will* hit you – she's one of those rare females who have absolutely no interest in me."

From the corner of his eye, he saw Hamish suck in his lips, trying manfully not to be hit. A very long pregnant moment passed, then Hamish dragged in a huge breath, and managed to get out, "Mayhap she's grown hardened to the Varisey charm, seeing as she's lived among you so long."

His voice had quavered only a little, not enough for Royce to retaliate. It had been decades since he'd felt that going a few rounds with Hamish – one of the few men he'd have to work to fight – might make him feel better. Might let him release some of the tension inside.

That tension sang in his voice as he replied, "Presumably. Regardless, all those facts rule out the easy way – I want no reluctant, sacrificial bride. She's not attracted to me, she wants me to marry appropriately so she can leave, yet if I offer for her, in the circumstances she might feel she has to, against all her expectations and inclinations, agree. I couldn't stomach that."

"Och, no." Hamish's expression suggested he couldn't stomach it, either.

"Unfortunately, her resistance to the Varisey charm rules out the not-quite-so-easy way, too."

Hamish frowned. "What's that?"

"Once I fill the position of my duchess, I'll be free to take a mistress, a long-term lover I can keep by my side."

"You'd think to make Minerva your lover?"

Royce nodded. "Yes."

He wasn't surprised by the silence that followed, but when it lengthened, he frowned and glanced at Hamish. "You were supposed to clout me over the ear and tell me I shouldn't have such lecherous thoughts about a lady like Minerva Chesterton."

Hamish glanced at him, then shrugged. "In that department, who am I to judge? I'm me, you're you, and our father was something else again. But" – tilting his head, he stared toward Wolverstone – "strange to say, I could see it might work – you marrying one of those hoity ton misses, and having Minerva as your lover-cum-chatelaine."

Royce grunted. "It *would* work, if she wasn't unresponsive to me."

Hamish frowned. "About that . . . have you tried?"

"To seduce her? *No.* Just think – I have to work closely with her, need to interact with her on a daily basis. If I made an advance and she rejected me, it would make life hellishly awkward for us both. And what if, after that, she decided to leave immediately despite her vows? I can't go that route."

He shifted on the wall. "Besides, if you want the honest truth, I've never seduced a woman in my life – I wouldn't have the first clue how to go about it."

Hamish overbalanced and fell off the wall again.

Where was Royce? What was his nemesis up to?

Although the bulk of the guests had left, Allardyce, thank heaven, among them, enough remained for him to feel confident he still had sufficient cover, but the thinning crowd should have made his cousin easier to see, to keep track of.

In the billiard room with his male cousins, he played, laughed, and joked, and inwardly obsessed over what Royce might be doing. He wasn't with Minerva, who was sitting with the grandes dames, and he wasn't in his study because his footman wasn't standing outside the door.

He hadn't wanted to come to Wolverstone, but now he was there, the opportunity to linger, mingling with his other cousins who, together with Royce's sisters, were planning what would amount to a highly select house party to capitalize on the fact they were there, together and out of sight of the ton, and, more importantly, their spouses, was tempting.

Yet his long-standing fear – that if Royce were to see him, were to look at him often enough, those all-seeing dark eyes would strike through his mask and Royce would see the truth, would know and act – remained, the nearness to his nemesis keeping it forever fermenting in one part of his brain.

From the first step he'd taken down the long road to becoming the successful – still living – traitorous spy he was, he'd known that the one being above all others he had to fear was Royce. Because once Royce knew, Royce would kill him without remorse. Not because he was an enemy, a traitor, not because he'd struck at Royce, but because he was family. Royce would not hesitate to erase such a blot on the family's escutcheon.

Royce was far more like his father than he believed.

For years he'd carried his fear inside him, held close, a smoldering, cankerous coal forever burning a hole in his gut.

Yet now temptation whispered. While so many of his cousins remained at Wolverstone, he, too, could stay.

And over the years of living with his fear, of coming to know it so intimately, he'd realized there was, in fact, one way to make the living torment end.

For years he'd thought it could only end with his death.

Recently he'd realized it could end with Royce's.

Chapter 6

Royce walked into the drawing room that evening more uncertain about a woman than he'd ever been in his life.

After Hamish had staggered to his feet a second time, he'd made a number of suggestions, not all of which had been in jest. Yet the instant Royce's gaze landed on Minerva, he rejected Hamish's principal thesis – that his chatelaine was no more immune to him than the average lady, but was concealing her reactions.

From him? Gauging others was one of his strengths, one he'd exercised daily over the past sixteen years; she'd have to possess the most amazing control to hide such an awareness of him, from him.

As if sensing his regard, she turned and saw him; leaving the group with whom she'd been conversing, she glided to him. "Did you find the more detailed list of candidates I left on your desk?"

Her voice was cool, serene. She was annoyed with his treatment of her initial list.

"Yes." There was nothing subtle about his tone.

Her eyes locked with his. "Have you read it?"

"No."

Her lips tightened, but she didn't press her luck. The drawing room was still comfortably well-populated; he'd thought more people would have left.

For an instant, she stood looking into his eyes, then she glanced around.

Backing down, thank God. He hadn't realized before how arousing it was to have a lady cross swords with him; no other ever had.

For a moment he stood looking down at her, letting his eyes, his senses, feast, then silently cleared his throat and followed her gaze . . . "Bloody hell!" he muttered. "They're *all* still here."

"The grandes dames? I did tell you they were staying until Monday."

"I thought you meant Therese Osbaldestone and maybe Helena and Horatia, not the whole damned pack."

She glanced at him, then past him. "Regardless, here's Retford." She met his eyes briefly. "You have Lady Augusta again, of course."

"Of. Course." He bit back the acid comments burning the tip of his tongue; no point expending energy over what he couldn't change. Besides, while the grandes dames might have stayed on, so, too, had many of his cousins, and some of his sisters' friends. Two of his uncles and their wives were still there; they'd mentioned they'd be leaving tomorrow.

There were enough gentlemen still present for him to escape with after dinner. Until then, he would deploy his considerable skills in deflecting all inquisition on the subject of his bride.

Locating Lady Augusta, he went to claim her hand.

Royce practiced the art of avoidance throughout the following day. He didn't disappear, but hid in plain sight.

In the morning, he confounded everyone by joining the group going to church; not one of the grandes dames was devoted to religion. He dallied after the service, chatting to the vicar and various locals, timing his return so that he walked into the castle as the luncheon gong rang.

He played the genial host throughout the informal meal, chatting easily about country pursuits. Considerate host that he was, the instant the platters were cleared he suggested a ride to a local waterfall.

His chatelaine looked at him, but said nothing.

They returned in the late afternoon. He'd managed to keep largely to himself; the others all thought that when he grew quiet, he was brooding over his father's death. Not grieving – for that, one had to love – but angry over being denied his long-awaited confrontation with his sire.

He walked with the others into the front hall. Seeing no sign of grandes dames – or his chatelaine – he parted from the rest and went up the main stairs, and into the keep.

He headed for his study. No one had mentioned the words "marriage," "bride," or "wedding" in his hearing all day; he was feeling sufficiently mellow to wonder if his chatelaine had left him another amended list. If she had, she would have found her second list sitting alongside the first by his blotter. He would read them, but in his own good time, not at the behest of a pack of ladies, even be they grandes dames.

His hand was on the study doorknob, opening the door, before he registered that Jeffers wasn't at his post. Not that he had to be when Royce wasn't in the study, but the man had an uncanny sense of when he would be coming to the room. Pushing the door wide, he walked in –

And halted. He'd walked into an ambush.

Seven grandes dames were seated in a semicircle before his desk, the chairs carefully arranged so he hadn't been able to see them, not until he'd walked too far in to retreat.

Only one lady – Therese Osbaldestone – turned her head to look at him. "Good afternoon, Wolverstone. We'd appreciate it if you would grant us a few minutes of your time."

No real question, and his title, not his name; stiffly, he inclined his head.

Therese glanced behind the door, to where Jeffers stood with his back to the wall. "You may go."

Jeffers looked at Royce. He endorsed the order with a curt nod.

As the door closed silently behind Jeffers, Royce walked forward. Slowly. Passing one end of the line of chairs, he rounded the desk, his gaze touching each determined face. Horatia, Helena, Therese, Augusta, Princess Esterhazy, Lady Holland, and Lady Melbourne. Behind the chairs to one side stood Letitia and Minerva.

Combining their various connections, with Letitia representing both the Vaux and Dearne, the group commanded the collective might of the upper echelons of the ton.

These were the ton's foremost female generals.

He inclined his head. "Ladies."

He sat, outwardly relaxed, and regarded them impassively.

Lady Osbaldestone was their elected speaker. "I've already discussed with you the reason you need to marry without delay." Her obsidian gaze lowered to the blotter, on which three sheets – a new and longer list – lay spread. "We have pooled our knowledge – we believe that list includes every gel you might consider for the position of your duchess, along with her antecedents, her expected fortune, and sundry information we thought helpful."

Her gaze rose from the list as Royce's did; she met and held his gaze. "You now have all the information you need to choose your bride, which, as we've all been at pains to impress on you, you need to do forthwith. *However*, what you may not yet perceive is what will occur if you do *not* act promptly. Should the ton not hear of your betrothal soon, then you and this castle are likely to be stormed by every even halfway eligible chit in Christendom." She rapped the floor with her cane. "And I can assure you they will be a great deal harder to repulse than any army!"

Spine straight, she looked him in the eye. "Is that what you want? Because if you fail to act, that is precisely what will happen."

The vision was enough to make him blanch, but . . . were they actually *threatening* him?

Lady Augusta shifted, drawing his attention. "That's *not* a threat – at least, not from us. It will, however, happen precisely

119

as Therese says, regardless of anything *we* may do, or indeed, anything you can do short of announcing your betrothal."

She hesitated, then went on, her tone more conciliatory, "If your father had lived, matters would be different. But he died, and so you are now Wolverstone, unmarried and childless, and with no direct heir – your marriage is urgent regardless. But for the reasons you now know of, that urgency has become acute. The matter of you choosing your bride has now become critical. And while we, and those others who would know, already recognize the urgency, the entire ton will become aware of it – of your need of a bride – sooner rather than later."

"Indeed," Princess Esterhazy said, in her accented voice, "it is a wonder you have not yet had a rash of carriages breaking down outside your gates."

"One would hope," Lady Osbaldestone said, "that they'll wait for at least a week after the funeral."

Royce studied her face, checked those of the others; she wasn't being facetious.

Helena, her normally clear eyes shadowed by concern, leaned forward. "We should perhaps make clear – we are not urging you to anything you would not at some point do. It is merely the timing that has changed." She pulled an expressive face. "Your family have always approached marriage as a means of alliance, of furthering the dukedom. All know that Variseys do not indulge in love matches. And while that may not be to the liking of all, we are none of us suggesting you change your spots. No. All we are saying is that you must make your choice – exactly the same choice you would at some point have made, *n'est-ce pas?* It is simply that the choice needs to be made with greater speed than you expected, yes?" She spread her hands. "That is all."

All? Before he could respond, Therese waved at the lists.

"Minerva gave you our initial recommendations, but these are more extensive. We've racked our brains, and included every possible potential candidate." She caught his eye. "Not one young lady on that list would turn down the position of your duchess should you choose to favor her by offering it. I realize – we all realize – that this situation has been forced on you, and that these ladies are not present for you to meet. However, in terms of the decision you must make, neither of those facts is relevant."

She drew a deep breath, held his gaze, her own weighty with the power she wielded. "We suggest you make your choice from these ladies – any one will make you an entirely acceptable bride." She paused, then went on, "I see no point in lecturing you, of all people, on the concept of duty – I accept you might well know more than even I of that quality. Be that as it may, there is no justifiable reason for you to drag your heels in this respect." Her hands tightened on the head of her cane. "Just do it, and it will be done."

She rose, bringing all the others to their feet. Royce eyed them, then slowly, stiffly, stood.

None of them were blind; not one had ever been foolish. They all sensed his temper, all inclined their heads to him and on a chorus of "Your Graces," turned, and filed out.

He stood, his face like stone, utterly expressionless, every instinct, every reaction, rigidly suppressed, and watched them go.

Minerva kept glancing at him. She was last in line for the door; she tried to hang back, but Lady Augusta, ahead of her, stepped back, took her arm in a viselike grip, and bundled her out before her.

Jeffers, in his usual position in the corridor outside, reached back and pulled the door closed; glancing back, Minerva caught a last glimpse of Royce, still standing behind his desk, looking down at her neat list.

She saw his lips curl in a soundless snarl.

She'd advised against it – the grandes dames' ambush – firmly and quite definitely, but they hadn't listened.

And then she'd stopped arguing because, suddenly, she hadn't been sure of her reasons, her motives in not wanting them to push him, not like that.

Was she arguing because of her burgeoning feelings for

him – was she trying to protect him, and if so, from what and why? – or was she right in thinking that them banding together in such a fashion and laying before him what he would certainly interpret – marcher lord that he was – as an ultimatum, was a very unwise, not to say outright bad, idea?

She now knew the answer. Very bad idea.

No one had seen him since that meeting in his study the previous afternoon. He hadn't come down to dinner, electing to dine alone in his apartments, and then this morning he'd – so she'd learned – got up at dawn, breakfasted in the kitchens, then gone to the stables, taken Sword, and disappeared.

He could be anywhere, including Scotland.

She stood in the front hall surrounded by the grandes dames' boxes and trunks, and took in the set, determined, positively mulish faces of those selfsame grandes dames as they perched on said trunks and boxes, having vowed not to stir a step further until Wolverstone – not one of them was calling him by his given name – gave them his decision.

They'd been sitting there for fully half an hour. Their carriages were lined up in the forecourt, ready to carry them away, but if they didn't leave soon, they wouldn't reach any major town before nightfall, so they would have to remain another night . . . she didn't know if their tempers or hers would stand it; she didn't want to think about Royce's.

Her hearing was more acute than theirs; she heard a distant creak, then a thump – the west courtyard door opening and closing. Quietly, she turned and slipped into the corridor behind her, the one leading to the west wing.

Once out of sight of the front hall, she picked up her skirts and hurried.

She rushed around a corner – and just managed not to collide with him again. His face still carved granite, he looked at her, then stepped around her and strode on.

Hauling in a breath, she whirled and hurried even more to catch up with him. "Royce – the grandes dames are waiting to leave."

His stride didn't falter. "So?"

"So you have to give them your decision."

"What decision?"

She mentally cursed; his tone was far too mild. "The name of which lady you've chosen as your bride."

The front hall loomed ahead. Voices carried in the corridors; the ladies had heard. They stirred, rising to their feet, looking at him expectantly.

He glanced back at her, then looked stonily at them. "No."

The word was an absolute, incontestable negative.

Without breaking his stride, he inclined his head coldly as he strode past the assembled female might of the ton. "I wish you Godspeed."

With that, he swung onto the main stairs, rapidly climbed them, and disappeared into the gallery above.

Leaving Minerva, and all the grandes dames, staring after him.

A moment of stunned silence ensued.

Dragging in a breath, she turned to the grandes dames – and discovered every eagle eye riveted on her.

Augusta gestured up the stairs. "Do you want to? Or should we?"

"No." She didn't want him saying something irretrievable and alienating any of them; they were, despite all, well disposed toward him, and their support would be invaluable – to him and even more to his chosen bride – in the years to come. She swung back to the stairs. "I'll talk to him."

Lifting her skirts, she climbed quickly up, then hurried after him into the keep. She needed to seize the moment, engage with him now, and get him to make some acceptable statement, or the grandes dames would stay. And stay. They were as determined as he was stubborn.

She assumed he would make for the study, but . . . "Damn!" She heard his footsteps change course for his apartments.

His *private* apartments; she recognized the implied warning, but had to ignore it. She'd failed to dissuade the grandes dames, so here she now was, chasing a snarling wolf into his lair.

No choice.

Royce swept into his sitting room, sending the door swinging wide. He fetched up in the middle of the Aubusson rug, listened intently, then cursed and left the door open; she was still coming on.

A very unwise decision.

All the turbulent emotions of the previous evening, barely calmed to manageable levels by his long, bruising ride, had roared back to furious, aggressive life at the sight of the grandes dames camped in his front hall – metaphorically at his gates – intent on forcing him to agree to marry one of the ciphers on their infernal list.

He'd studied the damned list. He had no idea in any personal sense of who any of the females were – they were all significantly younger than he – but how – *how?* – could the grandes dames imagine he could simply – so cold-bloodedly – just choose one, and then spend the rest of his life tied to her, condemning her to a life tied to him . . .

Condemning them both to living – no, existing – in exactly the same sort of married life his father and his mother had had.

Not the married life his friends enjoyed, not the supportive unions his ex-colleagues had forged, and nothing like the marriage Hamish had.

No. Because he was Wolverstone, he was to be denied any such comfort, condemned instead to the loveless union his family had traditionally engaged in, simply because of the name he bore.

Because they – all of them – thought they knew him, thought that, because of his name, they knew what sort of man he was.

He didn't know what sort of man he truly was – how could they?

Uncertainty had plagued him from the moment he'd stepped away from the created persona of Dalziel, then been compounded massively by his accession to the title so unexpectedly, so unprepared. At twenty-two he'd been entirely

124

certain who Royce Henry Varisey was, but when he'd looked again sixteen years later . . . none of his previous certainties had fitted.

He no longer fitted the construct of the man, the duke, he'd thought he would be.

Duty, however, was one guiding light he'd always recognized, and still did. So he'd tried. He'd spent all night poring over their list, trying to force himself to toe the expected line.

He'd failed. He couldn't do it – couldn't force himself to choose a woman he didn't want.

And the prime reason he couldn't was about to enter the room behind him.

He hauled in a massive breath, then snarled and flung himself into one of the large armchairs set before the windows, facing the open doorway.

Just as she sailed in.

Minerva knew from long experience of Variseys that this was no time for caution, much less meekness. The sight that met her eyes as she came to a halt inside the ducal sitting room – the wall of fury that assailed her senses – confirmed that; he'd roll right over her, smother her, if she gave him half a chance.

She fixed him with an exasperated, aggravated gaze. "You have to make a choice, make it and declare it – or else give me something I can take downstairs that will satisfy the ladies, or they're not going to leave." She folded her arms and stared him down. "And you'll like that even less."

A long silence ensued. She knew he used silences to undermine; she didn't budge an inch, just waited him out.

His eyes narrowed. Eventually, one dark, diabolically winged brow rose. "Are you really that keen to explore Egypt?"

She frowned. "What?" Then she made the connection. Tightened her lips. "Don't try to change the subject. In case you've forgotten, it's your bride."

His gaze remained fixed on her face, on her eyes. "Why are you so keen to have me declare who I'll wed?" His voice had lowered, softened, his tone growing strangely, insidiously suggestive. "Are you so eager to escape from Wolverstone and your duties, and all those here?"

The implication pricked a spot she hadn't, until that instant, realized was sensitive. Her temper flared, so quickly and completely she had no chance to rein it back. "As you know damned well" – her voice dripped fury, her eyes, she knew, would be all golden scorn – "Wolverstone is the only home I've ever known. It *is* my home. While you might know every rock, every stone, I know every single man, woman, and child on this estate." Her voice deepened, vibrating with emotion. "I know the seasons, and how each affects us. I know every facet of the dynamics of the castle community and how it runs. Wolverstone has been my *life* for more than twenty years, and loyalty to – and love for – it and its people is what has kept me here so long."

She dragged in a tight breath. His eyes dropped briefly to her breasts, mounding above her neckline; uncaring, she trapped his gaze as it returned to her face. "So no, I'm *not* keen to leave – I would much rather stay – but leave I must."

"Why?"

She flung up her hands. "Because you *have to marry* one of the ladies on that damned list! And once you do, there'll be no place for me here."

If he was taken aback by her outburst, she saw no hint of it; his face remained set, the lines chiseled stone. The only sense she gained from him was one of implacable, immovable opposition.

His gaze shifted from her to the mantelpiece, following the long line of armillary spheres she'd kept dusted and polished. His dark gaze rested on them for a long moment, then he murmured, "You're always telling me to go my own road."

She frowned. "This *is* your own road, the one you would naturally take – it's only the timing that's changed."

He looked at her; she tried, but, as usual, could read nothing in his dark eyes. "What," he asked, his voice very soft, "if that's not the road I want to take?"

She sighed through her teeth. "Royce, stop being difficult

for the sake of it. You know you're going to choose one of the ladies on that list. The list is extensive, indeed complete, so those are your choices. So just tell me the name and I'll take it downstairs, before the grandes dames decide to barge in here."

He studied her. "What about your alternative?"

It took her a moment to follow, then she held up her hands, conceding. "Fine – give me something to tell them that will satisfy them instead."

"All right."

She suppressed a frown. His gaze fixed on her, he looked like he was thinking, the wheels of his diabolical mind churning.

"You may announce to the ladies downstairs" – the words were slow, even, his tone dangerously mild – "that I've made up my mind which lady I'll wed. They can expect to see the announcement of our betrothal in a week or so, once the lady I've chosen agrees."

Her eyes locked with his, she replayed the declaration; it would, indeed, satisfy the grandes dames. It sounded sensible, rational – in fact, exactly what he should say.

But . . . she knew him far too well to accept the words at face value. He was up to something, but she couldn't think what.

Royce surged to his feet – before she could question him. Shrugging out of his hacking jacket, he walked toward his bedroom. "And now, if you'll excuse me, I must change."

She frowned, annoyed by his refusal to let her probe, but with no choice offering, she stiffly inclined her head, turned, and walked out, closing the door behind her.

Tugging loose his neckerchief, he watched the door shut, then strode into his bedroom. She would learn the answer to her question soon enough.

Chapter 7

The next morning, garbed in her riding habit, Minerva sat in the private breakfast parlor and consumed her marmaladed toast as quickly as she daintily could; she was intent on getting out on Rangonel as soon as possible.

She hadn't seen Royce since he'd sent her off with his response to the grandes dames' demand. He hadn't joined the guests still remaining for dinner; she hadn't been surprised. But she wasn't in any hurry to meet him, not until she felt more like herself, hence her wariness as, toast finished, tea drunk, she rose and headed for the stables.

Retford had confirmed that His Grace had breakfasted earlier and gone riding; he was most likely far away by now, but she didn't want to run into him if he'd cut short his ride and was returning to the keep. Avoiding the west courtyard, his favored route, she exited via the castle's east wing, and set off through the gardens.

She'd spent an unsettled evening, and an even more restless night, going over in her mind the ladies on the list, trying to predict whom he'd chosen. She'd met some of them during the seasons she and his mother had spent in the capital; while she couldn't imagine any of them as his duchess, that lack of enthusiasm didn't explain the hollow, deadening feeling that had, over the last days, been growing inside her.

That had intensified markedly after she'd delivered his declaration to the grandes dames and waved them on their way.

Certainly, being forced to state out aloud her unhappiness over leaving Wolverstone, giving voice to what she truly felt, hadn't helped. By the time she'd retreated to her room last night, that unexpected, welling emotion was approaching desolation. As if something was going *horribly* wrong.

It was nonsensical. She'd done what she'd had to do – what her vows had committed her to do – and she'd *succeeded*. Yet her emotions had swung crazily in the opposite direction; she didn't feel as if she'd won, but as if she'd lost.

Lost something vital.

Which was silly. She'd always known the time would come when she'd have to leave Wolverstone.

It had to be some irrational twisting of her emotions caused by the increasingly fraught battle she constantly had to wage to keep her frustrating and irritating, infatuation-obsession-driven physical reactions to Royce completely hidden – hidden so completely not even he would see.

The stables loomed ahead. She walked into the courtyard, smiling when she saw Rangonel waiting, saddled and patient by the mounting block, a groom at his head. She went forward – a flash of gray and the steel tattoo of dancing hooves had her glancing around.

Sword pranced on the other side of the yard, saddled and . . . waiting. She tried to tell herself Royce must have just ridden in . . . but the stallion looked fresh, impatient to be off.

Then she saw Royce – pushing away from the wall against which he'd been leaning chatting to Milbourne and Henry.

Henry went to calm Sword and untie his reins.

Milbourne rose from the bench on which he'd been sitting.

And Royce walked toward her.

Quickening her pace, she clambered onto the mounting block and scrambled, breathless, into her sidesaddle.

Royce halted a few paces away and looked up at her. "I need to talk to you."

Doubtless about his bride. Her lungs constricted; she felt literally ill.

He didn't wait for any agreement, but took the reins Henry offered, and swung up to Sword's back.

"Ah . . . we should discuss the mill. There are decisions that need to be made —"

"We can talk when we stop to rest the horses." His dark gaze raked her, then he turned Sword to the archway. "Come on."

This time, he led.

She had no option but to follow. Given the pace he set, that took all her concentration; only when he slowed as they started up Lord's Seat did she have wits to spare to start wondering what, exactly, he was going to say.

He led her up to a sheltered lookout. A grassy shelf on the side of the hill where a remnant of woodland enclosed a semicircular clearing, it had one of the best views in the area, looking south down the gorge through which the Coquet tumbled, to the castle, bathed in sunlight, set against the backdrop of the hills beyond.

Royce had chosen the spot deliberately; it gave the best, most complete view of the estate, the fields as well as the castle.

He rode Sword to the trees, swung down from the stallion's back, and tied the reins to a branch. On her bay, Minerva followed more slowly. Allowing her time to slip down from her saddle and tie her horse, he crossed the lush grass to the rim of the clearing; looking out over his lands, he seized the moment to rehearse his arguments one more time.

She didn't want to leave Wolverstone, and, as the pristine condition of his armillary spheres testified, she felt *something* for him. It might not be the counterpart of his desire for her, and she hadn't seen enough of him to have developed an admiration and appreciation of his talents reciprocal to his for hers. But it was enough.

Enough for him to work with, enough for him to suggest as a basis for their marriage. It was a damned sight more than could possibly exist between him and any of the ladies on the grandes dames' list.

He'd come prepared to persuade.

She was twenty-nine, and had admitted no man had offered her anything she valued.

She valued Wolverstone, and he would offer her that.

Indeed, he was willing to offer her anything it was in his power to give, just as long as she agreed to be his duchess.

She might not be as well-connected or well-dowered as the candidates on the list, but her birth and fortune were more than sufficient that she needn't fear the ton would consider their union a mésalliance.

More, in marrying him herself, she would be satisfying her vows to his parents in unarguably the most effective way – she was the only female who had ever stood up to him, ever faced him down.

As she'd proved yesterday, she would tell him whatever she deemed he needed to hear regardless of him wanting to hear it. And she would do so knowing that he could rip up at her, knowing how violent his temper could be. She already knew, was demonstrably confident, that he would never lose it with – loose it on – her.

That she knew him that well spoke volumes. That she had the courage to act on her knowledge said even more.

He needed a duchess who would be more than a cipher, a social ornament for his arm. He needed a helpmate, and she was uniquely qualified.

Her caring for the estate, her connection with it, was the complement of his; together, they would give Wolverstone – castle, estate, title, and family – the best governance it could have.

And when it came to the critical issue of his heirs, having her in his bed was something he craved; he desired her – more than he would any of the grandes dames' ciphers, no matter how beautiful. Physical beauty was the most minor attractant to a man like him. There had to be more, and in that respect Minerva was supremely well-endowed.

Yesterday, while she'd been insisting he appease the grandes dames, he'd finally accepted that, if he wanted a marriage like his friends', then, regardless of what he had to do to make it happen, it was Minerva he needed as his wife. That if he wanted something more than a loveless marriage, he would have to strike out, and, as he had with her help in other respects, try to find a new road.

With her.

The certainty that had gripped him, infused him, hadn't waned; with the passing hours, it had grown more intense. He'd never felt more certain, more set on any course, more confident it was the right one for him.

No matter what he had to do – no matter the hurdles she might place in his path, no matter where the road led or how fraught the journey might be, no matter what she or the world might demand of him – it was she he had to have.

He couldn't sit back and wait for it to happen; if he waited any longer, he'd be wed to someone else. So he would do whatever it took, swallow whatever elements of his pride he had to, learn to persuade, to seduce, to entice – do whatever he needed to to convince her to be his.

Mind and senses returning to the here and now, poised to speak, he mentally reached for her – and realized she hadn't yet joined him.

Turning, he saw her still sitting her horse. She'd swung the big bay to face the view. Hands folded before her, she looked past him down the valley.

He shifted, caught her eye. Beckoned. "Come down. I want to talk to you."

She looked at him for a moment, then nudged her horse forward. Halting the big bay alongside, she looked down at him. "I'm comfortable here. What did you want to talk about?"

He looked up at her. Proposing while she was perched above him was beyond preposterous. "Nothing I can discuss while you're up there."

She'd eased her boots from the stirrups. He reached up and plucked her from her saddle.

Minerva gasped. He'd moved so fast she'd had no time to

block him – to prevent him from closing his hands around her waist and lifting her . . .

Increasingly slowly, he lowered her to the ground.

The look on his face – utter, stunned disbelief – would have been priceless if she hadn't known what put it there.

She'd reacted to his touch. Decisively and definitely. She'd stiffened. Her lungs had seized; her breath had hitched in a wholly damning way. Focused on her, his hands tight about her waist, he hadn't missed any of the telltale signs.

Long before her feet got within a foot of the lush grass, he'd guessed her secret.

Knew it beyond question.

She read as much in the subtle shift of his features, in the suddenly intent – ruthlessly intent – look that flared in his eyes.

She panicked. The instant her feet touched earth, she forced in a breath, opened her lips –

He bent his head and kissed her.

Not gently.

Hard. Ravenously. Her lips had been parted; his tongue filled her mouth with no by-your-leave.

He marched in and laid claim. His lips commanded, demanded – rapaciously seized her wits. Captured her senses.

Desire rolled over her in a hot wave.

His, she realized on a mental gasp, not just hers.

The realization utterly dumbfounded her; since when had he desired her?

Yet the ability to think, to reason, to do anything other than feel and respond had flown.

She didn't at first realize she was kissing him back; once she did, she tried to stop – but couldn't. Couldn't drag her senses from their fascination, from their greedy excitement; this was better than she'd dreamed. Regardless of all wisdom, she wasn't able to disengage, not from him, not from this.

He made it harder yet when he angled his head, slanted his lips over hers, and deepened the kiss – not by degrees, but in one bold, senses-shattering leap.

Her hands had fallen to his shoulders; they gripped, clung as their mouths melded – as he relentlessly pressed his advantage, rolled over her defenses and drew her with him into the scorching, shatteringly intimate exchange. She couldn't comprehend how his rapacious kisses, his hard hungry lips, his bold thrusting tongue, caught her, trapped her, then delivered her up, captive to her own need to respond. It wasn't *his* will making her kiss him so damningly eagerly, as if despite all good sense, she couldn't get enough of his thinly veiled possession.

She'd always known he would be an aggressive lover; what she hadn't known, would never have guessed, was that she would respond so flagrantly, so invitingly – that she would welcome that aggression, seize it as her due and demand more.

Yet that was precisely what she was doing – and she couldn't stop.

Her experience with men was limited, but not nonexistent, yet this . . . was something entirely beyond her ken.

No other man had made her heart thud, made her blood sing, sent it racing through her body.

With his lips on hers, with just a kiss, he'd transformed her into a greedy wanton – and some part of her soul sang.

Royce knew. Sensed her response in every fiber of his being. He wanted more – of her, of her luscious mouth, of her blatantly inviting lips. Yet beyond his own hunger lay the wonder of hers, a temptation like no other, one every primitive instinct he possessed had fixed upon, unswervingly fastened on as the most direct and certain route to appeasing his own, already tumultuous needs.

Sunk in her mouth, he wasn't thinking. Only feelings registered – the spike of disbelief when he'd realized what she'd been hiding – that she did indeed respond to him vibrantly, instinctively, most importantly helplessly – that despite his experience, his skills, she'd pulled the wool thickly and completely over his eyes . . . and a wave of hard anger that the agonies he'd suffered over the past weeks while subduing his lust for her hadn't been necessary. That if he'd given in and kissed her, she'd have yielded.

As she was now.

She was helplessly in thrall to the desire, the passion, that had erupted between them, more powerful, more driven from having been denied.

Relief swam through him; he would no longer need to suppress his lust for her. Expectation flared at the prospect of giving it full rein. Of indulging it to the hilt. With her. In her.

In the instant before he'd kissed her, he'd looked into her face, into her gorgeous autumn-rich eyes – and had seen them widen. Not only with the realization that he'd learned what she'd been hiding, not just with apprehension over what he might do, but with sensual shock. That was what had sent her eyes flaring, all rich browns and welcoming golds; more than experienced enough to recognize it, he'd instantly taken advantage.

He'd seen her lips part, start to form some word; he hadn't been interested in listening. And now – now that she was trapped in the web of their desires – he was intent on only one thing. On possessing what he'd wanted to seize for the last too many days.

On possessing her.

She was clinging to his shoulders, as deeply ensnared in their kiss as he. Her knees had weakened; his hands locked about her waist, he held her upright.

He didn't even need to think to steer her back, shouldering her horse aside as he guided her back until her spine met the bole of the nearest useful tree.

She instinctively braced against it. He wedged his right knee between her thighs, the hard muscle of his thigh riding against hers, holding her in place as he released his grip about her waist, easing back from the kiss as, hard palms to the velvet of her habit, he skated his hands, slow and deliberate, up, over her ribs, and closed them possessively about her breasts.

He broke from the kiss, let their hungry lips part just enough to catch the shocked, delicious inward hiss of her breath as he eased his hands, then closed them again, then provocatively kneaded. Just enough to savor her half moan, half sob when he found her nipples and through the screening fabric circled the tight nubs with his thumbs.

Then he dove back into the kiss, reclaimed her mouth, sent her gathering wits spinning again while he set his hands to learn everything he needed to know to reduce her to the sensual wanton he had every intention of drawing forth.

She had it in her, he knew.

Even just from this kiss, he knew beyond question that she was not just more responsive than any woman he'd ever known, but specifically more responsive to him. If he managed her correctly, educated her properly, she would willingly cede him everything, anything and everything he wanted of her; he knew it to his bones.

There was nothing the marcher lord within him found more alluring than the prospect of absolute surrender.

He plundered her mouth, and reveled in the knowledge that, soon, she would be his. That, very soon, she would lie beneath him, heated and mindless as he sheathed himself in her.

As he took her, claimed her, and made her his.

He wouldn't even need to go slowly; she wouldn't be shocked by his demands. She knew him well, knew what to expect from him.

Closing his hands possessively about her breasts, squeezing her distended nipples between his fingers, he shifted his thigh so the long muscle rode more definitely against the soft flesh at the apex of hers, caught her muffled moan, and held her, with lips and tongue bound her ever more tightly to the increasingly explicit exchange.

Drew her ever more powerfully along the road to his goal.

Minerva knew his direction, felt it – ached for it – with every muscle, with every taut nerve, yet while most of her mind was deliriously following him, wantonly abandoned to his desire and hers, a small part remained lucid, detached, shrieking that this was more than dangerous, more than disastrous – that this was calamity about to strike.

It didn't matter; she couldn't break away. Her mind was overwhelmed, seduced in every way.

He, his kiss, was all power and passion, intertwined, entwined, inseparable.

The taste of him, of that senses-seducing combination, overrode all good sense, devastatingly easily. The edged desire in his kiss, dangerous and uncompromising, lured her on. He devoured, seized, claimed – and she kissed him back, wanting more, inviting more; his hands on her body, hard and possessive, set a fire burning within her she knew he could quench.

She needed to feel it, that fire, that life, needed to burn in its flames.

She knew that, craved it, even though she knew that with him, that fire would sear, scorch, and ultimately scar.

Yet the fact that he wanted her, and she knew enough to know that his want was as honest and real as hers, completely overset, overcame, overturned her carefully constructed defenses. His need, his raw hunger, was the most powerful weapon he could wield against her – as if he'd needed more.

She knew she was a fool for permitting the kiss to rage – although how she might have stopped him, stopped them, she had no clue. Yet even knowing how witless it was to so wantonly accept every potent caress, and mindless – abandoned to all good sense – yearn for more, she couldn't stop herself from seizing this, this moment, with both hands, and wringing from it all she could. Clinging to him, savoring every nuance, every evocative, provocative sweep of his tongue, of his bold fingers, seizing as much as she dared, surrendering whatever he asked. Taking from him, from the moment, as much as she possibly could.

It wasn't going to happen again.

It was he who broke the kiss, he who lifted his lips from hers. They were both breathing rapidly. After several breaths, her senses returned enough to inform her how heated, how pliant, how weak she'd become.

How helpless in his arms.

He glanced left, then right. Then he swore.

Grated, his voice a deep rumble, "Not here."

Her wits returned in a rush, and she realized what he meant. Felt panic rise as she looked where he had, and realized she owed her escape to the heavy dew that had left the lush grass sodden.

If not for that . . .

She quashed a telltale shuddery shiver as he stepped back.

Royce felt it – sensed it in his marrow – but clamped down hard on his inevitable reaction. The grass was too damned wet, and the trees all had rough, deeply etched bark, but quite aside from such logistical difficulties, ones he could yet have overcome, that part of him ruled by his more primitive self was insisting, dictatorially, that the first time he sank into his chatelaine she should be sprawled naked beneath him in his ducal bed – the massive four-poster in his room.

His mind could, and did, supply any number of pertinent benefits, and after his proven-to-be-unnecessary abstinence of the past weeks, he wasn't in any mood to stint himself.

Stepping back, he waited until she was steady on her feet, then towed her to her horse and lifted her to her saddle.

Blinking in surprise, Minerva desperately tried to reorder her senses and her wits. While he untied Sword's reins and swung up to the gray's back, she slid her boots into her stirrups, reclaimed her reins.

With just a look that said very clearly, "Follow me," he turned Sword and led the way down. Luckily, they had to go slowly down the hill; once they reached the flat and the horses stretched into a gallop, she'd recovered enough to cope.

Nevertheless, she was amazed she made it back to the castle without a stumble. By the time the stables rose before them, her mind had cleared, and her wits had reassembled. Her lips were still swollen, and her body still warm, and if she thought too much, remembered too much, she would blush, but she knew what she had to do.

They clattered into the stable yard and he fluidly dismounted. By the time she'd halted Rangonel and freed her feet from her stirrups, he was by her side; she surrendered to the inevitable and let him lift her down.

And discovered that, if she wasn't tensing, fighting to suppress her reaction, then the sensation of his hands gripping her waist, that instant of being completely in his power as he lifted her, held more delight than trauma.

138

She reminded herself that when it came to him, she no longer had anything to hide. Yet when he grasped her hand, engulfing it in his, she would have tugged it back – except he tightened his hold, threw her a look, and proceeded to hold her beside him as, with a curt nod to Milbourne, he stalked out of the yard.

Deciding that having a tug-of-war over her hand with His Grace of Wolverstone in his own stable yard, watched over by various of his and her staff, wasn't an endeavor she was likely to gain anything from, she held her tongue, and strove to keep up with his strides.

She had to pick her time, her moment. Her battleground.

He led her to the house via the west courtyard, but instead of taking his usual route to the front hall and the main stairs, he turned the other way; she realized he was making for the west turret stairs, a rarely used lesser staircase from which he could reach the gallery, not far from his rooms.

Until he'd headed that way, she hadn't been sure what he intended, but given his preference for the minor stairs . . . he was taking her to his rooms.

She chose the small hall at the foot of the turret stairs to make her stand. There were no servants about, no one else about to see, let alone interrupt. When he reached for the newel post, she halted. Held steady when he tried to draw her forward. He looked around, met her gaze – saw her determination. Arched one black brow.

"What you have in mind isn't going to happen." She made the statement clearly, evenly. Not a challenge, but a statement of fact. She wanted to draw her hand from his, to lose the sensation of his long, strong fingers locked about hers, but knew better than to trigger his reaction. Instead, she met his gaze with steadfast resolution. "You are not even going to kiss me again."

His eyes narrowed; turning to face her, he opened his mouth –

"No. You will not. You might lust after me, but that, as we both know, is merely a reaction to being forced to name your bride. It will last for all of a day or two, and then what? It's possible that the only reason your eye has fixed on me is that I'm one of the few ladies in the house not related to you. But I'm not going to tumble into your bed just because you've decided it suits you. I'm your chatelaine, not your lover, not your mistress." She drew in a breath, held his dark gaze. "So we're going to pretend, going to behave, as if what just happened on Lord's Seat . . . didn't."

That was the only way she could think of to survive, heart intact, to get through this time as his chatelaine, fulfill her vows to his parents, and then leave Wolverstone and start a new life.

Somewhere.

Somewhere a very long way from him, so she'd never have to meet him again, not even set eyes on him. Because after what had just happened on Lord's Seat, she was going to regret not letting matters take their course, to regret not letting him take her to his bed.

And that regret would last forever.

Royce watched her denial form on her lips – lips he'd just kissed, possessed, and now knew beyond question were his. He heard her words, could even make sense of them, but the reactions they called forth left him inwardly reeling. As if she'd picked up a broadsword and clouted him over the head.

She couldn't be serious – yet he could see she was.

He'd stopped thinking rationally the instant he'd possessed her lips, the instant he'd swept into her mouth and tasted her. Claimed her. He'd spent the ride home anticipating claiming her in a more absolute, biblical way – and now she was refusing.

More, she was insisting that their incendiary kiss should be ignored, as if she hadn't welcomed him, kissed him back, and clung.

Worse, she'd accused him of seducing her out of lust – that he would take her to his bed with no feeling whatever, that she was merely a convenient female body to him . . . inwardly he frowned. He felt offended, yet . . .

He was a Varisey, until now in this sphere archetypically so – she had every reason to believe any female would do.

Except no other would. He knew that to his bones.

He held her gaze. "You want me as much as I want you."

She lifted her chin. "Perhaps. But remember the reason I haven't accepted any offers – of any sort – from any gentlemen? Because they didn't offer anything I wanted." She looked directly into his eyes. "In this case, anything I want *enough*."

Her last word echoed in the stairwell, filling the silence that fell between them.

A clear, unequivocal challenge.

One that called to him on a level he couldn't deny, but he could see from her eyes, her calmly resolute mien, that she was unaware she'd issued it.

The marcher lord within him purred in anticipation. Inwardly he smiled; outwardly he maintained his impassive expression.

Desire, lust, and need still ran rampant through his veins, but he reined the unruly, tempestuous emotions in. He wanted her, and was determined to have her. He'd gone to the lookout already committed to doing whatever it took to convince her to be his – in all the relevant spheres, of which this was one. His first test, apparently, was to convince her that she wanted him *enough* – to wit, a great deal more than she knew.

The prospect of exerting himself over a woman felt alien, but he shook aside the niggle.

He'd been intending to offer her the dukedom, his duchess's coronet; he toyed with the idea of asking her if that would prove *enough*. But the challenge she'd issued had been based on the physical, not the material; he would answer her on the same plane. Time enough once she was gracing his bed to inform her of the permanent position he intended her to fill.

His gaze lowered to her hand, still resting in his. He needed to let her go – for now.

Forcing his fingers to ease, he let her hand, her fingers, slide from his grasp. Saw, because he was watching intently, her release the breath she'd been holding. She didn't step away; she lowered her arm, but otherwise remained still. Watching him.

Wise; his more primitive side wasn't happy about letting her go, and was just waiting for any excuse to override her wishes and the counsel of his wiser self.

Too conscious of that primitive self prowling just beneath his skin, he forced himself to turn away, to start up the stairs. He spoke without turning around. "I'll see you in the study in half an hour to discuss the mill."

That afternoon, Royce's last traitor lay naked on his back in Royce's younger sister's bed.

Equally naked, Susannah lolled on her stomach beside him. "I sent off that note with the post last evening – it should reach town later today."

"Good." Lifting an arm, he trailed his fingers over the quite delectable curve of her derriere. "It'll be amusing to see if dear Helen avails herself of your kind invitation."

"Poor Royce, forced by the grandes dames to choose a bride – the least I can do is arrange a little diversion."

"With luck, the beautiful countess will be here by Sunday."

"Hmm." Susannah looked pensive. "I really can't see him rushing to announce his betrothal, not given it was forced on him. Once she arrives, he might put it off indefinitely."

"Or even change his mind. Have you really no idea who he's chosen?"

"No. No one does. Even Minerva has no clue, which, as you might expect, is bothering her greatly."

"Can't you wheedle it out of him? You're his favorite sister, after all."

Susannah snorted. "This is Royce *Varisey* we're talking about. He might look on me more kindly than he does Margaret and Aurelia – and really, who wouldn't? – but 'wheedling' anything out of him would literally be the equivalent of getting blood from a stone."

"Ah, well – it seems we'll have to wait with everyone else to hear. A week or so . . . not that long."

Susannah sat up. "Wait a minute. He said the week's delay was to get the lady's agreement." She turned to him. "If we knew which lady he contacted . . ."

It was his turn to snort derisively. "Not even *I* would suggest you might induce Retford to tell you who his new master is corresponding with."

Susannah slapped his chest with the back of her hand. "Not me, silly – Minerva. I bet she's already thought of it." She grinned, then slid sinuously, sensuously, into his arms. "I'll ask her . . . later."

He pulled her over him, licked her lips, and slid his hand between her thighs. "Indeed. Later."

Chapter 8

Royce walked into the drawing room that evening, and calmly surveyed the remaining company. His sisters had stayed, although their husbands had departed; all three had, apparently, decided to indulge themselves with a few weeks' break, taking advantage of the, for them, freer, less restrictive structure of his essentially bachelor household.

All three were indulging in affairs under his roof – Aurelia and Susannah with two of his cousins, Margaret with the husband of one of her "friends," who was helpfully otherwise engaged with another of his cousins.

Luckily, he wasn't, wouldn't be held to be, responsible in any way for them, their sins, or their marriages. For the moment, at least, they could do as they pleased; they – his sisters, cousins, and their assorted friends – would provide cover for his pursuit of his chatelaine.

For that, he would tolerate them, at least for now. He was easy enough in their company; he could interact with them or ignore them as he chose.

Some had mentioned staying for the Alwinton Fair, a few weeks away. It was a highlight of the local year; their mother had often hosted house parties coinciding with the event. As he glanced around, noting bright eyes, flushed cheeks, and meaningful looks, it seemed his sisters and cousins were intent on recapturing those youthful, more carefree times.

He, in contrast, was intent on capturing Minerva. With luck, the fair and the company would distract his sisters from any further misplaced interest in *his* affairs.

Despite the frustration he'd recently endured having been to no real purpose, that frustration was still continuing. Not, however, for long. He'd forced himself to toe her line through a few hours of her company, discussing the mill and other estate matters – lulling her into a sense of safety.

Into believing she was safe with him. From him.

Nothing could be further from the truth, at least not with respect to their current point of contention. She was going to land in his bed – naked – sooner or later; he was intent on ensuring it was the former that applied.

He located her at the center of a group by the fireplace; she still wore her weeds, as did his sisters, but the other female guests had switched to gowns of lavender or gray. Minerva still shone like a beacon to him. He prowled through the guests, heading her way.

Minerva saw him coming; continuing to smile at Phillip Debraigh, who was entertaining the group with a tale, she forced herself to take slow, deep breaths, and a firmer grip on her composure. Royce had, without argument, behaved precisely as she'd stipulated for the rest of the morning and all the afternoon, adhering to both the letter and intent of her dictate. There was no reason to imagine he'd suddenly change tack . . .

Except that she couldn't bring herself to believe that he would meekly accept her dismissal and fall in with her specified line.

Which was why she tensed, lungs tightening, when he neared. Phillip ended his tale and excused himself, drifting off to join another group. The circle shuffled, adjusted, as Royce came to stand by her side.

He greeted the others with his customary, coolly urbane air; last of all, he looked at her – and smiled.

Pure wolf. That he planned something was patently clear from the expression in his dark eyes.

Lips lightly curved, she inclined her head serenely in reply.

One of the other ladies launched into the latest ton story.

Nerves flickering, her lungs too tight, Minerva seized the moment to murmur, "If you'll excuse me . . ." She stepped back –

Halted, nerves leaping, as long, hard fingers closed – gently, yet with underlying strength – about her elbow.

Royce turned with her, one dark brow arching. "Whither away?"

Away from him. She looked across the room. "I should see if Margaret needs anything."

"I thought, as my chatelaine, you're supposed to remain by my side."

"If you need me."

"I definitely need you."

She didn't dare look at his face. His tone was bad enough; the tenor of his deep voice sent a shivery tingle skating down her spine. "Well, then, you should probably speak with those cousins you've spent least time with. Henry and Arthur, for instance."

Releasing her, he waved her forward. "Lead on." He paced beside her as she glided through the guests toward the group with whom the two youngest Variseys present were standing. As they neared, he murmured, "Just don't try to slip away from me."

The undisguised warning had her plastering on a smile, engaging Henry and Arthur, and dutifully remaining beside Royce as they conversed.

She quickly realized why he'd appeared in the drawing room the full regulation half hour before dinner – so he could use the time to torture her with a thousand little touches. Nothing more than the polite, unremarkable, customary gestures a gentleman bestowed on a lady – his grip on her elbow, a touch on her arm, the sensation of his hand hovering at the back of her waist . . . then touching, lightly steering – *burning*.

Her pulse leapt every time; when Retford at last appeared to announce dinner, she was wishing she'd brought down her fan.

Under cover of the butler's stentorian announcement, she glanced at Royce, narrowed her eyes. Although his impassive mien didn't soften, with his eyes he managed to convey an expression of supreme innocence.

She narrowed her eyes to slits. "You haven't been innocent since birth."

He smiled – a gesture that, for her, didn't bode well – and took her arm.

Desperately tamping down her reaction, she indicated a lady across the room. "You should lead Caroline Courtney in."

"Lady Courtney can find her own partner. This is not a formal dinner." He looked down at her, his dark gaze suggestive. "I'd much rather lead you."

He deliberately omitted the "in," leaving her to supply the context – something the less sensible part of her mind was only too happy to do. Damn it. Damn him.

Reaching the dining table at the head of the line, he sat her to the left of his great chair. As he took his seat, she grasped the chance provided by the scrape of other chairs to murmur, "This ploy of yours won't work." She caught his eye. "I'm not going to change my mind."

He held her gaze, let a heartbeat pass, then slowly raised one brow. "Oh?"

She looked away, inwardly berating herself. She knew better than to fling gauntlets his way.

Predictably, he picked hers up.

She'd thought she would be reasonably safe at the table – the numbers had reduced so they weren't sitting overly close – but she quickly learned that he didn't need to physically touch her to affect her.

All he needed to do was fix his gaze on her mouth as she supped her soup, or as she closed her lips about a delicate fish dumpling; how he could communicate lascivious thoughts with just a glance from his dark eyes she didn't know, but he could.

She sat back, cleared her throat, reached for her wineglass. Took a sip, felt his gaze on her lips, then felt it lower as she

147

swallowed . . . as if he were tracking the liquid as it slid down her throat, traveled down inside her chest . . .

Desperate, she turned to the gentleman – Gordon Varisey – sitting on her other side, but he was engrossed in a discussion with Susannah. Across the table, Caroline, Lady Courtney, was more interested in making eyes at Phillip Debraigh than in distracting her host.

"Is my ploy working yet?"

The soft, taunting words slipped past her ear like a caress; turning to face Royce as he sat back in his chair, wineglass in hand, she fought to quell a reactive shiver, and didn't entirely succeed.

Her only consolation was that no one else seemed to have noticed the subtle battle being waged at the head of the table. That being so . . . she narrowed her eyes on his, succinctly stated, "Go to the devil."

His lips curved in an entirely genuine – devastatingly attractive – smile. His gaze locked with hers, he raised his wineglass, sipped. "I expect I will."

She looked away; she didn't need to see the sheen of red wine on the mobile lips she'd spent a good portion of her girlhood dreaming about. She reached for her wineglass.

Just as he added, "If nothing else for what I'm imagining doing to you."

Her fingers missed the glass bowl, bobbled the long stem; the wineglass tipped –

He caught it, his left hand reaching over hers, then curling over it as he pressed the stem into her all but nerveless fingers.

His hand rested, hard and strong, over hers, until she gripped the glass, then he withdrew his hand slowly, his fingers stroking over her hand and knuckles.

Her lungs had seized long ago.

He shifted, using the movement to lean closer and murmur, "Breathe, Minerva."

She did, hauling in a huge breath – refusing to notice that as he sat back, his gaze lowered to her breasts, half exposed by her evening gown.

She was ready to do murder by the time the meal ended. Rising with the other ladies, she followed Margaret to the drawing room.

Royce wasn't going to let her be. She'd been chased by gentlemen – even noblemen – before; any man but he and she would have simply stood her ground, confident of her ability to trump whatever move he made, but she knew her limits. She needed to escape while she could. He would lead the gentlemen back to rejoin the ladies all too soon.

Reaching the drawing room, the ladies filed in; she paused just inside the door, waiting until the others settled. She'd speak with Margaret, then –

"There you are." Susannah slipped her arm through hers and drew her toward the side of the room. "I wanted to ask" – Susannah leaned close – "whether you have any idea which lady Royce is corresponding with?"

She frowned. "Corresponding?"

"He said he'd make an announcement once the lady he'd chosen agreed." Halting, Susannah fixed her eyes – a lighter brown than her brother's – on Minerva's face. "So I presume he's asking her, and as she's not here, I assume he must have written to her."

"Ah, I see. I haven't seen him write any letter, but then he uses Handley for most of his correspondence, so I wouldn't necessarily know." Much to her relief, especially in this matter.

"Handley?" Susannah tapped her lips with one fingertip, then slanted a glance Minerva's way. "I haven't met him, but perhaps he might be persuaded to divulge what he knows?"

She shook her head. "I wouldn't bother trying. Aside from all else, he'll tell Royce." She hesitated, then added, "In fact, all Royce's personal staff are utterly devoted. You won't find any who'll discuss his private affairs."

Including her.

Susannah sighed. "I suppose we'll learn the truth soon enough."

"Indeed." She patted Susannah's arm as she drew hers free. "I have to speak with Margaret."

Susannah nodded and strolled off to join some others while Minerva headed for Margaret, enthroned in state on the chaise facing the hearth.

Susannah was right; Royce must have sent some communication to the lady he'd chosen as his duchess – a point she shouldn't have forgotten. In typical Varisey fashion, while waiting for his bride to agree to be his, he was intent on bedding his chatelaine.

If she needed any reminder of the unwisdom of letting him seduce her, recalling that she would learn any day who would be his duchess should help bolster her resolution.

She really didn't want to know; the thought curdled her stomach.

Refocusing on her plans to stay out of his arms, and out of his bed, she paused beside Margaret. "I have a headache," she lied. "Can you do the honors with the tea tray?"

"Yes, of course." Looking more relaxed than when her husband had been there, Margaret waved her away. "You should tell Royce not to work you so hard, dear. You need time for some distraction."

Minerva smiled and headed for the door; she understood perfectly what "distraction" Margaret was recommending – precisely the sort her brother had in mind. *Variseys!*

She didn't dally; she didn't trust Royce not to cut the men's drinking short, and under some pretext return to the drawing room early. Slipping out of the room, she went into the front hall, then quickly climbed the main stairs.

There was no one about. She heard no rumble of male voices; the gentlemen must still be in the dining room. Relieved, she walked into the keep, hesitated, debating, then headed for the duchess's morning room. It was too early for sleep, and her embroidery frame was there.

The morning room had been the late duchess's personal domain; her daughters had only intruded when invited. Since her death, they hadn't set foot there. Variseys had little interest in the dead; they never clung to memories.

That had suited Minerva. Over the last three years, the room had become her own.

Presumably it would remain so – until the next duchess arrived.

Opening the door, she went in. The room lay in darkness, but she knew it well. She walked toward the table that stood along the back of the nearer sofa, paused, then returned to the door and locked it. No sense taking any chances.

Smiling to herself, she strolled to the sofa table, set her hand on the tinderbox, and lit the lamp. The wick flared; she waited until it burned steadily, then set the glass in place, adjusted the flame – and suddenly felt – *knew* – that she wasn't alone . . . raising her gaze from the lamp, she looked –

At Royce, sitting at his negligent ease on the sofa opposite. Watching her.

"What are you doing here?" The words left her lips as her panicking mind assessed her options.

"Waiting for you."

She'd locked the door. Looking into his eyes, so dark, his gaze intent and unwavering, she knew that despite him being on the farther sofa, if she tried to reach the door, he'd be there ahead of her. "Why?"

Keeping him talking seemed her only option.

Assuming, of course, that he would oblige.

He didn't. Instead, he slowly rose. "Helpful of you to lock the door."

"I wasn't trying to help you." She watched him walk toward her, tamped down her flaring panic, reminded herself it was pointless to run. One did not turn and flee from a predator.

He rounded the sofa, and she swung to face him. He halted before her, looked into her face – as if studying it, her features, as if memorizing the details. "What you said – about me not kissing you again?"

She tensed. "What about it?"

His lips lifted fractionally. "I didn't agree."

She waited, beyond tense, for him to reach for her, to kiss her again, but he didn't. He stood looking down at her, watching her, his dark gaze intent, as if this were some game and it was her move.

Trapped in his gaze, she sensed heat stirring, rising between them; desperate, she searched for some way to distract him. "What about your bride? You're supposed to be arranging an announcement as we speak."

"I'm negotiating. Meanwhile . . ." He stepped forward; instinctively she stepped back. "I'm going to kiss you again."

That was what she was afraid of. He took another step, and she backed again.

"In fact," he murmured, closing the distance between them, "I'm going to kiss you more than just once, or even twice. And not just now, but later – whenever I feel like it."

Another step forward from him, another back for her.

"I intend to make a habit of kissing you."

She quickly took another step back as he continued to advance.

His gaze lowered to her lips, then flicked up to her eyes. "I'm going to spend a great deal of time savoring your lips, your mouth. And then . . ."

Her back hit the wall. Startled, she raised her hands to hold him off.

Smoothly, he caught them, one in each of his, and took one last step. Pinning her hands to the wall on either side of her head, he lowered his and looked into her eyes. Held her gaze relentlessly from a distance of mere inches.

"After *that*" – his voice had lowered to a senses-caressing purr – "I'm going to spend even more time savoring the rest of you. All of you. Every inch of skin, every hollow, every curve. I'm going to know you infinitely better than you know yourself."

She couldn't speak, couldn't breathe – couldn't think.

"I'm going to know you intimately." He savored the word. "I intend to explore you until there's nothing left to learn – until I know what makes you gasp, what makes you moan, what makes you scream. Then I'll make you do all three. Frequently."

Her spine was plastered to the wall; he wasn't leaning into her – yet – but with his arms raised, his coat had fallen open; there was barely an inch separating his chest and her breasts –

and she could feel his heat. All down the front of her, she could feel his nearness, the beckoning hardness.

Everything her wanton self needed for relief.

But . . . She swallowed, forced herself to hold his gaze, lifted her chin. "Why are you telling me this?"

His lips quirked. His gaze lowered, fastened on her lips. "Because I thought it only fair that you know."

She forced a laugh. A breathless one. "Variseys never play fair – I'm not sure you 'play' at all."

His lips twisted. "True." His gaze drifted back to her eyes.

She caught it. "So why did you tell me?"

One brow lifted devilishly. "Because I intend to seduce you, and I thought that might help. Is it working?"

"No."

He smiled then, slowly, his eyes locked on hers. He shifted one hand, turned it so, when she followed his sideways glance, she saw he had the tips of his long fingers clamped over the veins at her wrist.

"Your pulse says otherwise."

His absolute unshakable arrogance set spark to her temper. Swinging her gaze back to his face, she narrowed her eyes on his. "You are the most ruthless, conceited, diabolical –"

He cut her off, his lips closing on hers, drinking in her temper – diverting it with ruthless, diabolical efficiency into something even hotter.

Something that melted her bones, that she fought, but couldn't contain; the molten heat erupted and flooded through her, consuming intentions, inhibitions, all reservations.

Eradicating all good sense.

Leaving only hunger – blatant, explicit, ruthlessly seeking succor – in its wake.

The hard thrust of his tongue, the heavy, steely weight of him as he shifted closer and at last leaned in and pinned her body to the wall, was everything and more her witless senses wanted. Her tongue met his in a flagrant mating; her body strained, not to push him away but, every sense alive, to press against him.

To meet his hunger with hers.

To feed his desire with hers.

To meld the two, entwine them, until the power became too much for either of them to withstand.

This, now, was her only option; the rational part of her surrendered, and set her free to grasp the moment, and take from it all she could.

Wring from it every iota of pleasure.

He gave her no choice.

She left him with even less.

For long moments, mentally cursing, Royce kept both his hands locked about hers, safely pressed to the wall on either side of her head, for the simple reason that he didn't trust himself. And with her as she was, all but drunk on passion, he trusted her even less.

Her body was a heated feminine cushion pressed the length of his, her breasts firm against his chest, her long limbs riding against his, tempting and luring, the soft tautness of her belly caressing his already engorged shaft as if to urge him on.

He hadn't known she would respond as she had – instantly plunging them both into the fire. He recognized the flames well enough, but with her the conflagration threatened to run amok, to cinder his control.

That realization had been shocking enough to snap the hold combined lust and desire had gained – enough to allow him to reassert that essential element. Control, his control, was vital – not just for him, but even more for her.

So he held on, battled the temptation she wantonly lavished on him, until his mind rose above the fog of his wracked and wholly engaged senses.

Then, at last, he knew what he had to do.

He didn't abate the passion, the possessiveness, in his kisses – not in the least. He angled his head and deliberately pushed her harder, further. Gave no quarter, accepted no appeasement.

Wasn't entirely surprised when, instead of retreating to safety, she met him, took all his passion, absorbed it, and then turned it back on him.

This time he was ready. Shifting against her, he used his hips to trap her against the wall; releasing her hands, he lowered his arms, and set his fingers to the tiny jet buttons running from her scooped neckline to the raised waist of her black gown.

She was so engrossed in the kiss, in inciting and taunting him, she didn't notice as he opened her bodice, then eased the halves apart. A flick here, there, and the ribbon ties of her chemise were undone. He set both palms to her shoulders, pressing the bodice wide, pushing the fine fabric of her chemise down as he ran his hands down, over and around, then filled them with her breasts. She gasped, literally quaked as he blatantly possessed – as he took charge of the kiss again, filled her mouth again, then let his attention shift to the warm, firm mounds in his hands.

To doing as he willed with them, tactilely savoring the fine skin, using one blunt fingertip to trace the ring of each puckered aureola, arousing her even more.

Then he closed his hands again, felt her drag in a breath and hold it as he played, possessed, kneaded. She shifted, tentative, restless; he sensed something within her – in the tautness of her slender frame – ease, change. Her hands fluttered, one on either side of his head, then closed, settled, one sliding to his nape, fingers tangling in his hair, gripping convulsively as he closed finger and thumb about her nipples and squeezed. Her other hand gently touched, traced, then cradled his cheek, his jaw.

Gently holding him.

First surrender, but he wanted much more, even though, tonight, he wouldn't take all he wanted from her.

He broke the kiss. Before she could react, with his head he nudged hers to the side, set his lips to the sensitive spot beneath her ear, then traced down the long line of her throat, paused to lave the point at its base where her pulse thudded frantically, then swept lower, to with his lips and mouth, with tongue and teeth, claim what his hands already had.

Head back against the wall, eyes closed, Minerva gasped, shuddered, felt her mind and her senses fragment under the assault he waged upon them. The sweep of his hard lips over her skin, the wet heat of his mouth applied to her aching nipples, the rough rasp of his tongue, the hot torment when he suckled her, ripped what wits she'd retained away, scattered them far and wide, and effectively routed any will she might have summoned against him.

His teeth nipped; pain and pleasure briefly combined, flaring hotly.

She was panting, wanton and abandoned, unable to think, her senses awash in a flood of heat; need, desire and passion were a growling, gnawing hunger in her belly.

He drew back, raised his head. His hands reclaimed her breasts, his fingers replacing his lips, continuing to play, to distract her as through the heated dimness he studied her face, assessed . . .

She felt the weight of his gaze, sensed his command, but she didn't want to open her eyes . . . she raised the heavy lids just enough to, through the fringe of her lashes, see him looking at her.

His face was harder, harsher than she'd ever seen it, lust and desire etching the edges of the already sharp angles and planes.

He saw her looking, caught her gaze.

A heartbeat passed, then one of his hands left her breast and, palm pressed to her body, skated slowly down. He held her gaze as, hand splayed, he paused at her waist to press . . . then that questing hand slid lower, pressed again as if testing the tautness of her stomach, then slid lower still, the rustle of her gown an evocative warning as he pressed his long fingers into the hollow between her thighs.

She shuddered, bit her lip, had to close her eyes, would have swayed if he hadn't been holding her against the wall.

His fingers stroked, then pressed further, deeper; her skirts did little to mute the effect of the intimate caress. His hand at her breast continued to idly play, further ruffling her senses, yet most of her awareness had locked on the heat emanating from where he was caressing her between her thighs.

She released her lip, gulped in a desperate breath – felt his fingers probe, and clamped her teeth over her lower lip again as her senses literally spun.

He leaned closer, one hard hip anchoring her while his fingers continued to stroke her soft flesh. He lowered his head, whispered in her ear, "Moan for me, Minerva."

She was utterly sure she shouldn't, that that was one surrender he shouldn't win. Eyes still closed, she shook her head.

Even though she couldn't see it, she knew his lips curved as he said, "Just wait. You will."

He was right; she did. And not just once.

He knew far too much, was too expert, too experienced, for her to stand against him. His fingers stroked, teased, probed, languidly caressed until she was utterly and insensibly desperate, for what she didn't fully comprehend, not until, with her wanton acquiescence, he rucked up her skirts and set his hand, his fingers, skin to skin to her wet, swollen flesh.

Then she learned, then she knew. Then she discovered what could make her moan, what could make her senses stretch tight, taut, to the sensual limit, where, quivering, they waited for release.

He thrust his fingers, one, then another, boldly into her sheath, worked them deep, and gave her what she wanted.

More pleasure, more sensation, more delight; the intimate penetration, his hard fingers slick with her passion, repetitively thrusting deep, filled her, drove her, sent her soaring.

Beyond recall; her senses, her nerves, started to unravel.

He locked his lips over hers, took her breath, gave it back as his fingers stroked deeply inside her – and her world shattered. She came apart, nerves fracturing, heat and sensation fragmenting, flying through her body, rocketing down her veins like shards of molten glass, flaring hot and bright everywhere under her skin, before sinking in, ultimately pooling low in her belly.

Long moments passed before her senses returned. Her first thought was that, if he hadn't kissed her at the last, she would have screamed.

Then she realized he'd drawn back, withdrawn his hand from between her thighs, and let her skirts fall. He'd shifted so he was leaning on one shoulder, set beside hers against the wall. His other hand was still idly, languidly caressing her naked breast.

She forced open her lids, turned her head to look into his

face. He was watching his hand on her breast, but he felt her gaze and raised his heavy lids to meet her eyes.

She looked into his, and saw . . . shivered.

Royce didn't try to hide his intentions; he let them live in his eyes, let her see.

A frown swam over her face. She moistened her swollen lips.

Before she could say anything, he pushed away from the wall, shifting to stand in front of her; drawing his hand from the bounty of her breast, he set his fingers to quickly doing up the buttons he'd earlier undone.

He felt her gaze on his face, but didn't meet it, knew without looking that her mind was working again – that she would conclude, correctly, that he was playing a long game.

He didn't just want her beneath him, didn't simply want to sheath his aching erection in the soft flesh he'd just explored and claimed. He wanted her in his bed, willing and eager. Not because he'd overwhelmed her senses to the point where she didn't know what she was doing. He wanted to see her sprawled naked on his sheets, wanted her to hold out her arms, spread her long legs and welcome him into her body.

Knowingly. With full knowledge of her actions, and their repercussions.

He wanted that – her complete, absolute, unequivocal, and willing surrender – more than he needed temporary relief. Taking her, storming her castle now, wouldn't yield him the greater prize.

He was a tactician, a man of strategy first and last, even in this arena.

Her bodice reclosed, he glanced at her face, noted her deepening frown. He felt sure that, come morning, she'd have worked out his tack – much good would it do her.

She'd been a part of this household from the age of six; she was now twenty-nine. There was no chance that, over recent years, she hadn't taken – indeed, been encouraged by his mother to take – a lover.

Which meant that the interlude they'd just shared should have reawakened her passions.

Women, even those with sexual needs as strong as his own, could go much longer than men without relief. Almost as if they could make their passions lie dormant, put them into hibernation.

But once reawakened, once sexual release was again dangled before their senses . . .

All he had to do was keep up the pressure and she would come to him of her own accord.

Scripting, planning the interlude that would follow, allowed him to step back, to escort her – still stunned and wondering – from the room and across the corridor to her bedroom door.

He set it swinging wide and stepped back.

Minerva halted, looked him in the eye. "You are not coming in."

His lips quirked, but he inclined his head. "As you wish. Far be it from me to force myself on you."

She felt her cheeks heat. In what had just passed, while he might have been the instigator she'd been an equal participant throughout. But she certainly wasn't going to argue with whatever chivalrous streak had possessed him. As haughtily as she could, she inclined her head. "Good night."

"Until next time."

The dark murmur reached her as she went through the door. Clutching the edge, she swung around and looked back. Stated definitively, "There won't be a next time."

His soft, dark laugh slid like sin over her flushed skin.

"Good night, Minerva." He met her eyes. "Sleep well."

With that, he walked away, toward his apartments.

She shut the door, and leaned back against it.

For just one minute let the sensations he'd sent sweeping through her replay in her mind.

Felt again their power.

Heaven help her – how could she stand against him?

More to the point, how was she going to stand against herself?

Chapter 9

Despite the physical frustrations of the night, Royce was in an equable mood as, the next morning, he worked through his correspondence with Handley in the study.

While he had no experience seducing unwilling or uncertain ladies, his chatelaine, thank God, was neither. Convincing her to lie in his bed would require no sweet talk, cajoling, or longing looks, no playing to her sensitivities; last night, he'd simply been the man, the marcher lord, she already knew him to be, and had succeeded. Admirably.

She might not yet have lain in his bed, but he'd wager the dukedom that by now she'd thought of it. Considered it.

His way forward was now crystal clear, and once he'd bedded her thoroughly, once she knew she was his to the depths of her soul, he'd inform her that she was to be his duchess. He would couch his offer as a request for her hand, but he was adamant that by then there would be no real question, most especially not in her mind.

The more he dwelled on his plan, the more he liked it; with a female like her, the more strings he had linking her to him before he mentioned marriage, the better, the less likely she was to even quibble. The grandes dames might be certain that any of the ladies on their list would unhesitatingly accept his offer, but Minerva's name wasn't on that list, and – despite her comment to the contrary – he wasn't so conceited, so arrogant, that he was, even now, taking her agreement for granted.

But he had no intention of letting her refuse.

"That's all you have to deal with today." Handley, a quiet, determined man, an orphan recommended to Royce by the principal of Winchester Grammar School, who had subsequently proved to be entirely worthy of the considerable trust Royce placed in him, collected the various letters, notes, and documents they'd been dealing with. He glanced at Royce. "You wanted me to remind you about Hamilton and the Cleveland Row house."

"Ah, yes." He had to decide what to do with his town house now he'd inherited the family mansion in Grosvenor Square. "Tell Jeffers to fetch Miss Chesterton. And you'd better stay. There'll be letters and instructions to be sent south, no doubt."

After sending Jeffers for Minerva, Handley returned to the straight-backed chair he preferred, angled to one end of Royce's desk.

Minerva entered. Seeing Handley, she favored him with a smile, then looked at Royce.

No one else would have seen anything unusual in that look, but Royce knew she was wary, watching for any hint of sexual aggression from him.

He returned her look blandly, and waved her to her customary chair. "We need to discuss the Wolverstone House staff, and how best to merge the staff from my London house into the ducal households."

Minerva sat, noting that Handley, settled in his chair, a fresh sheet of paper on top of his pile, a pencil in his hand, was listening attentively. She switched her gaze to Royce. "You mentioned a butler."

He nodded. "Hamilton. He's been with me for sixteen years, and I wouldn't want to lose him."

"How old is he?"

Royce cocked a brow at Handley. "Forty-five?"

Handley nodded. "About that."

"In that case –"

161

She provided information on the existing Wolverstone households, while Royce, with Handley's additional observations, gave her an overview of the small staff he'd accumulated over his years of exile. Given he had no wish to keep the Cleveland Row house, she suggested that most of the staff be sent to Wolverstone House.

"Once you're married and take your seat in the Lords, you and your wife will entertain a great deal more there than has been the case in the last decade – you'll need the extra staff."

"Indeed." Royce's lips curved as if something amused him, but then he saw her noticing and glanced at his jottings. "That leaves only Hamilton's fate unresolved. I'm inclined to assign him to Wolverstone House in a supportive capacity to old Bridgethorpe. In time, Hamilton can take over there, but until Bridgethorpe is ready to retire, depending on how much I need to travel between the various estates, I may use Hamilton as a personal butler."

She raised her brows. "One who travels with you?"

"He knows my preferences better than anyone else."

She inclined her head. "True. And that will allow all the other butlers to remain in their roles without causing tension."

He nodded and looked at Handley. "Is there anything else?"

Handley shook his head and glanced at Minerva.

"Nothing more about the households," she said, "but I wondered if you'd thought further about the mill."

Royce frowned. "I'll have to speak with Falwell, and I suppose Kelso, too, before I make any decision." He glanced at Handley. "Send a message that I wish to see them tomorrow morning."

Handley nodded, making a note.

In the distance, a gong sounded.

"Luncheon." Minerva stood, surprised and relieved that she'd survived two full hours of Royce's company without blushing once. Then again, other than that initial assessing look, he'd been entirely neutral when interacting with her.

She smiled at Handley as he and Royce rose to their feet.

Handley smiled back. Gathering his papers, he nodded to

Royce. "I'll have those letters ready for you to sign later this afternoon."

"Leave them on the desk – I'll be in and out." Royce looked at Minerva, waved her to the door. "Go ahead – I'll join you at the table."

She inclined her head and left – feeling very like Little Red Riding Hood; avoiding walking alone through the keep's corridors with the big, bad wolf was obviously a wise idea.

She had to own to further surprise when Royce chose to sit between Lady Courtney and Susannah at the luncheon table. The meal was strictly informal, a cold collation laid out on a sideboard from which guests helped themselves, assisted by footmen and watched over by Retford, before taking what seats they wished at the long table.

Flanked by Gordon and Rohan Varisey, with the startlingly handsome Gregory Debraigh opposite, she had distraction enough without wondering about Royce and his machinations. Presumably during the day, while he was Wolverstone and she was his chatelaine, he intended to behave with circumspection.

The meal had ended, and she was strolling with the others through the front hall, when Royce walked up behind her. "Minerva."

When she halted and turned, brows rising, he said, "If you're free, I'd like to take a look at the mill. It would help if I have a better understanding of the problem before I see Falwell and Kelso tomorrow."

"Yes, of course." She was the one urging the matter be dealt with immediately. "Now?"

He nodded and waved her toward the west wing.

They walked through the corridors, the voices of the others fading as they turned into the north wing. A side hall at the north end led them to a door that gave onto the gardens beyond.

Lawns and shrub borders fell away to more rolling expanses hosting larger, mature trees. The ornamental stream burbled beside them as they followed the gravel path along its bank.

163

Ahead, the mill sat built over the stream; partially screened by a stand of willows, it was far enough from the house to be unobtrusive, yet was within walking distance.

As they approached, Royce studied the building, part stone, part timber. It sat squarely across the deep race, at that point only a few yards wide, through which the diverted waters of the Coquet rushed with sufficient force to spin the heavy waterwheel that turned the massive grinding stone.

The ground sloped upward, away from the castle toward the hills to the northwest, so the west bank of the race was significantly higher than the east bank. Spanning the race, the mill therefore was built on two levels. The higher and larger western section contained the grinding stone and the beams, levers, and gears that connected it to the waterwheel in the race.

The narrower, lower, eastern side through which he and Minerva entered contained beams and pulleys that raised and lowered the huge waterwheel; because of the bores that surged down the Coquet when the snows melted, it was essential the wheel could be lifted entirely free of the race. The eastern section also contained bins and storage cupboards set against the wooden railing that ran along the edge of the race.

The first crop of corn had already been ground; the second crop was yet to be harvested. For the moment, the mill stood silent and empty, with the wheel raised and braced above the race on massive beams.

"The problem's not hard to see." Minerva led the way into the soft shadows. The building had no windows, but light streamed in through the three open doorways – the one through which they'd entered, as well as the two at either end of the upper, western section.

Royce followed her along the continuation of the path, now paved; bins and cupboards formed a row on his left, the wood-and-stone outer wall to his right. The noise of rushing water was amplified inside, filling his ears. The cupboards were shoulder-height; when he looked over their tops, his eyes were level with the timber floor of the western section.

Ahead, beyond where the cupboards ended, Minerva had paused at the foot of a slanting gangplank connecting the two sections of the mill.

He nodded at the gangplank. "That's new." There'd always been a plank, but the ones he remembered had been literally planks, not this substantial timber board with cleats and a sturdy rail on one side. Halting beside Minerva, he studied the hinges, ropes, and pulleys attached to the plank, connecting it to the western section's floor and railing. "And it even swings out of the way."

In order for the waterwheel to be lowered and raised, the plank used to have to be removed altogether.

"After he'd replaced the old plank three times – you know how frequently they drop it in the race when they try to lift it away – Hancock designed this." Minerva started across the narrow platform. "He hasn't had to even repair it since."

"An estimable improvement." Royce followed her.

"Which is what we could do with up here." Stepping off the gangplank's upper end, Minerva swept her arms wide, encompassing the whole timber-floored western section in the middle of which sat the massive circular grinding stone supported by a stone plinth; the plinth continued through the floor into the earth beneath.

Letting his gaze travel around the otherwise empty area, Royce walked to the millstone, then cocked a brow at her.

"As I explained," she continued, "because we have to keep the doors open all the time, summer and winter, it's impossible to store anything here. The corn is ground, collected, and bagged – and then, each day, has to be moved, either to the castle cellars or back to farmers' holdings. If we close the doors to keep the animals out, the corn starts to mold by the next day. Bad enough, but preserving the millstone through winter is a never-ending battle. No matter what we've tried, it takes weeks of preparation every spring before we can use it without risking the corn."

"Mold again?" He walked back to the railing along the race.

"Mold, fungus, mildew – we've even had mushrooms growing on it."

Running a hand along the wide top rail, he grimaced. "Too damp."

"If we shut the doors, it sometimes gets so bad it drips."

He looked at her. "So what's your solution?"

"Hancock agrees that if we put up a timber wall all along the race, we can tar it and make it waterproof. We'd also need to fill the gaps in the outer walls and roof, and around the plinth, and put extra strips on the doors, to stop damp air getting in. And Hancock strongly recommends, as do I, putting in glass panes above the southern doors, so sun can shine in and help keep what's inside warm and dry."

Royce glanced around. "Shut those doors." He waved at the pair at the north end of the building, then walked to the larger set at the southern end. He waited until Minerva, frowning, shut both north doors, cutting off the light from that direction.

Sunshine coming through the doors in the eastern section didn't reach the western side. Royce swung one of the southern doors closed, blocking off half the sunshine that had been streaming in, then, more slowly, closed the other door, watching as the band of sunshine narrowed until it was a thin beam.

Shutting the door completely, he walked back along the line the sunshine had traced to where it had ended just before the millstone. Halting, he turned to look back toward the doors, at the wall above them reaching to the roof.

Minerva came to stand beside him.

"How much glass was Hancock thinking of?"

Glass was expensive. "He was thinking of at least two panes, one above each door, at least half the width of each door."

She watched as Royce studied the wall, then turned and looked at the millstone. "We'd be better off glazing as much of that wall as possible."

She blinked.

He glanced at her, arched a brow.

Quickly, she nodded. "That would definitely be best." She hadn't suggested it because she hadn't thought he would agree.

A subtle curving of his lips suggested he'd guessed as much, but all he said was, "Good." Turning, he looked at the mill-stone, then prowled around her, examining the stone.

She looked up at the area above the door, estimating the size, then deciding she might as well reopen the north doors, swung around and walked – into Royce.

Into his arms.

She was surprised.

He wasn't.

That last registered – along with the wicked glint in his eyes, the subtly triumphant lift to his lips, and that they were alone in the mill, acres from the castle, and the doors were closed –

He kissed her. Despite her racing thoughts, she had less than an instant's warning. She tried to resist – the intention formed; she tried to make herself stiffen as his arms slid around her, tried to make her hands, instinctively splayed on his chest, push him away . . .

Nothing happened. Or rather, for long moments she simply stood there and let him kiss her – savored again the pressure of his lips on hers, the subtle heat of them, and of his body so near, hard, and fascinating as he gathered her in, closer to that beckoning heat . . . she almost couldn't believe it was happening again. That he was kissing her again.

In a burst of startling clarity, she realized she hadn't truly believed what had happened the previous night. She'd been cautious, wary and watchful today, but she hadn't truly let herself acknowledge, not consciously, all that had happened in the morning room last night.

So it was going to happen again.

Before panic could gather wit and will, grab them back from where they'd wandered enough to mount any effective resistance, his lips firmed, hard and commanding, and hers parted. In the instant he surged, conquerorlike, into her mouth, she sensed his full intention – realized with absolute certainty that she had no hope of stopping him when fully half of her didn't want to.

When too much of her wanted. Wanted to know, to experience, to savor him and all he would show her, to embrace the moment, and the pleasure and delight it might bring.

To open herself to that, and him, to explore the possibilities she'd sensed last night – to follow the lingering urging of her infatuation-obsession and all the fanciful dreams she'd ever had . . . of just such an illicit moment as this.

With him.

Even as the thought resonated through her, she felt the dark silk of his hair sliding over and under her fingers, realized that, once again, she was kissing him back – that he'd succeeded once again in luring her – the inner wanton only he had ever touched – into coming out and playing with him.

And it was a game. A sudden sense of exhilaration gripped her and she shifted against him, then, utterly blatant, stroked her tongue boldly along his.

She felt his deep chuckle, then he returned the favor, his mouth, lips, and tongue doing things to hers that she felt perfectly certain ought to be banned. His arms tightened, steely bands closing to bring her body flush against his, then his hands went wandering, tracing, then evocatively sculpting her curves, sweeping over her hips and down, then drawing her closer, molding her hips against his hard thighs, the rigid rod of his erection impressing itself on her much softer belly.

Already lost in the kiss, to his embrace, she felt her inner flames leap from a smolder to a crackling blaze. Felt herself heat, then melt into them, become part of them as they spread and consumed her.

She felt like a fey creature as she let herself spin, senses alert, attuned, as she let the fiery, gathering vortex he was orchestrating draw her in.

At some point, his arms eased from her; hands gripping her waist, he turned with her, then drew her down to the millstone.

The next thing she knew – the next moment her senses surfaced from the firestorm of pleasure he wrought enough to know – she was lying on her back, the rough stone beneath her shoulders, hips, and thighs, her bodice wide open, and he was feasting on her naked breasts even more evocatively – more intently and expertly – than he had the previous night.

It was only because he'd drawn back to look down on the

flesh he'd so thoroughly possessed that she'd been able to rise above the pleasured haze he'd wrapped her in. Trapped her in – yet she couldn't deny she was a very willing prisoner.

She was panting, gasping; she knew she'd moaned. Her hands lay lax on his upper arms; they'd lost all strength, after all he'd wrung from her. His dark eyes were tracing; she could feel the heat of his gaze, so much hotter on her bare skin.

But it was his face that, in that moment, held her, the sharp angles and planes, the long hollows of his lean cheeks, the square chin and wide brow, the blade of his nose, the intent line of his lips – the expression that, for that one unchecked instant, screamed with possessive lust.

It was that, it had to be; recognition made her wantonly writhe inside. Beneath his hand, she shifted restlessly.

His gaze flicked up; his eyes met hers for an instant, then he looked back at her breasts, lowered his head – and with calculated intensity swept her back into the flames.

She was far beyond any protest when he drew her skirts and petticoats up – all the way up to her waist. The touch of air on her skin should have felt cool, but instead she was already burning.

Already yearning for the touch of his hand between her thighs; when it came, she sighed. But she couldn't relax, caught her breath on an urgent half sob, her fingers gripping his sleeve as her body arched, helplessly wantonly begged as he stroked, caressed, teased . . .

She wanted his fingers inside her again. That or . . . she'd always wondered why, how, women could be persuaded to accommodate the hard, heavy reality of a man's erection, what madness possessed them to permit, let alone invite, such a thing to penetrate them there . . . now she knew.

She definitely knew, definitely burned with a want she'd never thought to feel.

Breathless, her voice no longer hers to command, she was struggling to find a way to communicate that burning, increasingly urgent desire when he released the tortured nipple he'd been suckling, lifted his head, slid down alongside her, ducked

169

his head below the ridge of her rucked skirts – she gasped, shivered, as she felt his hot lips caress her navel.

Then she felt his tongue touch, caress, probe, then settle to a languid thrust and retreat; she shuddered and, eyes tightly closed, sank one hand in his hair, clinging to her whirling senses as between her thighs his fingers stroked in the same, evocative rhythm.

She was so deeply ensnared in the web of hot delight, of heated pleasure he sent coursing down her veins, that she was only dimly aware of him drawing back, of him easing her thighs wider apart.

What broke through the haze was the touch of his gaze, when, sensing it, faintly disbelieving, she cracked open her eyes and from beneath her lashes watched him studying, examining, the wet, swollen flesh his fingertips were tracing.

Her eyes locked on his face, captured by what she saw, sensed in the harsh, arrogant lines – the absolute drive, the all-consuming intent to possess her, all of her, that was engraved so clearly on his features.

The sight stole what little breath she had left, locked her lungs, left her giddy.

"Are you ready to scream?"

He hadn't looked up, hadn't met her eyes. She frowned; she hadn't screamed yet, or only in her mind.

He glanced up, met her gaze for a fleeting instant, then lowered his head. And replaced his fingers with his lips.

She gasped, arched, would have jerked away but he had her well anchored, her hips held immobile so he could lap, lick, and savor.

And taste her. The realization brought a moan to her lips. Lids falling, head back, she tried to breathe, tried to cope, had no other option but to, fists clenching in his hair, ride the wave of sharp delight he sent surging through her.

That with an expert's skill he crafted into a powerful, thunderous force that swept her into a fierce tempest of pleasure.

She battled to stifle a shriek as the tip of his tongue circled and stroked the tight bud of her desire, only partially succeeded. Her thighs trembled as his tongue continued to stroke . . .

Her spine arched helplessly as he eased it into her.

She shrieked, then screamed as he thrust it deep, then again more deeply into her.

Came apart in shuddering, sobbing waves as his mouth worked at her, on her, over her.

As the storm passed on and through her, leaving her utterly wracked and spent, Royce continued to lap at the nectar he'd drawn forth, savoring the gradual easing of her muscles, the slow roll of release as it swept through her.

Eventually, he drew back, looked at her face – that of a madonna pleasured to her toes – and smiled.

He reached for the buttons of her bodice and carefully did them up. A flick of his hand sent her skirts rustling down, covering her long, lithe legs. There was no sense in tormenting himself; this wasn't his bed.

Tactics, strategy, and above all else, winning the war.

He rose, and opened the northern doors, then, once he'd ensured her skirts were fully down, opened the big southern doors as well. The afternoon sun slanted in; he stood there for a moment, ignoring the persistent ache in his groin, and looked back at the castle. He could see the keep's battlements, private and out of bounds to all guests, but all the lower windows were screened by trees. Returning to the castle, they'd be safe from any even mildly interested eyes until they got much nearer the walls.

Given he wanted her to agree to their wedding solely because she desired him as much as he desired her, keeping their liaison a secret was imperative; he was determined that no social pressure of any stripe would work its way into their equation. Reassured, he returned to her.

The instant she blinked back to life, he took her hand and drew her to her feet, steadying her until, her arm tucked in his, she could walk beside him.

He led her out into the sunshine, heading back to the castle via the path along the western bank of the race.

Minerva felt . . . detached. Light, floating, glowing. Her limbs felt deliciously relaxed.

If nothing else, she now knew beyond question that Royce was expert at this game – which left her wondering why he hadn't taken advantage of what he had to have known was her acquiescence, and sought his own release in her wantonly willing body.

The body he'd reduced to wanton willingness with caresses that, for the rest of her life, would make her blush.

As heat rose in her cheeks, she inwardly frowned; her features were still too lax to manage the expression.

"Because I intend to have you naked – not a stitch on – in my ducal bed." He made the statement in an even, matter-of-fact voice as he strolled beside her, his gaze on the castle. "That's where I intend to sink into you, to fill you and have my fill of you, for the first time."

A spurt of irritation gave her strength enough to turn her head and narrow her eyes on his profile, until he, lips faintly curved, glanced her way.

She looked into his eyes, dark as sin and still far too molten, and discovered she had nothing to say. They'd reached a footbridge spanning the race, now a wider, burbling stream; drawing her arm from his, she reached for the railing and started across. She needed to put space between them.

"At the risk of sounding arrogantly smug, I got the impression you haven't been accustomed to . . . life's little subtleties."

His tone made it clear to what he was referring; life's little subtleties, indeed! "Of course not. I've been your mother's confidante and your father's chatelaine for the past eleven years. Why would I know of such things?"

She glanced his way, and saw a faintly puzzled, somewhat quizzical look on his face.

The same qualities resonated in his voice when he replied, "Strangely, those same criteria gave rise to my question."

She looked ahead, felt his gaze on her face.

"I take it your past lovers weren't . . . shall we say, imaginative?"

172

Her past lovers were nonexistent, but she wasn't going to tell him that – he who had known more women than he could count. Literally.

That he, expert that he was, hadn't detected her inexperience left her feeling faintly chuffed. She cast about in her mind for a suitable retort. As she stepped off the bridge and set off down the path, with every step closer to the castle feeling more like herself, she inclined her head in his direction. "I suspect few men are as imaginative as you."

She felt certain that was nothing more than the truth, and if it caused him to preen and think he'd advanced his cause, so much the better.

After the afternoon's debacle, she was going to have to give avoiding him much more serious thought.

He thought she'd had lovers.

Then again, Variseys were sneaky, underhanded, and utterly untrustworthy when it came to something they wanted; he was quite capable of paying her a roundabout compliment like that in the hopes of further softening her brain.

Which, where he was concerned, was already soft enough.

Late that night, so late the moon was riding an inky sky over the Cheviots, casting a pearlescent sheen over every tree and rock, Minerva stood at her bedroom window and, arms folded, stared unseeing at the evocative landscape.

The door was locked; she suspected Royce could pick locks, so she'd left the key in the hole and turned it fully, then wedged a handkerchief around it, just to be sure.

She'd spent the evening with the other ladies, metaphorically clinging to their skirts. Although her bedroom was in the keep proper, opposite the duchess's morning room, not all that far from the ducal apartments and Royce's ducal bed, by steering the guests up the main keep stairs, she'd been able to tag along, stopping at her door while the ladies with rooms in the east wing walked on.

Royce had noticed her strategy, but other than an appreciative quirk to his lips, had made nothing of it.

She, however, was clearly going to have to take a stand against him.

The speculation the assembled ladies had indulged in after dinner, in the drawing room before the men had rejoined them, had underscored what she shouldn't have needed to be reminded of; they were all waiting to learn who he'd chosen as his bride.

Any day now, they would hear.

And then where would she be?

"Damn all Variseys – especially *him*!" The muttered sentiment relieved a little of her ire, but the major part was self-directed. She'd known what he was like all along; what she hadn't known, hadn't realized, was that he could take her idiotic infatuation-obsession and with a few lustful kisses, a few illicit caresses, convert it into outright desire.

Flaming desire – the sort that burned.

She felt like she was smoldering, just waiting to ignite. If he touched her, kissed her, she would – and she knew where that would lead. He'd even told her – to his ducal bed.

"Humph!" Despite wanting – now, thanks to him and his expertise, wanting quite desperately – to experience in the flesh all that her fanciful imagination had ever dreamed, despite her smoldering desire to lie beneath him, there was one equally powerful consideration that, no matter that damning desire, had her holding adamantly, unwaveringly, to her original decision never to grace his bed.

If she did . . . would infatuation–obsession–smoldering desire convert to something more?

If it did . . .

If she ever did anything so foolish as to fall in love with a Varisey – and with him in particular – she would deserve every iota of the emotional devastation that was guaranteed to follow.

Variseys did not love. The entire ton knew that.

In Royce's case it was widely known that his lovers never lasted long, that he inevitably moved on to another, then another, with no lingering attachment of any kind. He was a Varisey to his toes, and he'd never pretended otherwise.

To fall in love with such a man would be unjustifiably stupid. She strongly suspected that, for her, it would be akin to emotional self-immolation.

So she wasn't going to – could not allow herself to – take the risk of falling in with his seduction, if it even could be called that – his highly charged sexual game.

And while she might be crossing swords with a master, she had a very good idea how to avoid his thrust – indeed, he'd told her himself.

Somewhat grimly, she considered ways and means. She wasn't, when she dwelled on it, as short of defenses as she'd thought.

Chapter 10

The next morning, she commenced her campaign to protect her heart from the temptation of falling in love with Royce Varisey.

Her strategy was simple; she had to keep as far as possible from his ducal bed.

She knew him; he was stubborn, not to say muleheaded, to a fault. Given he'd declared that he would first have her in the huge four-poster – even to denying himself over the point – as long as she kept clear of his bedroom and that bed, she would be safe.

After breakfasting with the other guests rather than in the keep's private parlor, she sent a message to the stables for the gig, went down to the kitchens and filled a basket with a selection of preserves made from fruit from the castle's orchards, then strolled out to the stables.

She was waiting for the gig's harness to be tightened when Sword came thundering in, Royce on his back.

Bringing the stallion under control, he raked her with his gaze. "Wither away?"

"There are some crofter families I need to call on."

"Where?"

"Up Blindburn way."

His gaze lowered to Sword. He'd ridden the stallion hard,

and would need another mount if he chose to come with her; the gig couldn't hold the basket and them both.

He glanced at her. "If you'll wait while they fetch my curricle, I'll drive us there. I should meet these crofters."

She considered, then nodded. "All right."

He dismounted, with a few orders dispatched Henry and two grooms to harness his blacks to his curricle, while others unharnessed the old cob from the gig.

When the curricle was ready, she let him take her basket and stow it beneath the seat, then hand her up; she'd remembered his demon-bred horses – with them between the shafts, he wouldn't be able to devote any attention to her.

To seducing her.

He climbed up beside her, and with a flick of his wrist, sent the blacks surging; the curricle rattled out of the stable yard and down the drive, then he headed the flighty pair up Clennell Street.

Twenty minutes later, they arrived at a group of low stone cottages huddled against a hillside. Royce was quietly relieved that his expensive pair had, once they'd accepted that he wasn't going to let them run, managed the less-than-even climb without breaking any legs.

He drew the horses to a halt at the edge of a flattened area between the three cottages. Children instantly appeared from every aperture, some literally tumbling out of windows. All were wide-eyed with wonder. They quickly gathered around, staring at the blacks.

"Coo – *oo!*" one boy reverently breathed. "Bet they go like the clappers."

Minerva climbed down, then reached in for her basket. She caught his eye. "I won't be too long."

A sudden feeling – it might have been panic – assailed him at the notion of being left at the mercy of a pack of children for hours. "How long is 'too long'?"

"Perhaps half an hour – no more." With a smile, she headed for the cottages. All the children chorused a polite "Good morning, Miss Chesterton," which Minerva answered with a smile, but the brats immediately returned their attention to him – or rather, his horses.

He eyed the motley crew gradually inching closer; they ranged from just walking to almost old enough to work in the fields – whatever ages those descriptions translated to. He'd had very little to do with children of any sort, not since he'd been one himself; he didn't know what to say, or do.

Their bright, eager gazes flicked from the horses to him, but the instant they saw him watching, they looked back at the horses. He revised his earlier conclusion; they were interested in him, but the horses were easier to approach.

He was their duke; they were his future workers.

Mentally girding his loins, moving slowly and deliberately, he tied off the reins, then stepped down and strolled to the horses' heads. Some of the children were quite small, and the blacks, although temporarily quiet, were completely untrustworthy.

The crowd drew back a step or two, the older boys and girls bobbing bows and curtsies. The younger ones weren't sure what to do or why. One girl hissed to her recalcitrant little brother, "He's the new dook, stoopid."

Royce pretended he hadn't heard. He nodded amiably – a general nod that included them all – then, catching his leader's bridle, reached up and smoothed a hand down the long arched neck.

An instant passed, then –

"Do you ride 'em, Y'r Grace? Or are they just for hauling th' carriage?"

"Have you won any races with 'em, Y'r Grace?"

"Is this here a curricle, or one of them phaetons, Y'r Grace?"

"How fast can they go, Y'r Grace?"

He very nearly told them to stop "Y'r Grace"-ing him, but realized it might sound like a reprimand. Instead, he set himself to answering their questions in a calm, unruffled manner.

Somewhat to his surprise, the approach he used with horses worked with children, too. They relaxed, and he had the chance to turn the tables enough to learn a little about the small settlement. Minerva had told him five families lived in the three cottages. The children confirmed that only the older women were at home; all the other adults and youths were in the fields, or working in the forge a little way farther along the track. They themselves weren't at school because there was no school nearby; they learned their letters and numbers from the older women.

After a few such exchanges, the children clearly felt the ice had been broken and their bona fides sufficiently established to ask about him.

"We did hear tell," the lad he thought was the oldest said, "that you was working in London for the government – that you were a *spy!*"

That surprised him; he'd thought his father would have ensured his occupation had remained a dim, dark secret.

"No, silly!" The oldest girl blushed when Royce and the others looked her way, but gamely went on, "Ma said as you were the *chief* spy – the one in charge – and that you were responsible for bringing down Boney."

"Well . . . not by myself. The men I organized did very dangerous things, and yes, they contributed to Napoleon's downfall, but it took Wellington and the whole army, and Blucher and the others, too, to finally get the deed done."

Naturally, they took that as an invitation to pepper him with questions about his men's missions; borrowing freely from otherwise classified exploits, it was easy enough to keep the expectant horde satisfied, although they were rather put out to learn he hadn't actually seen Napoleon dragged away in chains.

After delivering the preserves she'd brought, and being introduced to the latest addition to the combined households by its grandmother, juggling the swaddled infant in her arms, cooing while it batted at her hair, Minerva went to the window the better to see the child's eyes, glanced out – and tensed to hand the babe back so she could rush out and rescue its siblings.

Or Royce, whichever applied . . . but after an instant of

179

looking, taking in the tableau centered on the black horses, the curricle – and the most powerful duke in England, who appeared to be telling some tale – she relaxed and, smiling, turned back to the baby and cooed some more.

The baby's grandmother came to the window; she, too, took in the scene outside. Her brows rose. After a moment, she said, "Looking at that, if I couldn't see with my own eyes that he's the last lord's get, I'd be thinking some cuckoo had got into the ducal nest."

Minerva's smile deepened; the idea of Royce as a cuckoo . . . "He's definitely a Varisey, born and bred."

The old woman humphed. "Aye, we'll all be locking up our daughters, no doubt. Still . . ." She turned from the window and headed back to her work. "If that had been his father out there, he would have snarled at the brats and sent them scurrying – just because he could."

Minerva couldn't disagree, yet old Henry would never have even considered coming out with her on her rounds.

Nevertheless, she didn't tempt fate; handing the baby back to its grandmother, she collected her basket, and was saying her farewells when a large presence darkened the doorway. Royce had to duck low to enter.

The three women immediately bobbed curtsies; Minerva introduced them before he could make any abrupt demand that they leave.

He acknowledged the women smoothly, then his gaze flicked over her, taking in the empty basket in her hand. But again, before he could say anything, the matriarch, who'd seized the moment to size him up, came forward to show him her grandchild.

Minerva held her breath, sensed him tense to step back – retreating from the baby – but then he stiffened and held his ground. He nodded formally at the matriarch's words, then, about to turn and leave, hesitated.

He reached out and touched the back of one long finger to the baby's downy cheek. The baby gurgled and batted with tiny fists. The grandmother's face was wreathed in smiles.

180

She saw Royce notice, saw him take in the way the other women softened, too. Then he glanced at her.

She gestured with her basket. "We should be going."

He nodded, inclined his head to the women. "Ladies." Turning, he ducked out of the cottage.

After exchanging impressed looks with the crofter women, Minerva followed. Crossing the yard to the curricle, she saw and heard enough to know that the children had lost all fear of their duke; their eyes now shone with a species of hero worship more personal than simple awe.

His father had had no real relationship, no personal interaction, with his people; he'd managed them from a distance, through Falwell and Kelso, and had spoken with any directly only when absolutely necessary. He'd therefore only spoken to the senior men.

Royce, it seemed, might be different. He certainly lacked his father's insistence on a proper distance being preserved between his ducal self and the masses.

Once again he took the basket, stowed it, then handed her up. Retrieving the reins from the oldest lad, he joined her. She held her tongue and let him direct the children back. Round-eyed, they complied, watched as he carefully turned the skittish pair, then waved wildly and sang their farewells as he guided the curricle down the lane.

As the cottages fell behind, the peace, serenity – and isolation – of the hills closed around them. Reminded of her goal, she thought quickly, then said, "Now we're out this way, there's a well over toward Shillmoor that's been giving trouble." She met his hard gaze as his head swung her way. "We should take a look."

He held her gaze for an instant, then had to look back to his horses. The only reply he gave was a grunt, but when they reached the bottom of the lane, he turned the horses' heads west, toward Shillmoor.

Rather than, as she was perfectly certain he'd intended to, make for the nearest secluded lookout.

Sitting back, she hid a smile. As long as she avoided being

alone with him in a setting he could use, she would be safe, and he wouldn't be able to advance his cause.

It was early evening when Royce stalked into his dressing room and started stripping off his clothes while Trevor poured the last of a succession of buckets of steaming water into the bath in the bathing chamber beyond.

His mood was distinctly grim. His chatelaine had successfully filled their entire day; they'd left the little hamlet near Shillmoor with barely enough time to drive back to the castle and bathe before dinner.

And after overseeing the final stages of reconstruction of the well's crumbling walls and sagging roof, then taking an active part in reassembling and correctly recommissioning the mechanism for pulling water up from the depths of the very deep well, he needed a bath.

The local men had taken the day off from working their fields and had gathered to repair the aging well, a necessity before winter; when he and Minerva had driven up, they'd been well advanced with the repairs to the walls. Their ideas for shoring up the roof, however, were a recipe for disaster; he'd stepped in and used his unquestioned authority to redesign and direct the construction of a structure that would have some hope of withstanding the weight of snow they commonly experienced in those parts.

Far from resenting his interference, the men, and the women, too, had been relieved and sincerely grateful. They'd shared their lunch – cider, thick slabs of cheese, and freshly baked rye bread, which he and Minerva had graciously accepted – then been even more amazed when, after watching the men scratch their heads and mutter over the mechanism they'd disassembled, he'd shrugged out of his hacking jacket, rolled up his sleeves, and got to work with them, sorting the various parts and helping reassemble, realign, and reposition the mechanism – he was taller and stronger than any of those there – finally resulting in a rejuvenated and properly functioning well.

There'd been cheers all around as one of the women had pulled up the first brimming pail.

He and Minerva had left with a cacophony of thanks ringing in their ears, but it hadn't escaped his notice how surprised and intrigued by him the villagers had been. Clearly, his way of dealing with them was vastly different from that of his sire.

Minerva had told him he didn't need to be like his father; it seemed he was proving her correct. She should be pleased . . . and she was. Her excursions had ensured she won the day – that she had triumphed in the battle of wills, and wits, he and she were engaged in.

To him, the outcome was a foregone conclusion; he did not doubt she would end in his bed. Why she was resisting so strongly remained a mystery – and an ongoing challenge.

Boots removed, he stood and peeled off his breeches and stockings. Naked, he walked into the bathing chamber, and stood looking down at the steam wreathing above the water's surface.

His chatelaine was the first woman he'd ever had to exert himself to win, to battle for in even the most minor sense. Despite the annoyance, the frequent irritations, the constant irk of sexual denial, he couldn't deny he found the challenge – the chase – intriguing.

He glanced down. It was equally impossible to deny he found her challenge, and her, arousing.

Stepping into the tub, he sank down, leaned back, and closed his eyes. The day might have been hers, but the night would be his.

He walked into the drawing room feeling very much a wolf anticipating his next meal. He located his chatelaine, standing before the hearth in her black gown with its modestly cut neckline, and amended the thought: a hunger-ravaged wolf slavering in expectation.

He started toward her. Within two steps, he registered that something was afoot; his sisters, his cousins, and those others still at the castle were abuzz and atwitter, the excitement of their conversations a hum all around him.

Suspicions had started forming before he reached Minerva. Margaret stood beside her; his elder sister turned as he neared, her face alight in a way he'd forgotten it could be. "Royce – Minerva's made the most *wonderful* suggestion."

Even before Margaret rattled on, he knew to his bones that he wasn't going to share her sentiment.

"Plays – Shakespeare's plays. There's more than enough of us who've decided to stay to be able to perform one play each night – to entertain us until the fair. Aurelia and I felt that, as it's now a week since the funeral, and given this is as private a party as could be, then there really could be no objections on the grounds of propriety." Margaret looked at him, dark eyes alive. "What do you think?"

He thought his chatelaine had been exceedingly clever. He looked at her; she returned his gaze levelly, no hint of gloating in her expression.

Margaret and Aurelia especially, and Susannah, too, were all but addicted to amateur theatricals; while he'd been in the south at Eton, then Oxford, they'd had to endure many long winters holed up in the castle – hence their passion. He'd forgotten that, but his chatelaine hadn't.

His respect for her as an opponent rose a definite notch.

He shifted his gaze to Margaret. "I see no objection."

He could see no alternative; if he objected, put his foot down and vetoed the plays, his sisters would sulk and poke and prod at him until he changed his mind. Expression mild, he arched a brow. "Which play will you start with?"

Margaret glowed. "*Romeo and Juliet.* We still have all the abridged scripts, and the costumes and bits and pieces from when we used to do these long ago." She laid a hand on Royce's arm – in gratitude, he realized – then released him. "I must go and tell Susannah – she's to be Juliet."

Royce watched her go; from the questions thrown at her and the expressions evoked by her answers, everyone else was keen and eager to indulge in the amusement.

Minerva had remained, the dutiful chatelaine, beside him.
"I assume," he said, "that we're to be regaled with *Romeo and Juliet* tonight?"

"That's what they'd planned."

"Where?"

"The music room. It's where the plays were always held. The stage and even the curtain are still there."

"And" – the most telling question – "just when did you make this brilliant suggestion of yours?"

She hesitated, hearing the underlying displeasure in his voice. "This morning over breakfast. They were moaning about how bored they were growing."

He let a moment pass, then murmured, "If I might make a suggestion, the next time you consider how bored they might be, you might first like to consider how bored *I* might be."

Turning, he met her eyes, only to see her smile.

"You weren't bored today."

There was no point in lying. "Perhaps not, but I am going to be utterly bored tonight."

Her smile widened as she looked toward the door. "You can't have everything."

Retford's summons rolled out. With irresistible deliberation, Royce took her arm. Noted the sudden leap of her pulse. Lowered his head to murmur as he led her to the door, "But I do intend to have everything from you. Everything, and more."

Placing her beside him again at dinner, he took what revenge he could, his hand drifting over the back of her waist as he steered her to her chair, his fingers stroking over her hand as he released her.

Minerva weathered the moments with what fortitude she could muster; jangling nerves and skittish senses were a price she was prepared to pay to avoid his ducal bed.

Frustratingly, no one – not even Margaret – seemed to think Royce monopolizing her company at all odd. Then again, with him leaning back in his great carver, making her turn to face him, their conversation remained largely private; presumably the others thought they were discussing estate matters. Instead . . .

"I take it *Romeo and Juliet* was not your choice." He sat back, twirling his wineglass between his long fingers.

"No. It's Susannah's favorite – she was keen to play the part." She tried to keep her attention on her plate.

A moment passed. "How many of Shakespeare's plays involve lovers?"

Too many. She reached for her wineglass – slowed to make sure he wasn't going to say anything to make her jiggle it; when he kept silent, she gratefully grasped it and took a healthy sip.

"Do you intend to take part – to trip the stage in one of the roles?"

"That will depend on how many plays we do." She set her glass down, made a mental note to check which plays were safe to volunteer for.

By example, she tried to steer his attention to the conversations farther down the table; with the increasing informality, these were growing more general – and more rowdy.

Indeed, more salacious. Some of his male cousins were calling suggestions to Phillip – cast as Romeo – as to how best to sweep his Juliet into the lovers' bed.

To her consternation, Royce leaned forward, paying attention to the jocular repartee. Then he murmured, his voice so low only she could hear, "Perhaps I should make some suggestions?"

Her mind immediately conjured an all too evocative memory of his last attempt to sweep her into his bed; when her intellect leapt to the fore and hauled her mind away, it merely skittered to the time before that, to his lips on hers, to the pleasure his long fingers had wrought while he'd pinned her to the wall in the lust-heavy dark . . .

It took effort to wrestle her wits free, to focus on his words. "But you haven't succeeded."

She would have called back the words the instant she uttered them; they sounded collected and calm – nothing like what she felt.

Slowly, he turned his head and met her eyes. Smiled – that curving of his lips that carried a promise of lethal reaction rather than any soothing reassurance. "Not. Yet."

He dropped the quiet words like stones into the air between them; she felt the tension pull, then quiver. Felt something within her inwardly tremble – not with apprehension but a damning anticipation. She forced herself to arch a brow, then deliberately turned her attention back down the table.

As soon as dessert was consumed, Margaret dispatched Susannah, Phillip, and the rest of the cast to the music room to prepare. Everyone else remained at the table, finishing their wine, chatting – until Margaret declared the players had had time enough, and the entire company adjourned to the music room.

The music room lay in the west wing, at the point where the north wing joined it. Part of both wings, the room was an odd shape, having two doors, one opening to the north wing and one to the west wing corridors, and only one window – a wide one angled between the two outer walls. The shallow dais that formed the stage filled the floor before the window, a trapezoid that extended well into the room. The stage itself was the rectangle directly in front of the window, while the triangular areas to either side had been paneled off, blocking them off from the audience sitting in the main part of the room, creating wings in which the players could don the finery that made up their costumes, and stage props and furniture could be stored.

Thick velvet curtains concealed the stage. Footmen had set up four rows of gilt-backed chairs across the room before it. The crowd filed in, chatting and laughing, noting the closed curtains, and the dimness created by having only three candelabra on pedestals lighting the large room; a chandelier, fully lit, cast its light down upon the presently screened stage.

Minerva didn't even attempt to slip from Royce's side as he guided her to a seat in the second row, to the right of the center aisle. She sat, grateful to have survived the trip from the dining room with nothing more discomposing than the sensation of

187

his hand at her waist, and the curious aura he projected of hovering over and around her.

Both protectively and possessively.

She should take exception to the evolving habit, but her witless senses were intrigued and unhelpfully tantalized by the suggestive attention.

The rest of the group quickly took their seats. Someone peeked out through the curtains, then, slowly, the heavy curtains parted on the first scene.

The play began. In such situations, it was accepted practice for the audience to call comments, suggestions, and directions to the players – who might or might not respond. Whatever the true tone of the play, the result was always a comedy, something the abbreviated scripts were designed to enhance; the players were expected to overplay the parts to the top of their bent.

While most in the audience called their comments loud enough for all to hear, Royce made his to her alone. His observations, especially on Mercutio, played to the hilt and beyond by his cousin Rohan, were so dry, so acerbic and cuttingly witty, that he reduced her to helpless giggles in short order – something he observed with transparently genuine approval, and what looked very like self-congratulation.

When Susannah appeared as Juliet, waltzing through her family's ball, she returned the favor, making him smile, eventually surprising a laugh from him; she discovered she felt chuffed about that, too.

The balcony scene had them trying to outdo each other, just as Susannah and Phillip vied for the histrionic honors on stage.

When the curtain finally swished closed and the audience thundered their applause for a job well done, Royce discovered he had, entirely unexpectedly, enjoyed himself.

Unfortunately, as he looked around as footmen hurried in to light more candles, he realized the whole company had enjoyed themselves hugely – which augured very badly for him. They'd want to do a play every night until the fair; it took him only an instant to realize he'd have no hope of altering that.

He would have to find some way around his chatelaine's latest hurdle.

Both he and Minerva rose with the others, chatting and exchanging comments. Along with the other players, Susannah reappeared, stepping down from the stage to rejoin the company. Slowly, he made his way to her side.

She turned as he approached, arched one dark brow. "Did you enjoy my performance?"

He arched a brow back. "Was it all performance?"

Susannah opened her eyes wide.

Minerva had drifted from Royce's side. She'd been complimenting Rohan on his execution of Mercutio; she was standing only feet away from Susannah when Royce approached.

Close enough to see and hear as he complimented his sister, then more quietly said, "I take it Phillip is the latest to catch your eye. I wouldn't have thought him your type."

Susannah smiled archly and tapped his cheek. "Clearly, brother mine, you either don't know my type, or you don't know Phillip." She looked across to where Phillip was laughing with various others. "Indeed," Susannah continued, "we suit each other admirably well." She glanced up at Royce, smiled. "Well, at least for the moment."

Minerva inwardly frowned; she hadn't picked up any connection between Phillip and Susannah – indeed, she'd thought Susannah's interest lay elsewhere.

With a widening smile, Susannah waggled her fingers at Royce, then left him.

Royce watched her go, and inwardly shrugged; after his years in social exile, she was right – he couldn't know her adult tastes that well.

He was about to look around for his chatelaine when Margaret raised her voice, directing everyone back to the drawing room. He would have preferred to adjourn elsewhere, but seeing Minerva go ahead on Rohan's arm, fell in at the rear of the crowd.

The gathering in the drawing room was as uneventful as usual; rather than remind his chatelaine of his intentions, he bided his time, chatted with his cousins, and kept an eye on her from across the room.

Unfortunately, she wasn't lulled. She clung to the group of females, Susannah included, who had rooms in the east wing; she left with them, deftly steering them up the wide main stairs – he didn't bother following. He would have no chance of laying hands on her and diverting her to his room before she reached hers.

He retired soon after, considering his choices as he climbed the main stairs. He could join Minerva in her bed. She'd fuss, and try to order him out, shoo him away, but once he had her in his arms, all denial would be over.

There was a certain attraction in such a direct approach. However . . . he walked straight to his apartments, opened the door, went in, and closed it firmly behind him.

He walked into his bedroom, and looked at his bed.

And accepted that this time, she'd triumphed.

She'd won the battle, but it was hardly the war.

Walking into his dressing room, he shrugged out of his coat, and set it aside. Slowly undressing, he turned the reason he hadn't gone to her room over in his mind.

In London, he'd always gone to his lovers' beds. He'd never brought any lady home to his. Minerva, however, he wanted in his bed and no other.

Naked, he walked back into the bedroom, looked again at the bed. Yes, that bed. Lifting the luxurious covers, he slid between the silken sheets, lay back on the plump pillows, and stared up at the canopied ceiling.

This was where he wanted her, lying beside him, sunk in the down mattress within easy reach.

That was his vision, his goal, his dream.

Despite lust, desire, and all such weaknesses of the flesh, he wasn't going to settle for anything less.

Chapter 11

By lunchtime the next day, Royce was hot, flushed, sweaty –
and leaning against a railing with a group of men, all estate
workers, in a field on one of his tenant farms, sharing ale,
bread, and bits of crumbly local cheese.

The men around him had almost forgotten he was their
duke; he'd almost forgotten, too. With his hacking jacket and
neckerchief off, and his sleeves rolled up, his dark hair and all
else covered in the inevitable detritus of cutting and baling hay,
except for the quality of his clothes and his features, he could
have been a farmer who'd stopped by to help.

Instead, he was the ducal landowner lured there by his
chatelaine.

He'd wondered what she'd planned for the day – what her
chosen path to avoid him would be. He'd missed her at breakfast, but while pacing before the study window dictating to
Handley, he'd seen her riding off across his fields.

After finishing with Handley, he'd followed.

Of course, she hadn't expected him to turn up at the hay-
making, let alone that their day would evolve as it had, due to
the impulse that had prompted him to offer to help.

He'd cut hay before, long ago, sneaking out of the castle
and, against his father's wishes, rubbing shoulders with the
estate workers. His father had been a stickler for protocol and

propriety, but he had never felt the need to adhere to and insist on every single privilege at every turn.

Some of the men remembered him from long ago, and hadn't been backward over accepting his help – tendered, he had to admit, more to see how Minerva would react than anything else.

She'd met his gaze, then turned and offered to help the women. They'd worked alongside those they normally directed for the past several hours, he swinging a scythe in line with the men, she following with the women, gathering the hay and deftly binding it into sheaves.

What had started out as an unvoiced contest had evolved into a day of exhausting but satisfying labor. He'd never worked so physically hard in his life, but he, and his body, felt unexpectedly relaxed.

From where the women had gathered, Minerva watched Royce leaning against the fence enclosing the field they'd almost finished cutting, watched his throat – the long column bare – work as he swallowed ale from a mug topped up from a jug the men were passing around – and quietly marveled.

He was so unlike his father on so many different counts.

He stood among the men, sharing the camaraderie induced by joint labor, not the least concerned that his shirt, damp with honest sweat, clung to his chest, outlining the powerful muscles of his torso, flexing and shifting with every movement. His dark hair was not just rumpled, but dusty, his skin faintly flushed from the sun. His long, lean legs, encased in boots his precious Trevor would no doubt screech over later, were stretched out before him; as she watched he shifted, cocking one hard thigh against the fence behind.

With no coat and his shirt sticking, she could see his body clearly – could better appreciate the broad shoulders, the wide, sleekly muscled chest tapering to narrow hips and those long, strong, rider's legs.

To any female this side of the grave, the view was mouth-watering; she wasn't the only one drinking it in. With all ducal trappings stripped away, leaving only the man beneath, he looked more overtly earthily sexual than she'd ever seen him.

She forced herself to look away, to give her attention to the women and keep it there, pretending to be absorbed in their conversation. The quick glances the younger women cast toward the fence broke her resolve – and she found herself looking his way again. Wondering when he'd learned to use a scythe; his effortless swing wasn't something anyone just picked up.

Their lunch consumed, the men were talking to him avidly; from their gestures and his, he was engaging in one of his disguised interrogations.

If anything, she'd increased her assessment of his intelligence, and his ability to garner and catalog facts – and that assessment had already been high. While both were attributes he'd always had, they'd developed significantly over the years.

In contrast, his ability with children was a skill she never would have guessed he possessed. He certainly hadn't inherited it; his parents had adhered to the maxim that children should be seen and not heard. Yet when they'd broken for refreshment earlier, Royce had noticed the workers' children eyeing Sword, not so patiently waiting tied to a nearby post; waving aside their mothers' recommendations not to let them pester him, he'd walked over and let the children do precisely that.

He'd answered their questions with a patience she found remarkable in him, then, to everyone's surprise, he'd mounted and, one by one, taken each child up before him for a short walk.

The children now thought him a god. Their parents' estimation wasn't far behind.

She knew he'd had little to nothing to do with children; even those of his friends were yet babes in arms. Where he'd learned how to deal with youngsters, let alone acquired the requisite patience, a trait he in the main possessed very little of, she couldn't imagine.

Realizing she was still staring, broodingly, at him, she forced her gaze back to the women surrounding her. But their talk couldn't hold her interest, couldn't draw her senses, or even her mind, from him.

All of which ran directly counter to her intentions; out of the castle and surrounded by his workers, she'd thought she'd be safe from his seduction.

Physically, she'd been correct, but in other ways her attraction to him was deepening and broadening in ways she hadn't – couldn't have – foreseen. Worse, the unexpected allure was unintentional, uncalculated. It wasn't in his nature to radically alter his behavior to impress.

"Ah, well." The oldest woman stood. "Time to get back to it if we're to get all those sheaves stacked before dusk."

The other women rose and brushed off their aprons; the men saw, and stowed their mugs and jug, hitched up their trousers, and headed back into the field. Royce went with a group to one of the large drays; seizing the moment, Minerva went to check on Rangonel.

Satisfied he was comfortable, she headed to where the others were readying an area for the first haystack. Rounding a dray piled with sheaves, she halted – faced with a fascinating sight.

Royce stood five paces ahead of her, his back to her, looking down at a small girl, no more than five years old, planted directly in his path, nearly tipping backward as she looked all the way up into his face.

Minerva watched as he smoothly crouched before the girl, and waited.

Entirely at ease, the girl studied his face with open inquisitiveness. "What's your name?" she eventually lisped.

Royce hesitated; Minerva could imagine him sorting through the various answers he could give. But eventually he said, "Royce."

The girl tilted her head, frowned as she studied him. "Ma said you were a wolf."

Minerva couldn't resist shifting sideways, trying to see his face. His profile confirmed he was fighting not to smile – wolfishly.

"My teeth aren't big enough."

The poppet eyed him measuringly, then nodded sagely. "Your snout isn't long enough, either, and you're not hairy."

Her own lips compressed, Minerva saw his jaw clench, holding back a laugh. After an instant, he nodded. "Very true."

The girl reached out, with one small hand clasped two of his fingers. "We should go and help now. You can walk with me. I know how the haystack's made – I'll show you."

She tugged, and Royce obediently rose.

Minerva watched as the most powerful duke in all of England allowed a five-year-old poppet to lead him to where his workers had gathered, and blithely instruct him in how to stack sheaves.

Days passed, and Royce advanced his cause not one whit. No matter what he did, Minerva evaded him at every turn, surrounding herself with either the estate people or the castle's guests.

The plays had proved a major success; they now filled the evenings, allowing her to use the company of the other ladies to elude him every night. He'd reached the point of questioning his not exactly rational but unquestionably honorable disinclination to follow her into her room, trampling on her privacy to press his seduction, his suit.

While playing a long game was his forte, inaction was another matter; lack of progress on any front had always irked.

Lack of progress on this front positively hurt.

And today, the entire company had decided to go to church, presumably to atone for the many sins they'd committed. Despite none of those sins being his, he'd felt obliged to attend, too, especially as Minerva had been going, so what else was he to do?

Wallowing in bed when that bed was otherwise empty – devoid of soft, warm, willing female – had never appealed.

Seated in the front pew, Minerva beside him, with his sisters beyond her, he let the sermon roll over him, freeing his mind to range where it would – the latest prod to his escalating frustration was its first stop.

They'd chosen *Midsummer Night's Dream* for their play last night – and Minerva had suggested he play Oberon, a chant promptly taken up by the rest of the company in full voice. The twist of fate that had seen her caught by the same company's brilliant notion that she play Titania, queen to his king, had been, in his opinion, nothing more than her due.

Given their natures, given the situation, even though their exchanges on stage had been oblique, the palpable tension between them had puzzled a number of their audience.

That tension, and its inevitable effects, had resulted in another near-sleepless night.

He slanted a glance to his right, to where she, his fixation, sat, her gaze dutifully trained on Mr. Cribthorn, the vicar, rambling from his pulpit about long-dead Corinthians.

She knew who and what he was; no one knew him better. Yet she'd deliberately set out to cross swords with him – and thus far she was winning.

Accepting defeat on any stage had never come easily; his only recent failure had been over bringing to justice the last traitor he and his men knew lurked somewhere in the government. There were some things fate didn't allow.

Be that as it may, accepting defeat with Minerva was . . . entirely beyond his scope. One way or another she was going to be his – his lover first, then his wife.

Her capitulation on both counts would happen – had to happen – soon. He'd told the grandes dames a week, and that week was nearly past. While he doubted they'd haul themselves all the way back to Northumbria if they didn't see a notice in the *Gazette* this coming week, he wouldn't put it past them to start sending candidates north – in carriages designed to break axles and wheels as they neared Wolverstone's gates.

The vicar called the congregation to their feet for the benediction; everyone rose. Subsequently, once the vicar had passed on his way up the aisle, Royce stepped out of the pew, stepped back to let Minerva go ahead of him, then followed, leaving his sisters trailing shawls and reticules in his wake.

As usual, they were the first out of the church, but he'd

noticed one of his more affluent farmers among the worshippers; as they stepped down to the path, he bent his head close beside Minerva's. "I want to have a word with Cherry."

She glanced back and up at him.

And time stopped.

With Margaret and Aurelia distracting the vicar, they were the only two in the churchyard – and they were very close, their lips inches apart.

Her eyes, rich browns flecked with gold, widened; her breath caught, suspended. Her gaze lowered to his lips.

His dropped to hers . . .

He dragged in a breath and straightened.

She blinked, and stepped away. "Ah . . . I must speak with Mrs. Cribthorn, and some of the other ladies."

He nodded stiffly, forced himself to turn away. Just as the rest of the congregation came flooding down the steps.

Searching for Cherry, he set his jaw. *Soon.* She was going to lie beneath him very soon.

Minerva let a moment pass while her heart slowed and her breathing evened, then she drew a deep breath, plastered on a smile, and went to speak with the vicar's wife about the preparations for the fair.

She was turning from Mrs. Cribthorn when Susannah approached.

"There you are!" Susannah gestured to where the castle's guests were piling into various carriages. "We're heading back – do you want to come, or do you have to wait for Royce?"

Royce had taken her up in his curricle for the drive to the church. "I . . ." *Can't possibly leave yet.* Minerva swallowed the words. As a recognized representative of the castle, the largest and socially dominant house in the district, it simply wasn't done to leave without chatting with their neighbors; the locals would see that as a slight. Neither she nor Royce could yet leave, a fact Susannah should have known. "No. I'll wait."

Susannah shrugged, gathering her shawl. "Commendably dutiful – I hope Royce appreciates it, and that you aren't bored to tears." With a commiserating grimace, she headed for the carriages.

Her last comment had been entirely sincere; the late duke's daughters had adopted their father's social views. Old Henry had rarely come to church, leaving it to his wife, and later Minerva alone, to carry the castle flag.

More interesting to Minerva, Susannah's comments confirmed that, despite the near debacle of last night's play – she'd thought the lust that had burned in Royce's eyes, that had resonated beneath the smooth tenor of his voice, the breathlessness that had assailed her, the awareness that had invested her every action, would have utterly given them away – not a single guest had realized that his interest in her had any basis beyond castle business.

Admittedly, every single guest was distracted on his or her own account.

That, however, didn't explain the pervasive blindness. The truth was, regardless of his pursuit of her, Royce had unfailingly ensured that whenever they were not alone, their interaction projected the image of duke and dutiful chatelaine, and absolutely nothing more. All the guests, and even more his sisters, now had that image firmly fixed in their minds, and blithely ignored anything to the contrary.

Looking over the congregation, she located his dark head. He stood in a group of farmers, most but not all his tenants; as was becoming usual, they were talking and he was listening. Entirely approving, she surveyed the gathering, then went to do her own listening with a group of farmers' wives.

She left it to him to find her when he was ready to leave. He eventually did, and allowed her to introduce him to the wife of the local constable, and two other ladies. After suitable words had been exchanged, they made their farewells and he strolled beside her down the path to where Henry waited with the curricle and the by now restive blacks.

Curious, she glanced at his face. "You seem to be . . ." She waggled her head. "Unexpectedly amenable to the 'letting the locals get to know you' socializing."

He shrugged. "I intend to live here for the rest of my life. These are the people I'll see every day, the ones I'll be working with, and for. They might want to know more of me, but I definitely need to know more about them."

She let him hand her into the curricle. While she settled, she pondered his words. His father –

She broke off the thought. If there was one thing she should by now have realized it was that he wasn't like his father when it came to people. His temper, arrogance, and a great deal more, were very familiar, but his attitudes to others were almost universally different. On some aspects – for instance, children – even diametrically opposed.

They were on the road beyond the village when he said, "Kilworth told me there's no school in the district, not even at the most elementary level."

Timorous Mr. Kilworth, the deacon, would never have mentioned such a matter, not unless asked.

"I suppose I should have guessed," he continued, "but it never occurred to me before."

She regarded him with something close to fascination – safe enough with his attention focused on his horses as he steered them toward the bridge. "Are you thinking of starting a school here?"

He flicked her a glance. "I've heard talk among other peers – there's an evolving notion that having better educated workers benefits everyone."

And he'd seen a lot of croft and farm children in recent days.

"I wouldn't disagree." His father had – vociferously – when she'd suggested it.

"Any school shouldn't be solely for the estate families – it needs to be for the district, so we'd need to recruit wider support, but . . ." He sent the blacks rocketing across the stone bridge. "I think it's worthwhile pursuing."

As the horses thundered through the big gates and the wheels rolled more smoothly on the drive, he glanced at her. "Write down any thoughts you have." His eyes rested on hers.

"Once I have the matter of my bride settled, we'll be able to move forward with that."

She felt ecstatic on the one hand, unsettled and oddly cast down on the other.

Minerva was given no time to examine her contradictory feelings; she and Royce walked into the castle as the luncheon gong sounded, then during the meal the idea of a fishing expedition upstream along the Coquet was touted, and instantly found favor with all the men.

And all the women, although none had any intention of picking up a rod. But the day was fine, sunny with the barest breath of a breeze, and everyone agreed a walk would do them good.

She was tempted to cry off, to use her duties as an excuse to remain behind and try to untangle her emotions, but Royce paused beside her as the company rose from the table.

He spoke quietly, for her ears only. "Keep an eye on the ladies – make sure the more adventurous don't attempt to investigate the gorge."

Inwardly cursing, she nodded. It was just the sort of witless thing some of the ladies present might do, and the gorge was dangerous.

The fishing rods and tackle were stowed in the boathouse by the lake; Royce led the men down to make their choices while the ladies hurried to fetch bonnets, shawls, and parasols.

From the lake, rods over their shoulders, the men followed the path north along the stream. Feeling like a sheepdog, Minerva marshaled the ladies and herded them along the west and north wings and out along the route to the mill.

The men were a little way ahead; some ladies called, waved. The men glanced back, waved, but continued walking.

Among the ladies, Margaret and Caroline Courtney led the way, heads together as they shared secrets. The other ladies walked in twos and threes, chatting as they ambled in the sunshine.

Minerva kept to the rear, ensuring no stragglers got left

behind. The men crossed the bridge over the race; the ladies followed.

After passing the mill, the twin parties reached the end of the race where it came off the gorge, and turned north along the gorge. Minerva did, indeed, have to dissuade three ladies from descending into the gorge to investigate the rock pools. "I know you can't tell from up here, but the rocks are terribly slippery, and the stretches of water are treacherously deep."

She pointed to where the river ran strongly, gushing and churning over its rocky bed. "There's been rain on the Cheviots over the last weeks – the currents will be surprisingly strong. That's the biggest danger if you fall in – that you'll be dashed to death on the rocks."

In her experience, it never hurt to be specific; the ladies "oh"-ed and readily walked on.

The men drew ahead; the ladies loitered, pointing to this, examining that, but nevertheless drifting in the right direction. Minerva fell back, ambling even more slowly in her shepherdess role. Finally she had a moment to think.

Not that her thoughts were all that clear.

She was thrilled Royce wanted to establish a school in the village; she would cheer him on in that. More, she felt strangely proud of him, that he – a Varisey in so many ways – had thought of it on his own. She felt distinctly vindicated over encouraging him to turn from his father's example and forge his own way, follow his own inclinations; they were proving very sound.

But she wouldn't be around to see the outcome – and that galled her. Disappointment, dejection, dragged her down, as if some prize she'd worked for and deserved was, by fate's fickle decree, to be denied her. More, was to be granted to another, who wouldn't appreciate it given she wouldn't know him.

His bride still remained unnamed, and therefore nebulous; she couldn't fix a face on the female, so couldn't direct her anger at her.

Couldn't resent her.

She halted at the thought.

Shocked by the unhappy emotion she'd just put a name to.

Nonsensical, she chided herself; she'd always known his bride would arrive one day – and that, soon after, she'd leave.

Leave the place she called home.

Lips firming, she thrust the thought away. The others had wandered far ahead; they'd reached the end of the gorge and were continuing on, following the river path into more open meadows. Lifting her head, drawing in a deep breath, she lengthened her stride and set out to catch them up.

No more thinking allowed.

North of the gorge, the river was wider, wending down from the hills through fertile meadowland. It was still deep in the middle, and there it ran swiftly, but the spreading edges flowed more gently.

There was a particular spot where the river rounded a curve, then spread in a wide pool that was especially good for fishing. The men had descended the sloping bank; spreading out in a line along the pool's edge, casting lures into the stream, they talked only in murmurs as they waited for a bite.

Royce and his male cousins – Gordon, Rohan, Phillip, Arthur, Gregory, and Henry – stood shoulder to shoulder. All tall, dark-haired, and handsome, they were an arresting sight, reducing the other male guests to mere contrast.

The ladies gathered on the bank above. They knew enough to mute their voices; standing in a loose group, they enjoyed the sunshine and the light breeze, chatting quietly.

Minerva joined them. Susannah asked again whether she'd discovered whom Royce had chosen as his bride; Minerva shook her head, then stepped a little away from the group, her eye caught by a flash of color upriver.

From their position, the land rose gently; she could see another party enjoying a pleasant day by the banks two bends upstream.

One of the tenant farmers' families, plus their laborers' families as well; squinting, she saw a gaggle of children playing by the water's edge, laughing and shrieking, or so it seemed, as they played tag. The breeze was blowing northward, so no sound reached her, yet she had to wonder how many fish the men would catch with such a cacophony two hundred yards upstream.

She was about to look away when a girl standing by the stream's edge suddenly flailed her arms – and fell backward into the stream. The bank had crumbled beneath her heels; she fell with a splash – breath caught, Minerva watched, waiting to see . . .

The girl's white cap bobbed to the surface – in the middle of the stream. The current had caught her skirts; even as the adults rushed to the bank, she was whisked downriver, around the next curve.

Minerva looked down at the men. "Royce!"

He looked up, instantly alert.

She pointed upriver. "There's a girl in the water." She looked again, spotted the bobbing white cap. "Two bends upstream. She's in the center and coming down fast."

Before the last word had left her lips, Royce was giving orders. Rods were dropped; his cousins and the others gathered around him, then the whole group turned and ran downstream.

Royce paused only to call to Minerva, "Yell when she comes around that bend." He pointed at the last bend before the pool, then raced after the others.

From their vantage point, the ladies watched in horrified fascination. Minerva went as far down the bank as she could without losing sight of the girl. Susannah and two friends joined her, peering after the men. "What are they doing?" Susannah asked.

Minerva spared a quick glance downriver, saw where the men were going – Royce on his own, just beyond the pool, the others still hurrying, leaping over rocks and slipping over wet patches on their way farther down – then looked back at the girl. "Royce is going out on the nearer spit – he'll catch her. But he's likely to lose his footing when he does – the current's running strongly – it'll take both of them. The others will form a human chain farther down. It'll be up to them to grab Royce and haul him and the girl in."

Susannah knew the river; she blanched.

One of her friends frowned. "Why are they trying to catch him? He's so strong – surely he'll be able to –"

"It's the *gorge*." Susannah cut her off, her voice harsh. "Oh, God. If they miss him . . ."

She grabbed up her skirts, climbed the bank, and started running downstream.

"What is it?" Margaret called.

Susannah turned and called something back. Minerva stopped listening. The girl, still weakly struggling, cleared the bend.

She turned and looked downriver. "Royce! She's coming!"

Standing in the shallows around the next bend, just visible from where she was, he raised a hand in acknowledgment; no longer wearing his coat, he waded deeper into the river.

Minerva hurried down the bank, then along the water's edge, where the men had stood. Susannah's other friend, Anne, held her tongue and went with her. Minerva ran, but the current whisked the girl along faster; long braids floating on either side of her small white face, the poor child was almost spent. "Hold on!" Minerva called, and prayed the girl could hear. "He'll catch you in a minute."

She slipped and nearly fell; Anne, on her heels, caught her and steadied her, then they both dashed on.

The bobbing rag doll the girl had become was swept around the bend, out of their sight. Gasping, Minerva ran faster; she and Anne rounded the bend in time to see Royce, sunk chest-deep even though he stood on a spit in the streambed, lean far to his right, then launch himself across, into the swiftly running current; it caught him in the same moment he caught the girl, hoisting her up onto his chest, then onto his right shoulder where her head was at least partly clear of the increasingly turbulent water.

Minerva slowed, her fingers rising to her lips as she took in what lay beyond the pair. The river started narrowing, funneling toward the gorge, the water tumbling and churning as it battered its way on.

There was only one spot, another spit, where the pair, whisked along, could be caught, one chance before the building pressure of the water swept them into the gorge and almost certain death. On the spit, Royce's Varisey and Debraigh cousins were linking arms, forming a human chain, anchored by Henry and Arthur, the lightest, together on the bank. Each held on to one of Gregory's arms. Gregory had his other arm linked with Rohan's, who in turn was waiting for Gordon to link his arm with his, leaving Phillip at the end.

Minerva halted, put her hands about her mouth. "*Quickly!*" she screamed. "They're almost there!"

Phillip looked, then shoved Gordon toward Rohan, grabbed one of Gordon's arms, and waded into the stream.

The current swung away, around the spit, carrying Royce and his burden along the other side of the riverbed. Rohan yelled and the men all stretched . . . Phillip yelled to Gordon to hang on to his coat. As soon as he had, Phillip lunged out, stretching as far as he could, reaching out.

Just as it seemed the pair would be lost, Royce's arm lashed out of the water – and connected with Phillip's. They both gripped.

"Hold hard!" Phillip yelled.

The dragging weight – not just of Royce and the girl, but now Phillip as well, all drenched and sodden – tested the other men. Muscles bunched, locked. Henry's and Arthur's feet shifted; they both leaned back, faces grim and set as they hauled their kinsmen in.

Then it was over. Royce and Phillip, swung downstream and in toward the bank, got their feet under them.

Royce stood, breathing hard, then, shaking his head like a dog, he hoisted the girl free of the water, and holding her to his chest, walked, slowly and carefully, across the rocky riverbed. Phillip staggered up, then followed alongside. He reached over and lifted the girl's hair from her face, tapped her cheek – and she coughed. Weakly at first, but when Royce reached the bank and laid her on her side, she retched, coughed hard, then started to cry.

Minerva fell to her knees beside her. "It's all right. Your mother and father are coming – they'll be here soon." She glanced at Royce; his chest was rising and falling like a bellows, and water ran off him in streams, but he was unharmed, unhurt. Alive.

She looked up at the other ladies, gathering in an anxious, exclaiming knot on the bank above. Anne had come to stand beside her. Minerva pointed at the shawls some of the others carried. "Shawls – the woolen ones."

"Yes, of course." Anne climbed the bank partway and reached up, beckoning.

Two ladies surrendered their shawls readily, but Aurelia sniffed. "Not mine."

Royce had bent over, hands braced on his knees. He didn't bother looking up. "Aurelia."

His voice cut like a whip; Aurelia all but flinched. She paled. Her face set in sour lines, but she shrugged off her shawl and tossed it at Anne – who caught it, turned, and hurried back to Minerva.

She'd stripped off the girl's hat and sodden pinafore, and had been chafing her small icy hands. She stopped to take one of the shawls – Aurelia's large warm one. Shaking it out, with Anne's help she wrapped the girl tightly, then wound the other shawls about her hands and feet.

Then the girls' parents and the rest of the farmer's party arrived; they'd had to backtrack to cross the river by a wooden bridge higher up.

"She's all right," Minerva called as soon as she saw the parents' distraught faces.

Both rushed down the riverbank, eyes only for their child.

"Mary!" The mother dropped to her knees opposite Minerva. She placed a gentle hand on the girl's cheek. "Sweetheart?"

The girl's lashes fluttered; she tried to move her hands. "Ma?"

"Oh, thank God." The mother swept the girl up against her bosom. She looked at Minerva, then up at Royce. "Thank you – *thank you*, Your Grace. I don't know how we can ever repay you."

Her husband laid a shaking hand on his daughter's dark head. "Nor I. I thought she were –" He cut himself off, blinked rapidly. Shook his head and looked at Royce. Gruffly said, "Can't thank you enough, Your Grace."

One of his cousins had fetched Royce's coat; he'd been using it to mop his face. "If you want to thank me, take her home and get her warm – after hauling her out, I don't want her to take a chill."

"Yes – yes, we will." The mother struggled to her feet, lifting the girl. Her husband quickly took the child.

"And you may be sure," the mother said, tugging her damp clothes straight, "that none of that lot will ever play too close to the riverbanks again." Her severe look directed their gazes to the gaggle of children, watching round-eyed from up along the bank, their parents and the other adults at their backs.

"You might like to remind them," Royce said, "that if they do, there's unlikely to be a group of us here, in the right spot at the right time, to pull them out."

"Aye. We'll tell them, you may be sure." The father ducked his head as low as he could. "With your permission, Your Grace, we'll get her home."

Royce waved him up the slope.

The mother sighed and shook her head. She exchanged a glance with Minerva. "You tell them and tell them, but they never listen, do they?" With that, she followed her husband up the bank.

Royce watched them go, watched as the other farmers and their wives gathered around, offering comfort and support as they closed around the couple and their nearly lost daughter.

Beside him, Minerva slowly got to her feet. He waited while she thanked Anne for her help, then asked, "Who were they?"

"The Honeymans. They hold the farm up around Green Side." She paused, then added, "They would have seen you at church, but I don't think you've met them before."

He hadn't. He nodded. "Let's get back." He was chilled to

the bone, and there was no earthly way to get his coat –
expertly fitted by Shultz – on over his wet clothes.

Anne had joined the others, but now she came back. She
touched Minerva's arm. "Susannah and some of the other
ladies have started back with Phillip – his teeth are chattering.
I thought I'd run ahead and warn the household." Although in
her thirties, Anne was slim, fit, and swift on her feet.

"Thank you." Minerva lightly grasped Anne's fingers. "If
you could tell Retford we need hot baths for His Grace, and for
Phillip, and hot water for the others, too."

"I'll do that." Anne glanced at Royce, inclined her head,
then turned and climbed swiftly up the slope.

With Minerva beside him, Royce followed more slowly.

Minerva humphed. Looking ahead to where certain of the
ladies were still milling inconsequentially, some, with hands
clutched to their breasts, exclaiming as if the incident had
overset their delicate nerves, she muttered, "At least some
people keep their heads in a crisis."

She meant Anne. Royce looked at her, felt his lips curve.
"Indeed."

Arthur and Henry, together with the other male guests not
in some degree soaked, had gone back to fetch the discarded
rods and tackle.

As Royce and Minerva crested the slope, the remaining
ladies, apparently deciding that the excitement was now
entirely over, regrouped and started back to the castle.

With Minerva walking alongside, Royce found himself
nearing the rear of the group, and wished they'd walk faster.
He needed to keep moving, or he'd start shivering as badly as
Phillip. His skin was already icy, and the chill was sinking
deeper into his bones.

Margaret looked back at him a few times; he presumed she
was assuring herself he wasn't about to collapse.

He wasn't entirely surprised when she stepped sideways out
of the group and waited until he and Minerva drew level.

But it was Minerva to whom Margaret spoke. "If I could
have a word?"

"Yes. Of course." Minerva halted.

Royce walked on, but slowed. He didn't like the look in Margaret's eyes, or her expression, and even less her tone. Minerva was no servant, not even to the family. She wasn't a penniless relative, or anything of the sort.

She was his chatelaine, and rather more, even if Margaret didn't yet know it.

"Yes?"

That was Minerva prompting Margaret, who had thus far remained silent.

Margaret waited until he'd taken two more steps before saying – hissing – "How *dare* you?" There was a wealth of furious, frightened venom in her voice; it shook as she went on, "How *dare* you put the entire *dukedom* at risk for a crofter's brat!"

Royce halted.

"The Honeymans are your brother's tenants, but regardless, saving that girl was the right thing to do."

He turned.

Saw Margaret draw in a breath. Her color high, eyes locked on Minerva, she all but shrieked, "For some stupid, silly girl, you risked –"

"Margaret." Royce walked back toward her.

She spun to face him. "And *you*! You're no better! Did you spare so much as a thought for us – for me, Aurelia, and Susannah, your *sisters*! – before you –"

"Enough."

His tone was all cold steel; it had her clenching her fists and swallowing the rest of her tirade. He halted before her, close enough so she had to look up into his face – close enough that she was just a touch intimidated, as well she should be.

"No, I didn't think of you, Aurelia, or Susannah – you all have wealthy husbands to support you, regardless of my continuing health. I didn't put you in danger by saving that girl. Her *life* was in the balance, and I would have been greatly disappointed had Minerva not warned me. I was in a position to save her – a girl who was born on my lands."

He looked down into his sister's mulish face. "What Minerva did was right. What I did was right. What you appear to have forgotten is that my people – even silly young girls – are my responsibility."

Margaret drew in a long, tight breath. "Papa would never –"

"Indeed." This time his voice cut. "But I am not Papa."

For a moment, he held Margaret silent with his gaze, then, unhurriedly and deliberately, turned toward the castle. "Come, Minerva."

She quickly caught up to him, walking alongside.

He lengthened his stride; the other ladies were now far ahead. "I need to get out of these wet clothes." He spoke conversationally, signaling he intended to leave Margaret's little scene behind, metaphorically as well as physically.

Minerva nodded, tight-lipped. "Precisely." A heartbeat passed, then she went on, "I really don't know why Margaret couldn't have waited until later to rail at me – it's not as if I won't be around. If she was really worried about your health, she'd have done better not to delay us." She glanced sharply his way. "Can you go faster? Perhaps you ought to run?"

"Why?"

"So you'll warm up." They were nearing the mill. Raising a hand, she pushed his shoulder. "Go that way – through the mill and over the race. It's faster than going down to the bridge and across."

She usually avoided touching him, yet now she kept pushing, so he diverted onto the paved path leading into the mill. "Minerva –"

"We need to get you to the castle, out of those wet clothes and into a hot bath as soon as possible." She prodded him toward the gangplank. "So move!"

He almost saluted, but did as she ordered. From Margaret, who thought of no one but herself, to Minerva, who was totally focused . . . on him.

On his well-being.

It took an instant for that to fully sink in.

He glanced at her as, her hands now locked about one of his elbows, she hurried him out of the mill. Her focus was on the castle, on getting him – all but propelling him – as fast as possible inside. Her intensity wasn't just that of a chatelaine doing her duty; it was a great deal more.

"I'm not likely to take a fatal chill from a dip in the river." He tried to slow to a fast walk.

She set her jaw and all but hauled him on. "You're not a doctor – you can't know that. The prescribed treatment for immersion in an icy river is a hot bath, and that's what you have to have. Your mother would never forgive me if I let you expire because you wouldn't treat the risk with due seriousness."

His mother, who had never wasted a moment worrying about his health. Male Variseys were supposed to be tough, and, indeed, were. But he bowed to Minerva's tugging and resumed his faster pace. "I am taking this seriously."

Just not as seriously as she was.

Or, as it transpired, any of his staff were.

The instant Minerva pushed him through the door into the north wing, Trevor pounced.

"*No!*" His valet was literally aghast. "That's another pair of Hobys ruined – two pairs in three days. And, oh, my heavens! You're drenched!"

He refrained from saying he knew. "Is my bath ready?"

"It better be." Trevor exchanged a look with Minerva, still by Royce's side, still hurrying him along. "I'll go up and make sure." Trevor turned and all but fled before them, his footsteps clattering up the turret stairs.

Royce and Minerva followed, taking the shortcut to his rooms.

Minerva halted outside his sitting room door; he kept walking, to the useful new door into his dressing room and the bathing chamber beyond that Hancock, the castle carpenter, was just testing.

Hancock nodded. "Your new door as ordered, Your Grace. Just in time, it seems." Hancock swung the panel wide. "Your bath awaits."

Royce nodded. "Thank you." He looked over the door and its frame as he went through into the dressing room, then nodded again to Hancock. "That's exactly what I wanted."

Hancock saluted, picked up his toolbox, and walked off. Minerva appeared in the doorway – mouth a-cock, staring at the door, then at its frame. Then she looked at Royce.

"So Trevor and the footmen don't need to come through the bedroom to reach these rooms."

"Oh." She stood there, digesting that, while he started the difficult task of unwinding his sodden cravat.

Trevor appeared in the open doorway opposite, from which steam eddied as a footman poured what had to be a last pail of steaming water into the large bath; if any more was put in, it would slosh out when Royce got in. He signaled to the footman to stop.

His valet, meanwhile, was frowning at two glass-stoppered bottles he was holding. "Which would be better? Mint or peppermint?"

"Menthol." Snapping out of her trance, Minerva bustled in to join Trevor. "Pennyroyal is what you want – it's the best for warding off chills." She stepped around Trevor, let the footman squeeze past, then pointed to a rack of similar bottles set on a wooden table. "There should be some there."

"Pennyroyal. Right." Trevor went to the rack. "Here it is. How many drops?" He squinted at the tiny label.

"About a teaspoon, even two. Enough so you can smell it strongly."

Trevor took out the stopper, tipped a bit of the oil into the water. Minerva and he sniffed the steam. Both frowned.

Walking into the bathing chamber, Royce dropped his sodden cravat, which he'd finally managed to untangle, onto the floor; it landed with a splat, but neither his valet nor his chatelaine reacted.

He looked longingly at the hot water, felt ice seeping into his marrow – heard the other two arguing the merits of adding peppermint as well.

Lips setting, he yanked his shirttails free of his waistband, loosened the cords at his wrists and neck, then looked at his chatelaine. "Minerva."

She looked up, met his eyes.

"Leave. Now." He reached for the bottom of his shirt.

"Oh, yes – of course."

He pulled the shirt up, heard the flurry of her footsteps, then the door to the bathing chamber click shut. Grimly smiled. But wrestling free of the drenched folds was an exercise and a half; Trevor had to help – with that, his boots, and his breeches, designed to cling to him even when dry.

Finally naked, he stepped into the tub, sat, and leaned back, then sank right down. Felt the heat from the water slowly melt the ice in his flesh. Felt the warmth sink in.

Felt warmth of a different kind slowly expand from his center out.

His gaze on the door through which his chatelaine had fled, he slowly thawed.

Late that night, lounging shoulder to the wall in the darkness of an embrasure in the keep's gallery, Royce broodingly stared at Minerva's bedroom door.

The only thought in his mind was whether her caring about him as she clearly did was sufficient excuse for what he was about to do.

He understood perfectly well why the need to bed her had suddenly escalated to a level significantly beyond his control. Dicing with death had that effect, made one only too aware of one's mortality, and commensurately fired the need to live, to prove one was vitally alive in the most fundamental way.

What he was feeling, how he was reacting, was all perfectly natural, normal, logical. To be expected.

He wasn't at all sure she'd see it that way.

But he needed her tonight.

And not solely for his selfish self.

While in the matter of the rescue, he and she had been in the right, so, too, had Margaret. He'd accepted the need to secure the succession; he couldn't continue to put off speaking and gaining Minerva's agreement to be his bride.

To be the mother of his son – the eleventh Duke of Wolverstone.

At this moment in time, all roads in his life led to this place, and compelled him to act, to take the next step.

The castle had grown quiet; all the guests were abed, whoever's bed they were gracing that night. Within the keep, only he and Minerva remained; all the staff had long retired.

There was no sense dallying any longer.

He was about to push away from the wall, had tensed to take the first fateful step toward her door, when it opened.

He froze, watched through the darkness as Minerva came out. She was still fully dressed; clutching a shawl about her shoulders, she glanced right, then left. She didn't notice him, standing perfectly still in the enveloping shadows.

Quietly closing her door, she set off down the corridor.

Silent as a wraith, he followed.

Chapter 12

A full moon rode the sky; Minerva didn't need a candle to slip down the main stairs and follow the west wing corridor to the music room. Once on the ground floor, she walked quickly, openly; all the guests were on the floor above.

She'd loaned Cicely, a distant Varisey cousin, her mother's pearl brooch to anchor the spangled shawl Cicely had worn as the Princess of France in that evening's performance of *Love's Labour's Lost* – and had forgotten to take it back. The brooch was valuable, but much more than that, it was one of the few mementos she had of her mother; she wasn't of a mind to risk leaving it jumbled with the other pieces of finery in the costume box, not even just until tomorrow.

Not that she imagined anyone would steal it, but . . . she wouldn't be able to sleep until she had the brooch back.

Reaching the music room, she opened the door and went in. Moonlight streamed through the wide window, flooding the stage, providing more than enough light. As she walked up the aisle between the rows of chairs, her mind drifted to Royce – and the sharp clutch of fear, almost paralyzing in strength, that had gripped her when she'd seen him in the river, with his burden sweeping wide around the spit where his would-be rescuers had waited . . .

For one crystal-clear instant in time, she'd thought she –

215

they – would lose him. Even now . . . She slowed, closed her eyes, drew in a slow, steadying breath. All had turned out well – he was safe upstairs, and the girl was at her home, no doubt cosseted and warm in her bed.

Exhaling and opening her eyes, she continued on more briskly, stepping up onto the low stage. The trunk of costumes stood in the lee of the paneled left wing. Beside it sat a box full of shawls, scarves, kerchiefs, mixed with fake daggers, berets, a paste tiara and crown, all the smaller items that went with the costumes.

Crouching by the box, she started sorting through the materials, looking for the spangled shawl.

With hands and eyes engaged, her thoughts, prodded by Margaret's outburst, and by comments she'd subsequently heard, not just from the ladies but from some of the men as well, roamed, circling the question of whether she'd done the right thing in warning Royce of the girl's danger.

Not all who'd commented had assumed she'd expected him to rescue the girl, but she had. She'd expected him to act precisely as he had – not in the specifics, but in the sense that he would do all he could to save the child.

She *hadn't* expected him to risk his life, not to the point where his death had become a real possibility. She didn't think he'd foreseen that, either, but in such situations there never was time for cold-blooded calculations, weighing every chance.

When faced with life-and-death situations, one had to act – and trust that one's skills would see one through. As Royce's had. He'd given orders to his cousins and they'd instinctively obeyed; *now* they might question the wisdom of his act, but at the time they'd done as he'd asked.

Which was all that mattered. To her mind, the end result had been entirely satisfactory, yet of all those above stairs, only she, Royce, and a handful of others saw the matter in that light. The rest thought he, and she, had been wrong.

Of course, they wouldn't think so if the girl had been well-born.

Noblesse oblige; those dissenting others clearly interpreted the phrase in a different way from her and Royce.

The spangled shawl wasn't in the box. Frowning, she piled the other things back in, then lifted the lid of the trunk. "Aha."

She drew the soft folds out. As she'd suspected, Cicely had left the brooch pinned to the shawl; freeing it, she closed the clip, and slipped the brooch into her pocket. Dropping the shawl back into the trunk, she lowered the lid, and stood.

Just as footsteps sounded in the corridor beyond the open door.

Slow, steady, deliberate footsteps . . . Royce's.

They halted in the doorway.

Royce normally moved impossibly silently. Was he allowing his footsteps to be heard because he knew she was there? Or because he thought there was no one around to hear?

She edged deeper into the lee of the panel; the thick velvet curtain, currently drawn back, gave her extra cover, ensuring her outline wasn't etched in moonlight on the floor before the stage. Sliding her fingers between the curtain and the panel, she peeked out.

Royce stood in the doorway. He glanced around the room, then walked slowly in, leaving the door wide.

A great deal tenser than she had been, she watched as he paced down the center aisle. Halting halfway to the stage, he sat in a chair at the end of one row; the wooden legs scraped as he shifted, the small sound loud in the night. Thighs spread, he leaned his forearms along them, linked his hands between. Head angled down, he appeared to be studying his loosely interlocked fingers.

Royce thought – again – of what he intended to do, but need was a clamor filling his mind, drowning out, sweeping aside, all reservations.

Despite his nonchalance, he knew perfectly well he'd come within a whisker of dying that day. He'd waltzed close to Death before; he knew what the touch of her icy fingers felt like. What was different about this time was that – for the first time – he'd had regrets. Specific regrets that had leapt, sharp

217

and clear, to the forefront of his mind in the moment when Phillip's hand had seemed just too far away.

His principal regret had been over her. That if he died, he'd miss knowing her. Not just biblically, but in a deeper, broader sense, something he could put his hand on his heart and swear he'd never wanted with any other woman.

Yet another reason it was just as well he was set on having her as his wife. He'd have years to learn of, to explore, all her different facets, her character, her body, her mind.

That afternoon, while warming up in his bath, he'd considered the odd impulse her hurrying him back to the castle had evoked. He'd wanted to put his arm around her and openly accept her help, to lean on her − not physically − but for some other reason, some other solace. Not just for him, but for her, too. Accepting her help, acknowledging it − showing he welcomed it, that he was pleased, felt honored, that she cared.

He hadn't done it − because men like him never showed such weakness. Throughout his childhood, his schooling, through social pressure, such views had shaped him; he knew it, but that didn't mean he could escape the effects, no matter how powerful a duke he might be.

Indeed, because he'd been destined to be just such a powerful duke, the conditioning had reached even deeper.

Which, in many ways, explained tonight.

Beneath the flow of his thoughts, he'd been evaluating, assessing, deciding. Drawing in a long breath, he lifted his head and looked to the left of the stage. "Come out. I know you're there."

Minerva frowned, and stepped out from her hiding place. Tried to feel irritated; instead . . . she discovered it was possible to feel exceedingly vulnerable and irresistibly fascinated simultaneously.

Stepping off the stage, she told herself, her unruly senses, to concentrate on the former and forget the latter. To focus on all the reasons she had to feel vulnerable about him. About getting too close to him in any way.

Predictably, as she walked with feigned calmness down the aisle, her senses, skittering in breathless expectation, gained the ascendancy. Being within four feet of him was not a wise idea. Yet . . .

The light from the window behind her fell on him, illuminated his face as, remaining seated, he looked up at her.

There was something in his expression, usually so utterly uninformative. Not tiredness, more like resignation – along with a sense of . . . emotional tension.

The observation puzzled, just as another puzzling fact occurred. She fixed her gaze on his dark eyes. "How did you know I was here?"

"I was in the corridor outside your room. I saw you come out, and followed."

She halted in the aisle beside him. "Why?"

The moonlight didn't reach his eyes; they searched her face, but she couldn't read them, any more than she could tell what he was thinking from the chiseled perfection of his features, yet they still held that certain tension, a need, perhaps, or a hunger; as the silence stretched she sensed it more clearly – honest, sincere, direct.

Real.

A lock of sable hair had fallen across his brow; entirely without thinking, she reached out and smoothed it back. Fingertips seduced by the rich softness, by the sensual tingle, she hesitated, then started to withdraw her hand.

He caught it, trapped it in one of his.

Eyes widening, she met his gaze. Fell into it.

He held her ensorcelled for a long moment, then, uncurling her fingers with his, he turned his head and, slowly, deliberately, pressed his lips to her palm.

The shocking heat leapt like a spark into her; the blatantly intimate touch made her shiver.

He shifted his head; his lips drifted to her wrist, there to bestow an equally intimate lover's caress.

"I'm sorry." The words reached her on a dark whisper as his lips left her skin. His fingers shifted over hers, locking her hand in his. "I didn't intend it to be like this, but . . . I can't wait for you any longer."

Before her brain could take in his meaning, let alone react, he surged to his feet – angling his shoulder into her waist, using his hold on her hand to pull her forward – in one smooth move hoisting her up over his shoulder.

"What . . .?" Disoriented, she stared down his back.

He turned to the door.

She grabbed the back of his coat. "For God's sake, Royce – put me down!" She would have kicked, tried to lever herself off his hard shoulder, but he'd clamped a steely arm over the backs of her knees, locking her in position.

"I will. Just be quiet for a few minutes."

A few minutes? He'd already walked out into the corridor.

Clutching the back of his coat with both hands, she looked around, then braced as he started climbing; through the dimness she recognized the hall before the west turret stairs – watched it recede.

A scarifying thought formed. "Where are you taking me?"

"You already know. Do you want me to state it?"

"Yes!"

"To my bed."

"No!"

Silence. No response, no reply, no acknowledgment of any sort.

He reached the gallery and turned toward his rooms. Any doubt that he meant to do as he'd said evaporated. Realization of how helpless she was grew; she couldn't prevent what would follow because she simply wouldn't, not once he'd hauled her into his arms and kissed her.

Just the thought of his hands – his clever, wicked hands – on her skin again made her shiver with damning anticipation.

Desperate, she braced her hands on his back, struggled to push up enough to drag air into her lungs. "Royce, *stop*!" She poured every ounce of command she could muster into her tone. When he didn't so much as pause, she quickly continued, "If you don't set me down this instant, I'll scream."

"A piece of advice from one who knows – never threaten what you're not prepared to deliver."

Incensed, she drew in a massive breath, held it . . . waited.

His strides didn't falter.

But then he halted.

Hope flared – only to be drowned by a wave of disappointment.

Before she could decide what she truly felt, he walked forward again, then swung around. Her gaze raked the line of his armillary spheres. They were in his sitting room. Her last chance of being saved, by any means, died as she heard the door shut.

She waited, breath bated, to be put down. Instead, he walked through the next door, kicked it shut behind them, and continued on across his bedroom.

All the way to the foot of his massive four-poster bed.

Halting, he gripped her waist; dipping his shoulder, he slid her slowly down, breasts to his chest, until her toes touched the floor.

Valiantly ignoring the sudden rush of her pulse and her swooningly eager senses, she fixed her eyes, narrowed, on his as he straightened. "You can't do this." She made the statement absolute. "You cannot simply carry me in here, and" – she gestured wildly – "*ravish* me!"

It was the only word she could think of that matched the intent she could now see in his eyes.

He studied her for an instant, then raised his hands, framed her face. Tipped it up as he shifted closer, so their bodies touched, brushed, settled, as, eyes locked with hers, he bent his head. "Yes. I can."

His statement trumped hers. It rang with innate conviction, with the overwhelming confidence that had been his from birth.

Lids falling, she braced for an assault.

It didn't come.

Instead, he supped at her lips, a gentle, tantalizing, tempting caress.

221

Her lips already hungered, her body thrumming with awakening need when he lifted his head just enough to catch her eyes. "I'm going to ravish you – thoroughly. And I guarantee you'll enjoy every minute."

She would; she knew she would. And she no longer knew of any way to avoid it – was fast losing sight of why she should. She searched his eyes, his face. Moistened her lips. Looked at his, and didn't know what to say.

What reply she wanted to convey.

As she stared at them, his lips curved. Thin, hard, yet mobile, the ends curved up just slightly, invitingly.

"You don't have to say anything. You just have to accept. Just have to stop resisting . . ." He breathed the last words as his lips lowered to hers. "And let what we both want, simply be."

His lips closed on hers again, still gentle, still persuasive, yet she felt the barely leashed hunger in the hands cradling her face. Lifting one hand, she closed it over the back of one of his – and knew to her bones his gentleness was a façade.

Ravish he'd said, and ravish he meant.

As if to prove her correct, his lips hardened, firmed; she felt his hunger, tasted his passion. She expected him to press her lips apart, with no further invitation claim her mouth, then her – but abruptly he reined in the passion about to break free.

Enough for him to lift his lips an inch from hers and demand, "If you don't want to know what it would be like to lie with me, say so now."

She'd dreamed of it, fantasized about it, spent long hours wondering . . . looking into the dark richness of his eyes, at the heat already burning in their depths, she knew she should deny it, grasp the chance and flee, yet the lie simply wouldn't come.

"If you don't want me, tell me now."

The harsh words grated, deep and low.

His lips hovered over hers, waiting for her answer.

One of her hands lay on his chest, spread over his heart; she could feel the heavy, urgent thud, could see in his eyes, behind all the heat, a simple need – one that pleaded, that touched her.

That needed her to be assuaged.

If you don't want me . . .

He wanted her.

Tipping up her face, she closed the distance, and kissed him.

Sensed a fleeting moment of surprise, then he accepted – seized – the implied permission.

His lips closed on hers – ravenously. Hers were parted; he surged in and laid claim. Laid waste to any vestige of resistance, laid siege to her wits and flattened her defenses.

He filled her mouth, captured her tongue and caressed, seized her senses, engaged them with his. Commanded, demanded; even as his hands slid from her face and his arms closed around her, steely bands pulling her into him, locking her uncompromisingly against his hard frame, he lured her into a heated exchange that rapidly escalated, eager and urgent, onto another plane.

He fed her fire and passion, and more. He gave her, pressed on her, a taste of raw possession, an undisguised, shockingly explicit portent of what was to come, of his unleashed hunger, of her own heady response.

Of her ultimate surrender.

Of that last there was never any doubt.

Her shawl slid from her shoulders to the floor. She could barely find her wits in the maelstrom of her senses, could do little more in that first turbulent wash of passion and desire than cling to the kiss, to his lips, wind her arms about his neck and hang on for dear life.

For this was much more than he'd shared with her before. He'd let fall the reins he normally held, and let his desire loose to devour her.

That was how it felt when he closed one hand about her breast. There was nothing gentle in his touch; she gasped through the kiss, felt herself arch helplessly into the caress – all possessive passion, expertly wielded. His fingers closed and she shuddered, felt his palm burn even through the layers of fabric shielding her skin. Felt a hot wave of desire, as before his and hers combining, undeniably twining, rise up and fill her.

Take her. Compel her. Overwhelm her.

In that instant she set aside all restraint, gave herself up to the moment, and all it would bring. Set herself free to take all and everything he offered, to revel and seize whatever came her way. To seize the moment fate had granted her to live her dreams – even if only for one night.

The decision resonated within her.

This was what she'd wanted all her life.

She reached for it. Boldly slid her fingers into his hair, tightened them on his skull – and kissed him back. Let her own hunger rise up and answer his – let her own passion free to counter his. To balance the scales as much as she could.

As far as that was possible.

His response was so powerfully passionate it curled her toes. He angled his head, deepened the kiss, took complete and absolute possession of her mouth. The hand locked about her swollen breast eased, released; he sent it skating down, trailing fire wherever he touched, over her waist, her hip, around and down to close, flagrantly possessive, about one globe of her bottom.

He lifted her into him, drew her up against him so the hard ridge of his erection rode against her mons. Caught in the kiss, trapped in his arms, she was helpless to hold back the tide of sensation he sent crashing through her as with a deliberate, practiced roll of his hips, he thrust against her.

Barely able to breathe, she clung as, with that simple, explicitly repetitive action, he stoked her fire until it cindered her wits, then he continued to move deliberately against her with just the right amount of pressure to feed the flames . . . until she thought she would scream.

Royce wanted to be inside her, wanted to sink his throbbing staff deep into her luscious body, to feel her wet sheath close tightly about him and ease the fiery ache, then to possess her utterly; he needed that more than he'd needed anything in his life.

Hunger and need pounded through his veins, relentless and demanding; it would be so easy to lift her skirts, lift her, release his staff and impale her . . . but while he wanted with blinding urgency, some equally strong, equally violent instinct wanted to draw the moment out. Wanted to make it last – to stretch the anticipation until they were both mindless.

He'd never been mindless, never had a woman who could reduce him to that state . . . the primitive side of him knew he had the one woman who could in his arms that night.

It wasn't control that allowed him to draw back, wasn't anything like thought that guided him as he lowered her to her feet, snaring her senses once more in their kiss – an increasingly hot, evocatively explicit mating of mouths – then steered her around the end of his bed.

He backed her along, then turned into the high side; using his hips and thighs to pin her there, he set his fingers to the laces of her gown.

A heartbeat later, her hands eased from his skull, slid down and out across his shoulders, then swept in, reaching between them to the buttons of his coat.

Curious over how direct she would be, how openly demanding, he let her slide the large buttons free; when she slid her hand up the inner edges and tried to push the coat off his shoulders, he obligingly released her and shrugged it off, let it fall where it would as he found her laces again and tugged them free.

At no stage did he let her break from the kiss – their hungry, greedy, devouring kiss. He drew her back into the heat and the flames, drew her against him again as he reached behind her and parted the gaping halves of her gown, slid one palm beneath, but found the fine silk of her chemise a last barrier, separating his hand from her skin.

Impulse goaded him to rip the garment away; he shackled it, but the notion acted like a spur. He wasted no time stripping the gown from her shoulders and down her arms, pushing it over her hips, letting it swish to the floor while he tugged the ribbon ties at the shoulders of her chemise undone, and sent it even more swiftly down.

Lifting his head, he dragged in a breath and stepped back.

Shocked – by her suddenly exposed state, but even more by the loss of his hard heat and the elemental hunger of his mouth – Minerva swayed back against the bed, managed to remain upright as her senses whirled.

They locked on him, tall, broad-shouldered, powerfully built, handsome as sin and twice as dangerous – standing a mere pace away.

One part of her mind told her to run; another felt she should tense, use her hands to cover herself, at least make some show of modesty – she was standing utterly naked before him – but the heat in his dark eyes as they roamed her body was hot enough to scorch, to burn away all inhibitions and leave her wantonly curious.

Wantonly fascinated.

She reached for the waistcoat she'd already opened, but he blocked her, brushing her hand aside with a gesture that said, "Wait."

His eyes hadn't left her body. His gaze continued to trace her curves, the indentation of her waist, the flare of her hips, the long, smooth lines of her thighs. It lingered, hot, assessing, blatantly possessive on the curls at the juncture of her thighs.

After a moment, his gaze lowered.

And she realized she wasn't entirely naked; she still had on her garters, stockings, and slippers.

He shrugged out of the waistcoat, let it fall as he went to his knees before her. He gripped one bare hip, bent and pressed his lips to the curls he'd studied. She felt her insides melt, reached back with her hands to lean on the bed, let her head loll back as the heat of his lips sank in, then he deftly tongued her – one artful sweep of his educated tongue over her most sensitive flesh.

She jerked, caught her breath – just managed to stifle a shriek. Hauling in a breath, she looked down as he drew back, reminded herself he thought she was experienced.

He didn't look up to gauge her reaction but, sitting back on his ankles, set his fingers to one garter and slowly rolled it and her stocking down. Bent his head as he did and with his lips traced a line of small, tantalizing kisses down the inner face of her leg, from high on her thigh to just below her knee.

By the time he finished removing her slippers and stockings, only her braced arms were holding her upright.

Her lids were heavy; from beneath her lashes she watched as he looked up at her, then he rocked back on his heels and smoothly rose.

Pulling the gold pin from his cravat, he tossed it onto the tallboy nearby, then unwound the folds, his movements tense, taut. Tugging the long strip from his neck, he dropped it, flicked the ties loose at his neck and wrists, then grabbed fistfuls of his shirt and hauled the fine linen up, and off.

Revealing his chest.

Her mouth watered. She'd caught only a glimpse in his bathing chamber earlier. Her eyes skated, drinking in the vision, then settled to a leisurely appreciation of each evocatively masculine element – the wide, well-defined muscles stretching across his upper chest, the sculpted ridges of his abdomen, the band of crinkly black hair that swept across the width, and the narrower stripe that arrowed down, disappearing beneath his waistband.

She watched the shift and play of muscles beneath his taut skin as he bent and pulled off his shoes, dispensed with his stockings.

Then he straightened, his fingers slipping the buttons at his waistband free.

She felt a panicky urge to wave a hand and tell him to stop. To at least slow down and give her time to prepare herself.

His eyes on her body, he stripped off his trousers, tossed them aside, straightened and walked toward her.

Her gaze locked on his phallus, long, thick, and very erect, rising from the nest of black hair at his groin; her mouth dried completely. Her heart thudded in her ears, but he didn't seem to hear.

Like most men, he seemed to have no concept of modesty . . . then again, with a body like a god, why would he feel shy?

She felt . . . overwhelmed.

He was all hard, heavy muscle and bone – and he was large. Definitely large.

She had every confidence that he knew what he – they – were doing, would be doing, but she couldn't imagine how he – that – was going to fit inside her.

Just the thought made her giddy.

He halted before her, as close as he could given she hadn't shifted her gaze. She didn't lift her head, didn't – couldn't – peel her eyes from that impressive display of male desire.

Desire she'd evoked.

She licked her lips, boldly reached for the solid rod and wrapped one palm and her fingers about it mid-length. Felt it harden at her touch.

Sensed his body tighten, harden, too, glanced up in time to see his eyes close. Her fingers didn't meet, but she slid her hand down, absorbing the contradictory textures of velvet over steel, traced down to the base, looked down to see her hand brushing against his hair, then she reversed direction, eager to explore the wide head. He hissed in pleasure when she reached it, then she released her grip and trailed her fingertips over the swollen contours, then around the rim.

He caught her hand – tightly; when she jerked her gaze to his face he gentled his grip. "Later." His voice was a low growl.

She blinked.

His jaw set as he raised her hand to his shoulder. "You can touch and feel all you like later. Right now, I want to feel you."

His hands slid around her waist to her back. He brought her away from the bed – into him.

Nothing had prepared her for the tactile shock. For the jolt of pure sensation that streaked like lightning down every nerve, leaving their ends frazzled, leaving her gasping, struggling to get air into lungs locked tight.

He was so hot! His skin seared her, but enticingly – she couldn't get enough. Enough of his hard chest against her breasts, the crinkly hair lightly, unspeakably deliciously, abrading her furled nipples. Enough of the feel of the long length of his steely thighs against hers, enough of the promise of the rigid rod at his groin pressing into her belly.

The lack of air nearly made her swoon, but instinct pushed her into his embrace as his arms slid around her and locked, wanton instinct that had her squirming against him, instinctively seeking the best and closest fit, wanting the maximum contact, the absolute maximum of his masculine heat.

She wanted to bathe in it.

Royce bent his head and took her mouth again, filled it, claimed it, possessed the delectable softness just as he intended to possess her body – slowly, repetitively, and thoroughly.

At last, he had her where he wanted her, naked in his arms. The first small step to fulfillment. He didn't need to think to have the rest of his campaign blazoned in his brain; primitive instinct had already etched it there.

He wanted her naked, helplessly, shudderingly, sobbingly naked and begging for his touch.

He wanted her lying, utterly naked, sprawled on his silk sheets, her breasts swollen and peaked, with the marks of his possession clear on her flawless skin.

He wanted her panting, her white thighs spread wide, her folds pink and swollen, glistening with invitation as she begged him to fill her.

He wanted her writhing beneath him as he did.

He wanted her to climax, but not until he entered her – wanted her to fracture in the instant he sheathed himself within her. Wanted her to remember that moment, to have it engraved on her sensual memory – the time he first penetrated her, filled her, possessed her.

He was Wolverstone, unquestioned all-powerful lord of this domain.

What he wanted, he got.

He made sure of it.

Made sure that, using his hands, lips, and tongue, but lightly, he awakened every nerve ending she possessed, arousing her, feeding her hunger, stoking her desire, luring her passion, yet not satisfying those wants in the least.

Expertly he urged them to grow, to well, swell, and fill her.

Until, on a shuddering moan, she caught his hand and drew it to her breast. Pressed his fingers hard to her firm flesh. "Stop playing, you fiend."

He would have chuckled, but his throat was too tight with suppressed desire; instead, he did as ordered, and palmed her breast forcefully, kneading evocatively, then he backed her against the bed, propping her against it so he could use both hands on her at the same time.

Until she sobbed, and reached for his erection.

He caught her hand, held it as he swept the covers back and off the bed, then releasing her, he swept her up in his arms, and climbed onto the crimson silk sheets. Laying her down in the center of the bed, her head on the piled pillows, he stretched out beside her, set his lips and tongue to her breasts, and tortured himself by torturing her.

When she was moaning unrestrainedly, hands sunk in his hair, gripping tight as she writhed and held him to her, he slid lower in the bed, sampling her passion-damp skin as he would, spreading her thighs wide, settling between to lightly lave and lick, in between tracing her folds with his fingertips.

Until, panting, she lifted her head, looked down at him, and, eyes gleaming gold with unslaked desire, gasped, "For God's sake, touch me *properly.*"

His features were granite, but he inwardly grinned as she flopped back. Then he gave her what she'd asked for, inserting first one, then two fingers into her tight sheath, working them deep, but carefully avoiding giving her release.

Minerva shuddered; simply breathing was a battle as she struggled to absorb each blatantly intimate caress, as her senses, totally focused, strained, greedily seizing all they could from each slow, heavy thrust of his fingers into her body – and discovering that it never was enough.

Not enough to spring the catch on her overwound senses, not enough – nowhere near enough – to fill the throbbing, empty void that had opened at her core.

All her skin felt flushed; passion's flames greedily, hungrily, licked all over her just beneath her skin, but no matter how she burned, the furnace within her merely smoldered red hot, molten and waiting.

Some distant part of her mind knew what he was doing – was even aware enough to be grateful; if he was – as she knew he was – going to thrust his engorged phallus into her, she wanted to be as ready as humanly possible.

But . . . she was already sopping wet – and desperate. Frantically desperate to feel and experience all the rest. She *wanted* him atop her, wanted to feel him join with her.

Finally comprehended what drove otherwise sane women to crave a lover like him.

Her body writhed under his hands. She could barely find air enough to gasp, "Royce . . ." A half sob, half moan carried the rest of her wordless plea.

One he understood; one she had a sudden comprehension he'd been waiting for. Leaving his fingers buried within her sheath, he rose up, his long body sliding over hers as, bracing on one elbow, he fitted his hips between her widespread thighs.

He withdrew his fingers from her slick sheath, set the broad head of his erection within her folds, literally at her entrance, then he settled over her, looking down into her face.

From beneath her lashes, she looked into his dark eyes.

"Do you want me inside you?" His voice was so gravelly, she could barely make out the words.

Releasing the sheets her hands had fisted in, she reached up, sank her fingers into his upper arms, and pulled him down to her – or tried to. "Yes," she hissed. "Now!"

His features, locked in passion, didn't shift, but she sensed his immense satisfaction. Then – to her immense satisfaction – he obliged her in both her requests.

He let his body down on hers, and her senses sang in delirious delight – all that heat, all that solid muscle, all that heavy body pinning her to the bed. But then he lowered his head, and took her mouth again, filled it again – something she hadn't been expecting that momentarily distracted her.

Then he flexed his hips, and nothing could distract her from the pressure as he entered her – slowly, inexorably – then he paused.

She almost screamed; she did moan, the sound muffled by their locked lips. Suddenly more desperate than she'd thought she could be, she sank her nails into his arms, writhed and lifted against him, tipped her hips, trying to lure him deeper, needing, begging –

He thrust heavily, powerfully, into her. Filled her completely with that single forceful thrust.

And she couldn't absorb it all at once. The brief flash of pain, the overwhelming shock of the sensation of him so solid and heavy within her, the realization that this had really happened ... like an overwound skein, her senses started to unravel.

He held still for a long moment, then withdrew, almost to her entrance, then thrust powerfully into her again, even more deeply – and her senses fractured. She screamed as they shattered; he drank in the sound.

And she was swept high on a spiral of infinite ecstasy, senses expanding and expanding, bright, sharp, crystalline clear as waves of sensation, increasingly intense, rolled through her – as he filled her mouth and claimed her there, as his body moved heavily upon hers, and hers responded and danced under his, instinctively responding to the deep, driving rhythm as he possessed her utterly – ravished her thoroughly – and everything within her sang.

Then ecstasy sharpened, gripped her anew, and pushed her even higher – he growled in his throat, caught her tongue with his, stroked, then thrust deep into her mouth just as he thrust even more forcefully into her body.

And she came apart again.

All her senses, every particle of her awareness, imploded. Fragmented. Shards of pleasure so intense they felt like light speared down her veins, then melted and made her glow, made her soften beneath him, around him, made her clutch him and hold him as he thrust one last time, even more deeply, then he stiffened, groaned, shuddered as his release swept him, as deep and intense as hers, leaving him wracked, helpless in her arms.

All tension released, fell away, and they were floating in some blissful, bliss-filled void, surrounded by a golden glory she couldn't name.

It caught them, buoyed them, cushioned them as they spiraled slowly back to earth.

That golden rapture seeped into her, spread through her veins, through her body, sank deep into her heart, softly, slowly, infused her soul.

He'd lost himself in her.

That had never happened to him before; it left him wary.

Something had changed. He didn't know what, but she'd opened some door, led him down a new path, and his view of an activity he'd taken for granted for years had altered.

His experience of that activity had been rewritten, rescripted.

He was very familiar with sexual satiation, but this was much more. The release he'd found in her, with her, was infinitely more sating; the satisfaction he'd found with her had reached his soul.

Or so it felt.

Royce stood at the uncurtained window of his bedroom and looked out at the moonlit night. Raising the glass of water he held, he sipped, and wished it could cool the still smoldering heat inside him.

But only one thing could do that.

He glanced back at his bed, where Minerva lay sleeping. Her hair was a golden wave breaking over his pillows, her face madonna-peaceful, one white arm gracefully draped atop the crimson-and-gold covers he'd pulled up so she wouldn't get cold.

He'd memorized the sight of her lying naked and sated, sprawled on his crimson sheets, before he'd covered her. She'd bled hardly at all, just a few streaks on the inside of her thighs, enough to confirm her previous untouched state, but not, he hoped, enough to make her hesitate over taking him inside her again.

His primitive side had gloated; he'd wanted her then, wanted to wake her again, but had decided to play civilized and give her a little time to recover. He hadn't been inside her all that long; her sheath had been so incredibly tight her release had brought on his. Control in abeyance, he hadn't held back, but that also meant he hadn't pounded into her for long; with luck she wouldn't be too sore to let him inside her again.

At least she was where she was supposed to be.

Keeping her there, ensuring she remained, was his next step. One he'd never attempted – wished to take – with any other woman.

But she was his. He intended to point that out – to propose and be accepted – once she stirred.

In considering that proposal, and how best to phrase it, his mind circled back to the surprise she'd had for him – the little secret she'd been hiding so amazingly well.

She'd never had any previous lover. Despite being so focused on her, despite his expertise, he hadn't detected her inexperience; instead, he'd assumed, and been wrong.

Sunk in her mouth, as physically linked with her as it was possible to be, he hadn't missed that instant of pain as he'd thrust deeply inside her for the first time; he was too experienced not to recognize when a woman beneath him tensed in pain, rather than from pleasure.

But even as he'd registered the stunning fact that she'd been a virgin, she'd started to climax. Just as he'd intended.

The unexpected surge of primitive feelings knowing he'd taken her virginity had evoked, combining with the intense satisfaction of knowing he'd succeeded to the last detail with his plan, had detached him from all control. From that point on, he'd had none; he'd operated on instinct alone – that same powerful, primitive instinct that was even now prowling just beneath his skin, satisfied to a point, yet still hungry for her.

He tore his eyes from the bed, tried to focus on the night-shrouded landscape instead. If he'd known she'd been a virgin . . . not that he'd had much experience bedding virgins – only two, both when he'd been sixteen – but he would at least have tried to be less forceful, less vigorous. God knew he wasn't the easiest man for even experienced women to accommodate, yet . . . He glanced again at the bed, then took another sip of water.

As she'd done with him in every other arena, in lying beneath him, she'd coped, too.

Coped rather well, in fact.

The thought brought to mind her earlier fascination with his erection – a fascination he now better understood; she'd wanted to touch, to examine . . . the memory of her small hand and delicate fingers wrapped about his shaft had the inevitable effect.

Jaw setting, he drained the glass. Later, he'd said; it was later now.

She stirred even before he reached the bed. Setting the empty glass on the bedside table, he met her eyes as he let the silk robe he'd donned fall from his shoulders; lifting the covers, he climbed into the bed and laid down. She slid helpfully toward him; expecting that, raising one arm, he drew her closer; she hesitated, then came, tentatively settling against him. He waited, assessing yet again the possible tacks he might take in the discussion he was about to initiate.

Minerva found his heat, the solidity of his body and the warmth that emanated from his muscled flesh, both comforting and luring. Nerves that had tensed slightly relaxed again. Greatly daring, she sank deeper into his light embrace; his arm tightened about her, and it seemed only natural to raise her head and settle it in the hollow just below his shoulder, letting her hand rest, palm down, on his chest.

She quashed an impulse to snuggle her cheek into the pillowing muscle; he wasn't hers, not really – she should strive to remember that.

He lifted a strand of her hair from her face, smoothed it back.

She was wondering if she was supposed to say something – comment on his performance, perhaps – when he spoke.

"You should have told me you were a virgin."

The instant the words left his lips, Royce knew they'd been the wrong thing to say. The wrong tack to take in introducing his proposal.

She tensed, gradually but definitely, then raised her head and narrowed her eyes on his face. "Understand this, Royce Varisey – I do not, absolutely *do not want to hear* a single word about marriage. If you so much as mention the word in relation to me, I'll consider it the most *inexcusable* insult. Just because I was your mother's protégée and just happened – through no fault of mine or yours – to still be a virgin, is no reason at all for you to feel obliged to offer for my hand."

Oh, Christ. "But –"

"No." Lips set, eyes snapping, she pointed at his nose. "Keep quiet and listen! There's no point in offering for my hand – in even thinking of it – because even if you do, I will refuse you. As you're very well aware, I enjoyed the" – she paused, then waved – "*interlude* immensely, and I'm more than adult enough to take responsibility for my own actions, even if our recent actions were more yours than mine. Regardless, contrary to popular misconception, the last, very last thing a lady such as I want to hear after lying with a man for the first time is a proposal prompted by said man's misplaced notion of honor!"

Her voice had steadily gained in intensity. She glared at him, lips tight. "So don't make that mistake."

The tension investing her body, lying half atop his, was of entirely the wrong sort. His features impassive, he searched her eyes; he'd made a tactical blunder, and had to beat a strategic retreat. He nodded. "All right. I won't."

She narrowed her eyes even more. "And you won't try to manipulate me into it?"

He raised both brows. "Manipulate you into marriage because I took your virginity?" He shook his head. "I can assure you – I'll even promise on my honor – that I won't do that."

Eyes locked with his, she hesitated, almost as if she could detect the prevarication in his words. He steadily returned her

236

regard. Eventually she uttered a soft "humph," and swung away. "Good."

She pulled out of his arms, and started wrestling her way free of the covers.

He reached out and lightly clasped her wrist. "Where are you going?"

She glanced at him. "To my room, of course."

His fingers locked. "Why?"

She blinked at him. "Isn't that what I'm supposed to do?"

"No." His eyes on hers, he drew the hand he held back beneath the covers – down to where his erection stood at full attention. Curling her fingers about his rigid flesh, he watched her expression change to one of fascination. "This," he ground out, "is what you're supposed to do. What you're supposed to attend to."

Her gaze refocused on his face. She studied his eyes, then nodded. "All right." Swinging back to him, she switched her right hand for her left, smoothing her palm up his length before, as she leaned into him, closing her fingers. "If you insist."

He managed a grating "I do." Reaching up, he slid one hand behind her nape and pulled her lips down to his. "I insist you learn all you want to know."

She took him at his word, hands touching, caressing, squeezing, gliding, tracing as she would. The unconscious, unguarded sensuality in her face as, eyes closing as if to imprint the heft and weight, length and shape of him on her mind, she explored as she would, tried his control to its limit and beyond. To a chest-shuddering, muscle-quivering extent he'd never before had to endure.

He clung to his sanity by planning what came next. He favored sitting her astride him, impaling her, then teaching her to ride him, but discovered he lacked the strength to counter the urges her bold, innocently brazen caresses called forth. Then incited and ignited.

She connected with his more primitive side far more than any other woman ever had.

237

Reduced to the point where control was a thin and rapidly shredding veil, he brushed her hands aside, rolled her over, pinning her beneath him, spreading her thighs wide and cupping her, touching her, to find her wet once more. Hauling in a huge breath, he wedged his hips between her thighs and entered her – slowly, slowly, slowly, *slowly* – steady and inexorable so her breath strangled in her chest and she arched beneath him, a cry fracturing on her lips as with a final short thrust he sheathed himself fully within her.

Letting himself down on her, he anchored her hip with one hand, found her face with the other and, lowering his head, covered her lips with his, filled her mouth, and plundered to the same rhythm with which he settled to plunder her body.

A bare heartbeat passed, and then she was with him, her hands reaching around to spread on his back, holding him, clinging, her body undulating, caressing, her hips lifting to match his heavy driving rhythm. Releasing her hip, he reached down, found her knee, and lifted it over his hip.

Without further direction, she hooked that knee higher, then did the same with her other leg, opening herself to him so he could sink deeper into her, could without restraint drive them both even harder, even faster, to oblivion.

He did; when she shattered beneath him he intended to hold back, to extend the engagement and take more of her, but the temptation to fly with her was too great – he let go and followed close on her heels, into the senses-shattering glory of climax and on into the void.

Wrapped in her arms, with her wrapped in his, their hearts thundering, breaths sawing, then slowing, they gradually drifted back to reality.

As, all tension spent, she relaxed, boneless, beneath him, he saw a small, subtle smile curve her kiss-swollen lips. The sight warmed him, curiously touched him.

He watched until it faded as she slid into sated sleep.

Chapter 13

He woke her sometime before dawn, time enough to indulge his senses and hers in one last, brief, intense engagement, then let her recover enough to don her gown and walk back to her room.

He rose and helped her dress, then saw her out of his sitting room door. He would have preferred to escort her to her room, but if any others were drifting back to their beds and saw her, it was better they didn't see her with him.

She was the castle's chatelaine; there were any number of reasons she might be about early.

After listening to her footsteps fade, he returned to the bedroom, and his bed. Settling beneath the covers, sensing her warmth lingering beside him, conscious of her subtle perfume wreathing all about him, he folded his arms behind his head and fixed his gaze on the window across the room.

So what now? He'd made progress, real and definite progress, but then she'd stymied him in a way he hadn't been quick enough to foresee. While henceforth he could, and would, have her in his bed, he could no longer simply *ask* her to be his bride. There was no argument that stood any chance of convincing her he'd wanted to marry her *before* he'd taken her virginity. That he hadn't known she was a virgin meant nothing, and no matter how long he waited, she would still view his proposal as the insult she'd warned him not to offer her.

And she'd refuse. Adamantly. And she'd only grow more stubborn the harder he pressed.

Admittedly he had, for one foolish moment, considered using the age-old argument based on virginity and honor as a possible supporting reason for their wedding. He should have guessed how she would react.

He lay staring into space as his household slowly awakened, juggling possibilities, assessing tacks. If he'd asked her to marry him when he'd first set out to, rather than letting her distract him with her challenge into seducing her first, he wouldn't now be facing this complication, yet there was no point dwelling on what couldn't be changed.

He could see only one way forward. He would have to keep silent over his intention to marry her, and instead do every-thing in his considerable power to lead her to conclude of her own accord that marrying him was her true and natural des-tiny. More, her greatly desired destiny.

Once she'd realized that, he could offer for her hand, and she would accept.

If he applied himself to the task, how long could it take? A week?

The grandes dames had accepted the week he'd originally stipulated readily enough. That week had now passed, but he doubted any of them would hie north to castigate him – not yet. If he dallied too long, someone would turn up to lecture him again and exhort him to action, but he probably had another week up his sleeve.

A week he would devote to convincing Minerva that she should be his duchess.

A week to make it clear she already was, but just hadn't real-ized.

His lips curved, just as Trevor looked in from the dressing room.

His valet saw his smile, saw the bed. Raised his brows inquiringly.

Royce saw no reason to keep him in the dark. "My chatelaine – who will shortly be your mistress." He fixed his gaze on Trevor's face. "A fact she doesn't yet know, so no one will tell her."

Trevor smiled. "Naturally not, Your Grace." His expression one of the utmost equanimity, he started to pick up Royce's clothes.

Royce studied him. "You don't seem all that surprised."

Straightening, Trevor shook out his coat. "You have to choose a lady, and all things considered I find it hard to imagine you could do better than Miss Chesterton." He shrugged. "Nothing to be surprised about."

Royce humphed, and got out of the bed. "I will, of course, wish to know anything and everything you learn that might be pertinent. I take it you know her maid?"

Folding Royce's waistcoat, Trevor smiled. "A young person by the name of Lucy, Your Grace."

Belting his robe, Royce narrowed his eyes on that smile. "A word to the wise. I might bed the mistress, but you'd be ill-advised to try the same with the maid. She'll have your balls on a stick – the mistress, not the maid. And in the circumstances, I'd have to let her."

Trevor's eyes opened wide. "I'll bear that in mind, Your Grace. Now, do you wish to shave?"

Minerva awoke when Lucy, her maid, came bustling into the room.

After leaving Royce, she'd slipped back to her room without seeing anyone; she'd undressed, put on her nightgown, brushed out her tangled hair, got into bed – and to her surprise had fallen deeply asleep.

She yawned, stretched – and felt twinges where she never had before. She watched Lucy open the curtains, then shake out her gown; when Lucy turned to the armoire, she surreptitiously peeked down the front of her nightgown.

She blinked, then looked across the room. "The black with the buttons up the front, Lucy. Just leave it over the chair. I'll get up shortly, but you don't need to wait. I can manage that gown by myself."

And innocent Lucy didn't need to see the telltale marks on her breasts. She didn't want to think what she might discover farther down.

"I've brought up your washing water. Do you need me for anything else, ma'am?"

"No, thank you, Lucy. You can go and have your breakfast."

"Thank you, miss." With a cheery smile and a bobbed curtsy, Lucy took herself off. The door closed behind her.

Minerva exhaled, sank deeper into the mattress, and let her thoughts range over the previous night, and its entirely unexpected events. That Royce would act so directly – and that she would respond so definitely – had never entered her head. But he had, and she had, so where were they now?

She'd always assumed he'd be a vigorous lover. In that, he'd exceeded her expectations; her untutored self had never even imagined much of what, at his hands, she had now experienced. Yet despite her inexperience, she knew him – she hadn't missed the hunger, the real need that had had him carting her off to his bed, that had driven him as he'd ravished her.

Possessed her.

Repeatedly.

When she'd woken before dawn, just as, from behind, he'd filled her, and proceeded to demonstrate yet another way he could possess her – her body, her senses, and her mind – utterly and completely, with his lips in the hollow below her ear rather than on hers, she, her senses, had been freer to absorb the nuances of his loving.

That he wanted her, desired her, she accepted without question.

That that want ran deep, she now understood.

She'd never imagined being the focus of that degree of desire, having so much male passion concentrated on her; the recollection sent a delicious shiver through her. She couldn't deny she'd found it deeply satisfying; she'd be lying if she pretended she wouldn't be happy to lie with him again.

If he asked, which he would. He wasn't, she knew, finished with her; that had been explicit in their final moments that morning.

Thank God she'd had sufficient wit to seize the chance and make it plain that she neither expected nor wanted to receive an offer from him.

She hadn't forgotten that other offer he was due to make – to the lady he'd chosen as his duchess. Not knowing if he'd made a formal offer yet, she'd needed to ensure he wouldn't, in some Machiavellian moment, decide to use her virginity – the taking of it – as cause to marry her instead.

While he'd toed the grandes dames' line, he wasn't happy about it; he might well seize an opportunity to take a different tack. And to him, marrying her might be preferable to having to deal with some unknown young lady who would know very little about him.

She – Minerva – would be a more comfortable choice.

She didn't need to think to know her response to that. He would be a sound husband to any lady who accepted the loveless partnership he would offer; just as long as said lady didn't expect love or fidelity, all would be well.

For herself, love, real and abiding, was the only coin for which she would exchange her heart. Extensive experience of Varisey unions had bolstered her stance; their type of marriage was not for her. Avoiding, if necessary actively resisting, any suggestion of marrying Royce remained an unaltered, unalterable goal; nothing on that front had changed.

And, to her immense relief, spending the night in his bed hadn't seduced her heart into loving him; her feelings toward him hadn't changed all that much – or only on the lust side, not in terms of love.

Thinking of how she now felt about him . . . she frowned. Despite her resistance, she did feel something *more* for him – unexpected feelings that had developed since his return. Feelings that had driven her panic of yesterday, when she'd thought he would die.

Those new feelings had grown through seeing him with his

people, from his attitudes and actions toward those he deemed in his care. From all the decisions and acts that distinguished him so definitively from his father. The physical pleasure he'd introduced her to hadn't influenced her as much as all those things.

Yet while he might differ from his father in many ways, when it came to his wife and his marriage, he would revert to type. He'd demonstrated as much in his approach to his prospective bride.

If she let herself be bullied into marrying him, she would risk falling in love with him – irrevocably, irretrievably – and then like Caro Lamb she would pine, wither, and eventually go mad when he, not at all in love with her, left her for another. As he inevitably would.

She wasn't so foolish as to believe that she might, through loving him, change him. No; if she married him, he, indeed everyone, would expect her to stand meekly by while he indulged as he wished with an endless succession of other ladies.

She snorted, threw back the covers, and swung her legs out of bed. "That's not going to happen."

No matter what she felt for him, regardless of what evolved from her infatuation-obsession, no matter *what* new aspects of attraction developed over the however many nights she might spend in his bed, she would not fall in love with him, ergo she wouldn't marry him.

At least they were both now very clear on that last point.

Standing, she crossed to the basin and pitcher on her dresser; pouring water into the basin, she let her thoughts range ahead. As matters now stood . . .

Setting down the pitcher, she stared at the settling water as the immediate future cleared in her mind.

Of necessity her liaison with Royce would be short-lived – he would marry soon, and soon after, she would leave. A few days, a week. Two weeks at most.

Too short a time to fall in love.

Slipping her hands into the bowl, she splashed water on her

face, feeling increasingly bright. More alert and expectant, almost intrigued over what the day might bring – reassured and confident that there was no reason she couldn't indulge with him again.

The risk wasn't significant. Her heart would be safe.

Safe enough so she could enjoy without a care.

By evening, expectation had turned to impatience. Minerva sat in the music room, ostensibly watching yet another of Shakespeare's plays while she brooded on the shortcomings of her day.

A perfectly ordinary day, filled with nothing more than the customary events – which was the problem. She'd thought . . . but she'd been wrong.

Royce had summoned her to his study for their usual morning meeting with Handley; other than a fleeting moment when she'd walked into the room and their eyes had met – and he and she had both paused, both, she suspected, suddenly reminded of how the other's skin had felt against theirs . . . but then he'd blinked, looked down, and she'd walked forward and sat, and he'd subsequently treated her exactly as he had the previous day.

She'd followed his lead, then and later, as they'd parted, then met again, throughout the day, confident that at some point they would meet privately . . . but she was no longer so sure that would happen. She'd never engaged in a liaison before; she didn't know the script.

He did, but he was seated two rows in front of her, chatting to Caroline Courtney, who had claimed the chair beside him.

Under cover of the dinner conversations, he'd asked her if Cranny still kept stocks of the chicken essence she'd used to administer to them when they'd suffered childhood chills. She hadn't been sure, but when he'd suggested they send a bottle to the Honeymans for their daughter, she'd detoured to see the housekeeper before joining the company in the music room, thus missing her chance to sit next to him.

Narrowing her eyes on the back of his head, she wished she

245

could see inside. What was he thinking? Specifically, what was he thinking about her? *Was* he thinking about her?

Or had one night been enough?

The more confident part of her brazenly scoffed, but a more vulnerable part wondered.

At the end of the play, she clapped politely, caught Royce's eye for an instant, then excused herself and retired, leaving Margaret to manage the tea tray. She could do without spending the next half hour surrounded by the lascivious throng with him in the same room, aware of his gaze occasionally resting on her, fighting to keep hers from him – while every inch of her skin prickled with anticipation.

Reaching her room, willing her mind from the question of "Would he?" she stripped off her clothes, donned her nightgown, shrugged on her robe, then rang for Lucy.

She had a set of faint marks at the top of one thigh that was beyond her ability to explain.

Seated at her dressing table, she was brushing out her hair when Lucy breezed in.

"You're early tonight, ma'am." Lucy bent to pick up her gown. "Didn't you enjoy the play?"

She pulled a face. "They're becoming rather boring – just as well the fair's next week or I'd have to devise some other entertainment." She glanced at Lucy as the maid bustled to the armoire. "Did you learn anything?"

Opening the armoire, Lucy shook her dark head. "Mr. Handley's a quiet one – he's kind and smiles, but he's not one to talk. And of course he sits at the top end of the table. Trevor's closer to me, and he's a right chatterer, but although he natters on, he never really says anything, if you know what I mean."

"I can imagine." She hadn't really thought Royce would employ staff who didn't keep his secrets.

"The only thing any of us have got out of the pair of them is that His Grace is still negotiating with this lady he's chosen." Shutting the armoire, Lucy turned. "Not even a whisper and nary a hint of who the lady is. I suppose we'll just have to wait until we're told."

"Indeed." She inwardly grimaced.

Lucy turned down the bed, then returned and halted beside her. "Will there be anything else, ma'am?"

"No, thank you, Lucy – you may go."

"Thank you, ma'am. Good night."

Minerva murmured a "Good night," her mind once again running down the names on the grandes dames' list. Which one had Royce chosen? One of those she knew?

She was tempted to ask him outright – it would help if she knew how well-trained his duchess-to-be was so she would know how much she herself would need to impart before said duchess could manage on her own. The thought of handing her chatelaine's keys to some giggling ninnyhammer evoked a response very close to revulsion.

Rising, she snuffed the candelabra on the dressing table, leaving only the single candle burning by her bed. Drawing her robe closed, she belted it as she walked to the window.

If Royce wished to spend the night with her, he would come to her room; she might not have indulged in a liaison before, but she knew that much.

He would come. Or he wouldn't.

Perhaps he'd heard from the family of the lady for whom he'd offered.

Crossing her arms, she looked out at the night-shrouded landscape.

And waited.

And wondered.

"Royce!"

Halting under the archway leading into the keep's gallery, Royce let his head fall back, eyes closing in frustration.

That had been Margaret's voice; he could hear her rustling and puffing as she toiled up the main stairs behind him, along with some other lady.

Taking a firmer grip on his temper, he turned, and saw that Aurelia was Margaret's companion. "Wonderful."

The muttered sarcasm reached Margaret as she bustled up,

but only confused her. He waved aside her puzzled look. "What is it?"

She halted a pace away, glanced at Aurelia as she joined her, then, hands gripped before her, looked at him. "We wanted to ask if you would be agreeable to us inviting some others up for the fair."

"It used to be one of the highlights of our year when we lived here." Aurelia lifted her chin, her cold eyes fixing on his face. "We would like your permission to hold a house party, like Mama used to."

He looked from one hard, arrogantly aristocratic face to the other; he knew what those simple words had cost them. To have to ask their little brother, of whom they'd always disapproved, for permission to hold a party in their childhood home.

His first impulse was to tell them he'd rather all the visitors left – freeing him to pursue Minerva through the day as well as the night. But no matter his view of his sisters, this was their childhood home and he didn't feel justified in barring them from it – which meant having others about was necessary for cover, and to distract them.

Neither Margaret nor Aurelia was at all observant, and while Susannah was more so, not even she had yet divined the nature of his interest in Minerva. She was his chatelaine; they assumed that was the reason behind every word he and she exchanged.

Aurelia had grown restless. "We'd thought to ask no more than ten extra – those already here will stay."

"If you allow it," Margaret hurriedly added.

Aurelia's thin lips pressed together; she inclined her head. "Indeed. We thought . . ."

Tempting as it was to let them do more violence to their feelings, he'd much rather listen to Minerva gasping, sobbing, and moaning. He spoke over Aurelia. "Very well."

"You agree?" Margaret asked.

"Keep it within reason – nothing more than Mama used to do."

"Oh, we will." Aurelia's eyes lit, her face softening.

He didn't want to feel the spark of pity that flared as he looked at them; they were married, had position, houses, and families, yet still they were searching for . . . happiness. Nodding curtly, he turned on his heel. "Speak with Retford, then tell Minerva what you want to do. I'll warn her."

His sisters' thanks faded behind him as he strode into the keep proper.

Anticipation mounting, he headed for his rooms.

When, more than an hour later, he closed his hand about the knob of Minerva's door, frustration was riding him hard. He'd assumed she'd left the gathering early so she could slip into his rooms unseen; he'd expected to find her there, in his bed, waiting. As he'd walked through his sitting room, the image he'd expected to see had filled his mind . . .

Instead, for some misbegotten reason, she'd retired to *her* bed. Turning the knob, he stepped quickly inside and shut the door. She was leaning against the side of the window; arms folded, she'd been looking out at the night.

As he crossed the room, she pushed away from the window frame, with one hand pushed back the heavy fall of her hair, then delicately smothered a yawn. "I thought you'd be up earlier."

He halted before her; hands rising to his hips, he looked down at her. She appeared faintly tousled, her lids already heavy. He wanted nothing more than to haul her into his arms, but . . . "I *was* up earlier." He spoke quietly, but his tone made her blink. "I expected to find you gracing my bed. But you weren't there. Then I had to wait for all the others to go to their beds before I came here. I thought I'd made it plain *which* bed we'd be using."

She'd straightened; she narrowed her eyes on his. "That was last night. Correct me if I err" – her diction attained the same cutting precision as his – "but when engaged in an illicit liaison, it's customary for the gentleman to join the lady in her room. In *her* bed." She glanced at her bed, then looked pointedly at him.

Lips thinning, he held her gaze, then nodded curtly. "Perhaps. In this case, however −" He stepped smoothly around her and swept her up in his arms.

She gasped, clutched his coat, but didn't bother asking where he was taking her as he strode for the door.

He juggled her, reached for the knob.

"Wait! Someone might see."

"They're all in bed. Someone's bed." Enjoying themselves. "They won't be playing musical beds just yet." He grasped the knob.

"But I'll have to get back here in the morning! I never wander the corridors in just my robe."

He glanced around, and saw the coat stand in the corner. He carried her to it. "Get your cloak."

She did. Before she could raise any further objections he whisked her out of the door and strode across the wide gallery, then down the short corridor to his apartments. Deep shadows cloaked them all the way; he thought she sniffed as he heeled his sitting room door shut behind them, then carried her into his bedroom.

To his bed.

He dropped her on the crimson-and-gold counterpane, then looked down at her.

Narrow-eyed, she frowned at him. "Why is it so important we use your bed?"

"Because that's where I want you." Absolute truth − for once primitive instinct coincided with good strategy.

She heard his conviction. Opened her eyes wide. "*Why* for heaven's sake?"

Because she belonged there. As far as his primitive self was concerned, there was no question of that, and using his bed would subliminally underscore how he thought of her, what her true role vis-à-vis himself was − one front in his campaign to impress that true role on her. The usual events of castle life would further advance his cause, but the day had been unhelpfully quiet; he'd taken steps to ensure tomorrow would be different. Meanwhile . . .

250

Toeing off his shoes, he shrugged out of his coat and waist-coat, tossed both aside, then grasped her slender ankles and drew her toward him until her knees were at the edge of the bed. Leaving her calves and feet dangling, he caged her legs between his and leaned over her; setting his hands palms flat on either side of her shoulders, he trapped her widening eyes. "Because I want you here, naked in my bed, every night from now on. And I always get what I want."

She opened her mouth, but he had no interest in further discussion. He swooped and covered her lips with his, captured them, tasted them long and lingeringly, then dove into her waiting mouth.

Gloried in the welcome she was helpless to deny him; no matter what she thought, she was already his. Yet he found himself spending longer than he'd expected hotly wrestling for supremacy; despite her inexperience, she boldly challenged him, even though this was one battleground on which she could never hope to stand against him. Ruthlessly deploying skills he'd honed over decades, he drew forth her desire, lured her senses to him, then shackled them, subdued them, suborned them to his will.

So they were his to wield.

Only then did he ease back from the passion-laden exchange enough to shift his weight to one arm; with his other hand he grasped the tie of her robe.

Minerva couldn't believe how desperate she was – couldn't believe he'd so effortlessly reduced her to such a state of wanton yearning, where desire, hot and urgent, flowed swiftly down her veins, where passion spread beneath her skin, and smoldered more deeply within her.

Waiting to erupt, pour forth, and sweep her away.

She needed to feel his hands on her skin – needed to feel his body on hers.

Needed, with an urgent desperation she couldn't fathom, to feel him inside her, linked and joined with her.

And that need wasn't his; it was hers.

And it felt glorious.

Glorious to give herself up to the heat, to without reservation, or hesitation, wriggle and help him strip away her robe, help his clever hands divest her of her nightgown.

And then she lay naked on his brocaded bed – and she suddenly sensed one reason behind his insistence that he have her there.

She knew what sort of nobleman he really was – knew the impulses of a marcher lord still ran in his veins. Knew, sensed, had always on some level recognized the primitive sexual possessiveness and predatoriness that was an innate part of him. Unwrapped like a present, displayed naked on his bed, offered up for his delectation, his to use in whatever manner he wished . . . a subtle shiver wracked her – one part wholly feminine fear, the rest illicit excitement.

He sensed her awareness through the kiss, felt that evocative shiver; he closed one hand about her hip, anchoring her, his thumb cruising the sensitive skin of her stomach. His touch seared, branded; she knew he would brand her even more deeply before the night was out. That he intended just that.

Her breath hitched. Anticipation and a strange, unfamiliar need clashed, then washed, tumbling and jumbling, through her.

Leaning closer, he released her hip, coming down on one elbow to anchor her head between his large hands as he kissed her deeply, voraciously, ravenously, snaring her wits in a maelstrom of sensation. She had to engage with him; he gave her no option. Had to respond, to meet the challenge of his tongue, of his lips, of the hot wetness of his mouth.

Locked with her in the kiss, he speared his fingers into her hair, spread and drew them away from her head, letting the long tresses flow through his fingers, leaving them fanned to either side.

He seemed as fascinated with the silky texture of her locks as she was with his; instinctively she'd sunk her hands into his hair, feathering the dark silk with her fingers.

His body was close; hers sensed it and reacted, need swelling like a warm wave within, the rising tide a solid beat in her veins. His heat was near, yet muted by his clothes; he still had his shirt and trousers on.

She drew her hands from his hair, slid them down the long column of his throat, splayed her palms over his chest and ran them down until she could grip handfuls of his shirt and tug it free of his waistband. Succeeding, she ran her hands up under the loose fabric, palms and fingers greedy for the incomparable feel of his skin, hot and taut over the heavy ridges and planes of his magnificent chest.

All but purring, she let her senses feast; had she the time, she could have savored for hours, but that complex, complicated, increasingly urgent need pressed her on. Pressed her to run her hands down to his waistband, to find and release the buttons there.

She slipped only one free before he broke from the kiss, smoothly shifting to catch her hands, one in each of his.

"Later." He murmured the word against her throat, then set his lips to trace the arching line.

Hot, urgent, his mouth fired her senses. With nipping pecks, he captured her attention, effortlessly held it as with openmouthed kisses he branded her skin. Here, there, as he would.

She was heated and panting when he reached her breasts.

She was writhing and frantic when, after expertly claiming them, he moved on, his wicked lips trailing lower to explore her navel, then lower still, to the apex of her thighs.

By the time he drew back, grasped her knees and spread them wide, she was far beyond all modesty; she wanted nothing more than to feel him there, for him to take her, possess her, however he wished.

She felt his gaze on her face. Heated beyond measure, she sensed his command, hauled in a tight breath and cracked open her lids. Enough for him to catch her gaze, for her to see the dark promise in the depths of his eyes, then he looked down, at her body, displayed, wantonly wet and eager, slick and swollen, all but begging. For him.

Then he bent, set his mouth to her flesh and ripped every

sense she possessed away, ruthlessly took all she offered, all she had in her – then demanded more.

She sobbed and helplessly gave; as the second wave of unimaginable glory crashed through her veins, she screamed his name.

Even through the heated clouds of her release, she sensed his satisfaction.

Felt it in the touch of his hands as he rose, grasped her hips, and rolled her onto her stomach. He half lifted, half drew her toward him until her hips rested on the edge of the high mattress.

Awash in sensation, her skin flushed and damp, her wits still in abeyance, she wondered what . . . how . . .

He slid into her from behind, deep, then he pressed even deeper. She shuddered, gasped, felt her fingers close in the rumpled brocade cover. He gripped her hips and shifted her, positioned her, then he drew back, almost free of her clinging sheath, and thrust in again.

Hard. More powerfully.

Her breath puffed out on a shallow pant; her fingers tightened in the rough counterpane. He withdrew and thrust in again; eyes closing, she moaned. She could feel him high inside her, almost as if he were touching her lungs.

Then he settled to possess her, ruthlessly, relentlessly, thrusting deep and hard into her utterly willing body. Her wholly surrendered body. She moved fractionally under the force of the steady pounding, the subtle roughness of the brocade quickly becoming an excruciating abrasion against the peaks of her breasts.

Until she couldn't take any more. His hands locked about her hips, he held her captive for each forceful penetration. Her skin flaringly alive, she could feel his groin meet the globes of her bottom, feel his testes against the backs of her thighs as he pushed deep and deeper. The rough fabric of his trousers abraded her legs; the edge of his shirt drifted over her bare back.

A sudden vision of how they looked – her utterly naked, he mostly clothed – taking her like this, exploded in her mind.

Her senses let go. Unraveled, fragmented, flew apart in a shattering release of imploding heat and tension.

He continued to thrust into her, and the release went on and on . . . until she fell from the peak with one last smothered gasp, and the blessed void gathered her in.

Jaw clenched, Royce slowed. Eyes closed, head back, chest heaving, he clung to the last shreds of his will, of his control, and rode out the incredible ripples of sensation, the aftermath of her heightened release as her sheath contracted repetitively about him, and lured, begged, commanded him to lose himself in her.

He had other plans.

Deeper plans. Plans that came from that more primitive self that, when it came to her, he could no longer deny. Didn't want to deny.

When she finally slumped, her body utterly lax, he withdrew from her, shed his clothes in seconds, then lifted her. He stripped back the covers, then knelt on the bed and laid her down on her back, her head and shoulders cushioned by the plump pillows.

He seized the moment as he stretched alongside to drink in the sight – of her so utterly ravished, so surrendered, so possessed.

So his.

On the thought, he lifted over her, spread her thighs wide, and settled between. Covered her. Slid deeply into her, then lowered his head, captured her lips, and sank into her. Into her mouth, deep into her body, received within the silken embrace of her scalding sheath.

He started to ride her slowly, unhurriedly, senses wide, drinking in every iota of sensation. Of the inexpressible delight of her body cradling his, of her softness accepting his hardness, of the innumerable contrasts between their merging bodies.

His felt tight, nerves taut and flickering, seeking, wanting, needing. His mind was open, receptive, overwhelmingly aware of the breadth, depth, and incredible power of the need that swelled and welled inside him.

Then she joined him.

Her small hands found his face, framed it for a moment, then lowered to spread across his shoulders.

As the tempo of their joining inexorably rose, she gripped, clutched, her body undulating beneath his, dancing to a rhythm as old as time.

One he set, but she was with him, waltzing in the heat and the flames, in the scintillating fire of their shared passion.

And it was everything he'd wanted the moment to be – appeasement and acknowledgment, satiation and surrender, all in one.

She was everything he needed her to be – his lover, his bride, his wife.

His all.

In the moment when together they crested the last peak and found ecstasy waiting to claim them, he knew beyond question that he had all he needed of life in his arms. For this, she was the only woman for him, with him creating, then anchoring him in, this deeper, more heart-wrenching glory.

Submitting to him, surrendering to him.

Vanquishing him.

Now and forever.

The storm took them, and he surrendered, too, his fingers locked with hers as the fury of their joint passion wracked them, rocked them. Shattered and drained them, then left their senses to slowly fill again – with each other.

He'd never felt so close to any woman before, had never shared what he just had with any other.

When he finally summoned enough strength and will to move, he disengaged and lifted from her, then gathered her to him, into his arms, soothed when she came readily, snuggling close.

Through the darkness he touched his lips to her temple. "Sleep. I'll wake you in time to leave."

Her only reply was that her last lingering tension eased, then faded.

He closed his eyes and, utterly stated to the depths of his primitive soul, let sleep claim him.

Chapter 14

Royce woke her before dawn in predictable fashion; Minerva reached her room with barely enough time to fall into her bed and recover before Lucy arrived to draw back the curtains.

After washing and dressing, once again eschewing Lucy's assistance, she set about her usual routine with far more confidence than the day before. If Royce wanted her enough to insist she grace *his* bed, then he wasn't about to lose interest in her just yet. Indeed, if last night was anything to judge by, his desire for her seemed to be escalating, not fading.

She pondered that, and how she felt about it, over breakfast, then, leaving his sisters and their guests to their own devices, retreated to the duchess's morning room to prepare for their usual meeting in the study – and to consider what she might request of him.

If he could demand and insist on her physical surrender, then, she felt, some reward was her due. Some token of his appreciation.

When Jeffers arrived to summon her, she knew for what she would ask; the request would test Royce's desire, but who knew how long his interest would last? She should ask now; with Variseys it paid to be bold.

Jeffers opened the study door. Entering, she saw that Falwell,

257

as well as Handley, was present; the steward was sitting in the second chair before the desk.

Royce waved her to her usual seat. "Falwell has been describing the current state of the flocks and the clip. There appears to be some decline in quality."

"Nothing major, of course," Falwell quickly said, glancing, surprised, at Minerva. "Miss Chesterton has no doubt heard the farmers' rumblings –"

"Indeed." She cut off the rest of Falwell's justification for doing nothing over recent years. "I understand the problem lies in the breeding stock." Sitting, she met Royce's gaze.

"Be that as it may," Falwell said, "to get new breeding stock we'd have to go far south, and the expense –"

"Perhaps O'Loughlin could help?" She made the suggestion as innocently as she could. Royce had summoned her to join this discussion; presumably he wanted her opinions.

Falwell bridled; he didn't like Hamish, but then Hamish had no time for him.

He opened his mouth, but before he could speak, Royce did. "I'll speak to O'Loughlin next time I'm up that way. He might have some breeders we could buy."

Unsurprisingly, Falwell swallowed his words.

Royce glanced at the sheet on which he'd been making notes. "I need to speak with Miss Chesterton, Falwell, but if you would remain, once we've finished, you and I should look over the castle flocks."

Murmuring acquiescence, Falwell rose, and at Royce's direction retreated to a straight-backed chair against the wall.

Minerva inwardly cursed. She didn't want Falwell to hear her request.

"So what have we to deal with today?"

Royce's question refocused her attention. She looked down at her list, and swiftly went through Retford's warning that in the wake of the funeral they would need to replenish the cellar, and Cranny's request for new linens for the north wing bedrooms. "And while we're looking at fabrics, there are two rooms in the south wing that could use new curtains." Because of the castle's isolation, all such items were normally procured from London.

Royce looked at Handley as his secretary glanced up from his notes. "Hamilton can make himself useful – he knows what wines I prefer, and for the rest he could consult with my London housekeeper –" He glanced at Minerva.

"Mrs. Hardcastle," she supplied.

He looked at Handley. "Send a note to Hamilton about the wines and fabrics, and suggest he ask Mrs. Hardcastle to assist him with the latter. Regardless, he should purchase the materials subject to Miss Chesterton's and Mrs. Cranshaw's approval."

Handley nodded, swiftly scribbling.

"The curtains need to be damask, with apple-green the predominant color," Minerva said.

Handley nodded again.

Royce arched a brow at her. "Is there anything else?"

"Not about the household." She hesitated; she would have infinitely preferred not to have Falwell present, but she had to strike while this iron was hot. She drew breath. "However, there's a matter I've been meaning to bring to your attention."

Royce looked his invitation.

"There's a footbridge over the Coquet, further to the south, a little beyond Alwinton. It's been allowed to deteriorate and is now in very bad condition, a serious danger to all who have to use it –"

Falwell shot to his feet. "That's not on castle lands, Your Grace." He came forward. "It's Harbottle's responsibility, and if they choose to let it fall down, that's their decision, not ours."

Royce watched Falwell slant a glance at Minerva, sitting upright in her chair; her gaze was fixed on him, not the steward. Falwell tipped his head her way. "With all due respect to Miss Chesterton, Your Grace, we can't be fixing things beyond the estate, things that are in no way ours to fix."

Royce looked at Minerva. She met his eyes, and waited for his decision.

He knew why she'd asked. Other ladies coveted jewels; she

asked for a footbridge. And if it had been on his lands, he would have happily bestowed it.

Unfortunately, Falwell was unquestionably correct. The last thing the dukedom needed was to become seen as a general savior of last resort. Especially not to the towns, who were supposed to manage their responsibilities from the taxes they collected.

"In this matter, I must agree with Falwell. However, I will raise the matter, personally, with the appropriate authorities." He glanced at Handley. "Find out who I need to see."

"Yes, Your Grace."

He looked again at Minerva, met her gaze. "Is there anything else?"

She held his gaze long enough to make him wonder what was going through her head, but then she answered, "No, Your Grace. That's all."

Looking down, she gathered her papers, then stood, inclined her head to him, turned, and walked to the door.

As it closed behind her, he was already considering how to use the footbridge to his best advantage.

There was more than one way to skin a cat – Minerva wondered what approach Royce was considering. With the luncheon gong echoing through the corridors, she headed for the dining room, hoping she'd read him aright.

She hadn't been surprised by Falwell's comments; his role was to manage the estate as a business, rather than care for its people. The latter was in part her role, and even more so the duke's. Royce's. He'd said he would take up the issue – presenting her request more clearly in people terms might help. As she neared the dining room, Royce walked out of the parlor opposite. He'd heard her footsteps; he'd been waiting for her. He paused, met her gaze; when she reached him, without a word he waved her ahead of him through the dining room door.

The rest of the company were already at table, engrossed in a discussion of Margaret's and Susannah's plans for the six days remaining before the fair. She and Royce went to the laden side-board, helped themselves from the variety of cold meats, hams, and assorted delicacies displayed on the platters and dishes, then Royce steered her to the head of the table, to the chair beside his. Jeffers leapt to hold it for her.

By the time she'd sat and settled her skirts, Royce was seated in his great carver, by the angle of his shoulders, and the absolute focus of his attention on her, effectively cutting off the others – who read the signs and left them in peace.

They started eating, then he met her eyes. "Thank you for your help with the sheep."

"You knew Hamish was the best source for breeders – you didn't need me to tell you so."

"I needed you to tell Falwell so. If I'd suggested Hamish, he'd have tied himself in knots trying to acceptably say that my partiality for Hamish's stock was because of the connection." He took a sip from his wineglass. "But you aren't connected to Hamish."

"No, but Falwell knows I approve of Hamish."

"But not even Falwell would suggest that you – the farmers' champion – would urge me to get stock from anywhere that wasn't the best." Royce met her eyes, let his lips curve slightly. "Using you to suggest Hamish, having your reputation supporting the idea, saved time and a considerable amount of convoluted argument."

She smiled, pleased with the disguised compliment.

He let her preen for a moment, then followed up with, "Which raises a related issue – do you have any suggestions for a replacement for Falwell?"

She swallowed, nodded. "Evan Macgregor, Macgregor's third son."

"And why would he suit?"

She reached for her water glass. "He's young, but not too young, a gregarious soul who was born on the estate and knows – and is liked by – literally everyone on it. He was a scallywag when younger, but always good-hearted, and he's quick and clever – more than most. Now he's older, being the third son, and with Sean and Abel more than capable of taking on Macgregor's holding between them, Evan has too little to do." She sipped, then met his eyes. "He's in his late twenties, and is still helping on the farm, but I don't think he'll stay much longer unless he finds some better occupation."

"So at present he's wasted talent, and you think I should use him as steward."

"Yes. He'd work hard for you, and while he might make the odd mistake, he'll learn from them, and, most importantly, he'll never steer you wrongly over anything to do with the estate or its people." She set down her glass. "I haven't been able to say that of Falwell for more than a decade."

Royce nodded. "However, regardless of Falwell's shortcomings, I meant what I said about the footbridge being something the dukedom can't simply step in and fix."

She met his eyes, studied them, then faintly raised her brows. "So . . .?"

He let his lips curve in appreciation; she was starting to read him quite well. "So I need you to give me some urgent, preferably dramatic, reason to get on my ducal high horse and cow the aldermen of Harbottle into fixing it."

She held his gaze; her own grew distant, then she refocused – and smiled. "I can do that." When he arched a brow, she smoothly replied, "I believe we need to ride that way this afternoon."

He considered the logistics, then glanced at the others.

When he looked back at her, brows lifting, she nodded. "Leave them to me."

He sat back and watched with unfeigned appreciation as she leaned forward and, with a comment here, another there, slid smoothly into the discussions they had, until then, ignored. He hadn't noticed how she dealt with his sisters before; with an artful question followed by a vague suggestion, she deftly steered Susannah and Margaret – the ringleaders – into organizing the company to drive into Harbottle for the afternoon.

"Oh, before I forget, here's the guest list you wanted,

Minerva." Seated along the table, Susannah waved a sheet; the others passed it to Minerva.

She scanned it, then looked at Margaret, at the table's foot. "We'll need to open up more rooms. I'll speak with Cranny."

Margaret glanced at him. "Of course, we don't know how many of those will attend."

He let his lips curve cynically. "Given the . . . entertainments you have on offer, I suspect all those invited will jump at the chance to join the party."

Because they'd be keen to learn firsthand whom he'd chosen as his bride. Comprehension filled Margaret's face; grimacing lightly, she inclined her head. "I'd forgotten, but no doubt you're right."

The reminder that he would soon make that announcement, thus signaling the end of his liaison with her, bolstered Minerva's determination to act, decisively, today. While his desire for her was still rampant she stood an excellent chance of securing her boon; once it waned, her ability to influence him would fade.

Susannah was still expounding on the delights of Harbottle. "We can wander around the shops, and then take tea at the Ivy Branch." She looked at Minerva. "It's still there, isn't it?"

She nodded. "They still serve excellent teas and pastries."

Margaret had been counting heads and carriages. "Good – we can all fit." She glanced at Minerva. "Are you coming?"

She waved the list of guests. "I need to attend to this, and a few other things. I'll ride down later and perhaps join you for tea."

"Very well." Margaret looked to the table's head. "And you, Wolverstone?" Ever since he'd agreed to their house party, Margaret and Aurelia had been making an effort to accord him all due deference.

Royce shook his head. "I, too, have matters to deal with. I'll see you at dinner."

With that settled, the company rose from the table. Conscious of Royce's dark gaze, Minerva hung back, letting the others go ahead; he and she left the dining room at the rear of the group.

They halted in the hall. He met her eyes. "How long will you take?"

She'd been swiftly reviewing her list of chores. "I have to see the timber merchant in Alwinton – it might be best if you meet me in the field beyond the church at . . ." She narrowed her eyes, estimating. "Just after three."

"On horseback, beyond the church, at just after three."

"Yes." Turning away, she flung him a smile. "And to make it, I'll have to rush. I'll see you there."

Suiting action to her words, she hurried to the stairs and went quickly up – before he asked how she planned to motivate him to browbeat the aldermen into submission. The sharp jab she had in mind would, she thought, work best if he wasn't prepared.

After speaking with Cranny about rooms for the latest expected guests, and with Retford about the cellar and the depredations likely during the house party, she checked with Hancock over his requirements for the mill, then rode into Alwinton and spoke with the timber merchant. She finished earlier than she'd expected, so dallied in the village until just after three before remounting Rangonel and heading south.

As she'd expected, Royce was waiting in the designated field, both horse and rider showing their customary impatience. He turned Sword toward Harbottle as she ranged alongside. "Are you really planning on joining the others in Harbottle later?"

Looking ahead, lips curving, she shrugged lightly. "There's an interesting jeweler I could visit."

He smiled and followed her gaze. "How far is it to this footbridge?"

She grinned. "About half a mile." With a flick of her reins, she set Rangonel cantering, the big gelding's gait steady and sure. Royce held Sword alongside despite the stallion's obvious wish to run.

A wish shared by his rider. "We could gallop."

She shook her head. "No. We shouldn't get there too early."

"Why?"

"You'll see." She caught his disgruntled snort, but he didn't press her. They crossed the Alwin at the ford, water foaming about the horses' knees, then cantered on, cutting across the pastures.

A flash of white ahead was the first sign that her timing was correct. Cresting a low rise, she saw two young girls, pinafores flapping, books tied in small bundles on their backs, laughing as they skipped along a track that led down a shallow gully disappearing behind the next rise to their left.

Royce saw them, too. He shot her a suspicious, incipiently frowning glance, then tracked the pair as he and she headed down the slope. The girls passed out of sight behind the next rise; minutes later, the horses reached it, taking the upward slope in their stride, eager to reach the crest.

When they did, Royce looked down and along the gully – and swore. He hauled Sword to a halt, and grimly stared down.

Expressionless, she drew rein beside him, and watched a bevy of children crossing the Coquet, swollen by the additional waters of the Alwin to a turbulent, tempestuous, swiftly flowing river, using the rickety remnants of the footbridge.

"I thought there was no school in the area." His clipped accents underscored the temper he held leashed.

"There isn't, so Mrs. Cribthorn does what she can to teach the children their letters. She uses one of the cottages near the church." It was the minister's wife who had brought the execrable state of the footbridge to her attention. "The children include some from certain of Wolverstone's crofter families where the women have to work the fields alongside their men. Their parents can't afford the time to bring the children to the church via the road, and on foot, there is no other viable route the children could take."

The young girls they'd seen earlier had joined the group at the nearer end of the bridge; the older children organized the younger ones in a line before, one by one, they inched their way along the single remaining beam, holding the last horizontal timber left from the bridge's original rails.

Someone had strung a rough rope along the rail, giving the

children with smaller hands something they could cling to more tightly.

Royce growled another curse and lifted his reins.

"No." She caught his arm. "You'll distract them."

He didn't like it, but reined both himself and Sword in; drawing her hand from the rigid steel his arm had become, she knew how much it cost him.

Could sense how much, behind his stony face, he fumed and railed while being forced to watch the potential drama from a distance – a distance too great to help should one of the children slip and fall.

"What happened to the damned bridge, and when?"

"A bore last spring."

"And it's been like this ever since?"

"Yes. It's only used by the crofter children to get to the church, so . . ." She didn't need to tell him that the welfare of crofter children didn't rate highly with the aldermen of Harbottle.

The instant the last child stepped safely onto the opposite bank, Sword surged down the rise and thundered toward the bridge. The children heard; trudging over the field, they turned and looked, but after watching curiously for several minutes, continued homeward. By the time she and Rangonel reached the river, Royce was out of the saddle and clambering about the steep bank, studying the structure from below.

From Rangonel's back, she watched as he grabbed the remaining beam, using his weight to test it. It creaked; he swore and let go.

When he eventually climbed back up and came striding toward her, his expression was black.

The glare he bent on her was coldly furious. "Who are the aldermen of Harbottle?"

He knew she'd manipulated him; the instant he'd seen the two girls he'd known. Despite that, his irritation with her was relatively minor; he put it to one side and dealt with the issue of the rickety footbridge with a reined fury that brought vividly to mind ghosts from his ancestral past.

There was a wolf in the north again, and he was in a savage mood.

Even though she'd had high expectations, Minerva was impressed. Together they thundered into Harbottle; she introduced him to the senior alderman, who quickly saw the wisdom of summoning his peers. She'd stood back and watched Royce, with cutting exactitude, impress on those unwitting gentlemen first their shortcomings, then his expectations. Of the latter, he left them in absolutely no doubt.

They bowed and scraped, and swore they would attend to the footbridge expeditiously.

He eyed them coldly, then informed them he would be back in three days to view their progress.

Then he turned and stalked out; entirely satisfied, she followed.

Royce set a furious pace back to the castle. The dark look he cast her as he swung up to his saddle made it clear he hadn't forgotten her tweaking of his temper, but he'd wanted an urgent and dramatic reason to give him justification for browbeating the aldermen into fixing the footbridge, so she'd given him one. Her conscience was clear.

Something she suspected he realized, for even when they reached Wolverstone, left their horses with Milbourne, and started toward the castle, other than another of his piercing, dark looks, he said nothing.

By the time they reached the west wing and were approaching the turret stairs, she'd stopped expecting any reaction from him. She was deep in self-congratulation, pleased and eminently satisfied with her day's achievements, when his fingers locked about her elbow and he swung her into the shadowed hall at the bottom of the stairs. Her back met the paneled wall; he followed, pinning her.

Startled, her lips were parted when he crushed them beneath his and kissed her – filled her mouth, seized her wits, and stormed her senses.

It was a hard, bruising, conquering sort of kiss, one she responded to with damning ardor.

Her hands were sunk in the dark silk of his hair when he abruptly pulled back, leaving her gasping, her senses reeling.

From a distance of inches, his eyes bored into hers. "Next time, just *tell* me." A growled, direct order.

She hadn't yet regained breath enough to speak, managed to nod.

His eyes narrow, his lips grimly set, he drew back a little – as if realizing how hard it was for her to think with him so close. "Is there anything else that bad on my lands? Or not on my lands but affecting my people?"

He waited while she gathered her wits, and thought. "No."

He exhaled. "That's something, I suppose."

Stepping back, he drew her away from the wall, and urged her up the narrow stairs. She went, her heart beating just a little faster from knowing he was directly behind her and not in a predictable mood.

But when they reached the gallery, and she turned for her room, he let her go. He stepped up from the last stair, halted.

"Incidentally . . ." He waited until she paused and glanced back at him; he caught her eyes. "Tomorrow morning I'll want you to ride with me to Usway Burn – we can check on progress and I want to speak with Evan Macgregor."

She felt her brightest smile dawn, felt it light her eyes. "Yes, all right."

With a nod, he turned to his rooms.

Thoroughly pleased with her day, she continued to hers.

They next met in the drawing room, surrounded by the others all full of their day and their plans for the morrow. Walking into the large room, Royce located Minerva chatting in a group with Susannah, Phillip, Arthur, and Gregory. He met her eyes as Retford appeared behind him to announce dinner; stepping aside, he let the others go ahead, waiting until she joined him to claim her.

He wanted her with him, but hadn't yet decided what he wanted to say – or rather, how to say it. He sat her beside him; as he took his own seat at the table's head, she regarded him calmly, then turned to Gordon on her left and asked him about something.

The party had relaxed even further, all the members entirely comfortable in each other's company. He felt comfortable ignoring them all; sitting back, his fingers crooked about the stem of his wineglass, as the endless chatter flowed over and around him he let his gaze rest on his chatelaine's golden head while their day replayed in his mind.

All in all it had been a distinct success, yet he hadn't been – still wasn't – pleased by the way she'd evoked – deliberately and knowingly provoked – his temper over the bridge. He'd asked her to in a way, but he hadn't imagined she'd succeed to anything like the extent she had.

She had effectively manipulated him, albeit with his implied consent. He couldn't recall the last time anyone had successfully done so; that she had, and so easily, left him feeling oddly vulnerable – not a feeling with which he was familiar, one the marcher lord he truly was didn't approve of in the least.

However, against that stood the successes of the day. First in dealing with Falwell, then in deciding the steward's replacement, and lastly over the bridge. He'd wanted to illustrate one point, to demonstrate it in a way she, rational female that she was, couldn't fail to see, and between them they'd succeeded brilliantly.

Regardless . . . he let his gaze grow more intent, until she felt it and glanced his way. He shifted toward her; she turned back and excused herself to Gordon, then faced him and raised her brows.

He locked his eyes on hers. "Why didn't you simply tell me about the children using the bridge?"

She held his gaze. "If I had, the effect would have been . . . distanced. You asked for something dramatic, to give you something urgent to take to the aldermen – if you hadn't seen the children, but simply been told of them, it wouldn't have been the same." She smiled. "*You* wouldn't have been the same."

He wouldn't have felt like handing the aldermen their heads. He hesitated, then, still holding her gaze, inclined his head.

"True." Lifting his glass, he saluted her. "We make a good team."

Which was the point he'd been bent on illustrating.

He might tie her to him with passion, but to be sure of holding her he needed more. A lady like her needed occupation – an ability to achieve. As his wife, she'd be able to achieve even more than she currently could; when the time came, he wasn't going to be backward in pointing that out.

She smiled, lifted her glass, and touched the rim to his. "Indeed."

He watched her sip, then swallow, felt something in him tighten. "Incidentally . . ." He waited until her gaze returned to his eyes. "It's customary when a gentleman gives a lady a token of his appreciation, for that lady to show her appreciation in return."

Her brows rose, but she didn't look away. Instead, a faint – distinctly arousing – smile flirted about the corners of her lips. "I'll bear that in mind."

"Do."

Their gazes touched, locked; the connection deepened. Around them the company was in full voice, the bustle of the footmen serving, the clink of cutlery and the clatter of china a cacophony of sound and a sea of colorful movement swirling all about them, yet it all faded, grew distant, while between them that indefinable connection grew taut, gripped and held.

Expectation and anticipation flickered and sparked.

Her breasts swelled as she drew in a breath, then she looked away.

He glanced down, at his fingers curved about the bowl of the wineglass; setting it down, he shifted in his chair.

At least the company had tired of amateur theatricals; he inwardly gave thanks. The meal ended and Minerva left his side; he kept the passing of the port to the barest minimum, then led the gentlemen to rejoin the ladies in the drawing room.

After exchanging one look, he made no attempt to join her; with heightened passion all but arcing between them, it was simply too dangerous – not even this company were that blind.

Outwardly idly amiable, he chatted to some of his sisters' friends, yet he knew the instant Minerva slipped from the room.

She didn't return. He gave her half an hour, then left the garrulous gathering and followed her up the stairs into the keep. Slowing, he glanced at the shadows wreathing the corridor to her room, wondered, but then continued on. To his apartments, to his bedroom.

She was there, lying in his bed.

Halting in the doorway, he smiled, the gesture laden with every ounce of the predatory impulses coursing his veins.

She'd left no candles burning, but the moonlight streamed in, burnishing her hair as it rippled across his pillows, gilding the curves of her bare shoulders with a pearlescent sheen.

No nightgown, he noted.

She lay propped high amid the pillows; she'd been looking out at the moon-drenched night, but had turned her head to watch him. Through the dark, he felt her gaze slide over him – sensed anticipation heighten, tighten.

He remained where he was and let it build.

Let it grow and strengthen until, when he finally stirred and walked forward, it felt as if some invisible silken rope had looped around him and drew him on.

The sight of her lying there, a willing gift, a reward, racked the hunger within him up another notch, set a primitive thrum in his blood.

She was his for the taking. In whatever manner his ducal self decreed.

Her willing surrender was implicit in her silent waiting.

He walked to the tallboy by the wall. Shrugging off his coat, he tossed it on a nearby chair, unbuttoned his waistcoat as he planned how best to use the opportunity to further his aim.

To advance his campaign.

Undressing casually was an obvious first step; deliberately drawing out the moments before he joined her with an activity that underscored his intent would increase her already heightened awareness, of him and all he and she would shortly do.

Drawing the diamond pin from his cravat, he laid it on the tallboy, then unhurriedly unwound the linen band.

When he drew his shirt off, he heard her shift beneath the sheets.

When he tossed his trousers aside and turned, she stopped breathing.

His stride slow and deliberate, he walked to her side of the bed. For an instant, he stood looking down at her; her gaze slowly rose from his groin to his chest, then eventually to his face. Trapping her wide eyes, he reached for the covers, lifted them as he held out his hand. "Come. Get up."

Anticipation flashed through her, a sharp, fiery wave spreading beneath her skin. Her mouth dry, Minerva searched his face, all hard angles and shadowed planes, the unyielding, uninformative expression that simply stated: primitive male. She licked her lips, saw his eyes follow the small movement. "Why?"

His eyes returned to hers. He didn't answer, simply held the covers up, implacably held out his hand, and waited.

Cool air slipped beneath the raised sheets and found her skin. He, she knew, would be radiating heat; all she had to do to quell the shivers threatening was to stand and let him draw her near.

And then what?

An even bigger shiver of anticipation – a telltale sign he wouldn't miss – threatened to overwhelm her. Lifting her hand, she placed her fingers in his, and let him draw her out of the bed, off it and onto her feet.

He walked backward, drawing her with him, until they both stood within the shaft of silvery moonlight, until they were both bathed by the pale glow. Her breath suspended, trapped in her chest, she couldn't drag her eyes from him – a magnificent male animal, powerful and strong, every muscled curve, every ridge and line, etched in molten silver.

His fingers tightening on hers, he tugged her to him, drew her inexorably, irresistibly, into his arms. Into an embrace that was both cool and heated; his hands slid knowingly over her skin, assessing, caressing, as his arms slowly closed and trapped her, then cinched further, easing her against him, against the hot hardness of his utterly male frame.

His hands spread on her back, molded her to him; his dark eyes watched, drank in her expression as their bodies met, bare breasts to naked chest, her hips to his thighs . . . she closed her eyes and shivered.

The hard ridge of his erection seared like a branding rod against her taut belly.

She sucked in a breath, opened her eyes, only to find him closing the distance. His lips found hers, covered them, possessed them, not with any conquering force but with a languid passion, one all the more evocative, all the more compelling, for being so unhurried – a statement of intent he had no reason to make more stridently; she would be his however he wished – they both knew it.

The knowledge seeped into her even as she gave him her lips, then her mouth, then engaged in a hot, but undriven duel of tongues; she'd come to his room with the thought of rewarding him high in her mind. Rewarding him required no active action from her; she could simply let him take all he wished, follow his lead, and he'd be satisfied.

But would she?

Passivity wasn't her style, and she wanted this, tonight, to be a gift from her – something she gave him, not something she surrendered.

Because he wasn't whipping them along, the reins fast in his grasp, opportunity was hers for the taking. So she took – slid one hand between them and closed it firmly about the rod of his erection. Felt certainty bloom when he stilled, as if her touch held the power to completely distract him.

Taking advantage of the momentary hiatus, she eased her other hand down to join the first, linking them about his rigid member in tactile homage – and through the fading kiss sensed every last particle of his awareness center on where she held him.

Slowly breaking from the kiss, she moved her palms – watched his face, confirming that her touch, her caresses, possessed the power to capture him. His arms eased as his attention shifted; his hold on her weakened enough for her to ease back.

Far enough to look down, so she could see what she was doing and better experiment.

He'd let her touch him before, but then she'd been all but overwhelmed – there'd been so much of him to explore. Now, more familiar with his body, more comfortable standing naked before him, less distracted by the wonder of his chest, the heavy muscles of his arms, the long powerful columns of his thighs, no longer held in thrall by his lips, she could extend her explorations to what she most wanted to learn – what pleased him.

She stroked, then let her fingers wander; his chest swelled as he drew in a tight breath.

Glancing at his face, she saw his eyes, dark desire burning, glinting from beneath the thick fringe of his lashes. Took in his clenched jaw, the muscles taut with a tension that was slowly spreading through his body.

Knew he wouldn't let her play for long.

In a flash of recollection, she remembered a long-ago afternoon in London, and the illicit secrets shared by her wilder peers.

She smiled – and saw his gaze sharpen on her lips. Felt the rod between her hands jerk faintly.

Looking into those dark eyes lit by smoldering passion, she knew exactly what he was thinking.

Knew exactly what she wanted to do, needed to do, to balance the scales of give and take between them.

She took half a step back, lowered her gaze from his eyes to his lips, then ran it down the column of his throat and the long length of his chest, all the way down to where her palms and fingers were firmly locked about him, one hand above the other, one thumb cruising the sensitive edge of the broad bulbous head.

Before he could stop her, she sank to her knees.

Sensed his shock – compounded it by angling the stiff rod to her face, parting her lips, and sliding them over the luscious, delicate flesh, slowly taking him into the warm welcome of her mouth.

She'd heard enough of the theory to know what she should do; the practice was a trifle harder – he was large, long, and thick, but she was determined.

Royce finally managed to get his lungs to work, to haul in a desperate breath, but he couldn't drag his eyes from her, from the sight of her golden head bent to his groin as she worked her mouth over his straining erection.

The ache in his loins, in his balls and his shaft, intensified with every sweet lap of her tongue, every long, slow suck.

He felt he should stop her, bring the moment to a swift halt. It wasn't that he didn't like what she was doing – he loved every second of tactile delight, loved the sight of her on her knees before him, his shaft buried between her luscious lips – but . . . he neither expected nor generally had ladies service him in this way.

They were usually too exhausted after he'd had his way with them – and his way always came first.

He should, but wasn't going to, stop her. Instead, he accepted – accepted the pleasure she lavished on him, let his hands – hovering about her head – close, let his fingers tunnel through her silky hair and grip, gently guide . . .

She eased him deeper, then deeper still, until his engorged head was in her throat. Her tongue wrapped around his length and slowly rasped.

Chest swelling, eyes closing, he let his head tip back, fought to stifle a groan – fought to let her go on, to let her have her way.

To let her have him.

But there was only so far he could go. Only so much of the wet heaven of her mouth he could endure.

Her hands about the base of his shaft, she'd found her rhythm; her confidence had grown, and with it her dedication. Lungs screaming, nerves beyond taut, he fought to give her one more moment – then he forced himself to slip a thumb between her lips and draw his throbbing length from her mouth.

She looked up, licked her lips – started to frown.

He bent, gripped her waist, and lifted her – up and to him. "Wrap your legs about my waist."

She already was. He slid his hands down to grip her hips, positioned her so the heated head of his erection parted the scalding slickness of her folds and pressed against her entrance.

He looked at her face, caught her wide, desire-darkened eyes – watched as he drew her down, as he steadily, inexorably, impaled her. Watched her features ease, then blank, as her awareness turned inward to where he stretched her and filled her. Her lids lowered and she quivered in his arms, caught on the knife edge of surrender. He gripped more firmly, ruthlessly pulled her hips into his, tilting her so he could thrust the last inch and fill her completely.

Possess her completely.

He saw, felt, heard the breath shudder from her lungs. Shifting his grip, he took her weight on one arm, lifted his other hand to her face, framed her jaw, and kissed her.

Hungrily.

She surrendered her mouth, opened to his onslaught, and gave him, ceded to him, all he desired. For long moments, sunk in her body, he simply devoured, then she tried to move, tried to ease up and use her body to satisfy the rampant demand of his – and discovered she couldn't.

That she couldn't move at all unless he permitted it, that impaled as she was, she was wholly in his power.

That the rest of this script was entirely his to write – and hers to experience, to endure.

He showed her – showed her how he could lift her as little or as much as he wished, then lower her, as slowly or as rapidly as he wanted. That the power and depth of his penetration of her body was wholly his to decree.

That their journey to the top of the peak would be at his command.

She'd given herself to him, now he intended to take – all and everything he could from her.

He lifted her, and brought her down, one hand still at her nape, that arm wrapped about her body, pressing it to his so the movement of their joining made her breasts ride against his chest. With one arm about her hips, that hand spread beneath her bottom, her legs wrapped, now tight, about his waist, her arms slung around his shoulders, her hands spread on his back, he could feel her all around him, and she was wholly locked within his embrace.

A naked, primitive embrace that suited him well. That would deliver her to him – make her surrender to him – at an even deeper, more primal level.

Minerva drew back from the kiss on a gasping sob, head rising as, breasts swelling, she struggled to find breath.

He let her, then, hand firming at her nape, drew her back.

Kissed her again.

Took, seized, and devoured again.

His hands were suddenly much more demanding, their grip like fire, just this side of painful, elementally commanding as he moved her on him, against him, flayed her senses in every possible way inside and out until she wrenched back from the kiss, let her head fall back, and gave herself up to him.

To the fires that raged between them, building and growing, then erupting in molten passion so hot it seared and scalded, branded and marked.

Flames, hungry and greedy, rose up and washed over them, through them, spreading beneath their skins and consuming as the insistent, persistent, tempo of his possession escalated and claimed her anew.

Made her burn anew, made her fragment and scream, made her cling and sob as he joined her.

As, at the last, she felt him, hard and hot and undeniably real, undeniably him, buried deep within her, deeper than he'd ever been.

Deep enough to touch her heart.

Deep enough to lay claim to that, too.

The thought drifted through her mind, but she let it go, let it fade as he carried her to his bed, and collapsed with her across it.

Holding her against his heart.

At the very last, she heard him groan, "Especially in this, we make an *excellent* team."

Chapter 15

Two nights later, Minerva slipped into Royce's rooms, and gave thanks that Trevor was never there waiting. As per her recent habit, she'd left Royce and the rest of the company downstairs and slipped away – to come here, to his rooms, to his bed.

Walking into the now familiar bedroom, she found herself quietly amazed at how easy their liaison had become, how comfortable she'd grown over such a short time with the daily and nightly rhythms.

The last days had passed in a whirl of preparations, both for the house party and for the fair itself. As the major house in the district, the castle was always first in donating and participating, an association the household staff maintained regardless of the interest of their masters.

She'd always made time for the fair. Run under the auspices of the local church, the fair raised funds both for the upkeep of the church as well as for numerous projects for the betterment of the local flock. A flock the castle would always have a vested interest in, a fact she used to justify the expenditure of time and goods involved.

Stripping off her gown, she was aware of an unexpected contentment. Given Margaret's, Aurelia's, and Susannah's involvement this year, matters might have been much worse, but all was progressing smoothly on both the house party and the fair fronts.

Naked, her hair down around her shoulders, she lifted the crimson sheets and slid beneath the cool silk. If she was honest, her contentment, the depth of it, had a nearer, deeper, more powerful source. She knew their liaison would last for only a short while – in reality her time with him had to be more than half over – but rather than making her wary and reticent, rather than making her draw back from their engagements, the knowledge that her chance to experience all she might with him was strictly limited had served to spur her on. She was determined to live, whole and complete, to embrace the moment and seize the chance to be all the woman she could be, for however long his interest lasted. For however long he gave her.

It wouldn't be long enough for her to fall in love with him, for her to get trapped by unrequited emotion, and if she felt an unwelcome pang because she would never have the chance to know love in all its glory, she could accept and live with that.

She heard the sitting room door open, and close, heard his step on the floor – then he was there, powerful and dominant, literally darkening the doorway in the unlit room. He met her gaze; she sensed rather than saw his smile, his liking for the sight of her lying naked in his bed.

He moved forward, heading for his tallboy to undress; she literally licked her lips and waited. It was one of many individual moments she savored, watching him disrobe, watching his powerful body be revealed element by element to her hungry gaze.

Offered up, for her delectation.

He knew. She knew he did. Although he never gave any overt sign – never made any too obvious gesture or glanced at her to see how she was reacting – he artfully drew the moments out until, by the time he was naked and joined her in the bed, she was beyond desperate to get her hands on him.

To feel him against her, all that glorious muscle, all those heavy bones, to sense and feel the power inherent in his large frame.

To have that possess her, shatter her, and bring her unbounded, unfettered delight. Unrestricted, unrestrained pleasure.

She knew that was what would come to her as, finally naked, he crossed the room and lifted the sheets. She waited, breath bated, nerves taut, for that moment when the mattress sagged beneath his weight, and he reached for her, gathered her in, and their bodies met.

Skin to skin, heat to heat, desire to passion, wanting to yearning.

She came to him, and Royce drew her to him, half beneath him as he leaned over her. Her hand touched the side of his face, welcoming, encouraging, mirroring the messages her body gave as she sank against him, her softness molding instinctively to his hardness, giving against his heavier weight, cushioning and beckoning with sirenlike allure.

Without hesitation, without thought, he dove into her mouth, and found her waiting there, too. Waiting to engage, to meet and satisfy his every demand – to challenge him, did she but know it, with the ease with which she so effortlessly sated him.

Even after having her for more times than he'd ever had any woman, he still couldn't get enough of her – any more than he could solve the riddle of how having her had become such a bliss-filled act.

Why it so soothed his soul, both that of the man and that of the beast, the primitive being that lurked deep within him.

She embraced him all, and gave him surcease; in her arms he found an earthly heaven.

In search of it again, he drew his hand from her breast, reached down, caught her knee, and lifted it. Angling his hips, he nudged into her, then thrust deep. Seated fully within her, he rolled and settled fully upon her; wrapped in her arms and the billows of his bed, he savored her mouth as he savored her body, rocking them both with slow, deep thrusts, taking them both on a slow ride to paradise.

At the last, she clutched, arched beneath him as his name

ripped from her throat; he buried his head in the sweet curve of her shoulder and gave himself to her in a long, intense climax that rolled on and on.

Afterward, once he'd regained possession of sufficient wit to move, he lifted from her, settled beside her, and gathered her close, and she came, snuggling against him, her head on his shoulder, her hand on his chest, spread over his heart.

He didn't know if she knew she did that every night, that she slept with her hand just there. With her warmth against him and all tension released, he sank deeper into the mattress, and let the quiet joy he always found with her seep slowly to his bones. To his soul.

And wondered, again, why. Why what he found with her was so different. And why he felt as he now did about her.

She was the woman he wanted as his wife – so he'd let her close, closer than he'd ever let anyone else, and therefore she meant more than anyone else to him. He shouldn't be surprised that she awakened, called to, drew forth emotions no other ever had.

He'd never felt as possessive of any woman as he felt about her. Never felt as consumed by, as focused on, as connected to anyone as he did to her. She was rapidly becoming – had already become – someone he needed and wanted in his life forever . . .

What he felt for her, how he felt about her, mirrored how his friends felt about their wives.

Given he was a Varisey through and through – knew that to his bones – he didn't understand how that could be, yet it was. In his Varisey heart, he didn't approve of it – his feelings for her – any more than he approved of any other vulnerability; a vulnerability was a weakness, a chink in his armor – a sin for such as he. But . . . deep within was a yearning he'd only recently recognized.

His father's death had been the catalyst, the message he'd left with Minerva an unintended revelation. If he didn't need to be like his father in running the dukedom, perhaps he didn't need to be like him in other ways. Then his friends had arrived to comfort him, and had reminded him of what they'd found, what they had. And he'd seen his sisters and their Varisey marriages – and that hadn't been what he'd wanted, not anymore.

He now wanted a marriage like his friends had. Like his ex-colleagues of the Bastion Club had forged. That want, that need, had burgeoned and grown over the past nights, even more over the past days, until it was an ache – like a stomach-ache – lodged in his chest.

And in the dark of his bed in the depths of the night, he could admit that that want scared him.

He didn't know if he could achieve it – that if he reached for what he wanted, he could in fact secure it.

There were few arenas in life in which he doubted himself, but this newfound battleground was one.

Yet the one thing he now yearned for above all else was for the woman in his arms to love him. He wanted what his friends had found – lusted after her gentle affection if anything more intensely than he lusted after her body.

But if he asked for her love, and she gave it, she would ask for, and expect, his love in return. That's how love worked; that much he knew.

But he didn't know if he could love.

He could see that far, but no further.

If somewhere deep in his Varisey soul, so deep no other Varisey had ever found it, love lurked, a nascent possibility . . .

His problem was he didn't believe that was so.

"Ma'am?"

Minerva looked up from her desk in the duchess's morning room. "Yes, Retford?" The butler had entered and stood just inside the door.

"The Countess Ashton has arrived, ma'am – one of Lady Susannah's guests. Unfortunately, Lady Susannah is out riding."

Minerva inwardly grimaced. "I'll come down." Laying aside her pen, she rose. Royce had ridden over the border to visit Hamish, presumably to discuss sheep and the required breeders; she'd hoped to use the time to catch up with her correspondence, which she'd neglected of late.

But duty called.

She consulted the list lying on one side of her desk, then turned to the door. "We've put the countess in the west wing – I'm sure Cranny will have the room ready. Please ask her to send up a maid, or has the countess brought one?"

"No, ma'am." Retford retreated into the corridor. "I'll speak with Mrs. Cranshaw."

Retford followed at Minerva's heels as she went down the corridor and descended the main stairs. In the huge hall below, a lady, curvaceous and dark-haired, turned from examining her reflection in one of the large mirrors.

An extremely modish hat sat atop Lady Ashton's sleek head. Her carriage gown was the latest in fashionable luxury, beautifully cut from ivory silk twill with magenta silk trimming; the skirts swished as, an easy smile curving delicately tinted lips, her ladyship came forward to meet Minerva.

Stepping down from the last step, Minerva smiled. "Lady Ashton? I'm Miss Chesterton – I act as chatelaine here. Welcome to Wolverstone Castle."

"Thank you." Of similar height to Minerva, Lady Ashton possessed classical features, a porcelain complexion, and a pleasant, confident demeanor. "I gather Susannah is out gadding about, leaving me to impose on you."

Minerva's smile deepened. "It's no imposition, I assure you. It's been some years since the castle hosted a house party – the household is quite looking forward to the challenge."

The countess tilted her head. "House party?"

Minerva hesitated. "Yes – didn't Susannah mention it?"

A faint smile on her lips, the countess glanced down. "No, but there was no reason she should. She invited me to another end."

"Oh." Minerva wasn't sure what was going on. "I'm sure Susannah will tell you about the party when she returns. Meanwhile, if you'll come this way, I'll show you to your room."

The countess consented to climb the stairs beside her. Halfway up, she grew aware of Lady Ashton's sideways glance, and turned her head to meet it.

Her ladyship pulled a wry face. "I didn't like to ask the butler, but is Royce – I suppose I should call him Wolverstone, shouldn't I? Is he about?"

"I believe he's out riding at present."

"Ah." The countess looked ahead, then shrugged. "He'll have to cope with us meeting again with others about, then – or if you see him, you might mention I'm here. Susannah sent for me well over a week ago, but I wasn't in London, so it's taken a while for me to arrive."

Minerva wasn't sure what to make of that. She fastened on the most pertinent fact. "You know Royce."

The countess smiled, her face transforming into that of a stunning seductress. "Yes, indeed." Her voice lowered to a purr. "Royce and I know each other very well." She glanced at Minerva. "I'm sure that's no real surprise to you, my dear – you must know what he's like. And while it was Susannah who penned the invitation to me, she made it clear it was for Royce that she summoned me."

A cold, iron fist gripped Minerva's heart; her head spun. "I . . . see." The countess must be the lady Royce had chosen. Yet Susannah had asked if Minerva knew . . . but perhaps that was before he'd had Susannah write to the countess.

But why Susannah, rather than Handley?

And surely the countess was married . . . no, she wasn't; Minerva recalled hearing that the Earl of Ashton had died several years ago.

They'd strolled past the short corridor to the ducal apartments and into the west wing. Halting before the door of the room the countess had been assigned, Minerva dragged in a breath past the constriction banding her chest, and turned to her ladyship. "If you would like tea, I can have a tray brought up. Otherwise, the luncheon gong will ring in about an hour."

"I'll wait, I think. I take it Wolverstone will return for lunch?"

"I really can't say."

"No matter – I'll wait and see."

"The footmen will bring up your trunk. A maid will be with you shortly."

"Thank you." With an inclination of her head and a perfectly gracious smile, the countess opened the door and went inside.

Minerva turned away. Her head was spinning, but that was the least of it. She literally felt ill . . . because her heart was chilled and aching – and it wasn't supposed to be.

Neither Royce nor Susannah nor the rest of the company returned for luncheon, leaving Minerva to entertain the countess by herself.

Not that that was a difficult task; Lady Ashton – Helen as she asked to be called – was an extremely beautiful, sophisticated lady with an even temperament, gracious manners, and a ready smile.

No matter the circumstances, no matter the sudden agonies of her foolish, foolish heart, no matter her instinctive inclination, Minerva found it difficult to dislike Helen; she was, in the very essence of the word, charming.

Leaving the dining room, Helen smiled rather wistfully. "I wonder, Minerva, if I may truly impose on you and ask for a quick tour – or as quick a tour as can be – of this enormous pile?" She looked up at the vaulted ceiling of the front hall as it opened before them. "It's rather daunting to consider . . ."

She trailed off, shot a look at Minerva, then sighed. "I've never been much of a hand at subterfuge, so I may as well be plain. I have no idea where I stand with Royce, and I freely admit to a certain nervousness – which is really not my style."

Minerva frowned. "I thought . . ." She wasn't at all sure what to think. She led the way to the principal drawing room.

The countess strolled beside her. As they paused inside the long formal room, Helen continued, "I assume you know of his inviolable rule – that he never spends more than five nights with any lady?"

Expressionless, Minerva shook her head. "I hadn't heard."

"I assure you it's true – there are any number of ladies within the ton who can attest to his refusal to bend on that score, no matter the inducement. Five nights are all he allows any woman." The countess grimaced. "I suppose it was one way to ensure none of us ever got any ideas, as one might say, above our station."

Surreptitiously, Minerva counted on her fingers; last night had been her fifth – and therefore last – night. She hadn't even known. Inwardly reeling, she stepped back into the hall, then led the way toward the formal dining room.

Helen kept pace. "I was his lover before he left London – for just four nights. I hoped for a fifth, but then he disappeared from town. Later I heard about his father's death, and so believed our liaison was over – until I received Susannah's note. She seemed to think . . . and then I heard about the grandes dames and their decree, but no announcement came . . ." She glanced at Minerva. "Well, I did wonder." She shrugged. "So here I am, come to throw my hat in the ring, if there is a ring, that is. But he does have to marry, and we get along well enough . . . and I do want to marry again. Ashton and I weren't in love, but we liked each other. There's a great deal to be said for companionship I've discovered, now I no longer have it."

Helen gave a cynical laugh. "Of course, all depends on the whim of one Royce Varisey, but I thought he should know that he does have alternatives to the giddy young misses."

Thrusting her reeling emotions deep and slamming a mental door on them, Minerva forced herself to consider Helen's words. And who was she to answer for Royce? For all she knew, he might feel some real connection to Helen; it wasn't hard to picture her on his arm, as his duchess.

Dragging in a breath, she held it, then managed a mild smile. "If you like, I can show you around the main areas of the castle." As Royce had to marry someone, she'd rather it was Helen than some witless miss.

*

Later that evening, Minerva sat midway down the long dining table, conversing blithely with those around her while surreptitiously watching Helen sparkle, effervesce, and charm from her position at Royce's left.

The lovely countess had usurped her place there, and, it seemed, had displaced her in other ways, too. Royce hadn't spared so much as a glance for her since he'd walked into the drawing room and laid eyes on Helen, a stunning vision in rose-pink silk.

Feeling dull and drab in her weeds, she'd stood by the wall and watched, no longer sure of where *she* stood with Royce, and utterly unsure what to do.

She'd started her tour with Helen imagining there was, in the matter of Royce's bride, no worse candidate than a giddy young miss. After an hour of listening to Helen's views on the castle and the estate, and most importantly its people, she'd revised that opinion.

Helen would never rule as Royce's duchess at Wolverstone. Quite aside from all else, she didn't want to. She'd assumed Royce would spend most of his time in London, but he'd already declared he would follow in his father's and grandfather's – and even great-grandfather's – footsteps. His home would be here, not in the capital.

When she'd mentioned that, Helen had shrugged, smiled, and said, "We'll see." Helen couldn't imagine she would change Royce's mind, which had left Minerva wondering just what sort of marriage Helen envisioned – quite possibly one that might well suit Royce.

Which would compound the more serious problem, namely that Helen had absolutely no feeling for, no empathy with, the estate in general, much less the people on it. She'd already hinted that she assumed Minerva would stay on as chatelaine. Minerva couldn't, wouldn't, but she'd always imagined handing her keys to some woman with a heart, with compassion and interest in her staff and the wider community of which the castle was the hub.

Glancing up the table again, she saw Royce, lips subtly

curving, incline his head to the countess in response to some sally. Forcing her gaze to Rohan, seated opposite her, she smiled and nodded; she hadn't heard a word of his latest tale. She had to stop torturing herself; she had to be realistic – as realistic as the countess. But what did reality demand?

On a purely worldly level, she ought to step quietly aside and let Helen claim Royce, if he was willing. She'd already had her five nights with him, and, unlike her, Helen would make him an excellent wife within the parameters he'd set for his marriage.

On another level, however, one based on the emotional promptings of her witless heart, she'd like to haul Helen away and send her packing; she was wrong – all wrong – for the position of Royce's bride.

Yet when she rose and, with the other ladies, filed behind Margaret to the door, she let her senses open wide . . . and knew Royce didn't even glance at her. In the doorway, she glanced swiftly back, and saw the countess very prettily taking her leave of him; his dark eyes were all for her.

Minerva had had her five nights; he'd already forgotten her existence.

In that instant, she knew that no matter how much of a fool she would think him if he accepted Helen's transparent invitation and offered her his duchess's coronet, she wouldn't say a word against his decision.

On that subject, she could no longer claim to hold an unbiased opinion.

Turning away, she wondered how long she would have to endure in the drawing room until the tea tray arrived.

The answer was, a lot longer than she wanted. More than long enough to dwell on Royce's iniquities; from his continuing obliviousness, her time with him had come to an absolute end – he'd just forgotten to tell her. The fiend.

She was in no good mood, but clung to the knots of others as they chatted about this and that, and hid her reaction as best she could; there was no value in letting anyone else sense or suspect. She wished she didn't have to think about it herself, that she could somehow distance herself from the source of her distress, but she could hardly cut out her own heart. Contrary to her misguided hopes and beliefs, she could no longer pretend it had escaped involvement.

There was no other explanation for the deadening feeling deep in her chest, no other cause for the leaden lump that unruly organ had become.

Her own fault, of course, not that that made the dull twisting pain any less. She'd known from the start the dangers of falling in love – even a little bit in love – with him; she just hadn't thought it could happen so quickly, hadn't even realized it had.

"I say, Minerva."

She focused on Henry Varisey as he leaned conspiratorially close.

His gaze was fixed across the room. "Do you think the beautiful countess has any chance of learning what no one else yet has?"

It took a moment to realize he was alluding to the name of Royce's bride. She followed Henry's gaze to where Helen all but hung on Royce's arm. "I wish her luck – on that subject he's been as close-mouthed as an oyster."

Henry glanced at her, arched a brow. "You haven't heard anything?"

"Not a hint – no clue at all."

"Well." Straightening, Henry looked back across the room. "It appears our best hopes lie with Lady Ashton."

Assuming Lady Ashton's wasn't the name in question . . . Minerva frowned; Henry, at least, didn't see Helen as even a possibility as Royce's chosen bride.

Across the room, Royce forced himself to keep his gaze on Helen Ashton, or whoever else was near, and not allow his eyes to deflect to Minerva, as they constantly wanted to. He'd walked into the drawing room before dinner, anticipating another delightful evening of enjoying his chatelaine, only to find himself faced with Helen. The very last woman he'd expected to see.

He'd inwardly sworn, plastered on an unruffled expression, and battled not to seek help from the one person in the room he'd actually wanted to see. He had to deal with Helen first. An unwanted, uninvited irritation; he hadn't understood why the hell she was there until he'd heard her story.

Susannah. What the hell his sister had been thinking of he had no clue. He'd find out later. For that evening, however, he had to toe a fine line; Helen and too many others – all those who knew she'd been his recent mistress – expected him to pay attention to her now she was there.

Because as far as they knew, he hadn't had a woman in weeks. He didn't have a mistress at Wolverstone. True, and yet not.

With everyone watching him and Helen, if he so much as glanced at Minerva, someone would see – and someone would wonder. While he was working toward making their connection public through getting her to convince herself to accept his suit, he wasn't yet sure of success, and had no intention of risking his future with her because of his ex-mistress.

So he had to bide his time until he could confirm Helen's status directly with her. As she was the senior lady present, he'd had no choice but to escort her into dinner and seat her at his left – in some ways a boon, for that had kept Minerva at a distance.

He hoped – prayed – she would understand. At least once he explained . . .

He wasn't looking forward to that conversation, but then again, Minerva knew him very well. She would hardly be shocked to learn that Helen had been his mistress, and was now his *ex*-mistress. In their world, it was the *ex*- that counted.

Even with his outward attention elsewhere, he knew when Minerva left the room. A quick glance confirmed it, and sharpened the inner spur that impelled him to follow her.

But he had to settle matters with Helen first.

And Susannah. His sister swanned past beyond Helen; she caught his eye – no difficulty as it was fixed on her – and winked. Hiding his reaction behind an easy expression, he left

Helen to her conversation with Caroline Courtney; reaching out he closed his fingers about Susannah's elbow and drew her with him as he strolled a few paces.

Once they were sufficiently apart to speak privately, he released her and looked down as she looked up at him.

She smiled with childlike – childish – delight. "Well, brother dear, are you happier now?"

He read her sincerity in her eyes. Inwardly sighed. "Actually, no. Helen and I parted when I left London."

Susannah's face fell almost comically. "Oh." She looked thoroughly disconcerted. "I had no idea." She glanced at Helen. "I thought . . ."

"If I might ask, what, exactly, did you tell her?"

"Well, that you were here and alone, and having to make this dreadful decision of who to wed, and that if she came up, perhaps she might make your life easier, and, well . . . *those* sort of things."

Royce inwardly groaned, then sighed through his teeth. "Never mind. I'll speak with her and straighten things out."

At least he now knew his instincts had been right; Helen wasn't there to share just a night of passion. Thanks to Susannah's poor phrasing, Helen now harbored higher aspirations.

He let Susannah, rather subdued, go and returned to Helen's side, but had to wait until everyone else finally decided to retire to take her to a place where they could speak privately.

Leaving the drawing room at the rear of the crowd, he touched Helen's arm, and indicated the corridor leading away from the hall. "This way."

He led her to the library.

She passed through the door he held open for her, and came to a momentary halt; she was too experienced not to realize the significance of the venue. But then her spine straightened, and she walked further into the room. He followed and closed the door.

A candelabra on the mantelpiece was alight; a small fire blazed cheerily in the hearth. He waved Helen to the wingchair to one side of the hearth. She walked ahead of him to the fireplace, but then swung to face him, hands clasped before her, fingers twining.

She opened her mouth, but he held up a hand, staying her words.

"First, let me say that I was surprised to see you here – I had no idea Susannah had written to you." Halting on the other side of the hearth, he held Helen's blue gaze. "However, courtesy of what my sister wrote, I accept that you may be laboring under a misapprehension. To clarify matters –" He broke off, then let his lips twist cynically. "To be brutally frank, I'm currently negotiating for the hand of the lady I've chosen as my duchess, and am entirely uninterested in any dalliance."

And if she'd thought she had any chance at a more permanent connection, she now knew better.

To give her her due, and as he'd expected, Helen absorbed the reality well. She was a natural survivor in their world. Her eyes on his face, she drew a long breath as she digested his words, then she inclined her head, her lips twisting in a rueful grimace. "Good Lord – how very . . . awkward."

"Only as awkward as we wish to make it. No one will be surprised if we amicably part and move on."

She thought, then nodded. "True."

"I will, naturally, do everything within my power to ensure you're not made uncomfortable while here, and I hope, in the future, you will continue to regard me as a friend." He continued to hold her gaze, entirely confident she would understand the offer behind his words, and value it accordingly.

She didn't disappoint him. She was far from stupid, and if she couldn't have him as either lover or husband, then having him as a powerful, well-disposed acquaintance was the next best thing. Again she inclined her head, this time in a deeper obeisance. "Thank you, Your Grace." She hesitated, then lifted her head. "If it would not inconvenience you, I believe I'll remain for a few days – perhaps for the house party."

He knew about saving face. "By all means."

Their interview was at an end; he waved her to the door, falling in beside her as she walked down the room.

He halted before the door, waited until she looked at him. "If I might ask, was it purely distraction you came up to Northumberland to offer, or . . . ?"

She smiled. "Susannah apparently believed I had some chance of becoming your duchess." She met his eyes. "To be perfectly honest, I didn't think it likely."

"I apologize for Susannah – she's younger than I, and doesn't, in fact, know me as well as she thinks she does."

Helen laughed. "No one knows you as well as they think they do." She paused, then smiled – one of her gloriously charming smiles. "Good night, Royce. And good luck with your negotiations."

Opening the door, she went out.

Royce watched the door close behind her; he stood staring at the panels, his mind immediately refocusing on the one burning issue dominating his current existence – his negotiations with the lady he'd chosen as his duchess.

His campaign to ensure Minerva said yes.

Minerva lay alone in her bed – a perfectly good bed she'd slept comfortably in for years and years, but which now seemed entirely lacking.

She knew what was missing, what lack it was that somehow made it impossible to fall asleep, but why the simple presence of a male body over a handful of days should have made such a deep impression on her psyche to the extent she – her body – fretted at his absence, she simply could not comprehend.

If her body was restless, her mind was even more so. She had to stop thinking about all she'd learned – had to stop wondering if Helen had actually meant five interludes, or five intimacies; on both counts she and Royce had exceeded the limit. Yet perhaps he, being male, simply counted nights?

The deadening truth she had to accept was that according to his immutable rule – and she could see why he, heir to a massively wealthy and powerful dukedom, had instituted such a rule and stuck by it – her time with him had come to an end.

It was just as well Helen had arrived and explained; at least now she knew.

Sitting up, she pummeled her pillow, then slumped down and pulled the covers over her shoulders. She closed her eyes. She had to get some sleep.

She tried to compose her features, but they wouldn't relax. Her frown refused to smooth away.

In her heart, her gut, everything felt wrong. So utterly wrong.

The click of her door latch had her opening her eyes. The door swung inward – rather violently – then Royce was in the room, shutting the door forcefully, but silently.

He stalked to the bed. Halting beside it, he looked down at her; all she could see of his expression was that his lips were set in a grim line.

"I suppose I should have expected this." He shook his head, and reached for the covers.

He tugged. She clutched them tighter. "Wh –"

"Of course, I'd hoped my edict that you're supposed to be in *my* bed might have been strong enough to hold, but apparently not." His accents were clipped, a sure indication of strained temper. He jerked the covers from her grip and flung them off her.

He stopped and stared down at her. "Heaven preserve me, we're back to nightgowns."

The disgust in his voice would, in other circumstances, have made her laugh. She narrowed her eyes at him, then dove to scramble off the other side of the bed – but he was too fast.

He caught her, hauled her to him, then hoisted her in his arms.

He started for the door.

"Royce!"

"Shut up. I'm not in a good mood. First Susannah, then Helen, now you. Misogyny beckons."

She glanced at his face, at his adamantine expression, and

shut her lips. As she couldn't prevent him from carrying her to his room, she would argue once they got there.

He paused by the coat rack. "Grab your cloak."

She did and quickly flicked the folds over her; at least he'd remembered that.

He juggled her, opened her door, softly shut it behind them, then carried her swiftly through the shadows to his apartments, and on into his bedroom. All the way to his bed.

She pinned him with a stony glare. "What about the countess?"

Halting beside the bed, he met her gaze, his own hard. "What about her?"

"She's your mistress."

"*Ex*-mistress. The *ex-* is important – it defines that relationship."

"Does she know that?"

"Yes, she does. She knew it before she came here, and I've just confirmed for her that the situation hasn't changed." He'd held her gaze throughout. "Any more questions on that subject?"

She blinked. "No. Not at the moment."

"Good." He tossed her on the bed.

She bounced once. Before she could grab it, he whipped her cloak off and flung it across the room.

He paused, then stepped back. His hands going to his coat buttons, he toed off his shoes; his eyes on her, he shrugged out of his tight-fitting evening coat, then pointed at her nightgown. "Take that off. If I do, it won't survive."

She hesitated. If she was naked, and so was he, rational discussion wouldn't be high on his agenda. "First –"

"Minerva – take off the gown."

Chapter 16

Minerva – take off the gown.

The words resonated in the dimness between them. He'd packed them with more distilled power, more direct command, than he'd ever used with her before; his tone filled her female ears with primitive threat, and unstated promise.

A not-at-all-subtle reminder that he was the sort of nobleman no one even thought to deny. Certainly no woman. Of their own volition, her fingers shifted on the fine fabric draping her legs.

She realized and stilled them, then, hauling in a breath through lungs suddenly tight, sat up, curling her legs, faced him, and narrowed her eyes on his. "No." She set her jaw, if not as hard, then at least as belligerently as he. "You didn't so much as glance at me all evening, and now you want to see me naked?"

His implacability eased not one jot. He drew his cravat off, and dropped it. "Yes." A heartbeat passed. "I didn't glance at you – and I'm well aware it was for the whole damned evening – because everyone, literally everyone, was watching *me*, watching to see me and Helen, my recent mistress, interact, and if instead I'd looked at you, everyone else would have, too. And then they'd have wondered why – why instead of looking at my recent mistress I was looking at you. And not being entirely devoid of intelligence, they'd have guessed, correctly, that my distraction with you at such a moment was because *you're* sharing my bed."

He shrugged off his waistcoat. "I didn't look your way once the entire evening because I wanted to avoid the speculation I knew would ensue, and I know you won't like." He looked down as he dropped the waistcoat on top of his coat; he paused, then lifted his head and met her eyes. "I also didn't want my cousins getting any ideas about you – and they would if they knew you were sharing my bed."

Truth – all truth. She heard it ring in every clipped, precise vowel and consonant. And the thought of his cousins approaching her – all the males were as sexually aggressive as he – had been the prod that had affected him most powerfully.

Before she could consider what that might mean, with a barely restrained tug he pulled his shirttails from his waistband.

His gaze lowered to her body, to the offending nightgown. "Take that damned gown off. If it's still on you when I reach you, I'm going to shred it."

Not a warning, not a threat, not even a promise – just a pragmatic statement of fact.

He was barely two yards away. She mentally threw up her hands and turned to draw the covers down so she could slip beneath them.

"No. Stay where you are." His voice had lowered, deepened; his tone sent a primitive thrill racing up her spine. He spoke increasingly slowly. "Just take the gown off. Now."

She turned back to face him. Her lungs had constricted again. She drew in a tight breath, then reached for the hem of the fine lawn gown, and drew it up, exposing her calves, her knees, her thighs, then, still sitting, her eyes locked on him, she wriggled and tugged until the long gown was bunched around her waist.

The roughness of his brocade counterpane rasped the bare skin of her legs and bottom – and she suddenly had an inkling of why he might want her naked *on* the bed, rather than in it.

And she wasn't about to argue.

297

From the waist down, she was no longer sheathed in the gown, but the folds shielded her hips and stomach, and all the rest of her, from his gaze.

Her mouth suddenly dry, she swallowed, then said, "Take off the shirt, and I'll take off the gown."

His gaze lifted from her naked thighs, locked with hers for an instant, then he grabbed the hem of his shirt and hauled it up and over his head.

She seized the instant – the barest fleeting instant – to drink in the arresting, arousing sight of his heavily muscled chest. Then he tore his hands free of the sleeves, dropped the shirt. His fingers reaching for the buttons at his waist, he stepped toward the bed.

Grabbing the folds of her nightgown, she hauled it up and off.

He was on her before she could pull her hands free. In a surging, muscled wave, he flattened her back on the bed.

Before she could blink she was stretched naked on her back across the crimson-and-gold brocade, with him stretched over her, one heavy hand locked about her tangled ones, pinning them, leaving her with her arms stretched out above her head.

Lifting off her, he set his hip alongside hers; leaning on the arm holding her hands captive, he looked down on her body as she lay displayed, naked and helpless, for his delectation.

For his taking.

Raising his free hand, he set it to her flesh. Used it to quickly, efficiently, ruthlessly arouse her until she writhed, until her body lifted and arched helplessly into that too-knowing hand, seeking, wanting.

His hand cupped between her thighs, working the slick, swollen folds, with two long fingers buried in her sheath stroking deeply, he lowered his head and set his mouth to one breast.

He licked, lipped, nipped, then drew her furled nipple deep into his mouth and suckled so fiercely, body bowing, she shrieked.

Releasing her tortured flesh, he glanced at her face, caught her gaze, and thrust his fingers deep inside her – watched as she gasped and instinctively lifted her hips, wanting to, straining to, reach completion.

Through the pounding of her heartbeat in her ears, she heard him mutter something deep, dark, and guttural – she couldn't make out the words.

Her skin was so flushed, so excruciatingly sensitive, she felt like she was burning – literally burning with unslaked desire. Bare minutes had passed since he'd spread her beneath him on the bed, yet he'd reduced her to this – to needing him inside her more than she needed to breathe.

His fingers withdrew from her. She opened eyes she hadn't known she'd closed as he moved over her.

She tugged, wanting her hands free, but his hold didn't ease.

"Later," he ground out.

Then his body came down on hers and her lungs seized.

He was naked to the waist – the hair on his chest abraded her breasts, keeping her nipples painfully erect – but he still had his trousers on. The woolen fabric, finest worsted though it was, rasped the bare skin of her legs, made her gasp as it scraped along her inner thighs as with his legs he spread hers wide and wedged his hips between.

The skin on her back had already come alive, teased by the roughly textured counterpane. Her senses reeled under the concerted impact of so much sensory stimulation – of his weight pinning her to the bed, of the anticipation that soared as she felt him reach between her thighs and release his erection.

He set the broad head at her entrance, then gripped her hip, and thrust powerfully into her. Filled her with one long, forceful stroke, then withdrew and thrust in even more deeply.

He held her down and rode her, with long, powerful, pounding strokes; every thrust shifted her fractionally beneath him, every inch of her skin, every nerve, abraded each and every time.

Royce watched her, watched her body undulate beneath him, taking him in, wanting and accepting. He watched her face, saw passion overtake desire, saw it build and sweep her up, catch her in its heated coils, saw them tighten, gripping, driving.

He waited until she was nearing the peak. Releasing her hip, he closed his hand about her breast, lowered his head and took her mouth, claimed her, possessed her, there, too, as his body drove hers on.

She came apart beneath him more intensely than ever before.

Minerva gasped, sobbed as her world fractured, but the climax rolled on and on. He kept it going, thrusting deep within her, making her body shift slightly against the abrading fabrics, keeping her nerves flaring even as inner satiation swept through her.

It was like nothing they'd shared before. More blatant, more powerful.

More possessive.

She wasn't entirely surprised when, after she'd slumped, spent and done, yet with her nerves and senses still alive, still flickering, he slowed, then stopped and withdrew from her.

He left the bed, but she knew he wasn't done with her yet; he hadn't yet claimed his release. From the sounds that reached her, he was dispensing with his trousers.

Eyes closed, she lay sprawled, naked and ravished, across his bed and waited. She hadn't freed her hands from her night-gown, couldn't yet summon the energy.

And then he was back.

He knelt on the bed, grasped her hips, and flipped her over. She rolled bonelessly, wondering how . . . Straddling her legs, he slid one large hand down and around to splay over her lower belly, then he lifted her hips up and back so she was kneeling slumped forward before him.

Hands still tangled, she drew her arms in so she could lean on her forearms. He pressed close behind her, his knees outside hers, then she felt the engorged head of his erection nudge her entrance.

Then he was inside her.

300

Pressing deeper than he'd ever been. Her toes curled, then he withdrew and thrust in again, seating himself even more fully within her.

She struggled to catch her breath, lost all she'd gained as he again thrust into her hard and deep.

Holding her to him, open and helpless, he set up a steady, driving rhythm that had her fingers curling, sinking into and clutching the crimson-and-gold brocade as he pounded into her, then he varied the speed, then the depth, then rolling his hips, he somehow caressed her deep inside.

She could swear she could feel him at the back of her throat.

She wasn't sure she was going to survive this, not this degree of shuddering intimacy. This absolute degree of physical possession. She could feel the thunder in his blood, feel the wave of heated need and physical desperation rise and build.

When it crashed it would sweep them both away.

Gasping, frantic, she was clinging to reality when he leaned over her, one fist sinking into the bed alongside her shoulder. He still held her hips up, anchoring her, holding her captive for his relentless penetration

His belly curved over the back of her hips; she could feel the heat of his chest all across her back as he bowed his head. His breath sawed past her ear, then he nuzzled the curve of her neck.

"Just let go."

She heard the words from a long way away; they sounded like a plea.

"Just let it happen – let it come."

She heard his breath hitch, then he pressed deep inside her, shortened his thrusts so he was barely withdrawing at all, just moving deep within her, rolling his hips into hers, stroking her inside.

The climax hit her so hard, on so many levels, she screamed.

Her body seemed to pulse, and pulse, and pulse with successive waves of glory, each brighter, sharper, more glittering as sensation spiraled, erupted, splintered, then flashed down every overwrought nerve, sank and melted under every single inch of sensitized skin.

Completion had never been so absolute.

Royce held her through it. His erection sunk deep within her convulsing sheath, he felt every scalding ripple, every glorious moment of her release; eyes closed, he savored it, savored her, savored the fulfillment he found in her body, and in her.

His own release beckoned, tempted, lured, but while he'd wanted to take her like this, he also wanted more.

Greedy, but . . .

It took effort to rein his aroused and hungry body in, to gradually slow his deep but short thrusts until he held still within her. He took one last moment to drink in the sensation of her sheath gripping his erection all along its rigid length, the scalding velvet glove of all men's fantasies.

Only when he was sure he had his body under full control did he risk pulling back from her.

Bracing her body with one hand, with the other he wrestled the covers down, then scooped her up and laid her back down. High in his bed, her head and shoulders cushioned in the pile of pillows, her delicate, flushed skin soothed by the cool silk of his sheets.

He sat back on his ankles, and looked at her, some primitive part of his psyche gloating. He fixed the image in his mind – her hair a rumpled silken veil flung over his pillows, her lush body lax and sated, skin still flushed, nipples still peaked, her hips and breasts bearing the telltale marks of his possession.

Exactly as he always wanted to see her.

Her head tilted slightly on the pillows; from beneath her long lashes, her golden eyes glinted as she watched him studying her. Her gaze slowly trailed down his body.

Then she raised one arm, reached out, and closed her fingers about his aching erection. She stroked slowly down, then lightly up.

Then she released him, settled deeper into the pillows, held out her arms to him, and spread her legs wide.

He went to her, into her arms, settled between her widespread thighs, and sank, so easily, into her body, into her embrace.

Where he belonged.

He no longer doubted that; he buried his face in the hollow between her shoulder and throat, and with long, slow strokes, gave himself up to her.

Felt her accept him, her arms wrapping around his shoulders, her hands spread on his back, her legs rising to clasp his flanks as she tilted her hips and drew him yet deeper.

As she opened herself to him so he could even more deeply lose himself in her.

His release rolled over him in long shuddering waves.

Eyes closed, Minerva held him close, felt the golden joy of such passionate intimacy well and suffuse her. And knew in her heart, knew to her soul, that letting him go was going to slay her.

Devastate her.

She'd always known that would be the price for falling in love with him.

But she had.

She could swear and curse her own stupidity, but nothing could change reality. Their joint realities, which meant they would part.

Destinies weren't easily changed.

He'd slumped upon her, heavy beyond belief, yet she found his weight curiously comforting. As if her earlier physical surrender was balanced by his.

Their combined heat slowly dissipated and the night air wafted over their cooling bodies. Wriggling and reaching, she managed to snag the edge of the covers and, tugging and flicking, drew the sheet up over them both.

Closing her eyes, she let the familiar warmth enfold her, and drifted, but when he stirred and lifted from her, she came fully, determinedly awake.

He noticed. He met her gaze, then flopped back on the pillows alongside her, reaching to draw her to him, into his side, her head on his shoulder.

That was how they normally slept, but while she let him

hold her within his arm, she came up so she could look at his face.

He met her eyes, a faint lift to his brows; she sensed a certain wariness, although, as usual, nothing showed in his face.

Reminding herself she was dealing with a Varisey – a naked male one – and that subtlety therefore would be wasted, she went straight to the question she wanted to ask. "What happened to your five-nights rule?"

He blinked. Twice. But he didn't look away. "That doesn't apply to you."

She opened her eyes wide. "Indeed? So what rule does apply to me? Ten nights?"

His eyes narrowed fractionally. "The only rule that applies to you is that my bed – wherever it is – is yours. There is nowhere else I will allow you to sleep but with me." One dark brow arched, openly arrogant. "I trust that's clear?"

She stared into his dark eyes. He wasn't a fool; he had to marry – and she wouldn't stay; he knew that.

But had he accepted that?

After a long moment, she asked, "What aren't you telling me?"

It wasn't his face that gave him away; it was the faint but definite tension that infused the hard body beneath hers.

He half shrugged, then settled his shoulders deeper into the bed, urging her down again. "Earlier, when you weren't here, I thought you were sulking."

A change of subject, not an answer. "After learning about your five-nights rule, then having you ignore me all evening as if I didn't exist, I thought you were finished with me." Her tone stated very clearly how she'd felt about that.

Having relieved her lingering ire, she yielded to his importuning, slumped back into his arms and laid her head on his shoulder.

"No." His voice was low; his lips brushed her temple. "Never that."

The last words were soft, but definite – and that telltale tension hadn't left him.

Never?

What was he planning?

Given how she felt – how deeply he'd already unwittingly snared her – she had to know. Hands on his chest, she pushed up again. Tried to, but his arms didn't give. She wriggled, got nowhere, so she pinched him. Hard.

He flinched, muttered something distinctly uncomplimentary, but let her lift her shoulders enough to look into his face.

She searched his eyes, replayed all he'd said, and how he'd said it. His plan for her, whatever it was, revolved about one question. She narrowed her eyes on his. "Who have you decided to marry?"

If she could get him to declare that, she could accept it, know it for fact, and prepare herself to hand over her keys, relinquish her place in his bed to another, and leave Wolverstone. *That* was her destiny, but while he refused to name his bride, he could draw their liaison out indefinitely, and draw her ever deeper into love – so that when she did have to leave, leaving him would shatter her.

She had to make him define the end of their affair.

He held her gaze, utterly expressionless. Utterly implacable.

She refused to back down. "Lady Ashton confirmed that your failure to make the promised announcement has been widely noted. You're going to have to make it soon, or we'll have Lady Osbaldestone back up here, in a foul mood. And in case you're wondering, her foul mood will trump your temper. She will make you feel as small as a flea. So stop pretending you can change your destiny, and just tell me so we can announce it."

So she could organize to leave him.

Royce was too adept at reading between other people's lines to miss her underlying thoughts . . . but he had to tell her. She'd just handed him the perfect opening to break the news to her and propose, but . . . he didn't want to yet. Wasn't yet sure enough of her response. Of her.

Beneath the covers, she shifted, sliding one long leg over his waist, then easing across and sitting up, straddling him, the

305

better to look into his face. Her eyes, the glorious autumn hues still darkened by recent passion, narrowed and bored into his, golden sparks of will and determination flaring in their depths. "*Have* you chosen your bride?"

That he could answer. "Yes."

"Have you contacted her?"

"I'm negotiating with her as we speak."

"Who is she? Do I know her?"

She wasn't going to let him slide around her again. Jaw setting, eyes locked on hers, he ground out, "Yes."

When he didn't say anything more, she clutched his upper arms as if to shake him – or hold him so he couldn't escape. "What's her name?"

Her eyes held his. He was going to have to speak now. Engage with her now. He was going to have to find some way – forge some path through the mire . . . He searched her eyes, desperate for some hint of a way forward.

Her fingers tightened, nails digging in, then she uttered a frustrated sound; releasing him, she raised her palms, along with her face, to the canopy. "*Why* are you being so damned difficult about this?"

Something within him snapped. "Because it *is* difficult."

Her head came down; she pinned him with her eyes. "*Why*, for heaven's sake? *Who* is she?"

Lips thin, he locked his gaze with hers. "You."

All expression fled from her face, from her eyes. "What?"

"*You*." He poured every ounce of his certainty, his determination, into the words. "I've chosen you."

Her eyes flared wide; her expression wasn't one he could place – she wasn't afraid of him. She started to draw back, pull away; he locked his hands about her waist.

"No." The word was weak, her eyes still wide; her expression looked strangely bleak. Abruptly she dragged in a breath, and shook her head. "No, no, no. I told you –"

"Yes. I know." He made the words terse enough to cut her off. "But here's something – some things – *you* don't know." He caught her gaze. "I took you up to Lord's Seat lookout, but I

306

never told you why. I took you there to ask you to marry me – but I got distracted. I let you distract me into getting you into my bed first – and *then* you turned your virginity, the fact I'd taken it, into an even bigger hurdle."

She blinked at him. "You wanted to ask me then?"

"I'd planned to – on Lord's Seat, and then here on that first night. But your declaration . . ." He paused.

Her eyes narrowed again; her lips thinned. "You didn't give up – you never give up. You set out to manipulate me – that's what all this" – she waved her arms, encompassing the huge bed – "has been about, hasn't it? You've been working to change my mind!"

With a disgusted snort, she tried to get off him. He tightened his grip on her waist, kept her exactly where she was, straddling him. She tried to fight loose, tried to pry his fingers away, wriggled and squirmed.

"No." He bit the word off with sufficient force to have her look at him again – and grow still. He trapped her gaze, held it. "It wasn't like that – it was *never* about manipulating you. I don't want you by stealth – I want your willing agreement. All *this* has been about *convincing* you. About showing you how well you fit the position of my duchess."

Through his hands, he sensed her quietening, sensed that he'd caught her attention, however unwilling. He dragged in a breath. "Now you've forced my hand, the least you can do is listen. Listen to why I think we'd suit – why I want you and only you as my wife."

Trapped in his dark eyes, Minerva didn't know what to think. She couldn't tell what she felt; emotions roiled and churned and tumbled through her. She knew he was telling the truth; veracity rang in his tone. He rarely lied, and he was speaking in terms that were utterly unambiguous.

He took her silence as acquiescence. Still holding her captive, still holding her gaze, he went on, "I want you as my wife because you – and only you – can give me everything I need, and want, in my duchess. The socially prescribed aspects are the most minor – your birth is more than adequate, as is your fortune. While an announcement of our betrothal might take many by surprise, it won't in any way be considered a mésalliance – from society's perspective, you're entirely suitable."

Pausing, he drew breath, but his eyes never left hers; she had never before felt so much the absolute focus of his attention, his will, his very being. "While there are many ladies who would be suitable on those counts, it's in all the other aspects that you excel. I need – demonstrably need – a lady by my side who understands the prevailing social and political responsibilities and dynamics of the dukedom as, courtesy of my exile, I do not. I need someone I can trust implicitly to guide me through the shoals – as you did at the funeral. I need a lady I can rely on to have the backbone to confront me when I'm wrong – someone who isn't afraid of my temper. Almost everyone is, but you never have been – among females that alone makes you unique."

Royce didn't dare take his eyes from hers. She was listening, following – understanding. "I also need – and want – a duchess who is attuned to and devoted to the dukedom's interests, and first and last to Wolverstone itself. To the estate, the people, the community. Wolverstone is not just a castle – it never has been. I need a lady who understands that, who will be as committed to it as I am. As you already are."

The next breath he dragged in shook; his lungs were tight, his chest felt compressed, but he had to say the rest – had to step off the beaten path and take a chance. "Lastly, I . . ." He searched her autumn eyes. "Need – and want – a lady I care about. *Not* the customary Varisey bride. I want . . . to try and have more of a marriage, a more complete marriage – one based on more than calculation and convenience. For that I need a lady I can spend my life with, one I can share my life with from now into the future. I don't want to occasionally visit my duchess's bed – I want her in my bed, this bed, every night for all the nights to come." He paused, then said, "For all those reasons, I need *you* as my bride. Of all the women I might have, no other will do. I can't imagine . . . feeling as I do about any other. There never has been any other I've slept beside through the night, no other

I've ever wanted to keep with me through the dawn." He held her gaze. "I want you, I desire you – and only you will do."

Staring into his dark eyes, Minerva felt her emotions surge and swell; she was in very deep water, in danger of being swept away. Being pulled under; the tug of his words, of his lure, was that strong – strong enough to tempt her, even her, even though she knew the price . . . she frowned. "Are you saying that you'll remain faithful to your duchess?"

"Not to my duchess. But to you? Yes."

Oh, clever answer; her heart skipped a beat. She looked into his eyes, saw his implacable, immovable will looking back – and the room spun. She drew an unsteady breath; the planets had just realigned. A Varisey was promising fidelity. "What brought this on?"

What on earth had proved strong enough to bring him to this?

He didn't immediately answer, but his eyes remained steady on hers.

Eventually he said, "I've seen over the years what Rupert, Miles, and Gerald have found with Rose, Eleanor, and Alice. I've spent more time in their households than in this one – and what they have is what I want. I've more recently seen my ex-colleagues find their brides – and they, too, found wives and marriages that offered far more than convenience and dynastic advance."

He shifted slightly beneath her, for the first time glanced beyond her, but then he brought his gaze back to her face – forced it back. His jaw tightened. "Then the grandes dames came and made clear what they expected – and not one thought that I would want, much less deserved, anything better than the customary Varisey marriage." His voice hardened. "But they were wrong. I want *you* – and I want more."

She inwardly shivered. She would have sworn she didn't outwardly, but his hands, until then warm and strong about her waist, left her, and he reached for the counterpane, drew it up to drape around and over her shoulders. She caught the edges, drew them closer. She wasn't cold; she was emotionally shaken.

To her toes.

"I . . ." She refocused on him.

He was looking at his hands adjusting the counterpane around her. "Before you say anything . . . when I went to see Hamish today, I asked his advice about what I might say to you to convince you to accept my suit." His eyes lifted and met hers. "He told me I should tell you that I loved you."

She couldn't breathe; she was trapped in the unfathomable darkness of his eyes.

They remained locked with hers. "He told me that you would want me to say that – to claim I loved you." He drew breath, went on, "I will never lie to you – if I could tell you I loved you, I would. I will do *anything* I need to to make you mine, to have you as my duchess – *except* lie to you."

He seemed to have as much trouble breathing as she did; the next breath he drew shuddered. He let it out as his eyes searched hers. "I care for you, in a way and to a depth that I care for no one else. But we both know I can't say I love you. We both know why. As a Varisey I don't know the first thing about love, much less how to make it happen. I don't even know if the emotion exists within me. But what I can – and will – promise, is that I will try. For *you*, I will try – I will give you everything I have in me, but I can't promise it'll be enough. I can promise to try, but I can't promise I'll succeed." He held her gaze unflinchingly. "I can't promise to love you because I don't know if I can."

Moments passed; she remained immersed in his eyes, seeing, hearing, knowing. Finally she drew in a long, slow breath, refocused on his face, looked again into those dark, tempestuous eyes. "*If* I agree to marry you, will you promise me that? Promise you'll remain faithful, and that you'll try?"

The answer was immediate, uncompromising. "Yes. For you, I'll promise that, in whatever way, whatever words, you wish."

She felt strung tight, emotionally tense – poised on a wire above an abyss. Assessing her tension made her aware of his; beneath her thighs, her bottom, his muscles were all steel – he otherwise hid it well, his uncertainty.

310

Gazes locked, they were both teetering. She drew breath, and pulled back. "I need to think." She swiftly replayed his words, arched a brow. "You haven't actually proposed."

He was silent for a moment, then succinctly stated, "I'll propose when you're ready to accept."

"I'm not ready yet."

"I know."

She studied him, sensed his uncertainty, but even more his unwavering determination. "You've surprised me." She'd thought of marrying him, fantasized and dreamed of it, but she'd never thought it might come to be – any more than she'd thought she would share his bed, let alone on a regular basis, yet here she was – a warning in itself. "A large part of me wants to say yes, please ask, but becoming your duchess isn't something I can decide on impulse."

He'd offered her everything her heart could desire – *short* of promising her his. In one arrogant sweep, he'd moved them into a landscape she'd never imagined might exist – and in which there were no familiar landmarks.

"You've thrown me into complete mental turmoil." Her thoughts were chaotic, her emotions more so; her mind was a seething cauldron in which well-known fears battled unexpected hopes, uncataloged desires, unsuspected needs.

Still he said nothing, too wise to press.

Indeed. She couldn't let him, or her wilder self, rush her into this – a marriage that, if it went wrong, guaranteed emotional obliteration. "You're going to have to give me time. I need to think."

He didn't protest.

She dragged in a breath, threw him a warning look, then slid off him, back to her side of the bed; turning onto her side, facing away from him, she pulled the covers up over her shoulders and snuggled down.

After a moment of regarding her through the dark, Royce turned and slid down in the bed, spooning his body around hers. Sliding his arm over her waist, he eased her back against him.

311

She humphed softly, but wriggled back, setting her hips against his abdomen. With a small sigh, she relaxed slightly.

He was still tense, his gut still churning. So much of his life, his future, was now riding on this, on her; he'd just placed his life in her hands – at least she hadn't handed it straight back.

Which, realistically, was all he could ask of her at that point.

Lifting her hair aside, he pressed a kiss to her nape. "Go to sleep. You can take whatever time you need to think."

After a moment, he murmured, "But when Lady Osbaldestone comes back up here and demands who I've chosen as my bride, I'll have to tell her."

Minerva snorted. Her lips curved, then, against every last expectation, she did as he'd bid her and fell fast asleep.

Chapter 17

"Hamish O'Loughlin, you mangy Scot, how dare you tell Royce to tell me he loves me!"

"Huh?" Hamish looked up from the sheep he was examining.

Folding her arms, Minerva fell to pacing alongside the pen.

Hamish studied her face. "You didn't want to hear that he loves you?"

"Of *course* I would *love* to hear that he loves me – but how can he say such a thing? He's a Varisey, for heaven's sake."

"Hmm." Letting the sheep jump away, Hamish leaned against the railing. "Perhaps the same way I tell Moll that I love her."

"But that's *you*. You're not –" She broke off. Halting, head rising, she blinked at him.

He gave her a cynical smile. "Aye – think on it. I'm as much a Varisey as he is."

She frowned. "But you're not . . ." She waved south, over the hills.

"Castle-bred? True. But perhaps that just means I never believed I wouldn't love, not when the right woman came along." He studied her face. "He didn't tell you, did he?"

"No – he was honest. He says he'll try – that he wants more of his marriage, but" – she drew in a huge breath – "he can't promise to love me because he doesn't know if he can."

Hamish made a disgusted sound. "You're a right pair.

You've been in love with him – or at least waiting to fall in love with him – for decades, and now you have –"

"You can't know that." She stared at him.

"Of course, I can. Not that he's said all that much, but I can read between his lines, and yours, well enough – and you're here, aren't you?"

She frowned harder.

"Aye – it's as I thought." Hamish let himself out of the pen, latching the gate behind him. Leaning back against it, he looked at her. "You both need to take a good long look at each other. What do you think has made him even consider having a different sort of marriage? A love match – isn't that what society calls them? Why do you imagine they're called that?"

She scowled at him. "You're making it sound simple and easy."

Hamish nodded his great head. "Aye – that's how love is. Simple, straightforward, and easy. It just happens. Where it gets complicated is when you try to think too much, to ration-alize it, make sense of it, pick it apart – it's not like that." He pushed away from the gate, and started lumbering up the path; she fell in beside him. "But if you must keep thinking, think on this – love happens, just like a disease. And like any disease, the easiest way to tell someone's caught it is to look for the symp-toms. I've known Royce longer than you have, and he's got every last symptom. He might not *know* he loves you, but he feels it – he acts on it."

They'd reached the yard where she'd left Rangonel. Hamish halted and looked down at her. "The truth is, lass, he might never be able to honestly, knowingly, tell you he loves you – but that doesn't mean he doesn't."

She grimaced, rubbed a gloved finger in the center of her forehead. "You've only given me *more* to think about."

Hamish grinned. "Aye, well, if you must think, the least you can do is think of the right things."

As Minerva rode south across the border and down through the hills, she had plenty of time to think of Royce and his symptoms. Plenty of time to ponder all Hamish had said; while helping her to her saddle, he'd reminded her that the late duchess had been unwaveringly faithful, not to her husband, but to her longtime lover, Sidney Camberwell.

The duchess and Camberwell had been together for over twenty years; remembering all she'd seen of the pair, thinking of "symptoms," she had to conclude they'd been very much in love.

Perhaps Hamish was right; Royce could and might love her.

Regardless, she had to make up her mind, and soon – he hadn't been joking when he'd mentioned Lady Osbaldestone – which was why she'd come out riding; Hamish's farm had seemed an obvious destination.

Take whatever time you need to think.

She knew Royce far too well not to know that he'd meant: Take whatever time you need to think *as long as you agree to be my wife.*

He would do everything in his power to ensure she did; henceforth he would feel completely justified in doing whatever it took to make her agree.

In his case, "whatever it took" covered a great deal – as he'd demonstrated that morning, with shattering results. She'd escaped only because the sun had risen. If it hadn't, she would be at his mercy still.

In public, however, over breakfast, and then later when they'd met for their usual meeting in his study with Handley in attendance and Jeffers by the door, he'd behaved with exemplary decorum; she couldn't fault him in that – while in private he might pressure her to decide quickly in his favor, he did nothing to raise speculation in others.

"For which," she assured the hills at large, "I'm duly grateful. The last thing I need is Margaret, Aurelia, and Susannah hectoring me. I don't even know which way they'd fall – for or against."

An interesting question, but beside the point. She didn't care what they thought, and Royce cared even less.

For the umpteenth time, she replayed his arguments. Most confirmed what she'd seen from the start; marrying her would be the best option for him, especially given his commitment to Wolverstone and to the dukedom as a whole. What didn't fit the mold of convenience and comfort was his desire for a different sort of marriage; she couldn't question the reality of that – he'd had to force himself to reveal it, and she'd felt his sincerity to her bones.

And he did care for her, in his own arrogant, high-handed way. There was an undeniably seductive triumph in being the only woman to have ever made a Varisey think of anything even approaching love. And especially Royce – to claim him as her own . . . but that was a piece of self-seduction.

If he did love her, would it last?

If he loved her as she loved him . . .

She frowned at Rangonel's ears. "Regardless of Hamish's opinion, I still have a *lot* to think through."

Royce was in his study working through his correspondence with Handley when Jeffers tapped and opened the door. He looked up, arched a brow.

"Three ladies and a gentleman have arrived, Your Grace. The ladies are insisting on seeing you immediately."

He inwardly frowned. "Their names?"

"The Marchioness of Dearne, the Countess of Lostwithiel, and Lady Clarice Warnefleet, Your Grace. The gentleman is Lord Warnefleet."

"The gentleman isn't asking to see me as well?"

"No, Your Grace. Just the ladies."

Which was Jack Warnefleet's way of warning him what the subject his wife and her two cronies wished to discuss was. "Thank you, Jeffers. Show the ladies up. Tell Retford to make Lord Warnefleet comfortable in the library."

As the door closed, he glanced at Handley. "We'll have to continue this later. I'll ring when I'm free."

Handley nodded, gathered his papers, rose, and left. Royce stared at the closed door. There seemed little point in wondering what message Letitia, Penny, and Clarice had for him; he would know soon enough.

Less than a minute later, Jeffers opened the door, and the ladies – three of the seven wives of his ex-colleagues of the Bastion Club – swept in. Rising, he acknowledged their formal curtsies, then waved them to the chairs Jeffers angled before the desk.

He waited until they'd settled, then, dismissing Jeffers with a nod, resumed his seat. As the door closed, he let his gaze sweep the three striking faces before him. "Ladies. Permit me to guess – I owe this pleasure to Lady Osbaldestone."

"And all the others." Letitia, flanked by Penny and Clarice, flung her arms wide. "The entire pantheon of tonnish grandes dames."

He let his brows rise. "Why, if I might ask, you – more specifically, why all three of you?"

Letitia grimaced. "I was visiting Clarice and Jack in Gloucestershire while Christian dealt with business in London. Penny had come up to join us for a few days when Christian relayed a summons from Lady Osbaldestone insisting I attend her immediately in London on a matter of great urgency."

"Naturally," Clarice said, "Letitia had to go, and Penny and I decided we could do with a week in London, so we went, too."

"But," Penny took up the tale, "the instant Lady Osbaldestone laid eyes on us, she made us joint emissaries with Letitia to carry the collective message of the grandes dames to your ears."

"I suspect," Clarice said, "that she thought you might be able to avoid Letitia, but you wouldn't be able to slide around all three of us."

Clarice glanced at the other two, who returned her regard, then all three pairs of feminine eyes turned on him.

He raised his brows. "Your message?"

It was Letitia who answered. "You are hereby warned that unless you do as you intimated and announce your duchess-to-be forthwith, you will have to cope with a fleet of carriages turning up at your gates. And, of course, the occupants of those carriages won't be the sort you can easily turn away." She shrugged. "Their version was rather more formal, but that's the gist of it."

Penny frowned. "Actually, it seemed as if you have quite a few people in residence already – and more arriving."

"My sisters are hosting a house party coincident with the local parish fair. It used to be a family tradition, but lapsed after my mother died." He focused on Letitia. "Is there a time limit on the grandes dames' threat?"

Letitia glanced at Clarice.

"We got the impression the limit is now." Clarice widened her eyes at him. "Or more precisely, your period of grace expires at the time a missive from us confirming your non-compliance reaches Lady Osbaldestone."

He tapped a finger on his blotter, letting his gaze sweep their faces again. Lady Osbaldestone had chosen well; with these three, intimidation wouldn't work. And while he might have been able to divert – subvert – Letitia, with the three of them reinforcing each other, he stood not a chance.

Lips firming, he nodded. "You may report to the beldames that I have, indeed, chosen a bride –"

"Excellent!" Letitia beamed. "So you can draft an announcement, and we can take it back to London."

"However" – he continued as if she hadn't spoken – "the lady in question has yet to accept the position."

They stared at him.

Clarice recovered first. "What is she? Deaf, dumb, blind – or all three?"

That surprised a laugh from him, then he shook his head. "It's the reverse – she's too damned insightful for my good. And please do include that in your report – it will make her ladyship's day. Regardless, an announcement in the *Gazette* at this point could well prove inimical to our mutual goal."

All three ladies fixed intrigued gazes on him. He regarded them impassively. "Is there anything else?"

"Who is she?" Letitia demanded. "You can't just dangle a tale like that before us, and not give us her name."

"Actually, I can. You don't need to know." They'd guess very quickly; he had as much confidence in their intelligence – individually and collectively – as he had in their husbands'.

Three pairs of eyes narrowed; three expressions grew flinty.

Penny informed him, "We're under orders to remain here – under your feet – until you send a notice to the *Gazette*."

Their continued presence might well work in his favor. Their husbands weren't all that different from him – and Minerva had been starved of the companionship of females she could trust, confide in, and ask for advice. And these three might be disposed to help his cause.

Of course, they'd probably view it as assisting Cupid. Just as long as they succeeded, he didn't care. "You're very welcome to stay and join the festivities my sisters have planned." Rising, he crossed to the bellpull. "I believe my chatelaine, Minerva Chesterton, is presently out, but she should return shortly. Meanwhile I'm sure my staff will make you comfortable."

All three frowned.

Retford arrived, and he gave orders for their accommodation. They rose, distinctly haughty, and increasingly suspicious.

He ushered them to the door. "I'll leave you to get settled. No doubt Minerva will look in on you as soon as she returns. I'll see you at dinner – until then, you must excuse me. Business calls."

They narrowed their eyes at him, but consented to follow Retford.

Letitia, the last to leave, looked him in the eye. "You know we'll hound you until you tell us this amazingly insightful lady's name."

Unperturbed, he bowed her out; they'd know his lady's name before he reached the drawing room that evening.

With an irritated "humph!" Letitia went.

Closing the door, he turned back to his desk.

And let his brows rise. Lady Osbaldestone and the other beldames might just have helped.

Returning from her ride, Minerva walked into the front hall to discover a handsome gentleman ambling about admiring the paintings.

He turned at the sound of her boot steps, and smiled charmingly.

"Good morning." Despite his country-elegant attire, and that smile, she sensed a familiar hardness behind his façade. "Can I help you?"

He bowed. "Jack Warnefleet, ma'am."

She glanced around, wondering where Retford was. "Have you just arrived?"

"No." He smiled again. "I was shown into the library, but I've studied all the paintings there. My wife and two of her friends are upstairs, bearding Dal – Wolverstone – in his den." Hazel eyes twinkled. "I thought I ought to come out here in case a precipitous retreat was in order."

He'd nearly said Dalziel, which meant he was an acquaintance from Whitehall. She held out her hand. "I'm Miss Chesterton. I act as chatelaine here."

He bowed over her hand. "Delighted, my dear. I have to admit I have no idea whether we'll be staying or –" He broke off and looked up the stairs. "Ah – here they are."

They both turned as three ladies preceded Retford down the stairs. Minerva recognized Letitia and smiled.

Beside her, Jack Warnefleet murmured, "And from their frowns, I suspect we're staying."

She didn't get a chance to ask what he meant; Letitia, seeing her, dispensed with her frown and came hurrying down to embrace her.

"Minerva – just who we need." Letitia turned as the other two ladies joined them. "I don't believe you've met Lady Clarice, for her sins Lady Warnefleet, wife of this reprobate." She flicked a hand at Jack, who merely grinned. "And this is Lady Penelope, Countess of Lostwithiel – her

320

husband is Charles, another of Royce's ex-operatives, as is Jack here."

Minerva touched hands with the other two ladies. "Welcome to Wolverstone Castle. I gather you're staying." She glanced at Retford. "Rooms in the west wing, I think, Retford." The other guests were mostly in the south and east wings.

"Indeed, ma'am. I'll have the ladies' and gentleman's bags taken up immediately."

"Thank you." Linking arms, Letitia leaned close. "Is there somewhere we can talk privately?"

"Of course." Minerva glanced at Retford. "If you would bring tea to the duchess's morning room?"

"At once, ma'am."

She looked at Jack Warnefleet. "Sir?"

He smiled. "Jack. And I believe I'll follow the bags and find our room." He inclined his head to them all. "I'll catch up with you at luncheon."

"You'll hear the gong," she assured him.

With a salute, he started up the stairs in the wake of two footmen hefting a trunk.

Minerva waved the ladies up, too. "Come up, and we can be comfortable."

In the duchess's morning room, they sank onto the sofas, then Retford arrived with a tray. After pouring and handing around the cups and a plate of cakes, Minerva sat back, sipped, caught Letitia's eye, and raised her brows.

Letitia set down her cup. "The reason we're here is that the grandes dames have lost patience and are insisting Royce announce his betrothal forthwith." She grimaced. "Of course, he's now told us that the lady he's chosen has yet to accept his suit. Apparently she has reservations, but he refuses to tell us who she is." She fixed her brilliant hazel gaze on Minerva. "Do you know her name?"

She didn't know what to say. He'd said he would tell, but he hadn't. And she hadn't anticipated such a question, especially from a friend.

A frown started to form in Letitia's eyes, but it was Clarice who set her cup on her saucer and, staring at Minerva's face, said, "Aha! 'She' is *you*." Her brows rose. "Well, well."

Letitia's eyes flew wide. She read confirmation in Minerva's expression, and delight filled her face. "It *is* you! He's chosen you. Well! I would never have credited him with so much good sense."

Head tilted, Penny said, "We're not wrong, are we? He has asked you to be his bride?"

Minerva grimaced lightly. "Not exactly – not yet – but yes, he wants me to be his duchess."

Letitia's frown returned. "Pray excuse me if I'm wrong, but I always sensed that you . . . well, that you wouldn't reject his advances."

Minerva stared at her. "Please tell me I wasn't that obvious."

"No, you weren't – it was just something about the way you paid attention whenever he was mentioned." Letitia shrugged. "It was probably feeling the same way about Christian that made me notice."

Minerva felt mildly relieved.

"So," Clarice asked, "why are you hesitating over accepting his suit?"

Minerva looked from one face to the other. "He's a Varisey."

Letitia's face blanked. "Oh."

"Ah . . ." Penny grimaced.

Slowly, Clarice nodded. "I see. Not being a giddy miss with more hair than wit, you want . . ." She glanced at the other two. "What we've all been lucky enough to find."

Minerva exhaled. "Precisely." They understood.

After a moment, Penny frowned. "But you haven't refused him."

Minerva met Penny's eyes, then set down her cup and rose; swinging around behind the sofa, she started to pace. "It's not that simple." No matter what Hamish thought.

The others watched her, waited.

She needed help; Letitia was an old friend, and they all had marriages based on love – and they'd immediately understood. She halted, briefly closed her eyes. "I didn't mean to fall in love with him."

"We rarely do," Clarice murmured. "It simply happens."

Opening her eyes, she inclined her head. "So I've realized." She resumed her pacing. "Since he returned, well, he wanted me, and I am twenty-nine. I thought I could be . . . close to him for just a little while without risking my heart. But I was wrong."

"*Wrong?*" Letitia pityingly shook her head. "You've been infatuated with Royce Varisey for decades, and you thought you could be with him – by which I assume you mean you're sharing his bed – and *not* fall in love with him? My dear Minerva, you weren't just *mistaken*."

"No, I know. I was a fool. But falling in love with him wouldn't have mattered if he hadn't decided to make me his duchess."

Letitia frowned. "When did he decide that?"

"Weeks ago. After the grandes dames saw him in his study. But" – Minerva forced herself to go on – "that's not the whole of my problem."

She continued pacing, ordering the elements of her explanation in her mind. "I've always been set on a marriage based on love – I've had offers before, a good many, and never been tempted. My parents' marriage was based on love, and I've never wanted anything else. At first . . . I had no idea Royce had his eye on me. I thought I could hide my interest in him, be the dutiful chatelaine, and then leave once his wife took up the reins. Then . . . he wanted me, and I thought it would be safe enough, given his marriage was imminent. I thought love would need time to grow – but it didn't."

Letitia nodded. "It can strike in an instant."

"So I'd heard, but I never really believed . . . regardless, once I realized I'd fallen in love with him, I still thought, given his marriage had to occur soon, that I'd be able to leave, if not heart-whole, then at least with dignity. I've never been in love before, and if I never was again, no one would know but me."

Minerva paused in her pacing, and raised her head. "Then he told me I was the lady he wanted as his duchess."

"Of course he *told* you." Penny humphed.

Minerva nodded. "Indeed – but I'd always known that the last thing, the *very* last thing I should do if I wanted a marriage based on love, was to marry Royce, or any Varisey. No Varisey marriage in history has been based on love, or in any way included love." She drew a deep breath, her gaze fixed across the room. "Until last night, I believed that if I married Royce, ours would be a typical Varisey arrangement, and he, and everyone else – all the ton, in fact – would expect me to stand meekly by while he indulged as he wished with any lady who took his fancy."

Frowning, Letitia nodded. "The typical Varisey union."

Minerva inclined her head. "And I couldn't do that. Even before I fell in love with him, I knew I'd never be able to stand that – that knowing he didn't love me as I loved him, when he went to another's bed, and then another's, I'd wither, pine, and go mad like Caro Lamb."

Their expressions stated that they fully understood.

"So what happened last night?" Clarice asked.

That needed another deep breath. "Last night, Royce swore that if I agree to be his duchess, he'll be faithful."

Complete silence reigned for several minutes.

Eventually, Penny said, "I can see how that . . . changes things."

Clarice grimaced. "If it weren't Royce we were talking about, I'd ask if you believed him."

Letitia snorted. "If he says he will, let alone swears he will, he will."

Minerva nodded. "Exactly. And at first glance, that should make it easy for me to agree, but, as I realized once I managed to find time to think, while him being faithful clears away one problem, it creates another."

Gripping the back of the sofa, she focused on the tea tray on the low table between the sofas. "He says he will never lie to me, and that I accept. He says he cares for me as he cares for no other – and I accept that, too. But what happens when, if we wed, and a few years pass, and he no longer comes to my bed." She raised her gaze, and met Clarice's, then Penny's, then lastly Letitia's. "How am I going to feel then? Knowing he no longer desires me, but because of his vow, is simply . . ." She gestured. "*Existing*. Abstaining. Him, of all men."

They didn't rush to reassure her.

Eventually, Letitia sighed. "That's not a comforting – or comfortable – thought."

Clarice grimaced. Penny did, too.

"If he loved me," Minerva said, "the problem wouldn't exist. But he's been brutally honest – and I can't fault him in that. He will promise me all that's in his power to give, but he won't promise love. He can't. He admitted he doesn't know if he even has it in him to give."

Clarice humphed. "That's not so odd – they never do know."

"Which leads me to ask" – Letitia swung to look up at her – "are you *sure* he isn't in love with you, but doesn't know it?"

Penny leaned forward. "If you haven't been in love before . . . are you sure you would know if he was?"

Minerva was silent for a long moment. "Someone recently told me that love is like a disease, and the easiest way to know if someone's caught it is to look for the symptoms."

"Excellent advice," Clarice affirmed.

Penny nodded. "Love isn't a passive emotion – it makes you do things you wouldn't normally do."

"It makes you take risks you otherwise wouldn't." Letitia looked at Minerva. "So what do you think? Might Royce be in love with you, but not know?"

A catalog of minor incidents, comments, tiny revelations, all the little things about him that had surprised her, ran though her mind, but it was Hamish's comment echoing her own earlier thought that held most weight. What on earth had proved strong enough to move him, the man he was, to break with long tradition and actively seek – want enough to strive for – a different marriage, one that, if she'd understood him correctly, he hoped as much as she might come to encompass love?

"Yes." She slowly nodded. "He might."

If she accepted the position of Royce's duchess, from the instant she said "yes" there would be no turning back.

The luncheon gong had curtailed her discussion with the other ladies; neither Royce nor Jack Warnefleet had appeared, but the rest of the company had, making it impossible to further pursue their debate – at least not aloud.

She spent most of the meal mentally enumerating Royce's symptoms, but while indicative, neither singly nor collectively were they conclusive.

Retford waylaid her on her way back to the morning room; the others went ahead while she detoured to assess the spirits store. After conferring with Retford, Cranny, and Cook, on impulse she asked after Trevor.

Fate smiled, and she found him alone in the ironing room, busily ironing his master's cravats. He saw her as she entered, quickly set the iron down, and turned.

"No, no." She waved him back to the board. "Don't stop on my account."

Hesitantly, he picked up the iron from the stand perched above a fire in the small hearth. "Can I help you with something, ma'am?"

This could be supremely embarrassing, but she had to ask, had to know. She drew breath, and plunged in. "Trevor – you've been with His Grace for some time, have you not?"

"Over seventeen years, ma'am."

"Indeed. Just so. So you would know if there's anything in the way in which he behaves toward me that differs from how he's behaved in the past with other ladies."

The iron froze in midair. Trevor looked at her, and blinked.

Embarrassment clutched at her chest; she hurried to add, "Of course, I will understand completely if you feel your duty to His Grace precludes you from answering."

"No, no – I can answer." Trevor blinked again, and his expression eased. "My answer, ma'am, is that I really can't say."

"Oh." She deflated; all that whipping up her courage for nothing.

But Trevor hadn't finished. "I've never known about any other ladies, you see. He never brought any home."

"He didn't?"

His attention on the strip of linen he was carefully flattening, Trevor shook his head. "Never. Cardinal rule. Always their beds, never his."

Minerva stared at the valet for a long moment, then she nodded and turned away. "Thank you, Trevor."

"My pleasure, ma'am."

"*Well!* That's encouraging." Perched on the arm of one of the sofas, Clarice watched her pace. "Especially if he's been so adamant over using *his* bed, not yours."

Letitia and Penny, seated on the other sofa, nodded in agreement.

"Yes, *but*," Minerva said, "who's to say that it's not just him viewing me as his duchess. He'd made up his mind I should marry him before he seduced me, so it's entirely in character for him to insist on treating me as if I already were what he wants me to be – his wife."

Letitia made a rude sound. "If Royce decided to ignore your wishes and roll over you, horse, foot, and guns, he'd have simply sent a notice to the *Gazette* – and *then* informed you of your impending change in station. That really *would* be in character. No, this news is definitely encouraging, but" – she held up a hand to stay Minerva's protest – "I agree that, for your purpose, you need something more definite."

Penny nodded. "Something more cut and dried."

"Something," Minerva stated, "that's more than just indicative, or suggestive. Something that's not open to other interpretations." Halting, she threw up her hands. "At present, this is the equivalent of reading tea leaves. I need something he absolutely wouldn't do *unless* he loves me."

Clarice blew out a breath. "Well, there is one thing you might try. If you're game . . ."

Later that night, after a final consultation with her mentors, Minerva hurried back to her bedroom. The rest of the company had retired some time ago; she was late – Royce would be wondering where she was.

If he asked where she'd been, she could hardly tell him she'd been receiving instruction in the subtle art of how to lead a nobleman to reveal his heart.

Reaching her door, she opened it and rushed inside – and came up hard against his chest.

His hands closed on her shoulders and steadied her as the door swung shut behind her. He frowned down at her. "Where –"

She held up a hand. "If you must know, I've been dealing with your friends' wives." She whisked out of his hold and backed away, already unbuttoning her gown. "Go to your room – I'll follow as soon as I've changed."

He hesitated.

She got the impression he wanted to help her with her gown, but wasn't sure he trusted himself. She waved him off. "Go! I'll get there sooner if you do."

"All right." He turned to the door. "I'll be waiting."

The door shut soundlessly behind him just as she recalled she should have warned him not to undress.

"Damn!" Wrestling with her laces, she hurried even faster.

He was *not* happy. The last weeks had crawled by without any real satisfaction.

It had taken Lady Ashton longer than he'd expected to get here, and then, instead of creating any difficulty for Royce – not even the slightest scene – the damned woman had, so it appeared, accepted her congé without even a tantrum – not even a decent sulk!

That was one thing. Her rejection of *him* was quite another.

Seething, he stalked out of the west wing into the deeper shadows of the keep's gallery. He'd gone to her room assuming that, as Royce had declined to share her bed – a fact she'd made light of when, at his subtle prod, Susannah had asked – then the delectable Lady Ashton would be amenable to entertaining him. She had a mouth he'd fantasized about using ever since Royce's interest had focused his attention on her.

Instead, the lovely countess hadn't let him past her door.

She'd pleaded a migraine and stated her intention of leaving the next day as necessitating a good night's sleep.

He ground his teeth. To be fobbed off with such transparent and paltry excuses made his blood boil. He'd intended to return to his room for a stiff brandy, but he needed something more potent than alcohol to burn away the memory of Lady Ashton's blank politeness.

She'd looked at him, and coolly dismissed him as unworthy to take Royce's place.

To rid himself of the vision, he needed something to replace it. Something like the image of Susannah – Royce's favorite sister – on her knees before him. With him looking down at her, first from the front, then from the rear, as she serviced him,

If he pushed her hard, she might just be able to make him forget the countess.

Imagining doing to Royce's sister what he'd planned to do to Royce's mistress, he crossed the gallery. Susannah's room was in the east wing.

He was passing one of the deep embrasures slotted into the keep's walls when the sound of a door hurriedly opening had him instinctively sidestepping into the deeper shadows and halting.

Silently he waited for whoever it was to pass.

Light footsteps came pattering along the runner – a woman, hurrying.

She passed the opening of the embrasure; a glint of moonlight tangled in her hair. Minerva.

Seeing her hurrying about wasn't surprising, even late at night. Seeing her rush off in her nightgown, swinging a light cloak about her shoulders, was.

He'd been walking back from the countess's rooms for some minutes; in the pervasive silence he would have heard if any of the staff had knocked on Minerva's door.

He slipped out of the embrasure and followed at a distance, stopped breathing when she turned down the short corridor that led to the ducal apartments. He reached the corner in time to peer around and see her open the door leading into Royce's sitting room.

It shut silently behind her.

Despite the obvious implications, he couldn't quite believe it. So he waited. Waited for her to emerge with Royce, having summoned him to deal with some emergency . . .

In her nightgown?

Barging into Royce's bedroom?

A clock somewhere tolled the quarter hour; he'd been standing there watching the door for over fifteen minutes. Minerva wasn't coming out.

She was the reason Royce had dismissed the countess.

"Well, well, well, well, well." Lips curving, he slowly turned and walked on to Susannah's room.

Chapter 18

Minerva paused just inside Royce's sitting room to drag in a breath and steady her nerves.

A shadow across the room shifted. Her senses flared.

He emerged from the dimness, the shadows sliding away; he'd dispensed with his coat, waistcoat, and cravat, and was barefoot, but still had his shirt and trousers on. He set down the empty glass he carried on a side table. He didn't actually growl, "About time," but the sentiment invested every stride as he stalked toward her.

"Ah . . ." She grabbed her sliding wits and hauled them back, raised her hands to ward him off.

He reached for her, but not as she expected. His hands clamped about her head, angled it as he swooped and captured her lips with his.

The searing kiss overwhelmed all thought, submerged every last vestige of rationality beneath a scorching tide of desire. Of passion unleashed; the flames licked about them, crackling and hungry.

She was, as always, drawn into the sheer wonder of being wanted so blatantly, in this way, to this degree. His hands locked about her head, with his mouth, lips, and tongue, he claimed, possessed – and poured so much raw need, unfettered passion, and unrestrained desire into her, through her, that, swamped, submerged, instantly aroused, she swayed.

Her hands flattened on his chest; through the fine linen of his shirt she felt his heat and hardness. Unrelenting, demanding, commanding – she felt all he was beckon and lure. Sensed through her touch and the grip of his hands that amazing though it seemed he wanted her with an even greater passion than he had the night before.

Far from waning, a hunger gradually sated, his appetite – and hers – only grew. Escalated, deepened.

Fingers curling in his shirt, she kissed him back – an equal participant in the outrageously explicit kiss. If he never seemed able to get enough of her, she felt the same about him.

The thought reminded her of what she needed from the night. What more she wanted of him. The others had given her directions, not instructions. She knew what she had to achieve, had known she would have to improvise.

So how?

Before she could think, he released her head and drew his hands outward, letting her hair flow through his long fingers. Her cloak slipped from her shoulders, sliding down to puddle in a heap behind her. He broke from the kiss, reached for her body – and she'd run out of planning time.

"No!" Stepping back, palm braced on his chest, she tried to hold him off.

He halted, looked at her.

"I want to lead. For this dance, I want you to let me lead."

That was the critical point – he had to let her. Had to accept the passive role instead of the dominant, had to willingly relinquish the reins and let her drive.

He'd never shared the reins – not truly. He'd allowed her to explore, but it had always been a permission granted, time and duration limited, all subject to his rule. He was a marcher lord, a king in his domains; she'd never expected anything else from him.

But tonight she was asking – demanding – that he not just share, but cede her his crown. For tonight, in his room, in his bed.

Royce understood very well what she was asking. Something he'd never granted to any other – and never would grant, not even to her, if he had a choice. But it wasn't hard to guess from whom she'd got the idea, nor what, in her mind and theirs, it meant. What they thought his capitulation would mean.

And they were right.

Which meant he had no choice. Not if he wanted her to wear his duchess's coronet.

Desire had already locked his features; he felt them grow harder, felt his jaw tighten as he held her gaze – and forced himself to nod. "All right."

She blinked – he had to stop himself from scooping her up anyway and carrying her to his bed. He could rip away her wits, and her determination, but that way lay failure. This was a test – one he had to take. Easing back, he stretched his arms to either side. "So what now?"

A more cerebral part of him was intrigued to see what she would do.

Sensing his underlying challenge, she narrowed her eyes, then grabbed one hand, swung on her heel, and towed him into his bedroom.

His gaze locked on her hips, swaying naked beneath the near translucent poplin of an amazingly prim white nightgown. None of her nightgowns rated as provocative, but this one, with its long, gathered sleeves and high collar, closed all the way up to her chin with tiny buttons, seemed extreme – and erotic.

Because he knew the body inside the gown so well, the nunlike outer casing only spurred his imagination in picturing what it concealed.

She led him to the foot of his bed.

Releasing him, wordlessly she pushed until he stood with his back to the bed, his thighs against the mattress's edge. She positioned him in the center of the four-poster, then grasped one arm, raised and slapped his palm to the ornately carved post on that side.

"Hold that. Don't let go."

333

She did the same with his other arm, setting that hand, too, level with his shoulder, against the other carved post. The bed was wide, but his shoulders were broad, his arms long; he could reach both posts easily.

She stepped back, assessed, nodded. "Good. That will do."

For what? He was utterly intrigued over what she was planning. For all his experience, he'd never considered anything from a woman's perspective; it was a novel, and unexpectedly arousing experience, arousing in an unusual way.

He'd been aroused from the moment he'd closed his hands about her head, painfully so once his lips had found hers; he would have taken her against the door in his sitting room if she hadn't stopped him. Although she had, courtesy of her peculiar direction, the fire in his blood hadn't died.

She trapped his eyes. "Under no circumstance are you to let go of the posts – not until I give you leave."

Turning, she walked away from him, and the fires inside him burned brighter.

He tracked her across the room, aware of his hunger growing. Curiosity balanced it to some degree, let him wait with some semblance of patience.

Crossing to where he'd slung his clothes on a chair, she shifted things, then straightened; because of the sharp contrast between the shadows cloaking the room and the brilliance of the shaft of moonlight beaming like a searchlight on him, he couldn't make out what she held in her hands until she drew near.

His cravat. Two yards of white linen. Instinctively he shifted his weight to his toes, about to step away from the bed.

She halted, caught his eye – waited.

He eased back, gripped the posts more firmly.

She uttered a small "humph," and walked down the side of the bed. The covers rustled as she climbed up, then came silence. She was on the bed a little way behind him, doing something; her gaze wasn't on him. "I forgot to mention – you aren't allowed to speak. No words. This is my script, and there are no lines for you."

He inwardly snorted. He rarely used words in this arena; actions spoke louder.

Then she moved closer behind him. He sensed her rising high on her knees; her breath brushed his ear when she murmured, "I think this might be easier if you." He sensed her arms rising over his head. "Can't." His cravat, folded to a narrow band, appeared before his face. "See."

She settled the band over his eyes, then wound the long strip multiple times around his head before tying it off at the back.

A cravat made a damned fine blindfold. The material sank across his eyes; he couldn't lift his lids at all.

Effectively blind, his other senses instinctively expanded, heightened.

She spoke by his ear. "Remember – no speaking, and no releasing the posts."

Her scent. The brush of her breath across his earlobe. Inwardly he smiled cynically. How was she going to remove his shirt?

She slid from the bed, and came to stand before him. The subtle beckoning heat of her. Her light perfume. The more primitive, more evocative, infinitely more arousing fragrance of her – the one scent he hungered for most strongly, that of his woman aroused and ready for him.

He'd had that taste on his tongue; it was imprinted on his brain.

Every muscle hardened. His erection grew even more rigid.

She was two feet away. With his hands locked on the posts, she was out of his reach.

"Hmm. Where to start?"

At his waistband, then head down.

"Perhaps with the most obvious." She stepped into him, plastered her body against his, drew his head down, and kissed him.

She hadn't told him he couldn't kiss her back. He ravaged her mouth, seized a first taste of what he ached for.

For one heady moment, she clung, caught, helpless, in the passion he'd unleashed, her body instinctively sinking against his, yielding, promising to ease the ache in his groin, offering pleasure and earthly delight . . .

He sensed her find her feet, digging in so she could stand against him. On a gasp, she wrenched back. Broke the kiss.

Unable to see, he couldn't follow and reinstate the exchange. She was breathing rapidly. "You're hungry."

An indisputable fact.

He smothered a growl as her body left his, clenched his jaw to quell the impulse to seize her and haul her back.

From his shoulders, her hands trailed slowly down, over his chest, over his abdomen, provocatively assessing. One paused at his waist; the other continued on, to, through his trousers, outline his erection, fingers tracing across the broad head before her palm flattened, warm and supple, over the throbbing length.

"Impressive." She gripped, then removed her hand.

He bit back a hiss. His fingers sank into the posts' carving. "Wait."

She left him, got back on the bed behind him; her hands gripped the back of his shirt at his waist, yanked it free of his waistband. Without freeing the sides or front, she slid her hands under the fabric, pressed her palms to his back.

Ran them – slowly – over him.

Over his back, up and over his shoulders, around and across his chest. The peaks of her breasts rode against his shirt-clad back. Her knees bracketed his hips.

She was still fully covered. So was he, yet with his sight gone and his other senses alive, her blatantly possessive caresses seemed infinitely erotic.

He was a slave and she his mistress, intent on possessing him for the first time. He sucked in a deep breath, chest swelling under her hands. Splayed, one on either side, she ran them slowly down from upper chest to waist.

They hovered for a long moment.

She drew back, warm palms and fingers trailing back over his sensitized skin, withdrawing from under the fall of his shirt, now hanging loose all around him.

Blind, he turned his head the better to sense her.

Noting the movement, Minerva smiled; sinking back on her ankles, she picked at the side seam of his shirt. "Did you know that the best tailors always use weak thread in their shirt seams, so if the shirt catches or tugs, the seam gives rather than the material?"

He stilled. She gave an experimental tug; the seam gave with a satisfying sound. Tugging, she opened the side and sleeve seams to the laces at his cuffs. The laces undone, with a wrench she had one side of the shirt hanging free.

She repeated the exercise on the other side, then swung off the bed and sauntered up before him. She flicked the hanging ends of the shirt. "I wonder what Trevor will think when he sees this."

Decidedly pleased, she unknotted the loose laces at his throat. Excitement flashed through her as she lifted both hands, found the front center seam. "Now, let's see . . ." She ripped.

The shirt parted all the way down the front.

"Oh, yes." Eyes feasting on his bared chest, she let the ruined halves fall to frame the heavily muscled expanse. Bathed in silvery moonlight, every powerful ripple and curve sheened, every line of bone was gilt-edged.

He breathed in, muscles tensing. His hands gripped harder.

Slowly she circled and climbed up on the bed again. Close behind him on her knees, she caught the shirt at the shoulders, drew it back and off, tossed it on the floor.

Although his back was in shadow, there was light enough to see. The long muscles, the supple, powerful planes, the quintessentially male sculpture rendered in muscle and bone and hot taut skin. She traced each feature. His tension built. Pressing against his back, she touched her lips to his shoulder, trailed her fingers around and reached for his waistband.

His stomach pulled in, letting her fingers slide past the band as she slipped the buttons free.

Lips curving against his shoulder, she drew the halves of the front placket wide, releasing his erection; careful not to touch, she grasped his trousers, edged them over his hips, down his thighs until they fell to the floor.

Leaving his body displayed naked in the moonlight, arms wide, muscles bunched as he gripped the posts. The only thing he still wore was the blindfold.

Drawing breath through lungs suddenly tight, placing both palms on his shoulders, she stroked slowly down, following the long muscles bracketing his spine to the slope of his rear; pivoting her hands over the tight cheeks, she slid them still farther, pressing against the mattress to reach and caress as far as she could down his thighs.

His head tipped back; his breath shuddered.

Retrieving her hands, she gripped the sides of his waist, eased her thighs wide, fitted herself against his back. Her cheek to one shoulder blade, she sent her hands around, down; lids falling, she found his erection, closed her hand about the rigid length.

He breathed out, short, sharp, as she squeezed and released. With her other hand, she reached further, caressed his heavy testicles, cradled them, fondled.

Royce's lungs locked tight, his body as rigid as his erection as she worked him with one hand, with the other weighed his balls, assessed, played. The sense of possession escalated. Head back, he gritted his teeth against a curse.

He'd felt nothing like this. Ever before. Sight cut off, he was functioning on touch, and imagination. Her lascivious acts conjured the image of a sultry, sirenlike seductress who owned him. Who could make free with his body as she wished, with total impunity.

That it was he who granted that immunity, his hands so tightly locked on his carved bedposts his fingers felt fused with the wood, merely added another layer to the swelling sensuality.

Her hand closed firmly. His control shuddered. Jaw clenched, he fought the impulse to pump his hips, work his erection in her fist. He wanted, desperately, to turn to her, rip the prim nightgown away, exposing the siren before spreading her beneath him and sheathing himself in her.

338

He burned to possess her with the same calculated intensity with which she was possessing him.

Over recent nights she'd learned what strokes, what actions, most pleasured him. Now she applied the knowledge. Too well . . .

Head back, he fought . . . every muscle locked tight.

"*Minerva!*" The plea was wrenched from him.

Her grip eased, her strokes slowed. Her hand drifted from his balls and he could breathe again.

"No talking, remember. Well, not unless you want to beg."

He growled, "I'm begging."

Silence, then she laughed. Sultry, rich, a siren's laugh. "Oh, Royce – what a lie. You just want to take control – but not this time."

She shifted position; her grip changed. "Not tonight. Tonight, you've ceded control to me."

Head rising, she murmured beneath his ear, "Tonight, you're mine."

Her fingers closed around his erection. "Mine to take. Mine to sate." Her breath fanning his ear, she ran her thumb over the weeping head. "*All* mine."

Sensation lanced through him. He locked his knees, sucked in a breath. He'd agreed – now all he could do was endure.

Easing her grip, but without releasing his erection, she slipped under his braced arm and off the bed. Taking him firmly in hand again, she came to stand before him. The hem of her nightgown drifted over his feet.

Pressing herself to him, she reached up, drew his head down for a long, sultry kiss. Locked between them, her hand solidly fisted his erection. He let her dictate, did nothing but follow. She laughed softly into his mouth, then, lips locking on his, moved.

Sinuously, flagrantly, blatantly erotic, her breasts, hips and thighs caressed him, flooding his senses with images of her writhing against him, wanton and abandoned – as hungry, as urgent, as desperate as he.

She released his lips and sank slowly down, lips trailing

down . . . head back, jaw clenched tight, he waited, prayed, wanted – feared . . .

She slid her lips slowly over his erection, slowly, deliberately took him into her mouth. Deep, then deeper, until he was sunk to the balls in her wet heat.

Slowly, deliberately, she reduced him to quaking desperation.

And he couldn't stop her.

He wasn't in control. He was at her mercy, completely and absolutely.

Hands gripping the posts, unable to see, he had to surrender, cede his body and his senses to her, hers to do with as she pleased.

One heartbeat before the point of no return, she slowed her attentions, then drew back.

His chest heaved; the night air felt cool against his damp, heated skin. She released him, rocked back, rose.

Fingers loose around his straining erection, she reached up and drew his head down. Kissed him, but briefly; drawing back, with her teeth, she tugged his lower lip – refocusing his attention.

"You have a choice. You can have your sight, or your hands. Choose."

He wanted his hands on her, wanted to feel her skin, her curves, but if he couldn't see . . . "Take off the blindfold."

Minerva smiled. His gaze she could endure, but with his hands free, her remaining in control for much longer was unlikely.

And she wanted longer.

The air was heavy, thick, the scent of passion and desire a miasma about them. The salty taste of his arousal was fresh on her tongue; she'd wanted to lure him to completion, but the hollow ache between her thighs was too insistent. She needed him there as desperately as he wanted her sheath enclosing his erection.

They each needed the other to achieve their ultimate in completion.

340

She reached up as he lowered his head. She picked the knot free, unwound the folds, drew the long strip away and stepped back. He blinked, focused.

His dark gaze burned, scorching, piercing.

She caught it, refused to think about his strength, that it was *his* control that gave her any chance of controlling him. "Put the insides of your wrists together in front of you."

Slowly he eased his fingers from their death grips on the posts, flexed his arms, then set his wrists together as she'd asked.

She bound them with the linen band. Releasing the trailing ends, she placed her splayed fingertips on his chest, pushed. "Sit on the bed, then lie back."

He sat, then let himself fall back onto the crimson-and-gold brocade.

Grasping one bedpost, raising the nightgown, she clambered up, kneeling, looking down at him. "Put your hands on the bed above your head."

In seconds he was lying stretched out on the bed, hands above his head, calves and feet dangling over the edge.

He lay there, naked, delectable, heavily aroused, hers for the taking.

Trapping his gaze, she wrapped one hand about his erection, with the other raised her nightgown so she could swing her thigh over his hips. Sinking down on her knees, she released the gown; the folds fell to his belly, screening her actions as she guided the blunt head of his erection between her slick folds, then eased back.

Releasing him, she sank slowly back, down, smoothly taking his turgid length into her body.

She shifted, sank further still, until she'd taken him all. Until she sat across his hips, impaled, full of him. He stretched her, completed her; the length and strength of him at her core felt indisputably right.

Her gaze locked with his, she rose slowly up, then slowly sank down.

Fingers braced on his chest, she changed angle, pace, found the rhythm she wanted, one she could maintain, sliding him deeply in, then almost completely out. He clenched his jaw, clenched his fists. His muscles hardened, tightened, as she devoted herself to taking every iota of sensual pleasure she could.

It wasn't enough.

Wrapped in his gaze, acutely aware of all she could see blazing in the dark depths of his eyes as his body strained, fought his control – as he battled his own instincts to give her all she wanted . . .

In that moment, she knew. For her, with him, taking would never be enough. She had to give – give him, show him, all she was. All that with him, for him, she could be.

All she could gift him with.

All that blossomed inside her.

She reached down, grasped her nightgown, drew it up, off, flung it aside. His gaze instantly lowered to where they joined. She couldn't see what he could, imagining was enough; the heat between her thighs flared. Within her, he grew larger, harder; she felt the change in his body between her thighs, deep inside her.

He glanced briefly at her face, then looked down again. His hips undulated beneath hers.

She should have ordered him to stop, to lie still. She didn't. Breath sawing in her throat, she arched back; head up, arms crossed behind, her hair a wild cascade about her, eyes closed, she gave herself up to the bucking ride, to the overwhelming pleasure, and rode him hard, then harder.

It still wasn't enough; she needed him deeper.

She sobbed, slowed, desperate . . .

He swore. Surged up from the waist, his bound wrists passing over her head, trapping her within the circle of his arms. Turning his palms, setting them to her back, his gaze locked with hers, he shifted between her thighs, then thrust up harder, deeper, higher with her.

He settled to a solid, heavy rhythm. His gaze lowered to her lips, inches from his. "You're still in control." He glanced up, caught her gaze. "Tell me if you like this."

342

He bent, set his lips to her ruched nipple. She cried out. He suckled; she gasped. Sinking her hands in his hair, she held him to her. Held him while he rocked her, pleasured her, while they came together and the sounds and scents of their joining wreathed through her brain, filling, reassuring, exciting.

She wanted more.

More of him.

All of him.

She wanted what he did.

Catching his head between her hands, she urged him to look up.

When he did, dark eyes heavy-lidded, lips rich, fine, wicked, she caught his gaze. Gasped, "Enough. Take me. Finish this."

His steady thrusting between her thighs didn't ease. He looked deep. "Are you sure?"

"Yes." Surer than of anything in the world. Slowing her own rhythm, she lost herself in his eyes. "However you wish, however you want."

For one long moment, he held her gaze.

Then she was on her back, flung across his bed, clinging to sanity as with her thighs pressed wide, his bound hands beneath her head, palms cradling it, he thrust into her body, hard, deep –

Sanity fractured and she flew apart.

Royce gasped, fought to hold still so he could savor her release, but the contractions were so strong they ruthlessly, relentlessly drew him on, until with a muffled roar he followed her into oblivion, his release, so long denied, rolling over and through him, powerfully raking him, wrecking him, leaving him drained, a husk buoyed on a welling emotional tide, coming back to life as glory seeped in, and filled him.

As his heart swelled, and he drew in a shuddering breath, through the haze in his brain, he felt her lips caress his temple.

"Thank you."

The words were a ghost of a whisper, but he heard, slowly smiled.

She had it arse over tit; it was he who should thank her.

*

343

A significant time later, he finally summoned sufficient strength to lift from her, roll onto his back, and with his teeth pick apart the knot at his wrists.

She lay slumped alongside him, but she wasn't asleep. Still smiling, he scooped her up, dragged down the covers, then collapsed on the pillows, arranged her in his arms, and tugged the covers over them.

Without a word, she snuggled against him, all but boneless.

Pleasure, of a depth and quality he'd never thought to feel, rolled over and through him. And sank to his bones.

Tilting his head, he looked into her face. "Did I pass your test?"

"Humph. Somewhere through all that" – she waved weakly toward the end of the bed – "I realized it was a test for me as much as you."

His lips curved more deeply; he'd wondered if she'd seen that.

Curiously clearheaded, he revisited the events, and even more the emotions – all they'd broached, drawn on, used, revealed, over the last hour.

She was still awake. Waiting to hear what he would say.

He touched his lips to her temple. "Know this." He kept his voice low; she would hear all he wanted her to hear in his tone. "I will give you anything. Anything and everything I have to give. There is nothing you can ask for that I will not grant you – whatever I have, whatever I am, is yours."

Each word rang with absolute, unshakable commitment.

A long moment passed. "Do you believe me?"

"Yes." The answer came without hesitation.

"Good." Lips curving, settling his head on the pillow, he closed his arms about her. "Go to sleep."

He knew it was a command, didn't care. He felt her sigh, felt the last of her tension fade, felt sleep claim her. Taking his own advice, contented to his toes, he surrendered to his dreams.

Chapter 19

At a smidgen before dawn, Minerva floated back to her room, flopped into her bed, and sighed. She couldn't stop smiling. Royce had more than passed her test with flying colors; even if he couldn't promise love, what he had promised had more than reassured. He'd given her everything she'd asked for.

So what now? What next?

She still had no assurance that at some point what presently flared so hotly between them wouldn't die . . . Could she risk accepting his offer?

Could she risk not?

She blinked, felt a cold chill wash through her. Frowned as, for the first time, the alternative to accepting – refusing him, turning her back on all that might be and walking away – formed in her mind.

The truth dawned.

"Damn that mangy Scot." She slumped back on her pillows. "He's right!" Why had it taken her so long to see it?

"Because I've been looking at Royce, not me. *I* love him." To the depths of her soul. "No matter how many symptoms of love he has, *my* heart won't change."

Infatuation-obsession had grown to something a great deal more – more powerful, deeper, impossible to deny, and immutable, set in stone. Whatever trials she staged, even when he passed with flying colors, were no more than reassurance. Comforting, enlightening, and supportive, yes, but in the end, beside the point. *She* loved him, and as Penny had said, love was not a passive emotion.

Love would never allow her to turn her back on him and walk away, would never allow her to be so cowardly as not to risk her heart.

Love would – and did – demand her heart.

If she wanted love, she had to risk it. Had to give it. Had to surrender it.

Her way forward was suddenly crystal clear.

"Your Grace, I will be honored to accept your offer."

Her heart literally soared at the sound of the words – words she'd never thought to say. Her lips curved, and curved; she smiled gloriously.

The door opened; Lucy breezed in. "Good morning, ma'am. Ready for the big day? Everyone's already bustling below stairs."

"Oh. Yes." Her smile waned. She inwardly swore; it was the day before the fair. The one day of the year in which she would have not a moment to call her own.

Or Royce's.

She swore again, and got up.

And plunged into the day – into a whirlpool of frenetic activity and concerted organization.

Breakfast for her was rushed. Royce, wisely, had come down early, and already ridden out. All the guests had arrived; the parlor was a sea of chatter and greetings. Of course, her three mentors were agog to hear her news; given the company, the best she could do was reconjure her radiant smile.

They saw it, interpreted it accurately – and beamed back.

Letitia patted her arm. "That's wonderful! You can tell us the details later."

Later it would have to be. It had been too many years since the staff had coped with a house party and the fair simultaneously; panic threatened on more than one front.

Tea and toast downed, Minerva rushed up to the morning

room. She and Cranny spent a frantic hour making sure their days' schedules included all that needed doing. The housekeeper had just left when a tap on the door heralded Letitia, Penny, and Clarice.

"Oh." Meeting Letitia's bright gaze, Minerva tried to refocus her mind.

"No, no." Grinning, Letitia waved aside her efforts. "Much as we'd like to hear all – in salacious detail – now is clearly not the time. Apropos of which, we've come to offer our services."

Minerva blinked; as Letitia sat, she glanced at Penny and Clarice.

"There is nothing worse," Penny declared, "than idly waiting, kicking one's heels, with nothing to do."

"Especially," Clarice added, "when there's obvious employment in which our particular talents might assist – namely, your fair." She sank onto the sofa. "So share – what's on your list that we can help with?"

Minerva took in their patently eager expressions, then looked down at her lists. "There's the archery contests, and . . ."

They divided up the tasks, then she ordered the landau to be brought around. While the others fetched bonnets and shawls, she grabbed hers and rushed down to speak with Retford. He and she discussed entertainments for the castle's guests, most of whom would remain about the castle that day, then she hurried to join the others in the front hall.

On the way to the fairground – the field beyond the church – they went over the details of the tasks each would pursue. Reaching the field, already a sea of activity, they exchanged glances, and determinedly plunged in.

Even delegating as she had, getting through her list of activities to be checked, organized or discussed took hours. The Alwinton Fair was the largest in the region; crofters came from miles around, out of the hills and dales of the Borders, and travelers, tradesmen, and craftsmen came from as far afield as Edinburgh to sell their wares.

On top of that, the agricultural side was extensive.

Although Penny was overseeing the preparations for the animal contests, Minerva had kept the produce section under her purview; there were too many locals involved, too many local rivalries to navigate.

And then there was the handfasting; the fair was one of the events at which the Border folk traditionally made their declarations before a priest, then jumped over a broomstick, signaling their intention of sharing an abode for the next year. She came upon Reverend Cribthorn in the melee.

"Nine couples this year." He beamed. "Always a delight to see the beginnings of new families. I regard it as one of my most pleasurable duties, even if the church pretends not to know."

After confirming time and place for the ceremonies, she turned away – and through a gap in the milling throng, spotted Royce. He was surrounded by a bevy of children, all chattering up at him.

He'd been about all day, directing and, to their astonishment, often assisting various groups of males engaged in setting up booths and tents, stages and holding pens. Although he and she had exchanged numerous glances, he'd refrained from approaching her – from distracting her.

She'd still felt his gaze, had known that at times he'd passed close by in the crowd.

Given he was absorbed, she allowed herself to stare, to drink in the sight of him dealing with what she'd come to realize he saw as his youngest responsibilities. He hadn't forgotten the footbridge, and therefore the aldermen of Harbottle hadn't forgotten, either. Hancock, the castle carpenter, had been dispatched to oversee the reconstruction, and reported daily to Royce.

Every local, on first setting eyes on him – a tall, commanding figure in his well-cut coat, buckskin breeches, and top boots – stopped and stared. As she watched, Mrs. Critchley from beyond Alwinton halted in her tracks, and all but gawped.

His father hadn't attended the fair in living memory, but

even more telling, his father would never, ever have assisted – have counted himself as one of this community. He'd been their ruler, but never one of them.

Royce would rule as his ancestors had before him, but not distantly, aloofly; he was one with the noisy horde around him. She no longer needed to think to know his views; his sense of duty toward those he ruled – to his people – infused all he did. It was a fundamental part of who he was.

Confident, arrogant, assured to his toes, he was Wolverstone, marcher lord incarnate – and using that power that by birth was his to wield, he'd rescripted the role, far more thoroughly, more fundamentally and progressively, than she'd dared hope.

Watching him with the children, seeing him turn his head and exchange a laughing comment with Mr. Cribthorn, she felt her heart grow wings.

That was the man she loved.

He was who he was, he still had his flaws, but she loved him with all her heart.

She had to turn away, had to battle to suppress the emotion welling inside so she could smile and function and do what needed doing. Irrepressibly smiling, she lifted her head, drew breath, and plunged back into the crowd, immersed herself in all she'd come there to do.

Later.

Later she would speak with him, accept his offer – and offer him her heart, without reservation.

"It's entirely thanks to you three that I'm heading home before dusk, let alone in time for afternoon tea." At ease in the landau, Minerva smiled at Letitia, Clarice, and Penny, all, like her, exhausted, but satisfied with their day.

"It was our pleasure," Penny returned. "Indeed, I think I'll suggest Charles investigates getting some ewes from that breeder, O'Loughlin."

She grinned, but didn't get to mention Hamish's background, distracted instead by Clarice's account of what she'd

349

discovered among the craft stalls. By the time they reached the castle, she'd been amply reassured that her friends hadn't found their assumed duties too onerous. Alighting, they went indoors to join the company for afternoon tea.

All the ladies were present, but only a handful of the gentlemen, most having taken out rods or guns and disappeared for the day.

"It seemed wise to encourage them," Margaret said. "Especially as we want them to dance attendance on us tomorrow at the fair."

Smiling to herself, Minerva quit the gathering and climbed the main stairs. She wasn't sure she'd dealt with everything within the castle itself; she'd left those lists in the morning room.

She was reaching for the knob of the morning room door when it opened.

Royce stood framed in the doorway. "There you are."

"I've just got back. Or rather" – she tipped her head downward – "just finished afternoon tea. Everything seems to be proceeding smoothly."

"As, under your guidance, things always do." Taking her arm, he moved her back, joining her and pulling the door closed behind him. "That being the case . . . come walk with me."

He wound her arm in his, setting his hand over hers. She glanced at his face – uninformative as ever – as she strolled beside him. "Where to?"

"I thought . . ." He'd led her back into the keep; now he turned down the short corridor to his apartments – not entirely to her surprise.

But he halted a few paces along, looked at the wall, then put out his hand, depressed a catch; the door to the keep's battlements sprang open. "I thought," he repeated, meeting her gaze as he held the door wide, "that the view from the battlements might entice."

She laughed, and readily went through. "Along with the peace up there, plus the fact it's entirely private?"

Perhaps she could tell him her decision up there?

"Indeed." Royce followed her into the stairway built into the keep's wall. Once she'd climbed to the top of the steep flight and pushed open the door, letting light flood down, he closed the corridor door, then took the stairs three at a time, emerging to join her on the open battlements.

They were the original battlements, the highest part of the castle. The view was spectacular, but by long tradition was enjoyed by only the family, more particularly those residing within the keep; guests had never been permitted up there, on the walks where, over the centuries, the family's most trusted guards had kept watch for their enemies.

The breeze was brisker than in the fields below; it tugged and flirted with Minerva's hair as she stood in one of the gaps in the crenellations, looking north, over the gardens, the bridge, the mill, and the gorge.

As he neared, she lifted her face, shook back her hair. "I'd forgotten how fresh it is up here."

"Are you cold?" He closed his hands about her shoulders.

She glanced into his face, smiled. "No, not really."

"Good. Nevertheless . . ." He slid his arms around her and drew her back against him, settling her back to his chest, enveloping her in his greater warmth. She sighed and relaxed into his embrace, leaning against him, crossing her arms, her hands curving over his as she looked out. His chin beside her topknot, he, too, gazed out over his fields.

The unfulfilled impulse that had prompted him to take her to Lord's Seat lookout weeks before had prodded him to bring her here – for the same reason.

"All you can see," he said, "as far as you can see, all the lands beneath your gaze are mine. All that lies beneath our feet – that, too, is mine. My heritage, under my rule, under my absolute authority. The people are mine, too – mine to protect, to watch over – their welfare my responsibility, all part of the same whole." He drew breath, then went on, "What you see before you is the greater part of what my life will be. What it will encompass. And you're already an integral part of it. The

351

day I took you to Lord's Seat, this is what I wanted to show you – all that I want to share with you."

He glanced at her profile. "I want to share all of my life with you, not just the customary parts. Not just the social and familial arenas, but all this, too." Tightening his arms, laying his jaw against her hair, he found the words he'd been searching for. "I want you by my side in everything, not just my duchess, but my helpmate, my partner, my guide. I will welcome you gladly into whatever spheres of my life you wish to grace.

"If you consent to be my wife, I will willingly give to you not just my affection, not just my protection, but the right to stand beside me in everything I do. As my duchess, you will not be an adjunct, but an integral part of all that, together, we will be."

Minerva couldn't keep the smile from her face. He was who he was, manipulative to his toes; he'd eloquently laid before her what he knew to be the most potent inducement he could offer – but he was sincere. Totally, unquestionably, speaking from his heart.

If she'd needed further convincing that she could have faith and go forward, that she should accept his suit and become his duchess, he'd just supplied it; all he'd said was predicated on, based on, built upon an "affection" he believed was sound, solid, as unshakable as the foundations of his keep.

She already knew the counter to that emotion lived, strong and vital, in her. To have such a fate, such a challenge, such a destiny offered her so freely . . . that was more than she'd ever dared dream.

Turning in his arms, she looked into his face, met his dark eyes. They were as unreadable as ever, but his lips twisted wryly.

"I know I shouldn't push – shouldn't press." He held her gaze. "I know you still need time to assimilate all I've said, all that's happened between us, but I wanted you to know how much you mean to me, so your deliberations will be . . . fully informed."

She smiled at his phrasing; despite his undoubted intelligence, he hadn't yet realized that love didn't need that much thought.

He smiled back. "And now I'm going to give you all the time you want to decide. I won't say more, not until you tell me I should."

Lowering his head, he brushed her lips lightly in an undemanding caress.

It wasn't something he meant to do, but there was enough in his tone to remind her that, from a man like him, granting her time was a gift.

Her declaration hovered in the forefront of her mind, yet his unstated boon – unneeded though it might be – deserved some acknowledgment; as their lips parted, she rose on her toes, pressed her lips to his, parted them – invited. They were alone, private; no one could see.

Lifting her arms, she wound them about his neck, pressed herself to him. His hands fastened about her waist, held her for an instant, then he laughed softly, angled his head, and took the kiss deeper.

Took her deeper, into the familiar richness of their mutual desire.

For long moments, they savored – each other, the warmth of the exchange, the inherent comfort.

Then the fire took hold.

Neither had summoned it; the flames were suddenly simply there, greedily licking all around them, tempting, luring . . .

Both hesitated, sensing, seeking the other's direction . . .

Both surrendered. Grasped. Seized.

His hands, spread, moved over her back, his touch possessive and sure. She sank her hands into his hair, held him to the suddenly rapacious kiss, and flagrantly demanded more.

Kneading her breasts, kissing her with slow, relentless promise, he backed her against the ungiving stone of his battlements.

Mutual need fired their blood, had her reaching for his waistband, had him raising her skirts.

Mutual passion had them gasping, hungry and greedy as he lifted her, braced her against the stone, sank into her, then thrust deep.

Mutual pleasure caught them; panting, chests heaving, they froze, forehead to forehead, breaths mingling, heated gazes touching, and drank in the exquisite sensation of their joining. Let it sink to their respective bones.

Then he closed his eyes and groaned, she moaned, and each sought the others' lips.

And let mutual surrender have them, take them.

A click was all the warning they had.

"Oh, my *God*!"

The shrill exclamation fell like a bucket of icy water over them.

It was followed by a chorus of gasps, and more muted expressions of shock.

Head up, spine rigid, Royce thought faster than he ever had in his life.

Women, ladies, an untold number, stood clustered in the doorway five yards behind his back.

Someone had brought them up here, but who had wasn't his first concern.

Locked in his arms, supported by his hand beneath her bottom and braced by his body sunk deeply in hers, Minerva was rigid. Hands fisted in his lapels, she'd ducked her head to his chest.

He felt like he'd been clouted with a battle mace.

His shoulders were broad; the women behind him couldn't see her, at least not her face or body. They would be able to see her topknot, telltale wheat-gold, over his shoulder, and even more damningly her stocking-clad legs clasped about his hips.

There was not a hope in hell of disguising their occupation.

A kiss would have been bad enough, but this . . .

There was only one course of action open to him.

Easing Minerva from him, he withdrew from her; given his size, that necessitated a maneuver that even viewed from behind was impossible to mistake. Her knees slid from his hips, he lowered her until her feet touched the ground. Her skirts tumbled straight of their own accord.

"Don't move," he murmured, quickly doing up the placket of his breeches. "Don't say a word."

She looked at him through wide, utterly stunned eyes.

Uncaring of the crowd, he bent his head and kissed her, a swift, reassuring kiss, then he straightened and turned to face their fate.

His expression aloof and cold, his gaze pure ice, he regarded the knot of ladies, round-eyed, hands at their breasts, their expressions as stunned as Minerva's . . . except for Susannah's. She stood at the rear, peering past the others.

Refocusing on those in the front of the group – a cluster of his sisters' London friends – he drew breath, then said the words he had to say. "Ladies. Miss Chesterton has just done me the honor of agreeing to be my wife."

"*Well!* It's Miss Chesterton! Whoever would have thought!" Caroline Courtney, all agog, broke the news as he circled the billiard table. With the other men present, most Royce's cousins, he halted and listened as Caroline blurted out the juicy details of how Royce and his chatelaine had been caught *in flagrante delicto* on the battlements.

"There was absolutely no doubt about it," she assured them. "We all saw."

He frowned. "Was she who Royce intended to marry all along?"

Caroline shrugged. "Who can say? Regardless, she's the one he'll have to marry now."

Frowning, Gordon stated, "I can't imagine Royce letting himself be trapped like that." Then he realized what he'd said, and colored. "Not that Minerva won't make a perfectly acceptable duchess."

Inwardly smiling, he mentally thanked Susannah; outwardly calm, he turned back to the table, savoring his victory.

The news would reach London as fast as the mail coach could carry it; he wouldn't need to lift so much as a finger.

So Royce would now have to marry his chatelaine – be *forced* to marry her, and that he wouldn't like.

Even worse would be the whispers traded behind scented hands, the sniggers, the unsavory speculation directed at his duchess.

Unavoidable within the ton.

And Royce wouldn't like that *at all*.

Smiling, he leaned over the table and sent one ball neatly into a pocket, then he straightened and, slowly circling the table, surveyed the possibilities.

In the duchess's morning room, Letitia watched Minerva pace. "I appreciate that it's the *very* last thing you would have wished to happen, but believe me, in the circumstances, there was nothing else he could have done."

"I know." Her tone clipped, Minerva swung on her heel. "I was there. It was *awful*."

"Here." Penny held out a glass containing at least three fingers of brandy. "Charles swears it always helps." She took a sip from her own glass. "And he's right."

Minerva seized the glass, took a healthy swallow, and felt the fiery liquid sear her throat, but then the warmth spread lower, loosening some of her icy rage. "I felt so damned *helpless*! I couldn't even think."

"Take it from a Vaux, that scene would have taxed my histrionic capabilities." Letitia, too, was sipping brandy. She shook her head. "There wasn't anything you could have done to change the outcome."

Rendered more furious than she'd ever been in her life, Minerva could barely recall descending from the battlements. In a voice that dripped icicles, Royce had, entirely unsubtly, informed the importunate ladies that the battlements, like the keep itself, were private; they'd all but tripped over each other fleeing back down the stairs. Once they were gone, he'd turned, taken her hand, led her down, and brought her here.

She'd been trembling – with rage.

He'd been incandescent with fury, but, as usual, very little showed. He'd kissed her lightly, squeezed her hand, said, "Wait here." Then he'd left.

Minutes later, Letitia had arrived, fired with concern, ready to offer comfort and support; she'd lent a sympathetic ear while Minerva had ranted, literally raved over being denied her declaration, her supreme moment when she accepted Royce and pledged her love.

Penny had joined them a few minutes ago, bearing a tray with the brandy decanter and four glasses. She'd listened for a moment, then set down the tray and poured.

The door opened, and Clarice came in. Penny held out the fourth glass; Clarice thanked her with a nod as she took it, sipped, then sank down onto the sofa opposite Letitia. She met their gazes. "Between us – Royce, Penny, Jack, and me – and surprisingly enough, Susannah – I think we've got everything smoothed over. Our story is that the three of us knew of the engagement – which, given your state this morning and what would naturally have followed from that, is the truth. And, indeed, that's why we're here, to witness the announcement for the grandes dames."

Minerva scowled, sipped. "I vaguely recall Royce muttering something about wringing Susannah's neck. Wasn't she the one who brought the ladies up to the battlements? If she was, and he hasn't, I will."

"She was." Penny sat beside Clarice. "But believe it or not, she thought she was helping. Being Cupid's assistant, so to speak. She'd learned, somehow, that you were Royce's lover, and decided she much preferred you as her sister-in-law over any other, so . . ." Penny shrugged. "Of course, she thought it was Royce dragging his heels."

Minerva grimaced. "She and I were much closer when we were young – we've always been friendly, although recently, of course, the connection's been more distant." She sighed, and dropped onto the sofa beside Letitia. "I suppose that explains it."

Penny's Charles was right; the brandy helped, but anger still coursed her veins. Thanks to Susannah, she and even more Royce had lost what should have been a treasured moment. "Damn!" She took another sip.

Luckily, the incident on the battlements and its outcome had changed nothing beyond that; she literally thanked heaven that she'd already made up her mind. If she hadn't . . .

Letitia stood. "I must go and speak with Royce."

"You know," Clarice said, "I always thought our husbands treated him with a respect that was somewhat overstated – as if they credited him with more power, more ability, than he or any man could possibly have." She raised her brows. "After seeing him in action downstairs, I've revised my opinion."

"Was he diabolical?" Letitia asked.

Clarice considered. "Mildly so. It was more a case of everyone being suddenly reminded of the Wolverstone family emblem – that it has teeth."

"Well," Penny said, "for my money, he has every right to feel savage."

"Be that as it may," Letitia said, "I have to go and bait the wolf."

"He's shut up in his study," Clarice told her. "'_'Ware the snarls."

"He might snarl, but he won't bite. At least, not me." Letitia paused at the door. "I hope."

On that note, she left.

Minerva frowned into her glass, now less than half full – then set it aside. After a moment, she rose and tugged the bellpull; when a footman arrived, she said, "Please inform Lady Margaret, Lady Aurelia, and Lady Susannah that I wish to speak with them. Here. Immediately."

The footman bowed – lower than normal; clearly the household already knew of her impending change in station – and withdrew.

Meeting Clarice's inquiring glance, Minerva smiled – intently. "I believe it's time I clarified matters. Aside from all else, with a ducal wedding to organize, the house party ends tomorrow night."

Royce was standing at the window when Jeffers entered to announce Letitia; he turned as she came in. "How is she?"

Letitia arched a brow. "Upset, of course."

The fury he'd been holding at bay – clamped tight inside – rose up at the thought, the confirmation. He turned back to look blindly out at his fields. After a long moment, during which Letitia wisely remained silent and still, he bit off, "It wasn't supposed to be like this."

Every word was invested with cold, hard rage.

The same words that had rung in his head as he'd driven back to Wolverstone after so many years away.

When he'd driven home to bury his father.

This time, the rage was even greater. "I can't believe – can't understand why – Susannah would do such a thing, even if, as she claims, she was trying to help." That was the other element that was eating at him. He raked a hand through his hair. "What help is this – essentially forcing us into marriage?"

Letitia saw the tremble in his hand, didn't mistake it for weakness; it was pure rage distilled. But he wouldn't be so angry, so close to true rage, if he didn't care – deeply – about Minerva's feelings. If he didn't have deep feelings of his own.

She was a Vaux – an expert in emotional scenes, in reading the undercurrents, the real passions beneath. Yet if she told him how pleased she was to see him so distraught, he'd bite her head off.

Besides, she had another role to fill. Lifting her head, she imperiously asked, "The announcement – have you written it?"

She hoped her tone would refocus his attention.

He continued to stare out. A minute ticked by. She waited.

"No." After a moment, he added, "I will."

"Just do it." She softened her voice. "You know it has to be done, and urgently." Realizing that he was at sea – on a storm-tossed emotional ocean he, of all men, was poorly equipped to navigate – she went on, "Get your secretary to pen it, then show it to Minerva and get her consent. Regardless, it must be on the mail coach to London tonight."

He didn't immediately respond, but then he nodded. Curtly. "It will be."

"Good." She bobbed a curtsy, turned, and walked to the door.

He stirred, glanced at her. "Can you tell Margaret she's hostess tonight?"

Her hand on the doorknob, she looked at him. "Yes, of course."

His chest swelled; for the first time he met her eyes. "Tell Minerva I'll come and see her in a little while – once I've got the announcement drafted."

Once he had his temper in hand. As a Vaux, Letitia knew all about temper – and she could see his roiling in his eyes.

He went on, "We'll dine in my apartments."

"I'll keep her company until then. Clarice, Jack, and Penny are going to mingle, to make sure there's no . . . uninformed talk." She smiled, anticipating doing the same herself – and putting a not-so-tiny flea in Susannah's ear. "I'll join them once you come for Minerva."

"Thank you. All of you."

Turning to the door, she smiled rather more delightedly, knowing he couldn't see. "Believe me, it's our pleasure." She paused, hand on the knob. "We can discuss the wedding tomorrow."

He grunted.

At least it wasn't a snarl. She let herself out, closing the door behind her. Glancing at Royce's footman standing utterly blank-faced along the wall, she smiled gloriously. "Despite all, this is going to work out very well."

With that, she hurried back to the morning room, to relate to Minerva all she'd seen, heard – and deduced.

Minerva had assuaged a great deal of her anger by the time Royce joined her in the morning room. Having successfully dealt first with his sisters, and then the assembled ladies, having ensured all knew precisely how unamused she was over Susannah's misplaced meddling, and having made her expectations, as the soon-to-be Duchess of Wolverstone, of their behavior over the matter abundantly plain, she was feeling much more settled as she stood looking out of the window, idly surveying his domain.

Royce's gaze locked on her the instant he opened the door, but she didn't turn around.

Seated on the sofa facing the door, Letitia rose. "I was about to go down." She glided forward.

Royce held the door open for her. She touched his arm, glanced back at Minerva. "I'll see you in the morning."

Without looking around, Minerva nodded – a tense, brief nod.

With a pat for him, Letitia left. He closed the door, hesitated – sent a prayer winging to any god that might be listening that Minerva wouldn't cry. Feminine tears usually left him unaffected, but her tears would shred his control, rupture his tenuous hold on his temper – and the gods alone knew who he'd strike out at, or how. Not her, of course, but . . .

Breathing in, mentally shoring up his defenses, emotional ones he rarely used, he walked to her side.

It was early evening; beyond the window, the shadows were lengthening, laying a purple wash over his lands. Spine poker straight, arms crossed, she was looking out, but he'd swear not seeing.

Halting beside her, he angled his head the better to see her features. She turned her head and met his gaze.

Her expression was controlled, composed, more so than he'd expected; her eyes . . . were unusually hard, and more unreadable than he'd ever seen, but . . . he could detect not a hint of tears.

Chin firm, she tipped her head toward the door. "They're really quite remarkable – Letitia, Penny, Clarice, and Jack. I'm sure between them they'll have the entire company in well-rehearsed order come morning."

Her tone was crisp, briskly businesslike. Determined. Steady assurance shone through her composed façade.

Confusion swamped him. Didn't she feel . . . *betrayed*? By fate, by his sister, by circumstance? By him? He drew in a

361

breath. "I'm sorry." He felt his jaw harden. "It wasn't supposed to have been like this."

Her eyes locked on his. "No, it wasn't, but what happened was neither my fault nor yours. Regardless, however much we may wish matters otherwise, we're faced with the situation as is, and we need to deal with it – to make the best of it. To take control and make it work for us, not against us."

He mentally blinked. She was behaving as if what had occurred was some minor hiccup along their road. A challenge they'd deal with, vanquish, and leave behind.

She couldn't be that understanding. She had to feel forced . . . had to resent the situation as much as he. He was missing something here; he didn't try to hide his frown. "You're a lot less upset than I expected."

The look she returned was all cold, hard steel. Her features tightened; her diction grew more precise. "I am *not* pleased – I'm angry, nay *furious, but* I am *not* of a mind to allow Susannah to play fast and loose with our lives." Strength of a kind he'd assumed was there but had never before encountered in her – the kind he associated with Lady Osbaldestone – radiated from her. "I am *not* going to let Susannah steal from us what we, both you and I, deserve. I know you don't understand, but I'll explain later." Alight with purpose, her eyes lowered. "Is that our announcement?"

He glanced down at the sheet of paper he'd forgotten he held. "Yes."

She held out her hand, fingers wiggling.

He handed over the excruciatingly generically worded statement he and Handley had labored over.

Turning, she held it so light from the window washed over it. "Royce Henry Varisey, tenth Duke of Wolverstone, son of the late Henry Varisey, ninth Duke of Wolverstone and the late Lady Catherine Debraigh, daughter of the fourth Earl of Catersham, announces his betrothal to Miss Minerva Miranda Chesterton, daughter of the late Lieutenant Michael Chesterton and the late Marjorie Dalkeith."

She frowned. "A lot of lates, but . . ." Face clearing, she

handed the announcement back, met his eyes. "That will do."

"So why, exactly, are you nothing more than 'not pleased'? What is it I don't understand?"

Halting before the wide window in Royce's bedroom, facing the night-shrouded hills, Minerva let her watchful tension ease. *Finally.*

Finally they were alone; finally she could tell him on her own terms, as she'd intended.

At his decree, they'd dined privately in his sitting room; she'd come into the bedroom to allow Jeffers to clear the table and set the room to rights. Royce had followed; closing the door on the clink of cutlery and plates, he'd prowled to halt just behind her.

She drew a deep breath. "I know you thought, by remaining apart, to spare me the ordeal of facing the undoubtedly avidly curious company downstairs – I agreed *not* because I felt fragile or distressed, but because *your* temper was so aroused that I had no faith whatever that your sisters or one of their friends wouldn't have said something to make you lash out – and that wouldn't have aided our cause." She swung to face him. "*Our* cause. From this morning on, it's been *our* cause."

She tilted her head, considered him. When he'd joined her in the morning room, his rage had been palpable, resonating in the words he'd ground out: *It wasn't supposed to have been like this.* "I understand why you were so angry. Being forced, trapped, into marriage shouldn't have mattered to you, but it did. Because you knew it mattered to me. You were enraged on my behalf – yours, too, but less directly."

The incident had delivered to him exactly what he'd wanted and had been working to gain – her agreement to their wedding. Yet instead of being pleased, he, a nobleman who rarely if ever apologized, had abjectly apologized for something that hadn't been his fault.

Because it was something she hadn't wanted, and so something the protector in him felt he should have prevented, but hadn't.

All day, in him, she'd been viewing love in action. Since that moment on the battlements, she'd watched love reduce a man accustomed to commanding all in his life to a wounded, potentially vicious beast.

While some intensely female part of her had gloated over such violent championing, she'd had to defuse his temper rather than encourage it. She'd been waiting for it to cool to have a better chance of him believing the truth of what she was about to say.

She locked her eyes on his, as always too dark to read. "I'd planned to speak now – this evening, once we were alone." She glanced around. "Here – in your room." She brought her gaze back to his face. "In your ducal apartments."

Stepping forward, eyes locked with his, she placed one hand over his heart. "I was going to tell you, just like this. Tell you that, as of this morning, I'd decided to accept your offer – when you make it. That you could feel free to offer, knowing I'll accept."

A long moment passed. He remained very still. "This morning?"

Hope warred with skepticism, but hope was winning. She smiled. "You can ask Letitia, Clarice, or Penny for confirmation – they knew. But that's why I'm not overwrought, distraught, unhappy. I'm none of those things – I'm *angry*, yes, but against that . . ." She let her smile deepen, let him see the depth of her understanding, and the sheer certainty and joy that was in her heart. "I'm thrilled, ecstatic, *delighted*. No matter Susannah's actions, no matter their outcome, in reality, between us, nothing has changed."

His hands slid about her waist. She raised hers, framed his face, looked deep into his fathomless eyes. "The only thing we might have lost was this moment, but I wasn't of a mind to let that go, to let it be taken from us. From this morning, for me, it's been *us* – *our* cause – and from this moment on, now that you know, there will be only one cause for us both – *ours*. It's the right cause for both of us to give our lives to – we both know that. From this moment on, we'll devote ourselves to it, work at it, if necessary fight for it – our joint life." Lost in his eyes, she let a heartbeat pass. "I wanted – needed – to tell you if that's what you want – if that's what your offer can and will encompass – then I'll accept. That's what I want, too."

A long moment passed, then his chest swelled as he drew in a huge breath. "You truly are happy to put this . . . hiccup behind us, consign it to history, and go forward?"

"Yes. Exactly as we would have."

He held her gaze for another long moment, then his lips, his features, eased. Her hands fell to his shoulders; he caught one of them, carried it to his lips. Eyes locked with hers, he kissed her fingertips.

Slowly.

In that instant he truly was mesmerizing; she couldn't have torn her gaze from his had flames leapt about them.

"Minerva, my lover. My lady. My heart. Will you marry me?"

She blinked once, twice, felt her heart literally swell. "Yes."

Such a little word, and although she'd poured every ounce of her certainty, resolution, and joy into it, there was more she had to say. Raising her other hand, she laid her fingers against his lean cheek, lightly traced the angular planes that gave so little away, even now.

Felt her heart overflow as she looked into his eyes, smiled. "I'll marry you, Royce Varisey, and fill the place by your side. I'll bear your children, and with my hand in yours, face whatever the future might bring, and make the most of it that, together, we can . . . for Wolverstone – and you."

He was Wolverstone, but that wasn't all he was. Underneath was a man who deserved her love. So she gave it, let him see it in her eyes.

Royce studied the autumn hues, the brilliant golds, the passionate browns, the mysterious agate-green, knew to his soul how much she meant to him – and knew he was the luckiest man alive. Slowly bending his head, he waited until she tipped her face up to his, then lowered his lips to hers.

And let a simple kiss seal their pact.

The loving that followed mirrored that kiss – simple, uncomplicated, undisguised. And she was right – nothing had changed. The passion, the heat, the fervor were the same. If anything deeper, broader, more intense, brought to burgeoning richness by acceptance, by the simple declarations that had committed them both, minds, bodies, hearts, and souls, to facing their future together.

That pledged them to the adventure of forging something new, something never before known in his family. To forging a marriage founded on, anchored in, held together by love.

Spread naked beneath him on his crimson silk sheets, she wrapped her arms about him and arched in welcome; poised above her, as heated and urgent as she, he slid into the haven of her body, and felt her clasp him tightly, embracing him, holding him. On a soundless gasp, head rising, he closed his eyes – held still, muscles bunched and quivering as he fought to give them that moment, that instant of indescribable sensation as their bodies locked, that instant of flagrant intimacy before the dance began.

Sensing the reins slipping, sliding from his grasp, he hauled in a breath and looked down. Saw her eyes glint gold from beneath her lashes.

I love you. He wanted to say the words, they hovered on his tongue, yet he didn't know, even now, if they were true. He wanted them to be, but . . .

Her lips curved as if she understood; reaching up with one hand, she cupped his nape, drew his lips to hers.

And kissed him – a blatant invitation to abandon.

He accepted and let go, let passion take and fuse them. Let their bodies surge, merge, surrendering to need, hunger, and wanting.

Opening his eyes, he looked down at her face, glowing with passion, rapturous in surrender, the face of his woman, his lady, soon his wife, utterly and unreservedly his.

Given to him.

He put aside the torment of the day, let their joint passion swamp it, drown it, wash it away. Let himself free and sealed their pact.

And gave himself unreservedly to her.

Chapter 20

The next morning, Minerva stood beside Royce as, with the cheers of the crowd for the nine handfasted couples gradually fading, he stepped to the front of the dais from which, earlier, he'd opened the fair.

Quietening, the crowd regarded him expectantly. He let his gaze roam the upturned faces, then said, "Wolverstone, too, has an announcement to make." He glanced at her, with his gaze drew her closer. His smile was all she would ever hope to see; the undisguised warmth in his eyes held her as, capturing her hand, he raised it to his lips, and in full view of the assembled company, pressed a kiss to her knuckles. "Miss Chesterton has done me the honor of agreeing to be my duchess."

He hadn't spoken loudly, yet his voice carried clearly over the hushed crowd . . .

The crowd erupted. Cheers, huzzahs, triumphant yells, whoops, and shrieks; noise rose in a wave of unalloyed happiness and washed over the scene. Minerva looked, and saw Hamish and Molly, who they'd found and told earlier, beaming up at them. The castle's staff were all there – Retford, Cranny, Cook, Jeffers, Milbourne, Lucy, Trevor, and all the rest – all looking fit to burst with pride and joy. Looking further, she saw the faces of many of Wolverstone's people, all delighted, all thrilled. Saw happy, joyous, pleased expressions, clapping hands, laughter, happy tears. Even those from the house party, scattered here and there among the throng, looked pleased to be part of the upwelling gladness.

Royce held up a hand; the cheers and whistles died. "Our wedding will be held in the church here, in just over three weeks' time. As many of you know, I returned only recently to take up the reins of the dukedom – in just a few weeks I've learned a great deal about what has changed, and what yet needs changing. Just as I'll make my vows to my duchess, and she to me, together we'll stand committed to you, to Wolverstone, to forging ahead into our joint future."

"Wolverstone!" With one voice, the crowd roared its approval. "Wolverstone! *Wolverstone!*"

Minerva surveyed the sea of happy faces, felt the warmth of their people reaching for them, embracing, buoying; turning her head, she met Royce's eyes, smiled.

His hand tightened about hers and he smiled back, openly, honestly, his customary shields lowered, for once set aside.

No! No, no, no, no – how could this have happened?

Deep in the crowd, surrounded by, jostled by, the raucous, gibbering throng, all transported with delight over the news of Royce's wedding, he stood stunned, unable to think – unable to drag his eyes from the picture of Royce and Minerva standing on the dais, lost in each other's eyes.

Royce was an excellent actor when he wanted to be – he knew that. Minerva could hold her own, too . . .

He shook his head, wished he could deny what his eyes were telling him. Neither was acting – what he was seeing, what the entire crowd about him was taking in and responding to, was *real*.

Royce wanted to marry Minerva.

And she wanted to marry him.

She was in love with him – nothing else could account for the softness in her face.

And while Royce couldn't possibly love her, he definitely

cared for her – in a far warmer way than he'd ever have thought possible.

Minerva wasn't, had never been, just another of Royce's legion of lovers. She'd been the one, all along – the lady he'd wanted as his wife . . .

"*It wasn't supposed to be like this*." He ground the words out through clenched teeth, fighting to keep his face a mask of utter blankness.

Their marriage was supposed to be a farce, a travesty – it was supposed to be *painful*. Instead, all his maneuvering had done was hand Royce precisely what he'd wanted.

He, through Susannah, had been instrumental in giving Royce the last thing he needed to complete the tapestry of an already rich and satisfying existence. He'd been instrumental in giving Royce something he craved, something he treasured . . .

Suddenly, he knew. Suddenly, he saw.

His features eased.

Then, slowly, he smiled, too.

Increasingly delightedly. He laughed, and clapped Rohan on the back when he passed him in the crowd.

Yes, of course. Now he saw it.

Royce had been the motive, the cause in bringing him his treasure – only then to take it away.

So fitting, then, that he would be the one to give Royce his greatest treasure – so he could return the favor.

Royce had taken his treasure.

Now he would take Royce's.

That evening, Royce, Minerva, Letitia, Clarice, Penny, and Handley met in the duchess's morning room. In the wake of the hugely successful fair – made even more notable by the news they'd shared – dinner had been an informal affair. After refreshing themselves, they'd left the relaxed and apparently pleasantly exhausted company downstairs, and retired to address the logistics of a ducal wedding.

While the others settled, Royce, subsiding beside Minerva on one of the sofas, considered his wife-to-be. "Did you say something to the others downstairs? They seem strangely unexercised by our betrothal."

"I simply explained that Susannah's intervention was misjudged, and that as your duchess, I would be severely displeased were anyone to paint our betrothal in anything other than the correct light."

Sinking onto the sofa opposite, Penny chuckled. "It was masterful. She made Susannah's action appear a childish prank – one of those occurrences that are so excruciatingly awkward that it would be a kindness to Susannah to pretend it never happened."

Joining Penny on the sofa, Letitia added, "She only had to speak to the ladies – Jack reported that as none of the men were on the battlements, they were very ready to pretend it never happened. But turning the event around so it reflected on Susannah was a master stroke. I would never have thought of it, but it served wonderfully well."

"No doubt," Clarice said, settling on the end of the sofa, "your facility comes from having to deal with Variseys for decades."

"Indeed." Minerva turned to Royce, met his eyes. "Now, for our wedding."

Very early that morning, he'd suggested as soon as possible, and been informed that wasn't in his cards. When he'd grumbled, he'd been further informed, at length, why. "Three weeks, I believe you said?"

Her eyes lit. "Indeed. Three weeks – and we'll need every minute from now until then." She looked at Handley, seated before her desk. "What date are we looking at?"

Resigned – and inwardly happier than he'd ever felt in his life – Royce sat back and let them organize; his only task was to approve when applied to, which he duly did. They were the experts. Letitia knew everything about staging events in the ton. Although in semiretirement, Clarice was renowned as a manipulator of ton sentiments. Penny, like Minerva, understood the dynamics of major estates, of country and county, while Minerva knew everything there was to know about Wolverstone and the Variseys.

Together, they made a formidable team. In short order, they had the framework settled.

"So" – Minerva caught Handley's eye – "the banns will be read over the next three Sundays, and we'll be married the following Thursday."

Handley nodded and made a note. "I'll ask Mr. Cribthorn to call tomorrow." He glanced at Royce.

"I'll be here all day. We've rather a lot to get into place." The marriage settlements, among other things. "You'd better summon Montague."

Handley furiously wrote. "And your solicitors?"

"Yes – them, too." Royce glanced at Minerva. "I've been racking my brains, but can't find the answer – who will give you away? And as you keep reminding me, this is a ducal union, so who do you want to act for you?"

She blinked. "I'll have to think about it." She glanced at Handley. "I'll give you the names and directions of my agent and solicitor so you can tell Royce's who to contact."

"Yes, ma'am."

Various other details were discussed and decided. The announcement for the news sheets completed, Handley left to ferry it to Retford for dispatch.

"The guest list," Clarice warned, "is going to be the biggest challenge."

"Just thinking of it makes the mind boggle." Letitia shook her head. "I thought my second wedding was big, but this . . ."

"We'll simply have to be highly selective," Minerva stated. "Which, to my mind, is no bad thing." She looked at Penny. "I'm inclined to set the number by the size of the church."

Penny considered, then shook her head. "You won't get away with that – not if by that you mean after you've accommodated the locals?"

"I did mean that." Minerva sighed. "So how many do you think?"

She'd wrestled the number down to five hundred when Royce decided he'd heard enough. *Five hundred?* Rising, he inclined his head. "Ladies, I believe I can leave the details in your capable hands." He glanced at Minerva. "If you need me, I'll be in the study, and then later in my apartments."

Waiting for her.

She smiled. "Yes, of course."

Smiling himself, he left them.

Minerva watched him go, sensing his inner peace, then, inwardly glowing herself, refocused on her list. "All right – how many do we need to allow for Carlton House?"

An hour later, with the major groups of guests identified and estimated, they called a halt. Retford had already delivered a tea tray; as they sat sipping, Letitia listed the areas they'd covered. "I really don't think there's much else we can assist you with, at least not at this time." She met Minerva's eyes. "We were thinking of leaving tomorrow at first light."

"Earlier than all the others, so we won't get caught up in their chaos," Penny said.

Clarice studied Minerva. "But if you truly need us, you only have to say."

She smiled, shook her head. "You've been . . ." She included the other two in her glance. "Immensely helpful, incredibly supportive. I honestly don't know how I would have got through all this without your help."

Letitia grinned. "You'd have managed. Given you can – demonstrably – manage your soon-to-be husband, I find it difficult to believe there's any situation you won't be able to overcome."

"I have to ask," Clarice said. "How did you get him to accept the three weeks so readily? We came prepared with a list of arguments, but you already had him agreeing."

"He's very predictable in some ways. I simply pointed out that our marriage should, by rights, be a major local event, and how disappointed everyone on the estate would be to be short-changed."

Letitia grinned. "Oh, yes – I can see that would work." She gave a delighted quiver. "Ooh! You've no idea how much good it does to see the master manipulator manipulated."

"But he knows I'm doing it," Minerva pointed out.

"Yes, indeed, and that makes it all the more delightful." Letitia set down her cup. "My dear, is there anything else, anything at all, that we can help you with before we leave?"

Minerva thought, then said, "If you will, answer me this: What moved your husbands to recognize they loved you?"

"You mean what wrung that word from their lips?" Letitia grimaced. "I was dangling from battlements, literally held from Death's jaws by his grip alone, before he thought to utter the word. I wouldn't recommend it."

Clarice frowned. "In my case, too, it was after a brush with death – with the iniquitous last traitor's henchman. Again, not an activity I'd recommend."

"As I recall," Penny said, "it was after we assisted Royce in apprehending a murderous French spy. There was a certain amount of life-threatening danger, none of which came to pass, but it opened *my* eyes, so I declared I would marry him – and then he was quite put out that I hadn't forced a grand declaration from him. He considered the point obvious, but had convinced himself that I'd claim my due." She smiled, sipped. "He gave it to me, anyway." Lowering her cup, she added, "Then again, he's half French."

Minerva frowned. "There seems to be a consistent trend with our sort of men."

Clarice nodded. "They seem to require a life-and-death situation to prod them into listening to their hearts."

Penny frowned. "But you already know Royce is head-over-ears in love with you, don't you? It really is rather blatantly obvious."

"Yes, *I* know." Minerva sighed. "I know, you know, even his sisters are starting to see it. But the one person who doesn't yet know is the tenth Duke of Wolverstone himself. And I honestly don't know how to open his eyes."

Three full weeks had come and gone. Sitting in the keep's breakfast parlor, Royce was quietly amazed; he'd thought the time would drag, but instead, it had flown.

On his left, a sunbeam glinting in her hair, Minerva was

engrossed in yet more lists; he smiled, savoring as he did count-less times a day the warmth and enfolding comfort of what he mentally termed his new existence.

His life as the tenth Duke of Wolverstone; it would be rad-ically different from that of his father's, and the cornerstone of that difference was his impending marriage.

Minerva humphed. "Thank heavens Prinny balked at the distance. Accommodating him and his toadies would have been a nightmare." She glanced up, smiled as Hamilton placed a fresh teapot before her. "We'll finalize the assignment of rooms this morning – Retford will need a list by noon."

"Indeed, ma'am. Retford and I have devised a plan of the castle, which will help."

"Excellent! If you come to the morning room once you're finished here, that should give me time to finish with Cranny, and check the mail to make sure we have no unexpected addi-tions." She glanced at Royce. "Unless you need Hamilton?"

He shook his head. "I'll be finalizing matters with Killsythe this morning." His solicitors, Killsythe and Killsythe, had finally wrested control of the last legal matters pertaining to the dukedom from Collier, Collier, and Whitticombe, so at last such issues were proceeding smoothly. "Incidentally" – with his finger he tapped a missive he'd earlier read – "Montague sent word that all is in place. He was very complimentary about your previous agent's efforts, but believes he can do better."

Minerva smiled. "I have high expectations." Reaching for the teapot, she surveyed the seven lists arrayed before her. "I can barely recall when I last had a chance to think of such mundane things as investments."

Royce raised his coffee cup, hid a smile. One thing he'd learned about his wife-to-be was that she thrived on challenge. As with his father's funeral, the principal guests would be accommodated at the castle, as would the majority of both sides of his family, virtually all of whom had sent word they would attend. While he'd been engulfed in legal and business matters, some still pending from his father's death but most part of the preparation necessary for the execution of the marriage settlements, Minerva's time had been swallowed up by preparations for the wedding itself.

Hamilton had proved a godsend; after discussions with Minerva and Retford, Royce had summoned him north to act as his personal butler, freeing Retford for the wider castle duties, increased dramatically because of the wedding. As Hamilton was younger and perfectly willing to defer to Retford, the arrangement was working well, to everyone's benefit.

Royce turned to the social page of yesterday's *Gazette*; he'd religiously perused every column inch devoted to their upcoming union ever since the news had broken. Far from being cast in any unflattering light, somewhat to his disgust their wedding was being touted as the romantic event of the year.

"What's today's effort like?" Minerva didn't take her eyes from her lists. When he'd first remarked on the slant all the news sheets had taken, she'd merely said, "I did wonder what they'd do." She'd been referring to the grandes dames.

Royce perused the five inches of column devoted to their event, then snorted. "This one goes even further. It reads like a fairy tale – wellborn but orphaned beauty slaves for decades as the chatelaine of a ducal castle, then on the death of the crusty old duke, catches the roving eye of said duke's mysterious exiled son, now her new lord, and a marcher lord at that, but instead of suffering the indignity of a slip on the shoulder, as one might expect, she succeeds in winning the hardened heart of her new duke and ends as his duchess."

With a sound very like "pshaw," he tossed the paper on the table. Regarded it with open disgust. "While that might contain elements of the truth, they've reduced it to the bizarre."

Minerva grinned. At one point she'd wondered whether he might realize the fundamental truth underlying the reports – that dissecting news sheet inanity might reveal to him what she and many others already knew of him – but it hadn't happened. As the days passed, it seemed increasingly likely that nothing less than long, frequent, and deepening exposure to his own emotions was likely to open his eyes.

Eyes that were so sharply observant when trained on anyone and anything else, but when it came to himself, to his inner self, simply did not see.

Sitting back, she considered her own efforts; ducal weddings in the country had to top the list of the most complicated events to manage. He rose to leave; she looked up, pinned him with a direct look. "You'll need to be available from noon today, and throughout tomorrow and the next day, to greet the more important guests as they arrive."

He held her gaze, then looked at Jeffers and Hamilton, standing by the wall behind her chair. "Send one of the footmen, one who can recognize crests, up to the battlements with a spyglass."

"Yes, Your Grace." Jeffers hesitated, then added, "If I might suggest, we could send one of the lads to the bridge with a list of those it would be helpful to know are approaching – he could wave a flag. That would be easily seen from the battlements."

"An excellent idea!" Seeing Royce's nod, Minerva turned to Hamilton. "Once we've done the rooms, you and Retford could make up a list. I'll check it, then Handley can make copies." She glanced at Royce, brows rising.

He nodded. "Handley will be with me in the study for most of the day, but he'll have time in the afternoon to do the lists."

Minerva smiled. Letitia had been right; there was very little she couldn't overcome – not with Royce, and the entire household, at her back. There was something intensely satisfying about being the general at the head of the troops; she'd always loved her chatelaine role, but she was going to enjoy being a duchess even more.

Royce's eyes held hers, then his lips kicked up at the ends. With a last glance, and a salute, he left her. Reaching for her cup, she returned to her lists.

The next morning they tumbled out of his bed early, and together rode up Usway Burn. Against everyone's but Royce's expectations, the cottages were nearing completion; after glancing over the improvements, Minerva sat on a bench against the front wall of the largest cottage while Royce made a more detailed inspection, old Macgregor at his elbow.

Of the major projects Royce had approved since he'd taken up the ducal reins, the footbridge over the Coquet had had first call on Hancock's time. The bridge was now a proper footbridge, raised higher to avoid bores, rebuilt, and properly braced. The cottages had come next, and they were nearly finished; another week would see them done. After that, Hancock and his team would start on the mill – not a moment too soon, but luckily the weather had held, and all the wood and even more importantly the glass had already been procured. The mill would be sealed before winter, which, aside from all the rest, was a great deal more than she'd thought to achieve before his father had died.

She looked up, watched as Royce and Macgregor, deep in discussion, paced slowly across to the cottage on the left. She smiled as they disappeared, then let her mind slide to its present preoccupation.

The first guests, all family, had arrived yesterday. Today, his friends and hers would drive up. He'd chosen Rupert, Miles, Gerald, and Christian as his groomsmen; against that, she'd chosen Letitia, Rose, an old friend Ellen, Lady Ambervale, and Susannah as her matrons-of-honor. She'd felt obliged to have one of his sisters, and despite Susannah's idiotic attempt at manipulation, she'd meant well, and Margaret or Aurelia would have been too grim.

All three of his sisters had arrived yesterday; all three were being very careful around her, aware that not only did she now have their all-powerful brother's ear, she also knew virtually all their secrets. Not that she was likely to do anything with the knowledge, but they didn't know that.

One part of the guest list that he'd supplied had pleased her enormously; he'd invited eight of his ex-colleagues. From Letitia, Penny, and Clarice she'd heard much about the group – the members of the Bastion Club plus Jack, Lord Hendon, and all their wives; she'd heard that Royce had declined to attend their weddings, and hadn't been the least surprised to receive instant acceptances from the respective ladies. She suspected they intended to make a point by dancing joyously at *his* wedding.

Regardless, she was looking forward to meeting them all, those who had been closest to Royce professionally over the last years.

Over the few hours they'd managed to steal for their own – those not spent in his bed – she'd encouraged him to tell her more of the activities that had filled his lost years, those years of his life that had been lost to her, and his parents. After an initial hesitation, he'd gradually relaxed his guard, speaking increasingly freely of various missions, and the numerous threads he'd woven into a net for gathering intelligence, both military and civilian.

He'd described it all well enough for her, knowing him, to see it, feel it, understand how and in what way the activity of those years had impacted on him. He'd admitted he'd killed, in cold blood, not on foreign soil, but here in England. He'd expected her to be shocked, had tensed, but had relaxed, relieved, when, after he'd confirmed such deaths had been essential for national safety, she'd merely blinked, and nodded.

He'd told her of the Bastion Club members' recent adventures. He'd also told her about the man they'd termed "the last traitor" – the fiend Clarice had mentioned – an Englishman, a gentleman of the ton, most likely someone with a connection to the War Office, who'd betrayed his country for French treasure, and had killed and killed again to escape Royce and his men.

After the war's end, Royce had lingered in London, pursuing every last avenue in an attempt to learn the last traitor's identity. He'd cited that as his only failure.

To her relief, he'd clearly put that unfulfilled chase behind him; he spoke of it as history, not a current activity. That he could accept such a failure was reassuring; she knew enough to appreciate that, in a man as powerful as he, knowing when to walk away was a strength, not a weakness.

That over the last weeks he'd talked to her so openly, and in return had elicited from her details of how she'd spent the same years, had left her feeling increasingly confident of the strength that would underpin their marriage – had left her ever more secure in the reality of his love.

A love he, still, could not see.

Emerging from the cottage, he exchanged farewells with Macgregor, shaking the old man's hand. Turning to her, he met her eyes, arched a brow. "Are you ready?"

She smiled, rose, and gave him her hand. "Yes. Lead on."

He was back at Wolverstone, under his nemesis's roof once more. Even though he had to share a room with Rohan, he didn't care. He was there, close, and invisible among the gathering throng. Everyone could see him, yet no one really could – not the real him. He was hidden, forever concealed.

No one would ever know.

His plans were well advanced, at least in theory. All he had to do now was find the right place to stage his ultimate victory.

It shouldn't be too hard; the castle was huge, and there were various buildings people paid little attention to dotted through the gardens. He had two days to find the perfect place.

Two days before he would act.

And finally win free of the torment.

Of the black, corrosive fear.

By Wednesday afternoon, the castle was full, literally to the rafters. With so many members of the haut ton attending, the number of visiting servants had stretched the accommodations below stairs – or rather in the attics – to their limit.

"We've even put cots in the ironing room," Trevor told Minerva when she met him in the gallery reverently ferrying a stack of perfectly ironed cravats. "We've moved the ironing boards into the laundry – unlikely we'll be doing much washing over the next two days."

She grimaced. "At least this time everyone is leaving the next day."

"Just as well," Trevor grimly declared. "There's a limit to how much mayhem one household can withstand."

She laughed and turned away. In reality the household was managing well, even though the castle was as full as she'd ever known it. Every guest chamber was in use, even the rooms in the keep. The only rooms on that level that had been spared were her morning room, Royce's sitting room, and the study.

Her morning room. Royce had started calling it that a few weeks ago, and she'd fallen into the habit.

Smiling, she continued around the gallery; it was late afternoon, almost early evening, and the guests were either resting or conversing quietly somewhere before dressing for dinner. For the first time that day, she had the opportunity to draw an unhurried breath.

"Minerva."

She stopped, turned, a smile already on her lips. Royce stood before the corridor to his apartments; he held out his hand.

There was nothing she had to do at that moment. Or rather . . . smile deepening, she went to join him.

Her smile mirrored in his eyes, he grasped her hand, turned down the corridor, stopped before the door to the battlements. As before, he released the catch, then let her go up before following.

She walked to the battlements, spread her arms wide and breathed . . . then turned to face him as he neared. "Just what I needed – fresh and *uncrowded* air."

His lips quirked. "The castle's all but humming with humanity. It's a living, breathing hive."

She laughed, swung again to the view, set her hands on the ancient stone of the battlements – and felt as if through the touch they grounded her. She looked out – and saw. Familiar sights, a familiar landscape. "When you brought me up here, and showed me this, and told me that this is what you would share . . . even though I'd been chatelaine for over a decade, I . . . it feels different, somehow, now." His hands slid about her waist; she glanced up and back at his face. "Now I'm to be your duchess."

Royce nodded; as she looked back at the hills, he dropped a kiss below her ear. "Before you weren't ultimately responsible – you were still one step removed. But now you're starting to see the fields as I do." He lifted his head, looking out over his lands. "You're starting to feel what I feel when I stand here and look out at my domain – and sense what that really means."

She leaned back against him. He settled his arms about her, felt her arms, her hands, settle over his.

For a moment, they were silent, seeing, sensing, feeling, then he said, "The message my father left me – that I didn't need to be like him. You took it to mean the dukedom, and the way I dealt with that. But the more I realize how much like him I am – and therefore how much like me he was – I think – believe – that he meant the comment more widely."

She tilted her head, listening, but didn't interrupt.

"I think," he said, his arms tightening about her, feeling her, a warm, vibrant presence anchoring him, "that in those last minutes, he tried to address the regrets of his life – and from all I've learned, how he managed the dukedom wasn't high on that list. How he lived, I think, was. I think he regretted, to his dying breath, not making the effort to make more of his life – he had chances, but didn't seize them. Didn't try to forge more than the usual Varisey life – a life that was handed to him on a silver platter.

"He didn't try to forge what I'm trying to forge with you. Every day that passes, every hour we spend together, whether alone and looking inward, or dealing with our people, our responsibilities, is like another brick, another section of our foundations solidly laid. We're building something together that wasn't here before . . . I think that's what he meant. That I didn't have to follow in his footsteps, didn't have to marry as he had, didn't have to turn my back on the chance to build something more, something stronger, more enduring."

"Something more supportive." She turned in his arms, looked up at his face, met his eyes. Considered, then nodded. "You might well be right. Thinking back . . . he'd been waiting to speak to you, rehearsing for weeks, and then . . . he knew he didn't have much time."

"So he said the most important thing."

She nodded. "He meant life, not just the dukedom." She hesitated, then said, "I know you never realized, but his breach with you . . . opened his eyes. You holding firm was the catalyst – that was when he started to change. When he started to think. Your mother noticed, and so did I. He'd never been introspective before."

His lips quirked, half grimace, half smile. "At least he should feel pleased that, at last, I've taken his advice."

Minerva smiled, warm and deep. "He'd be unbearable – and unbearably proud."

He raised his brows, deprecatingly skeptical.

The deep bong of a gong floated up from below.

He held her before him, looked down at her face. "I suppose we should go and dress for dinner."

She nodded. "Yes, we should."

He sighed, bent his head and kissed her. Lightly . . .

Their lips clung, parted reluctantly. He lifted his head just an inch, breathed against her lips, "I don't suppose we can be late?"

Her hand had remained, splayed against his chest. It firmed. "No. We can't."

His sigh as he straightened was a great deal more heartfelt. "At least they'll all be gone the day after tomorrow."

She laughed, took his hand, and led him back to the stairs. "Incidentally, don't be late tonight."

Pausing at the head of the stairs, she met his eyes. "Actually, tradition dictates that the bride and groom should spend the night before the wedding apart."

"In case you haven't noticed, I'm not wedded to tradition – and there's something I want to give you. Unless you wish to be carried through the gallery again – this time with every room around it occupied – I suggest you find your way to my rooms early rather than late."

She held his gaze, narrowed her eyes, then, struggling not to smile, humphed and turned down the stairs. "In case you haven't noticed, there are some Varisey traits you're very definitely wedded to."

Inwardly smiling, Royce followed her down the stairs.

"So what was it you wished to give me?" Minerva flicked her hair out of her eyes, struggled to lift her head enough to squint at him. "Or have I just received it?"

Royce laughed. He hugged her briefly, then hauled himself up. "No – there really is something." He had to sit on the edge of the bed for a moment until blood found its way back to his head, then he rose and crossed to the nearer tallboy. Opening the top drawer, he withdrew the package that had been delivered by special courier earlier that day. Carrying it back to the bed, he laid it on the sheet before her. "From me, to you, on the occasion of our wedding."

Minerva looked up at him, then, ignoring her unclad state, sat up amid the rumpled covers and eagerly unwrapped the odd-shaped parcel; it was vaguely triangular on one side, falling away . . . "Oh. My." The last piece of tissue fell away, leaving her round-eyed. "It's . . . *fabulous*."

That in no way did justice to the diadem that nestled in the layers of soft paper. Gold filigree of a complexity and fineness she'd never before seen wound its way around the band, rising in the front to support a plethora of . . . "Diamonds?"

The jewels didn't wink and blink; they burned with white fire.

"I had the whole cleaned and the stones reset." Royce dropped back on the bed, looked into her face. "Do you like it?"

"Oh, *yes*." Minerva reverently placed her hands around the delicate crown, then lifted it, glanced at him. "Can I put it on?"

"It's yours."

Raising her hands, she carefully placed the circlet atop her head. It sank just slightly, fitting neatly above her ears. She moved her head. "It fits."

His smile deepened. "Perfectly. I thought it would."

Uncaring of her naked state, she scrambled off the bed, and walked to the other tallboy so she could admire the coronet. The gold was just one shade darker than her hair, presently down and streaming over her bare shoulders.

Turning, she removed the crown; holding it between her hands, she examined it as she returned to the bed. "This isn't new – the design's old. Very old." She glanced at him. "I know it's not the Wolverstone duchess's coronet, at least not the one your mother had. Where did you get it?"

He met her eyes. "Prinny."

"Prinny?" She stared anew at the diadem. "But . . . this must be worth a small fortune. I can't imagine him parting with such a thing willingly."

"He wasn't exactly willing, but . . . I consider it ironically fitting that having pressured me into finding my bride, he should provide her wedding crown."

She sank back on the bed, carefully settling the crown back in its paper nest. "Irony aside, cut line – how and why did he come to give you such a thing?"

Royce stretched out on his back, crossed his arms behind his head. "You remember I told you about the treasure the last traitor had acquired from the French authorities?"

She nodded. "His payment for spying."

"Exactly. Not all of it was recovered from the wreck of the smuggling ship bringing it to England, but some pieces were found – among them, that crown. When the authorities matched it to the list of antiquities the French were missing, they discovered it was, in fact, Varisey property." He met her startled gaze. "It was made for one Hugo Varisey in the fifteen hundreds. It remained in the hands of the principal line of the family in France, until it fell into the hands of the revolutionary authorities. Thereafter it was considered property of the French state – until it was given in exchange for information to our last traitor – who we know is an Englishman. Now the war is over, the French, of course, want the crown back, but the government in Whitehall see no reason to hand it over. However, to end any discussion, and as it was felt I was owed

384

some recognition for my service, they had Prinny present it to me – the head of the only branch of the Varisey family still extant."

She smiled. "So Prinny really had no choice?"

"I daresay he protested, but no." Royce watched as she carefully lifted the crown in its papers. "That's now mine – the oldest piece of Varisey family jewelry – and I'm gifting it to you."

Minerva set crown and papers on the bedside table, then turned and crawled back to him, a smile of explicit promise curving her lips. Reaching him, she framed his face and kissed him – long, lingeringly – as she slowly slid one leg over him. When she lifted her head, she was straddling him. "Thank you." Her smile deepened as she looked into his eyes. "And that's just the beginning of my thanks."

He looked back at her with open anticipation – and something very close to challenge. "I was hoping you'd say that." He settled back. "Feel free."

She did – free to thank him to the top of her bent.

Later, when she lay pleasantly exhausted beside him, pleasured to her toes, she murmured, "You know, if it hadn't been for Prinny and his machinations . . ."

Royce thought, then shook his head. "No. Even if I'd taken longer to realize, I would still have set my heart on you."

Everything was ready. He'd found the right spot, worked through every detail of his plan. Nothing would go wrong.

Tomorrow would be his triumph. Tomorrow would see him win.

Tomorrow he'd break Royce.

And then he'd kill him.

Chapter 21

The clamor was deafening.

Royce leaned forward and spoke to Henry. "Pull up."

Bedecked in full livery, garlanded with white ribbon – as was the open carriage – Henry eased the heavy horses to a halt in the middle of the road leading through Alwinton village.

The cheering crowd pressed closer, waving, calling.

Royce threw Minerva a glance, a smile, then rose, and drew her up with him; her hand clasped in his, he raised it high. "I give you your new duchess!"

The crowd roared its approval.

Minerva fought to contain the flood of emotion that welled and swelled inside her; looking out, she saw so many familiar faces – all so pleased that she was Royce's bride.

His wife.

She stood by his side and waved; the beaming smile on her face had taken up residence when he'd turned her from the altar to walk back up the aisle, and hadn't yet waned.

The crowd satisfied, he drew her back down; once she sat, he told Henry to drive on.

Still smiling, she relaxed against Royce's shoulder, her mind reaching back to the ceremony, then ranging ahead to the wedding breakfast to come.

The same carriage, freshly painted with the Wolverstone

crest blazing on the doors and with ribbons woven through the reins, had carried her, the Earl of Catersham, and her matrons-of-honor to the church. Her gown of finest Brussels lace softly shushing, the delicate veil anchored by the Varisey diadem, she'd walked down the aisle on the earl's arm oblivious to the horde packed into the church – held by a pair of intense dark eyes.

In an exquisitely cut morning coat, Royce had waited for her before the altar; even though she'd seen him mere hours before, it seemed as if something had changed. As if their worlds changed in the instant she placed her hand in his and together they turned to face Mr. Cribthorn.

The service had gone smoothly; at least, she thought it had. She could remember very little, caught up, swept along, on a tide of emotion.

A tide of happiness that had welled as they'd exchanged their vows, peaked when Royce had slipped the simple gold band on her finger, overflowed when she'd heard the words, "I now pronounce you man and wife."

Duke and duchess.

The same, yet more. A fact that had been amply illustrated from the instant Royce had released her from the utterly chaste kiss they'd shared. A kiss that had carried both acknowledgment and promise, acceptance and commitment, from them both.

Their eyes had touched, then, as one, they'd turned and faced their future. Faced first the assembled throng, all of whom had wanted to congratulate them personally. Luckily, the others – his friends and the Bastion Club couples – had formed something of a guard, and helped them move reasonably smoothly up the aisle.

The roar as they'd emerged from the church into the weak sunshine had echoed from the hills. Hamish and Molly had been waiting by the steps; she'd hugged Molly, then turned to Hamish to see him hesitating – awed by the delicacy of her gown and the brilliance of the diadem's diamonds. She'd hugged him; awkwardly, he'd patted her with his huge hands.

"You were right," she'd whispered. "Love really is simple – no thinking required."

He'd chuckled, bussed her check, then released her to all the others waiting to press her hand, shake Royce's, and wish them well.

An hour had passed before they'd been able to leave the churchyard; the guests and the rest of the wedding party had gone ahead, to the wedding breakfast waiting in the castle's huge ballroom, a long-ago addition built out at the back of the keep.

The carriage rolled across the stone bridge; a minute later, they passed through the heavy gates with their snarling wolf's heads. The castle rose before them; it was as much home to her as it was to Royce. She glanced at him, found his gaze dwelling on the gray stone of the façade.

Retford, Hamilton, Cranny, and Handley were waiting to meet them just inside the front door; all were beaming, but trying to keep their delight within bounds. "Your Grace." Retford bowed low; it took her a moment to realize he was addressing her.

Hamilton, Cranny, and Handley, too, all greeted her formally. "Everything's in readiness, ma'am," Cranny assured her.

"I take it everyone is here?" Royce asked.

Handley nodded. "Lord Haworth and Lord Chesterfield will need to leave in a few hours – I'll make sure to remind them."

Royce glanced at Minerva. "Any others we need to pay early attention to?"

She mentioned five others, representatives of king, regent, and Parliament, all of whom had to leave for London later that day. "Other than that, we'd be wise to give the grandes dames their due."

He snorted. "It's always wise to give those beldames due attention." Taking her arm, he led her toward the ballroom.

"I suspect I should mention, Your Grace, that as from today, *I* am classed among the grandes dames."

He grinned. "My own grande dame. If that means that

from now on I'll only have to deal with you" – he met her gaze as they paused outside the ballroom door – "I have no complaints."

Jeffers, liveried, proud, and bursting with delight, was waiting to open the door. Royce held her autumn eyes – eyes that saw him, all of him, and understood. He raised her hand, pressed a kiss to her fingertips. "Are you ready?"

She smiled a touch mistily. "Indeed, Your Grace. Lead on."

He did, ceremonially leading her into the huge ballroom where the entire company rose and applauded. They paraded down the long room to the table at the end; a smile wreathing every face, the company clapped until he seated her in the center of the main table, and sat beside her, then everyone followed suit and the festivities began.

It was a day of unalloyed happiness. Of enfolding warmth as the breakfast rolled on – through the long meal, the customary speeches, the first waltz. After that, the company rose and mingled freely.

Returning from doing his duty with the representatives of Crown and government, Royce resumed his chair at the high table. Content, aware of a depth of inner peace he'd never before known, he looked over the crowd, smiling at the undisguised joy apparent on so many faces. A moment to savor, to fix in his memory. The only friends missing were Hamish and Molly; both he and Minerva had wanted them to attend, but hadn't pressed, understanding that, in this milieu, Hamish and Molly would feel awkward.

Instead, he and Minerva planned to ride over the border tomorrow.

He wondered how much longer it would be wise for her to ride, especially long distances. He slanted a glance at her, in her chair beside him; as she hadn't yet actually *told* him anything, he suspected he'd be wise to hold his tongue, at least until she did.

A frisson of uncertainty rippled through him; he had absolutely no experience of ladies in delicate conditions. However, he knew several men who did – several, indeed, who were in much the same straits as he. Leaning closer to Minerva, deep in conversation with Rose and Alice, he touched her wrist. "I'm going to mingle. I'll catch up with you later."

She glanced at him, smiled, then turned back to his friends' wives.

Rising, he went looking for his ex-colleagues.

He found them in a knot in one corner of the room. All had glasses in their hands; all were sipping while they chatted, their gazes, one and all, trained in various directions – resting on their ladies scattered about the hall.

Accepting a glass from one of his footmen, he joined them.

"Ah – just the man!" Jack Hendon beamed. "Finally, you're here to join us – about time."

"I often wondered," Tony mused, "whether it was *our* weddings you eschewed, or weddings per se."

"The latter." Royce sipped. "The excuse of not being Winchelsea was exceedingly convenient. I used it to avoid all wider ton gatherings."

They considered, then all grimaced. "Any of us," Tristan admitted, "would have done the same."

"But we always have a toast," Gervase said. "What's it to be today?" They all looked at Charles.

Who grinned. Irrepressibly. He'd clearly been waiting for the moment. He raised his glass to Royce; the others did the same. "To the end of Dalziel's reign," he began. "To the beginning of yours – and even more importantly, to the beginning of *hers*."

The others cheered and drank.

Royce grimaced, sipped, then eyed them. "You perceive me in the unusual position of seeking advice from your greater collective experience." They all looked intrigued. "How," he continued, "do you . . . corral and restrain, for want of better words, your spouses when they're in what is commonly termed 'a delicate condition'?"

The only one of their wives not yet obviously blooming – and he suspected it truly was not *yet* – was Letitia.

390

Somewhat to his surprise, all his men looked pained. He looked at Jack Hendon. "You're an old hand – any tips?"

Jack closed his eyes, shuddered, then opening them, shook his head. "Don't remind me – I never figured it out."

"The difficulty," Jack Warnefleet said, "is in being subtle when what you want to do is put your foot down and state categorically that they can't do that – whatever 'that' is at the time."

Deverell nodded. "No matter what you say, how tactfully you try to put it, they look at you as if you have the intelligence of a flea – and then just do whatever they were going to."

"Why is it," Christian asked, "that we, the other half of the equation as it were, are considered to have no valid opinions on such matters?"

"Probably because," Tony replied, "our opinions are ill-informed, being based on a woeful lack of intelligence."

"Not to mention," Gervase added, "us having no experience in the field."

Royce glanced at them. "Those sound like quotes."

Tony and Gervase answered as one. "They are."

"What worries me even more," Tristan said, "is what comes next."

They all looked at Jack Hendon.

He looked back at them, then slowly shook his head. "You really don't want to know."

All considered it, but none of them pressed.

Royce smiled wryly. "What cowards we are."

"When it comes to that . . . yes." Christian drained his glass, then turned the conversation to the recent developments surrounding the Corn Laws. They were all peers, all managed estates of various sizes, all had communities under their protection; Royce listened, learned, contributed what he knew, his gaze resting on Minerva as she stood chatting with Letitia and Rose halfway down the room.

Another lady approached – Ellen, Minerva's friend, one of her matrons-of-honor; Ellen joined the group, then spoke specifically to Minerva and indicated one of the side doors.

Minerva nodded, then excused herself to Letitia and Rose and, alone, went to the door.

Royce wondered what household emergency she'd been summoned to deal with . . . but why would Cranny or Retford or any of the others use Ellen to ferry a message? The summons had to be about something else . . .

He told himself it was their recent discussion of delicate conditions and their primitive responses that was playing on his mind, but . . . with a nod he excused himself and started moving through the crowd.

He felt Christian glance at him, sensed his gaze following as he made his way to where Letitia and Rose were still talking. They looked up as he halted beside them.

"Where's Minerva?"

Letitia smiled at him. "She just stepped outside to meet someone."

"They had a message from your half brother, or something like that." Rose tipped her head toward the side door. "They were waiting out there."

Royce looked toward the door – and knew Minerva wasn't in the hallway beyond it. Every instinct he possessed was alive, pricking. Leaving the ladies without a word, he moved toward the door.

Christian drew near as he opened it.

The hallway beyond was empty.

He walked into the narrow space; to his right the hall led back into the house while to his left it ran along the ballroom a little way, then ended in a door to the gardens. Common sense suggested Minerva had gone into the house; he prowled left, drawn by a white clump on the floor before the door.

Christian followed.

Royce stooped to pick up a beribboned band covered with white silk flowers – Minerva's mother's wedding favor; Minerva had worn it on her wrist. Bent over, he froze, sniffed. Turning his head, he crouched, looked; from the base of the umbrella stand he teased out a scrap of linen . . . a handkerchief.

Without even raising it to their faces, both he and Christian, drawing near, recognized the smell. "Ether." Rising, he stared out of the glassed doors into the gardens, but all looked peaceful, serene.

"She's been *taken*." He barely recognized his voice. His fist closed on the handkerchief. Lips curling in a snarl, he swung around –

Christian caught his arm. "Wait! *Think*. This was planned. Who are your enemies? Who are hers?"

He frowned. It was a huge effort to get his mind to function; he'd never felt such scalding rage – such icy terror. "We don't have any . . . not that I know of. Not here . . ."

"You do. You have one. And he *could* be here."

He met Christian's eyes. "The last traitor?"

"He's the one person who has most to fear from you."

He shook his head. "I'm no longer Dalziel – he won. He got away."

"Dalziel may be gone, but you're here – and *you* never, ever, give up. He's someone who knows that, so he'll never feel safe." Christian released him. "He's taken her, but it's you he wants."

That was undeniably true.

"She's the lure." Christian spoke quickly, urgently. "He'll keep her alive until you come. But if you alert everyone, send everyone searching . . . he might feel forced to kill her before you or any of us can get to her."

The thought helped him force the terror-driven rage down, caging it like a beast, deep inside, letting his mind, his well-honed faculties, rise above it and take command. "Yes. You're right." Hauling in a tight breath, he lifted his head. "Yet we need to search."

Christian nodded. "But only with those capable of acting and rescuing her if they find her."

Royce glanced outside. "He couldn't have imagined we'd realize so soon."

"No. We've got time to do this properly, so we can get her back alive."

"You seven," he said. "Hendon, Cynster, Rupert, Miles, and Gerald – they were all in the Guards at one time."

"I'll fetch them." Christian caught his eyes. "While I do, you *have* to think. You're the only one who knows this terrain – and you're the one who knows this enemy best. You are the best at planning battles like this – so *think*, Royce. We need a plan, and you're the only one who can supply it."

Minerva's life – and that of their unborn child – depended on it. He nodded curtly.

Christian left him to it, and went quickly back into the ballroom.

Two minutes later, Royce returned to the ballroom. He saw Christian moving smoothly through the crowd, surreptitiously tapping shoulders. His plan was taking shape in his mind, but there was something he needed to know.

Last time he and the last traitor had crossed swords, the traitor had won. That wasn't going to happen this time, not with what was at risk; he wanted to learn everything he possibly could before he took the field.

Letitia, still standing with Rose, was already alerted, restive and restless, when he halted beside her. "Can you and Rose find Ellen, and bring her to me in the hallway beyond the side door?" Briefly he met her eyes. "Don't ask, but hurry – and don't alert anyone else bar the other Bastion Club wives." He glanced at Rose. "Or Alice and Eleanor. No one else."

Both wanted to ask why; neither did. Lips tightening, they nodded, exchanged glances, then separated and slipped through the crowd.

Searching. He searched, too, but, finding it harder and harder to keep his expression impassive, he went back into the hallway and left the hunt to the women.

Minutes later, Leonora slipped through the door. "They've found her, but she was conversing with others. Eleanor, Madeline, and Alicia are extracting her."

He nodded, pacing, too tense to remain still.

The other ladies joined them, one by one slipping into the hallway, all aware something was amiss. They threw him searching glances, but none asked. Last to join them were

Eleanor, Alicia, and Madeline, shepherding Ellen, wide-eyed, before them.

She didn't know him; sensing the anger he was trying to contain, she was already skittish.

"Just ignore the growling," Letitia curtly advised her. "He won't bite."

Ellen's eyes widened even more.

"I don't have time to explain," Royce said, speaking to them all, "but I need to know who Minerva came out here to meet."

Ellen blinked. "One of your cousins asked me to tell her your half brother's children were here, asking to speak with her. Apparently they had a gift they'd made her. He said they were waiting in the garden." She nodded down the corridor. "Out there."

Royce felt a sudden sense of inevitability. "Which of my cousins?"

Ellen shook her head. "I'm sorry, I can't say. I don't know them, and you all look so alike."

Phoebe stirred. "How old?"

Ellen glanced at Royce. "Of similar age to His Grace."

Letitia looked at Royce. "How many is that?"

"Three." But he already knew which one it was, which one it had to be.

The door to the ballroom cracked open; Susannah peered around it. She took in the ladies, then focused on him. "What's going on?"

He didn't answer, instead said, "I need to know if Gordon, Phillip, and Gregory are in the ballroom. Don't speak to them, just go and check. Now."

She stared at him, then closed her mouth and went.

Clarice, Letitia, and Penny headed for the door. "We know them, too," Penny said as she passed him.

Bare minutes later, all four came back. "Gordon and Gregory are in there," Susannah reported. "Not Phillip."

Royce nodded, half turned away, his mind churning.

Alicia said, "That's not conclusive. Phillip might be any-where – the castle is huge."

395

Mystified, Susannah appealed to the others; Letitia explained they were trying to learn which of the cousins had lured Minerva away.

"It'll be Phillip." Susannah was definite. Royce looked at her; she went on, "I don't know what bee he's got in his bonnet about you, but for years he's always wanted to know every last thing about you and your doings – and recently . . . it was he who suggested I invite Helen Ashton. He who told me Minerva was your lover and . . . not suggested but led me to think that engineering a situation might be a good thing. Of course, he never dreamed you loved her –" She broke off, paled. "Oh, God – he's taken her, hasn't he?"

For a long moment, no one answered, then Royce slowly nodded. "Yes, he has."

He glanced at Alicia. "The last traitor we've been hunting over the last year? We concluded he had some connection with the War Office. Of all my cousins, of all those here, only Phillip qualifies."

He felt a certain sureness infuse him. It always helped to know who he was hunting.

Minerva struggled through clouds of unconsciousness. Her head felt woolly; thoughts half formed, then slipped away, sank into the murk. She couldn't think – couldn't concentrate, couldn't formulate a coherent wish, much less open her eyes. But inside, where a cold kernel of panicked helplessness clung to reality, she knew.

Someone had seized her and carried her away. She'd gone to the door, looking for Hamish's children – and someone, some man, had come up behind her. She'd sensed him an instant before he'd grabbed her, tried to turn her head, but he'd slapped a handkerchief over her nose and mouth . . .

It had smelled sickly sweet, cloying . . .

Reality inched closer, seeped into her mind. She breathed in, carefully, but that horrible, nauseating smell was gone.

Someone – the man – was talking, the sound distant, fading in and out.

Familiar. *He* was familiar.

She would have frowned, but her features were still not her own. She was lying on her back . . . on stone, its rough surface beneath her fingers, under one palm . . . she'd been here before, lain just like this not long ago . . .

The millstone. She was lying on the grinding stone in the mill.

The realization evoked an inpouring of awareness; the clouds dissipated; she came fully awake.

Just as the man halted beside her. She sensed him looking down at her; instinct kept her perfectly still.

"Damn you – wake *up!*"

He'd spoken through clenched teeth, yet she placed him. *Phillip.* What the devil was he up to?

With a muttered curse, he swung away. Her hearing focused, her mind followed; still too weak to move, she listened as he paced, talking to himself.

"It's all *right*. I have time. *Plenty* of time to set the stage – to rape her, and beat her, then kill her – perhaps slit her throat, let her blood flow artistically over the stone – yes!"

His shoes scraped on the floor as if he'd swung around. She sensed him looking at her; she didn't move a muscle.

"Damn!" he muttered. "I forgot to bring my knife." He paused, then said, "No matter. I've ball and powder – I can shoot her as many times, in as many places, as I like."

Again she felt him studying her, then he started pacing again.

"Yes, that will do nicely. I'll rip her gown to shreds, shoot her in the head, then again in the belly, and place that damned crown in the blood." He laughed. "Oh, *yes*, that will work. He has to be shattered by the sight. Completely and utterly *broken*. He has to finally see that *I'm* more powerful. That because he took my treasure, I've taken something he valued from him – that in our game, *I'll* always win. That I'm the truly clever one. When he comes in here, and sees what I've done to her – his new duchess, the woman he today vowed to honor and protect – he'll know I've won. He'll know that *everyone* will know

397

what a failure he is – that he wasn't even clever enough, strong enough, powerful enough, to protect *her*."

His long strides brought him to the millstone again; again she felt his gaze. Unlike Royce's, his made her skin crawl. She fought to remain lifeless, utterly lax – battled the compulsion to tense, to hold her breath, to raise her lids enough to see.

She nearly sighed with relief when he said, "Time's on my side." He moved away again. "I've got more than an hour before that valet gives Royce the note. Plenty of time to enjoy debauching and killing her, and then get ready to welcome him."

Facts fell into place with a suddenness that left her mentally reeling. *Treasure.* Phillip had said treasure. *He* was Royce's last traitor.

That's what this was all about. He thought to use her to break Royce.

The fight she had to wage to suppress her reaction – not to let her jaw, her features, set, *not* to let her hands curl into fists, not to reach for the knife she had, for an entirely different reason, strapped to her thigh – was immense.

She could kill him with that knife, but Phillip was strong – he was like Royce in that. Yet while he believed her unconscious, it seemed she was safe. Just as long as he kept believing he had time, her best strategy was to simply lie there and let him rant.

And give Royce time to reach her.

She knew he would.

How long had she been unconscious? How long was it since she'd left the ballroom? Phillip's plan had a large hole in it, one he'd never see. He might not be a Varisey, yet he was just like Royce in not understanding what love actually was.

He didn't comprehend that Royce would simply know, that he was always aware of her – even in a crowded ballroom. He'd never wait an hour before checking where she'd gone. She seriously doubted he'd have waited ten minutes. Which meant rescue was afoot.

Phillip was now ranting about his father, and his grandfather,

398

how they'd always lauded Royce and never him. How they would now see that Royce was nothing, powerless . . .

Royce's maternal grandfather was long dead.

Not that she needed any further proof of the state of Phillip's mind.

Nevertheless, she forced herself to listen so she could track his movements; when she was sure he was pacing away from her, she quickly cracked open her lids – immediately closed them again and heaved a mental sigh of relief. He'd closed the mill doors.

Resisting the urge to smile intently, she worked on keeping every muscle flaccid.

Not so easy when Phillip stopped talking, then halted beside the millstone. She was fully awake now, could sense his physical closeness. Like Royce, he was large, well-muscled, and radiated heat – and quelling her revulsion and lying quiescent with him near was the hardest thing she'd ever had to do.

Then she heard a rustle; his arms moved.

Then he leaned near. "Come on, damn you! Wake up."

And then she discovered there were harder things to quell than mere revulsion.

Instinct had her peeking through her lashes. She only had an instant's warning, only an instant to scream at herself to relax, relax, *for God's sake don't react!* – then he jabbed her in the arm with his cravat pin.

Royce waited in the hallway until all the men had gathered. The ladies remained, too – they were all too sober to go back into the ballroom; if they did, they'd cause comment.

Christian slipped through the door. "That's all of us."

Royce raked the ranks of deadly serious faces. "My cousin, Phillip Debraigh, has seized Minerva. He's our last traitor – the one I failed to apprehend. As far as I can judge, he's set on wreaking vengeance of a sort on me – the diadem she was wearing" – *that he, Royce, had given her* – "was part of his thirty pieces of silver. He's taken her somewhere outside. Although the castle is huge, with it packed with guests there are staff constantly

399

scurrying everywhere – something he knows. He won't have risked staging anything indoors." He glanced outside. "But there are only so many places he could use outside – which gives us a chance to rescue Minerva, and capture him."

He brought his gaze back to the grave faces. "He took her less than fifteen minutes ago – he won't be expecting us to have even noticed her absence yet, so we have a small amount of time to plan."

Rupert, on his left, shifted, caught Royce's eyes when he glanced his way. "Whatever we do, secrecy is imperative. No matter he's a traitor, and deserves to be brought down, you can't bring down the Debraighs as a family. You, especially, can't do that."

Because the Debraighs, his mother's family, had always supported him. Because his Debraigh grandfather had been so much a part of his formative life. Jaw set, Royce nodded. "As far as possible, we'll try to keep this secret, but I won't risk Minerva's safety, not even for the Debraighs."

He looked at the grouped ladies, at Letitia, Clarice, Rose, and all the rest. "You ladies are going to have to give us cover. You're going to have to go back into the ballroom and spread some story – of how we've adjourned for a meeting on whatever topic your imaginations can devise. You're going to have to hide your apprehension – make it appear as irritation, annoyance, resignation – anything. But we'll never keep this concealed without you."

Clarice nodded. "We'll manage. Just go" – she waved them off – "do what you're so good at, and get Minerva back."

Her waspish tone was reinforced by the looks on the other ladies' faces. Royce nodded grimly, and looked at the men. "Come up to the battlements."

He led them up the battlement stairs in a thunder of heavy feet. Just in case he'd guessed wrongly and Phillip was somewhere in the house, Handley, Trevor, Jeffers, Retford, and Hamilton were alerted, and a quiet search was under way. But as he walked to the battlements, waited while the others joined him, he knew he was right. Phillip was outside – somewhere in the grounds, all the relevant parts of which were visible from this vantage point.

Bracing his hands on the stone, he looked out. "He'll have taken her to one of the structures. There's not that many. There's –" He broke off. He'd come to the same spot to which he'd brought Minerva, twice. The view was to the north, up the gorge to the Cheviots and Scotland beyond.

The mill was in the foreground.

He straightened, his gaze locked on the building. "He's taken her to the mill."

All the others crowded the battlements, looking.

Before any could ask, he went on, "There is no one on the entire estate who would close those doors – for excellent reasons, they're *always* left open."

Christian was assessing the terrain, as were the others. "Two levels."

"Can he get out along the stream?" Tony asked.

"Not easily – not safely."

"So." Devil Cynster straightened, cocked a brow his way. "How are we going to do this?"

In a few succinct phrases, he told them.

They weren't entirely happy, but no one argued.

Minutes later, they were streaming from the house, slipping into the gardens, a silent, deadly force intent on only one thing – ending the last traitor's reign.

Royce was at the head of the pack, saving Minerva his only real aim.

Chapter 22

Minerva had weathered the prick of the cravat pin – more through sheer terror than anything else. She'd managed not to flinch, but her muscles had tensed. Phillip had noticed; he'd nudged her, slapped her cheeks, but when she'd stirred, mumbled, then slumped as if comatose again, he'd muttered a raw expletive and swung viciously away.

He'd fallen to pacing again, but closer, watching her all the while. "Damn you, wake *up*! I want you awake so you'll know what I'm doing to you – I want you to fight me. I want to hear you *scream* as I force my way inside you. I specifically brought you here – far enough from the house and with the noise of the water to cover all sounds – just so I could enjoy your sobbing and pleading. And your screaming – above all, your screaming. I want to see your eyes, I want to feel your fear. I want you to know every little thing I'm going to do to you before I do it – and for every second while I am."

He suddenly swooped close. "You won't be dying anytime soon."

She jerked her head away from the hot waft of his crooning breath, tried to disguise the instinctive flinch as restlessness.

He drew back, his gaze heavy on her face. Then, "You aren't *pretending* to still be asleep, are you, Minerva?"

His tone was taunting; he slapped her cheek again. Then he sneered. "Let's see if this will wake you up."

He roughly seized her breast, hard fingers searching for, then framing her nipple. Her breasts were tender; she cracked open her lids, looked up –

Saw him above her, one knee on the millstone beside her, his features distorted into a mask of pure evil, looking down to where his hand imprisoned her flesh. His eyes glittered; his other hand rose, holding his cravat pin.

Her hands came up; with all her strength, she pushed him off.

Releasing her breast, he rocked back – laughed in triumph. Before she could move, he swooped and seized her arm.

He dragged her half upright, shook her like a doll. "You *bitch!* Time for your punishment to begin."

She fought him; he shook her viciously, then slapped her hard.

The crack of his palm on her cheek echoed sharply through the mill.

Something fell to the ground.

Phillip froze. Standing with his knees against the side of the millstone, with her on the stone before him, her legs trapped in the lace froth of her wedding gown, one of her arms locked in a painful, unbreakable grip, he stopped breathing and stared across the race.

The sound had come from the east side – the lower side of the mill. There were no doors on that side of the building; if anyone was going to come in unremarked, they would have to come that way.

"Royce?" Phillip waited, but no answer came. No hint of movement. No further sound.

He glanced down at her, but immediately snapped his gaze up again, locked it on the gangplank, presently set over the race connecting the two levels; his eyes searched the clear space on the lower side beyond it.

Minerva felt him shift his weight from one foot to the other; he was uncertain – this wasn't what he'd planned. Her gaze

403

fixed on him, her senses locked on him, she waited for her chance.

Royce was somewhere on the lower level; her senses told her he was there. But Phillip couldn't see him because of the cupboards lining the race, not unless – until – Royce wanted to be seen.

Apparently realizing, Phillip snarled, and grabbed her with both hands; hauling her off the millstone, he dragged her up against him, her back to his chest. With one arm, he locked her there; he held her so tightly she could barely breathe. With his other hand he fished in his pocket; turning her head to the side, she saw him pull out a pistol.

He held it down, at his side. His body at her back was unbelievably tense.

He was using her as a shield, and she couldn't do anything; her arms were trapped against her body. If she struggled he'd just lift her off her feet. All she could do was grasp her skirts in her hands, hold them as high as she could – at least enough for her feet to be free – and wait for an opening. Wait for the right moment.

Phillip was muttering beneath his breath; she forced herself to focus, to listen. He was talking to himself, reworking his plan; he was ignoring her as if she were some inanimate pawn – no threat whatsoever.

"He's down there somewhere, but that's all right. As long as he knows I've killed her, I still win. And then I'll kill him." He hauled her with him as he edged around the huge circular stone. "I'll get into position, shoot her, then I'll have to grab the gangplank and swing it to this side – he'll be shocked, he won't be expecting that, I can have it done by the time she hits the ground."

His whispered words tripped over themselves as he frantically rehearsed. "Then I'll reload – and shoot him when he comes for me . . ."

She felt him look up; she looked where he did – at the big beams forming the heavy structure supporting the waterwheel.

"With the gangplank gone, he'll have to come that way. He might not love her, but he won't let me get away with killing his duchess. So he'll come for me – and I'll have more than enough time to reload and shoot him before he can reach me."

She sensed welling triumph in his tone.

"Yes! That's what I'll do. So first, I get in place." Renewed confidence infused him. He tightened his arm, lifted her from her feet, and walked forward – toward the upper end of the gangplank.

She'd run out of time, but with her arms locked to her body there was nothing she could do.

Above her head, Phillip muttered, so low she could barely hear him. "Close enough to the plank ropes, close enough to my powder and shot."

He moved her forward. And she saw the powder horn and shot canister he'd left on the flat top railing, a few feet left of the gangplank.

She couldn't use her arms, but could she possibly raise her feet high enough to kick powder or shot away? Either would do – then he'd have only one shot. Only one person he could kill.

If he shot her, he couldn't kill Royce. Phillip slowed as he maneuvered into position; she was gauging the distance, tensing to try to kick up –

Something flashed across in front of them, right to left – and hit the powder horn and canister, sending both spinning.

The powder horn spun off the railing and fell into the race.

Something clattered on the wooden floor. Both she and Phillip instinctively looked.

And saw a knife. Royce's knife.

Like most gentlemen, he always had one somewhere about him – but she'd only known him ever to have one.

A thump had their heads snapping around –

Royce had leapt onto the lower end of the gangplank.

He stood directly before them, his gaze locked on Phillip's face. "Let her go, Phillip – it's me you want."

Phillip snarled; backing quickly, he pressed the muzzle of the cocked pistol to Minerva's temple. "I'm going to kill her – and you're going to watch."

"You've only got one shot, Phillip – who are you going to kill? Her . . . or me?"

Phillip halted. He rocked back and forth, heels to toes, indecisive, undecided.

Then his chest swelled; with a roar, he flung Minerva to the side, and swung his pistol up to aim at Royce. "*You!*" he screamed. "I'm going to kill *you!*"

"*Run*, Minerva!" Royce didn't even glance at her. "Through the doors. The others are outside."

Then he charged up the gangplank.

Having landed on her side on the millstone, she was frantically hauling up her skirts.

She sat up – saw Phillip brace his pistol arm with his other hand. His face aglow with maniacal joy, laughing, he aimed for Royce's chest.

Her fingers closed about the hilt of her knife. She didn't think, didn't blink, just threw it.

The hilt appeared on the side of Phillip's neck.

He choked, pulled the trigger.

The shot rang out, filling the enclosed space.

Phillip started to crumple.

Minerva scrambled off the millstone. Her eyes locked on Royce as he halted before Phillip, looking down on his cousin as he slumped to the floor. Her gaze raced over Royce, seeking the wound . . . she nearly swooned with relief when she finally accepted that there wasn't one. Phillip's shot had gone wide.

Her gaze returned to Royce's face; behind his mask, he was stunned. In that instant she knew he hadn't expected to survive.

He could have run for cover, but he'd run toward Phillip to give her time to get away, to make sure Phillip shot at him, and not her.

Dragging in a deep breath, she went to join him.

Just as the doors at both ends of the mill swung open, and Christian and Miles appeared at the lower end of the gangplank.

Reaching Royce, she laid a hand on his arm. He looked at her then, met her eyes, then he looked down at the knife in Phillip's throat, and didn't say anything.

The others gathered around; what expressions were discernable were unrelentingly grim. She glimpsed pistols being slipped back into pockets, the flash of knives being put away.

Royce drew in a breath – almost unable to believe he could. Almost unable to believe that Minerva stood, shaken but otherwise well, beside him – that he could sense her there, steady and sure, that he was still alive to feel her comforting warmth, her vital presence.

The emotions churning inside him were staggeringly strong, but he battened them down, left them for later. There was one more thing he had to do.

Something only he could.

The others had formed a rough circle about them. Phillip lay sprawled, twisted half on his back, his head not far from Royce's right shoe. The knife wound would eventually kill him, but he wasn't dead yet.

He shifted to his right, crouched down. "Phillip – can you hear me?"

Phillip's lips twisted. "Almost got you. Almost . . . did it."

The words were barely a whisper, but in the intent silence, they were audible enough.

"You were the traitor, weren't you, Phillip? The one in the War Office. The one who sent God knows how many Englishmen to their deaths, and who the French paid in a treasure most of which lies at the bottom of the Channel."

Although his eyes remained closed, Phillip's lips curved in an unholy smile. "You'll never know how successful I was."

"No." Royce curved one hand about Phillip's chin, with his other hand grasped the top of his skull. "We won't."

He sensed Minerva draw close, from the corner of his eye glimpsed the ivory lace of her gown. He turned his head her way. "Look away."

Phillip dragged in a hissing breath. He frowned. "Hurts."

Royce looked down at him. "Sadly nowhere near as much as you deserve." With an abrupt twist, he snapped Phillip's neck.

He released him. The features so like his own eased, fell slack. He reached for the knife hilt, jerked the blade free. With

Phillip's heart already stopped, the wound bled only slightly. He wiped the blade on Phillip's lapel, then rose, sliding the knife into his pocket.

Minerva's hand slipped into his, her fingers twining, gripping.

Christian stepped forward; so did Miles and Devil Cynster.

"Leave this to us," Christian said.

"You've tidied up after us often enough," Charles said. "Allow us to return the favor."

There was a growl of agreement from the other Bastion Club members.

"I hate to sound like a grande dame," Devil said, "but you need to get back to your wedding celebration."

Miles glanced at Rupert and Gerald. "Gerald and I will stay and help – we know the estate fairly well. Enough, at least, to help stage a fatal accident – I presume that's what we need?"

"Yes," Rupert, Devil, and Christian answered as one.

Rupert caught Royce eye. "You and Minerva need to get back."

They took over and, for once, Royce let them. Devil, Rupert, Christian, Tony, and both Jacks accompanied him and Minerva back to the house, leaving the others to stage Phillip's accident. Royce knew what they would do; the gorge was both close and convenient, and disguising the knife wound as a wound from a sharp stick wouldn't be hard – but he appreciated their tact in not discussing the details in front of Minerva.

She hurried beside him, her skirts looped over her arm so they could stride faster.

The instant they came within sight of the house, the ladies – who had been banned absolutely from setting foot in the gardens until their husbands returned, and who, for once, had obeyed – broke ranks and came pouring out of the north wing to meet them.

They had, it transpired, been operating in shifts – some on watch, while the others did duty in the ballroom. Letitia, Phoebe, Alice, Penny, Leonora, and Alicia had just resumed the watch – they flocked around Minerva, reporting that all was under control, that although the grandes dames were suspicious, none had yet demanded to be told what was going on, then they announced that Minerva's gown would no longer pass muster – she would have to change.

"And that," Leonora declared, "is our perfect excuse for where you've been. This gown looks so delicate, no one will be surprised that you've chosen to change, even in the middle of your wedding breakfast."

"But we'll have to make it quick." Alice beckoned them back into the house. "Let's go."

In a flurry of silks and satins, the ladies whisked Minerva up the west turret stairs.

Royce and the other men exchanged glances, drew in deep breaths, then headed back to the ballroom. Pausing before the door, they donned expressions of relaxed jocularity, then, with a nod, Royce led them back into the melee.

No one knew, no one guessed; gradually all those involved slipped back into the ballroom, the men returning in jovial groups of three or more, the ladies ferrying Minerva back, ready with their tale to explain her absence.

And if the grandes dames wondered why Royce thereafter kept Minerva so closely beside him, why he so often drew her within the circle of his arm, if they wondered why she showed no inclination to stray, but instead often touched a hand to his arm, none of them voiced so much as a vague query.

The wedding celebrations of the tenth Duke and Duchess of Wolverstone were widely reported to have passed joyously, and – sadly for the gossipmongers – entirely without incident.

About a third of the guests left late that afternoon. It was evening before Royce and Minerva could disappear, could close the door of his sitting room on the world – and finally take stock.

She halted in the middle of the room, stood for one moment, then drew in a huge breath, raised her head, whirled – and plowed her fist into his arm. "Don't you *dare* do such a thing again!"

As immovable as rock, and equally impassive, he merely looked down at her, arched an arrogant brow.

She wasn't having that. She narrowed her eyes on his, stepped close and pointed a finger at his nose. "Don't you *dare* pretend you don't know what I'm talking about. What sort of maniac *invites* a deranged killer to shoot him?"

For a long moment, he looked down at her, then, his eyes locked on hers, he caught her hand, raised it, and pressed a kiss to her palm. "A maniac who loves you. To the depths of his cold, hardened, uninformed heart."

Her lungs seized. She searched his eyes, replayed his words – savored the certainty that rang in them. Then she drew in a shaky breath, nodded. "I'm glad you've realized that. Phillip was useful for that much, at least."

His lips quirked, but then he sobered. "Phillip." He shook his head, his expression turning grim. "I suspected the last traitor was someone I knew, but . . ."

"You never imagined the traitor had become a traitor *because* of you, so you never suspected anyone so close." She stepped back, with the hand he still held drew him with her. "There's more – Phillip ranted a lot while he was waiting for me to recover. I already had, but was pretending to be unconscious, so I heard. Come and sit down, and I'll tell you. You need to hear."

He sank heavily into one of the armchairs, pulled her down onto his lap. "Tell me."

Leaning against his chest, his arms around her, she recounted as much as she could remember.

"So it was his father's and my grandfather's attention he craved?"

"Not just their attention – their appreciation and acknowledgment that he was your equal. He felt . . . impotent when it came to them – no matter what he did, what he achieved, they never noticed him."

Royce shook his head. "I never saw it." He grimaced. "At least not that they lauded me and not Phillip, but I was rarely there to hear either." He shook his head again. "My uncle and grandfather would be horrified to know they were the cause of such traitorous acts."

"The underlying cause," she sternly corrected him. "*They*

were entirely unwitting – it was Phillip's mania, first to last. He twisted his mind – no one else can be blamed."

He cocked a brow at her. "Not even me?"

"Least of all you."

The fierceness in her tone, in her eyes as she turned her head to meet his, warmed him.

Then she frowned. "One thing I've been puzzling over – if Phillip wanted you dead, and he definitely did, more than anything else, then why did he help rescue you from the river? Surely it would have been easy to miss catching you, and then your death would have been a sad accident."

He sighed. "In hindsight, I think he did intend to let me drown. He couldn't not help in the rescue because all the others were there, but by being the last in the line . . ." He tightened his arms about her, as ever anchored by her warmth, her physical presence. "At the time, I thought I wouldn't be able to reach his hand. It was just out of my reach – or so I thought. In desperation I made a herculean effort – and managed to grab his wrist. And once I had, he couldn't easily have broken my hold – not without being obvious. So he had to pull me in – an opportunity he missed, by pure luck."

Her head shifted against his coat as she shook it. "No. You weren't meant to die – he was. His time for being the last traitor had run out."

He let her certainty seep into him, soothing, reassuring. Then he shifted. "Incidentally . . ." Reaching into his pocket, he withdrew her knife. Held it up where both of them could see it. "This, as I recall, was once mine."

She took it, turned it in her hands. "Yes, it was."

"What on earth made you wear it – today, of all days?"

He'd tipped his head so he could see her face. Her lips curved in pure affection. "_'Something old, something new, something borrowed, something blue.' I had the crown as something very old, my gown as the new, my mother's wedding favor as something borrowed, but I didn't have anything blue." She pointed to the cornflower-blue sapphire set in the dagger's hilt. "Except for this – and it seemed oddly fitting." Her smile deepened; slanting her eyes sideways, she caught his gaze. "I thought of you discovering it when we came back here to continue our celebrations."

He laughed; he hadn't thought it possible after all that had happened, but the look in her eyes – the pure suggestion – made him laugh. He refocused on the blade. "I gave it to you when you were what? Nine?"

"Eight. You were sixteen. You gave it to me that summer and taught me how to throw it."

"There was an element of blackmail involved, as I recall."

She snorted. "You were sixteen – there was a girl involved. Not me."

He remembered, smiled. "The blacksmith's daughter. It's coming back to me."

Minerva eyed his smile, waiting . . . he saw her looking, quirked an arrogantly amused brow. She smiled back – intently. "Keep remembering."

She watched as he did. His smile faltered, then disappeared.

Expression inscrutable, he met her eyes. "You never told me how much you actually saw."

It was her turn to smile in fond reminiscence. "Enough." She added, "Enough to know your technique has improved significantly since then."

"I should bloody well hope so. That was twenty-one years ago."

"And you haven't been living in a monastery."

He ignored that. Frowned. "Another thing I didn't think to ask all those years ago – did you often follow me?"

She shrugged. "Not when you rode – you would have seen me."

A short silence ensued, then he quietly asked, "How often did you spy on me?"

She glanced at his face, arched a brow. "You're starting to look as stunned as you did in the mill."

He met her eyes. "It's a reaction to the revelation that I was singlehandedly if unwittingly responsible for my wife's extensive sexual education at a precocious age."

412

She smiled. "You don't seem to have any objection to the outcome."

He hesitated, then said, "Just tell me one thing – it was singlehandedly, wasn't it?"

She laughed, leaned back in his arms. "I may have been precocious, but I was only interested in you."

He humphed, hugged her tight.

After a moment, he nuzzled her neck. "Perhaps it's time I reminded you of some of the technical improvements I've assimilated over the years."

"Hmm. Perhaps." She shifted sinuously against him, her derriere caressing his erection. "And perhaps you might include something new, something more novel and adventurous." Glancing over her shoulder, she caught his eye. "Perhaps you should extend my horizons."

Her tone made that last an imperious, definitely duchessy demand.

He laughed and rose, sweeping her up in his arms. He carried her into the bedroom; halting beside the bed with her cradled in his arms, he looked down. Met her eyes. Held them. "I love you – I really do." The words were low, heartfelt, resonating with feeling – with discovery, joy, and unfettered belief. "Even when you refuse to do as I say – perhaps even because you refused to look away, to not see the violent side of me."

Her words were as heartfelt as his. "I love all of you – your worst, your best, and everything in between." Laying a palm against his cheek, she smiled into his eyes. "I even love your temper."

He snorted. "I should have you put that in writing."

She laughed, reached further, and drew his head to hers. He kissed her, followed her down as he laid her on his bed, on the crimson-and-gold brocade.

His. His duchess.

His life. His all.

Later, much later, Minerva lolled naked on the crimson silk sheets, and watched the last of the light fade over the distant hills. Beside her, Royce lay slumped on his back, one arm crooked behind his head, the other draped loosely around her.

He was at peace, and so was she. She was precisely where she was meant to be.

His parents, she thought, would have been pleased; she'd fulfilled her vows to them – quite possibly in the way they'd always intended. They'd known her well, and, she'd come to realize, had understood Royce better than he'd known.

She stirred, shifting closer to his muscled body – a body she'd explored at length, claimed beyond question, and now considered uniquely hers. Eyes still on the far-reaching view, she murmured, "Hamish told me that love was a disease, and you could tell who'd caught it by looking for the symptoms."

Even though she couldn't see it, she knew his lips curved.

"Hamish is frequently a font of worldly wisdom. But don't tell him I said that."

"I love you." A statement, no longer any great revelation.

"I know."

"When did you know?" One thing she'd yet to discover. "I tried so hard to deny it, to hide it – to call it something else." She turned in his arms to look into his face. "What did I do that first made you suspect that I felt anything at all for you?"

"I knew . . ." He brought his gaze down to meet her eyes. "The afternoon that I arrived back here, when I realized you'd polished my armillary spheres."

She arched her brows, considered, then persisted, "And now I know that *you* know you love me."

"Hmm." The sound was full of purring content.

"So confess – when did you first realize?"

His lips curved; drawing the arm from behind his head, he caught a stray lock of her hair, gently tucked it behind her ear. "I knew I felt *something*, more or less from that first night. It kept getting stronger, no matter what I did, but I didn't realize, didn't even imagine, for obvious reasons, that it might be love. I thought it was . . . lust at first, then caring, then a whole host of similar, connected emotions, most of which I wasn't in the habit of feeling. Yet I knew what they were, I could name them, but I didn't know it was love that made me feel them." He looked into her eyes. "Until today, I didn't know that I loved you – that I would, without thought or hesitation, lay down my life for you."

Through her happiness, she managed a frown. "Incidentally, I was serious. Don't ever, *ever* do that again – put your life before mine. Why would I want to live if you die?" She narrowed her eyes on his. "Much as I value the sentiment – and I do, nothing more highly – promise me you will never give up your life for mine."

He held her gaze steadily, as serious as she. "If you promise not to get caught by a murderous maniac."

She thought, then nodded. "I'll promise that, as far as I'm able."

"Then I'll promise what you ask, as far as *I'm* able."

She looked into his dark eyes, and knew that would never hold. "Humph!"

Royce grinned, bent, and kissed her nose. "Go to sleep."

That was one order he seemed always to get away with. As if she'd heard his thought, she humphed again, less forcefully, and snuggled down, within his arm, her head on his shoulder, her hand over his heart.

He felt her relax, felt the soothing warmth of her sink to his marrow, reassuring, almost stroking, the primitive being within.

Closing his eyes, he let sleep creep up, in, over him.

In the now peaceful stillness of his mind, the thought that had jarred and jangled as, weeks before, he'd raced back to Wolverstone to bury his father and assume the ducal mantle echoed, reminded him of the uncertainties, the loneliness, he'd left behind.

Since then, through Minerva, Fate had laid her hands on him. Now, at long last, he could surrender; at last he was at peace.

At last he could love, had found his love, and his love had found him.

It wasn't supposed to have been like this.

That's what he had thought, but now he knew better.

This was precisely how it *was* supposed to be.

Something New From

Stephanie

LAURENS

Four ex-Guardsmen on a deadly mission from India
to England, carrying vital evidence to convict a powerful
fiend to the Duke of Wolverstone, aka Dalziel.

Four ladies unwittingly caught up
in their dangerous journeys.

The members of the Bastion Club waiting at four
English ports to assist in repelling the enemy.

The Cynsters, all six cousins and their wives, gathered for
Christmas at Somersham Place, as the first ex-Guardsman
and Devil Cynster's close friend draws near . . .

This Cynster Christmas is sure to be filled with
excitement, adventure – and passion.

LOOK FOR THE FIRST VOLUME IN THE
BLACK COBRA QUARTET

The Untamed Bride

ON SHELVES EVERYWHERE OCTOBER 27, 2009

For more details on The Black Cobra Quartet visit
www.stephanielaurens.com.

The following is a preview of

Temptation and Surrender

The newest Cynster novel
from *New York Times* bestselling author

Stephanie

LAURENS

On sale in paperback September 29, 2009
from

Piatkus Books

I feel like tearing my hair out – not that that would do any good."

The dark hair in question fell in elegantly unruly locks about Jonas Tallent's handsome head. His brown eyes filled with disgusted irritation, he slumped back in the armchair behind the desk in the library of the Grange, the paternal home he would eventually inherit, a fact that accounted in multiple ways for his current, sorely frustrated state.

At ease in the chair facing the desk, Lucifer Cynster, Jonas's brother-in-law, smiled in wry commisseration. "Without intending to add to the burden weighing so heavily upon you, I feel I should mention that expectations are only rising with the passage of time."

Jonas humphed. "Hardly surprising – Juggs' demise, while being no loss whatsoever, has raised the specter of something better at the Red Bells. When Edgar found the old sot dead in a puddle of ale, I swear the entire village heaved a sigh of relief – and then immediately fell to speculating on what might be if the Red Bells had a *competent* innkeeper."

Juggs had been the innkeeper of the Red Bells for nearly a

decade; he'd been found dead by the barman, Edgar Hills, two months ago.

Jonas settled deeper into his chair. "I have to admit I was first among the speculators, but that was before Uncle Martin expired of overwork and the pater went off to sort out Aunt Eliza and her horde, leaving the matter of the new incumbent at the Red Bells in my lap."

If truth be told, he'd welcomed the opportunity to return from London and assume full management of the estate. He'd been trained to the task throughout his youth, and while his father was still hale, he was becoming less robust; his unexpected and likely to be lengthy absence had seemed the perfect opportunity to step in and take up the reins.

That, however, hadn't been the principal reason he'd so readily kicked London's dust from his heels.

Over the last months he'd grown increasingly disaffected with the life he'd more or less fallen into in town. The clubs, the theaters, the dinners and balls, the soirees and select gatherings – the bucks and bloods, and the haughty matrons so many of whom were only too happy to welcome a handsome, independently wealthy, well bred gentleman into their beds.

When he'd first gone on the town, shortly after Phyllida, his twin sister, had married Lucifer, a life built around such diversions had been his goal. With his innate and inherited attributes – and, courtesy of his connection with Lucifer the imprimatur of the Cynsters – achieving all he'd desired hadn't been all that hard. However, having attained his goal and moved in tonnish circles for the past several years, he'd discovered that life on that gilded stage left him hollow, strangely empty.

Unsatisfied. Unfulfilled.

In reality, unengaged.

He'd been very ready to come home to Devon and assume control of the Grange and the estate while his father hied to Norfolk to support Eliza in her time of need.

He'd wondered whether life in Devon, too, would now feel empty, devoid of challenge. In the back of his mind had hovered the question of whether the deadening void within was entirely an effect of tonnish life or, far more worrying, was the symptom of some deeper inner malaise.

Within days of returning to the Grange he'd been reassured on that point at least. His life was suddenly overflowing with purpose. He hadn't had a moment when one challenge or another hadn't been front and center before him, clamoring for attention. Demanding action. Since returning home and seeing his father off, he'd barely had time to think.

That unsettling sense of disconnection and emptiness had evaporated, leaving only a novel restlessness beneath.

He no longer felt useless – clearly the life of a country gentleman, the life he'd been born and bred to, was his true calling – yet still there was something missing from his life.

Currently, however, it was the missing link at the Red Bells Inn that most severely exercised him. Replacing the unlamented Juggs had proved to be very far from a simple matter.

He shook his head in disgusted disbelief. "Whoever would have imagined finding a decent innkeeper would prove so damned difficult?"

"How far afield have you searched?"

"I've had notices posted throughout the shire and beyond – as far as Plymouth, Bristol, and Southampton." He pulled a face. "I could send to one of the London agencies, but we did that last time and they landed us with Juggs. If I had my choice, I'd have a local in the job, or at least a Westcountryman." Determination hardening his face, he sat up. "And if I can't have that, then at the very least I want to interview the applicant before I offer them the job. If we'd seen Juggs before the agency hired him, we'd never have contemplated foisting him on the village."

His long legs stretched before him, still very much the startlingly handsome, dark-haired devil who years before had made the ton's matrons swoon, Lucifer frowned. "It seems odd you've had no takers."

Jonas sighed. "It's the village – the smallness of it – that makes all the good applicants shy away. The countering facts – that when you add the surrounding houses and estates we're a decent-sized community, and with no other inn or hostelry in the vicinty we're assured a good trade – aren't sufficient, it seems, to weigh against the drawbacks of no shops and a small population." With one long finger, he flicked a sheaf of papers. "Once they learn the truth of Colyton, all the decent applicants take flight."

He grimaced and met Lucifer's dark blue eyes. "If they're good candidates, they're ambitious, and Colyton, so they believe, has nothing to offer them by way of advancement."

Lucifer grimaced back. "It seems you're looking for a rare bird – someone capable of managing an inn who wants to live in a backwater like Colyton."

Jonas eyed him speculatively. "You live in this backwater – can I tempt you to try your hand at managing an inn?"

Lucifer's grin flashed. "Thank you, but no. I've an estate to manage, just like you."

"Quite aside from the fact neither you nor I know the first thing about the domestic side of running an inn."

Lucifer nodded. "Aside from that."

"Mind you, Phyllida could probably manage the inn with her eyes closed."

"Except she's already got her hands full."

"Thanks to you." Jonas bent a mock-censorious look on his brother-in-law. Lucifer and Phyllida already had two children – Aiden and Evan, two very active little boys – and Phyllida had recently deigned to confirm that she was carrying their third child. Despite numerous other hands always about to help, Phyllida's own hands were indeed full.

Lucifer grinned unrepentantly. "Given you thoroughly enjoy playing uncle, that condemnatory look lacks bite."

Lips twisting in a rueful smile, Jonas let his gaze fall to the small pile of letters that were all that had come of the notices with which he'd papered the shire. "It's a sad situation when the best applicant is an ex-inmate of Newgate."

Lucifer let out a bark of laughter. He rose, stretched, then smiled at Jonas. "Something – or someone – will turn up."

"I daresay," Jonas returned. "But *when*? As you pointed out, the expectations are only escalating. As the inn's owner and

424

therefore the person everyone deems responsible for fulfilling said expectations, time is not on my side."

Lucifer's smile was understanding if unhelpful. "I'll have to leave you to it. I promised I'd be home in good time to play pirates with my sons."

Jonas noted that, as always, Lucifer took special delight in saying that last word, all but rolling it on his tongue, savoring all that it meant.

With a jaunty salute, his brother-in-law departed, leaving him staring at the pile of dire applications for the post of innkeeper at the Red Bells Inn.

He wished he could leave to play pirates, too.

The thought vividly brought to mind what he knew would be waiting for Lucifer at the end of his short trek along the woodland path linking the back of the Grange to the back of Colyton Manor, the house Lucifer had inherited and now shared with Phyllida – and Aidan and Evan and a small company of staff. The manor was perennially filled with warmth and life, an energy – something tangible – that grew from shared contentment and happiness and filled the soul.

Anchored it.

While Jonas was entirely comfortable at the Grange – it was home, and the staff were excellent and had known him all his life – he was conscious – perhaps more so after his recent introspections on the shortfalls of tonnish life – of a wish that a warmth, a glow of happiness similar to that at the Manor, would take root at the Grange, and embrace him.

Fill his soul and anchor him.

For long moments, he stared unseeing across the room, then he mentally shook himself and lowered his gaze once more to the pile of useless applications.

The people of Colyton deserved a good inn.

Heaving a sigh, he shifted the pile to the middle of the blotter, and forced himself to comb through it one last time.

Emily Ann Beauregard Colyton stood just beyond the last curve in the winding drive leading to the Grange on the southern outskirts of Colyton village, and peered at the house that sat in comfortable solidity fifty yards away.

Of worn red brick, it looked peaceful, serene, its roots sunk deep in the rich soil on which it sat. Unpretentious yet carrying a certain charm, the many-gabled slate roof sat over attic windows above two stories of wider, white-painted frames. Steps led up to the front porch. From where she hovered, Em could just see the front door, sitting back in shadowed majesty.

Neatly tended gardens spread to either side of the wide front façade. Beyond the lawns to her left, she spotted a rose garden, bright splashes of color, lush and inviting, bobbing against darker foliage.

She felt compelled to look again at the paper in her hand – a copy of the notice she'd spotted on the board in the posting inn at Axminster advertising the position of innkeeper-manager of the Red Bells Inn at Colyton. When she'd first set eyes on the notice, it had seemed expressly designed to be the answer to her prayers.

She and her brother and sisters had been wasting time waiting for the merchant who'd agreed to take them on his delivery dray when he made his round to Colyton. Over the previous week and a half, ever since her twenty-fifth birthday when, by virtue of her advanced age and her late father's farsighted will, she'd assumed guardianship of her brother and three sisters, they'd traveled from her uncle's house in Leicestershire by way of London to eventually reach Axminster – and finally, via the merchant's dray, Colyton.

The journey had cost much more than she'd expected, eating all of her meager savings and nearly all of the funds – her portion of their father's estate – that their family's solicitor, Mr. Cunningham, had arranged for her to receive. He alone knew she and her siblings had upped stakes and relocated to the tiny village of Colyton, deep in rural Devon.

Their uncle, and all those he might compel or persuade to his cause – that of feathering his own nest by dint of their free labor – had not been informed of their destination.

Which meant they were once again very much on their

own – or, to be more precise, that the welfare of Isobel, Henry and the twins, Gertrude and Beatrice, now rested firmly on Em's slight shoulders.

She didn't mind the burden, not in the least; she'd taken it up willingly. Continuing a day longer than absolutely necessary in their uncle's house had been beyond impossible; only the promise of eventual, and then imminent, departure had allowed any of the five Colytons to endure for so long under Harold Potheridge's exploitative thumb, but until Em had turned twenty-five, he – their late mother's brother – had been their co-guardian along with Mr. Cunningham.

On the day of her twenty-fifth birthday, Em had legally replaced her uncle. On that day, she and her siblings had taken their few worldly possessions – they'd packed days before – and departed Runcorn, their uncle's manor house. She'd steeled herself to face her uncle and explain their decision, but as matters had transpired Harold had gone to a race meeting that day and hadn't been there to witness their departure.

All well and good, but she knew he would come after them, as far as he was able. They were worth quite a lot to him – his unpaid household staff. So travelling quickly down to London had been vital, and that had necessitated a coach and four, and that, as she'd discovered, had been expensive.

Then they'd had to cross London in hackneys, and stay two nights in a decent hotel, one in which they'd felt sufficiently safe to sleep. Although she'd thereafter economized and they'd traveled by mail-coach, what with five tickets and the necessary meals and nights at various inns, her funds had dwindled, then shrunk alarmingly.

By the time they'd reached Axminster, she'd known she, and perhaps even Issy, twenty-three years old, would need to find work, although what work they might find, daughters of the gentry that they were, she hadn't been able to imagine.

Until she'd seen the notice on the board.

She scanned her copy again, rehearsing, as she had for the past hours, the right phrases and assurances with which to convince the owner of the Grange – who was also the owner of

427

the Red Bells Inn – that she, Emily Beauregard – no one needed to know they were Colytons, at least not yet – was precisely the right person to whom he should entrust the running of his inn.

When she'd shown her siblings the notice, and informed them of her intention to apply for the position, they had – as they always did, bless them – fallen in unquestioningly and enthusiastically with her scheme. She now had in her reticule three glowing references for Emily Beauregard, written by the invented proprietors of inns they'd passed on their journey. She'd written one, Issy another, and Henry, fifteen and so painfully wanting to be helpful, had penned the third, all while they'd waited for the merchant and his dray.

The merchant had dropped them off outside the Red Bells. To her immense relief, there'd been a notice on the wall beside the door stating "Innkeeper Wanted" in bold black letters; the position hadn't yet been filled. She'd settled the others in a corner of the large common room, and given them coins enough to have glasses of lemonade. All the while she'd surveyed the inn, evaluating all she could see, noting that the shutters were in need of a coat of paint, and that the interior was sadly dusty and grimy, but there was nothing she could see amiss within doors that wouldn't yield to a cloth and a bit of determination.

She'd watched the somewhat dour man behind the bar. Although he was manning the tap, his demeanor had suggested he was thinking of other things in a rather desultory way. The notice had given an address for applications, not the inn but the Grange, Colyton, doubtless expecting said applications to come through the post. Girding her loins, hearing the crinkle of her "references" in her reticule, she'd taken the first step, walked up to the bar, and asked the man the way to the Grange.

Which was how she'd come to be there, dithering in the drive. She told herself she was only being sensible by trying to gauge the type of man the owner was by examining his house.

Older, she thought – and settled; there was something about

the house that suggested as much. Comfortable. Married for many years, perhaps a widower, or at least with a wife as old and as comfortable as he. He would be gentry, certainly, very likely of the sort they called the backbone of the counties. Paternalistic – she could be absolutely sure he would be that – which would doubtless prove useful. She would have to remember to invoke that emotion if she needed help getting him to give her the position.

She wished she'd been able to ask the barman about the owner, but given she intended to apply for the position of his superior that might have proved awkward, and she hadn't wanted to call attention to herself in any way.

The truth was she needed this position. Needed it quite desperately. Quite aside from the issue of replenishing her funds, she and her siblings needed somewhere to stay. She'd assumed there would be various types of accommodation available in the village, only to discover that the only place in Colyton able to house all five of them was the inn. And she couldn't afford to stay at any inn longer than one night.

Bad enough, but in the absence of an innkeeper, the inn wasn't housing paying guests. Only the bar was operating; there hadn't even been food on offer. As an inn, the Red Bells was barely functioning – all for want of an innkeeper.

Her Grand Plan – the goal that had kept her going for the last eight years – had involved returning to Colyton, to the home of their forebears, and finding the Colyton treasure. Family lore held that the treasure, expressly hidden against the need of future generations, was hidden there, at a location handed down in a cryptic rhyme.

Her grandmother had believed unswervingly in the treasure, and had taught Em and Issy the rhyme.

Her grandfather and father had laughed. They hadn't believed.

She'd held to her belief through thick and thin; for her and Issy, and later Henry and the twins, the promise of the treasure had held them together, held their spirits up, for the past eight years.

The treasure was there. She wouldn't – couldn't – believe otherwise.

She'd never kept an inn in her life, but having run her uncle's house from attics to cellars for eight years, including the numerous weeks he'd had his bachelor friends to stay for the hunting, she was, she felt sure, more than qualified to run a quiet inn in a sleepy little village like Colyton.

How difficult could it be?

There would no doubt be minor challenges, but with Issy's and Henry's support she'd overcome them. Even the twins, ten years old and mischievous, could be a real help.

She'd hovered long enough. She had to do this – had to march up to the front door, knock, and convince the old gentleman to hire her as the new innkeeper of the Red Bells.

She and her generation of Colytons had made it to the village. It was up to her to gain them the time, and the facility, to search for and find the treasure.

To search for and secure their futures.

Drawing in a deep breath, she held it and, putting one foot determinedly in front of the other, marched steadily on down the drive.

She climbed the front steps and without giving herself even a second to think again, she raised her hand and beat a sharp rat-a-tat-tat on the white-painted front door.

Lowering her hand, she noticed a bell pull. She debated whether to tug that, too, but then approaching footsteps fixed her attention on the door.

It was opened by a butler, one of the more imposing sort. Having moved within the upper circles of York society prior to her father's death, she recognized the species. His back was ramrod straight, his girth impressive. His gaze initially passed over her head, but then lowered.

He considered her with a steady, even gaze. "Yes, miss?"

She took heart from the man's kindly mein. "I wish to speak with the owner of the Red Bells Inn. I'm here to apply for the position of innkeeper."

Surprise flitted over the butler's face, followed by a slight frown. He hesitated, regarding her, then asked, "Is this a joke, miss?"

She felt her lips tighten, her eyes narrow. "No. I'm perfectly serious." Jaw firming, she took the bull by the horns. "Yes, I know what I look like." Soft light brown hair with a tendency to curl and a face everyone – simply everyone – saw as sweet, combined with a slight stature and a height on the short side of average didn't add up to the general notion of a forceful presence – the sort needed to run an inn. "Be that as it may, I have experience aplenty, and I understand the position is still vacant."

The butler looked taken aback by her fierceness. He studied her for a moment more, taking in her high-necked olive green walking dress – she'd tidied herself as best she could while at Axminster – then asked, "If you're sure . . .?"

She frowned. "Well, of course I'm sure. I'm here, aren't I?"

He acknowledged that with a slight nod, yet still he hesitated.

She lifted her chin. "I have written references – three of them." She tapped her reticule. As she did so, memories of the inn, and the notices – and their curling edges – flashed through her mind. Fixing her gaze on the butler's face, she risked a deductive leap. "It's clear your master has had difficulty filling the position. I'm sure he wishes to have his inn operating again. Here I am, a perfectly worthy applicant. Are you sure you want to turn me away, rather than inform him I am here and wish to speak with him?"

The butler considered her with a more measuring eye; she wondered if the flash she'd seen in his eyes might have been respect.

Regardless, at long last he inclined his head. "I will inform Mr. Tallent that you are here, miss. What name shall I say?"

"Miss Emily Beauregard."

"Who?" Looking up from the depressing pile of applications, Jonas stared at Mortimer. "A young woman?"

"Well . . . a young female person, sir." Mortimer was clearly in two minds about the social standing of Miss Emily

Beauregard, which in itself was remarkable. He'd been in his present position for decades, and was well-versed in identifying the various levels of persons who presented themselves at the local magistrate's door. "She seemed . . . very set on applying for the position. I thought, all things considered, that perhaps you should see her."

Sitting back in his chair, Jonas studied Mortimer, and wondered what had got into the man. Miss Emily Beauregard had clearly made an impression, enough to have Mortimer espouse her cause. But the idea of a female managing the Red Bells . . . then again, not even half an hour ago he himself had acknowledged that Phyllida could have run the inn with barely half her highly capable brain.

The position was for an innkeeper-*manager*, after all, and certain females were very good at managing.

He sat up. "Very well. Show her in." She had to be an improvement over the applicant from Newgate.

"Indeed, sir." Mortimer turned to the door. "She said she has written references – three of them."

Jonas raised his brows. Apparently Miss Beauregard had come well-prepared.

He looked at the sheaf of applications before him, then tapped them together and set the pile aside. Not that he had any great hopes of Miss Beauregard proving the answer to his prayers; he was simply sick of looking at the dismal outcome of his recent efforts.

A footstep in the doorway had him glancing up.

A young lady stepped into the room; Mortimer hovered behind her.

Instinct took hold, bringing Jonas to his feet.

Em's first thought on setting eyes on the gentleman behind the desk in the well-stocked library was: He's too young.

Far too young to feel paternalistic toward her.

Of quite the wrong sort to feel paternalistic at all.

Unexpected – unprecedented – panic tugged at her; this man – about thirty years old and as attractive as sin – was not the sort of man she'd expected to have to deal with.

Yet there was no one else in the room, and the butler had returned from this room to fetch her; presumably he knew who she was supposed to see.

Given the gentleman, now on his feet, was staring at her, she dragged in a breath, forced her wits to steady, and grasped the opportunity to study him.

He was over six feet tall, long limbed and rangy; broad shoulders stretched his well-cut coat. Dark, sable-brown hair fell in elegantly rumpled locks about a well-shaped head; his features bore the aquiline cast common among the aristocracy, reinforcing her increasing certainty that the owner of the Grange sat rather higher on the social scale than a mere squire.

His face was riveting. Dark brown eyes, more alive than soulful, well set under dark slashes of brows, commanded her attention even though he hadn't yet met her gaze. He was looking *at* her, at all of her; she saw his gaze travel down her frame, and had to suppress an unexpected shiver.

She drew in another breath, held it. Absorbed the implication of a broad forehead, a strong nose and an even stronger, squarish jaw, all suggesting strength of character, firmness, and resolution.

His lips ... were utterly, comprehensively distracting. Narrowish, their lines hinted at a mobility that would soften the angular, almost austere planes of his face.

She dragged her gaze from them, lowering it to take in his subtle sartorial perfection. She'd seen London dandies before, and while he wasn't in any way overdressed, his clothes were of excellent quality, his cravat expertly tied in a deceptively simple knot.

Beneath the fine linen of his shirt, his chest was well-muscled, but he was all lean sleekness. As he came to life and slowly, smoothly, moved around the desk, he reminded her of a predatory animal, one that stalked with a dangerous, overtly athletic grace.

She blinked. Couldn't help asking, "You're the owner of the Red Bells Inn?"

433

He halted by the front corner of the desk and finally met her gaze.

She felt as if something hot had pierced her, making her breath hitch.

"I'm Mr. Tallent – Mr. Jonas Tallent." His voice was deep but clear, his accents the clipped speech of their class. "My father's Sir Jasper Tallent, owner of the inn. He's currently away and I'm managing the estate in his absence. Please – take a seat."

Jonas waved her to the chair before his desk. He had to stifle the urge to go forward and hold it while she sat.

If she'd been a man, he would have left her standing, but she wasn't a man. She was definitely female. The thought of having her standing before him while he sat and read her references and interrogated her about her background was simply unacceptable.

She subsided, with a practised hand tucking her olive green skirts beneath her. Over her head he met Morti_mer's gaze. He now understood Mortimer's hesitation in labeling Miss Beauregard a "young woman." Whatever else Miss Emily Beauregard was, she was a lady.

Her antecedents were there in every line of her slight form, in every unconsciously graceful movement. She possessed a small-boned, almost delicate frame; her face was heart-stoppingly fine, with a pale, blush cream porcelain complexion and features that – if he'd had a poetic turn of mind – he would have described as being sculpted by a master.

Lush, pale rose lips were the least of them; perfectly molded, they were presently set in an uncompromising line, one he felt compelled to make soften and curve. Her nose was small and straight, her lashes long and lush, a brown fringe framing large eyes of the most vibrant hazel he'd ever seen. Those arresting eyes sat beneath delicately arched brown brows, while her forehead was framed by soft curls of gleaming light brown; she'd attempted to force her hair into a severe bun at the nape of her neck, but the shining curls had a mind of their own, escaping to curl lovingly about her face.

Her chin, gently rounded, was the only element that gave any hint of underlying strength.

As he returned to his chair, the thought uppermost in his mind was: What the devil was she doing applying to be an innkeeper?

Dismissing Mortimer with a nod, he resumed his seat. As the door gently closed, he settled his gaze on the lady before him. "Miss Beauregard –"

"I have three references you'll want to read." She was already hunting in her reticule. Freeing three folded sheets, she leaned forward and held them out.

He had to take them. "Miss Beauregard –"

"If you read them" – folding her hands over the reticule in her lap, with a nod she indicated the references – "I believe you will see that I have experience aplenty, more than enough to qualify for the position of innkeeper of the Red Bells." She didn't give him time to respond, but fixed her vivid eyes on his and calmly stated, "I believe the position has been vacant for some time."

Pinned by that direct, surprisingly acute hazel gaze, he found his assumptions about Miss Emily Beauregard subtly altering. "Indeed."

She held his gaze calmly. Appearances aside, she was clearly no meek miss.

A pregnant moment passed, then her gaze flicked down to the references in his hands, then returned to his face. "I could read those for you, if you prefer?"

He mentally shook himself. Lips firming, he looked down – and dutifully smoothed open the first folded sheet.

While he read through the three neatly folded – identically folded – sheets, she filled his ears with a litany of her virtues – her experiences managing households as well as inns. Her voice was pleasant, soothing. He glanced up now and then, struck by a slight change in her tone; after the third instance he realized the change occurred when she was speaking of some event and calling on her memory.

Those aspects of her tale, he decided, were true; she had

had experience running houses and catering for parties of guests.

When it came to her experience running inns, however . . .

"While at the Three Feathers in Hampstead, I . . ."

He looked down, again scanned the reference for her time at the Three Feathers. Her account mirrored what was written; she told him nothing more.

Glancing at her again, watching her face – an almost angelic vision – he toyed with the idea of telling her he knew her references were fake. While they were written in three different hands, he'd take an oath two were female – unlikely if they were, as stated, from the male owners of inns – and the third, while male, was not entirely consistent – a young male whose handwriting was still changing.

The most telling fact, however, was that all three references – supposedly from three geographically distant inns over a span of five years – were on the exact same paper, written in the same ink, with the same pen, one that had a slight scratch across the nib.

And they appeared the same age. Fresh and new.

Looking across his desk at Miss Emily Beauregard, he wondered why he didn't simply ring for Mortimer and have her shown out. He should – he knew it – yet he didn't.

He couldn't let her go without knowing the answer to his initial question. Why the devil was a lady of her ilk applying for a position as an innkeeper?

She eventually ended her recitation and looked at him, brows rising in faintly haughty query.

He tossed the three references on his blotter and met her bright eyes directly. "To be blunt, Miss Beauregard, I hadn't thought to give the position to a female, let alone one of your relative youth."

For a moment, she simply looked at him, then she drew in a breath and lifted her head a touch higher. Chin firming, she held his gaze. "If I may be blunt in return, Mr. Tallent, I took a quick look at the inn on my way here. The external shutters need painting, and the interior appears not to have been adequately cleaned for at least five years. No woman would sit in your common room by choice, yet it's the only public area you have. There is presently no food served at all, nor accommodation offered. In short, the inn is currently operating as no more than a bar-tavern. If you are indeed in charge of your father's estate, then you will have to admit that as an investment the Red Bells Inn is presently returning only a fraction of its true worth."

Her voice remained pleasant, her tones perfectly modulated; just like her face, it disguised the underlying strength – the underlying sharp edge.

She tilted her head, her eyes still locked with his. "I understand the inn has been without a manager for some months?"

Lips tightening, he conceded the point. "Several months."

Far too many months.

"I daresay you're keen to see it operating adequately as soon as may be, especially as I noted there is no other tavern or gathering place in the village. The locals, too, must be anxious to have their inn properly functioning again."

Why did he feel as if he were being herded?

It was plainly time to reassert control of the interview and find out what he wanted to know. "If you could enlighten me, Miss Beauregard, as to what brought you to Colyton?"

"I saw a copy of your notice at the inn in Axminster."

"And what brought you to Axminster?"

She shrugged lightly. "I was . . ." She paused, considering him, then amended, "*We* – my brother and sisters and I – were merely passing through." Her gaze flickered; she glanced down at her hands, lightly clasped on her reticule. "We've been traveling through the summer, but now it's time to get back to work."

And that, Jonas would swear, was a lie. They hadn't been traveling over summer . . . but, if he was reading her correctly, she did have a brother and sisters with her. She knew he would find out about them if she got the job, so had told the truth on that score.

A reason for her wanting the innkeeper's job flared in his

mind, growing stronger as he swiftly assessed her gown –
serviceable, good quality, but not of recent vintage. "*Younger*
brother and sisters?"

Her head came up; she regarded him closely. "Indeed." She
hesitated, then asked, "Would that be a problem? It's never
been before. They're hardly babes. The youngest is . . .
twelve."

That latter hesitation was so slight he only caught it because
he was listening as closely as she was watching him. Not
twelve – perhaps a precocious ten. "Your parents?"

"Both dead. They have been for many years."

Truth again. He was getting a clearer picture of why Emily
Beauregard wanted the innkeeper's job. But . . .

He sighed and sat forward, leaning both forearms on the
desk, loosely clasping his hands. "Miss Beauregard –"

"Mr. Tallent."

Struck by her crisp tone, he broke off and looked up, into
her bright hazel eyes.

Once he had, she continued, "I believe we've wasted
enough time in roundaboutation. The truth is you need an
innkeeper quite desperately, and here I am, willing and very
able to take on the job. Are you really going to turn me away
just because I'm female and have younger family members in
my train? My eldest sister is twenty-three, and assists me with
whatever work I undertake. Likewise my brother is fifteen, and
apart from the time given to his studies, works alongside us. My
youngest sisters are twins, and even they lend a hand. If you
hire me, you get their labor as well."

"So you and your family are a bargain?"

"Indeed, not that we work for nothing. I would expect a
salary equal to a twentieth of the takings, or a tenth of the
profits per month, and in addition to that, room and board
supplied through the inn." She rattled on with barely a pause
for breath. "I assume you wish the innkeeper to live on site. I
noticed that there's attic rooms above, which appear to be
unoccupied and would do perfectly for me and my siblings. As
we're here, I could take up the position immediately –"

"Miss Beauregard." This time he let steel infuse his voice, enough so that she stopped, and didn't try to speak over him. He caught her gaze, held it. "I haven't yet agreed to give you the position."

Her gaze didn't flinch, didn't waver. The desk may have been between them, yet it felt as if they were toe-to-toe. When she spoke, her voice was even, if tight. "You're desperate to have someone take the inn in hand. I want the job. Are you really going to turn me away?"

The question hovered between them, all but blazoned in the air. Lips thinning, he held her gaze, equally unwaveringly. He *was* desperate for any capable innkeeper – she had that right – and she was there, offering . . .

And if he turned her away, what would she do? She and her family, who she was supporting and protecting.

He didn't need to think to know she'd never turned to the petticoat line, which meant her younger sister hadn't either. What if he turned her away and she – they – were forced, at some point, to . . .

No! Taking such a risk was out of the question; he couldn't live with such a possibility on his conscience. Even if he never knew, just the thought, the chance, would drive him demented.

He narrowed his eyes on hers. It didn't sit well to be jock-eyed into hiring her, which was what she'd effectively done. Regardless . . .

Breaking eye contact, he reached for a fresh sheet of paper. Setting it on the desk, he didn't glance at her as he picked up his pen, checked the nib, then flipped open the ink pot, dipped and rapidly scrawled.

No matter that her references were fake, she was better than no one, and she wanted the job. Lord knew she was a managing enough female to get it done. He'd simply keep a very close eye on her, make sure she correctly accounted for the takings and didn't otherwise do anything untoward. He doubted she'd drink down the cellar as Juggs had.

Finishing his brief note, he blotted it, then folded it. Only then did he look up and meet her wide, now curious, eyes.

"This" – he held out the sheet – "is a note for Edgar Hills, the barman, introducing you as the new innkeeper. He and John Ostler are, at present, the only staff."

Her fingers closed about the other end of the note and her face softened. Not just her lips; her whole face softly glowed. He recalled he'd wanted to make that happen, wondered what her lips – now irresistibly appealing – would taste like . . .

She gently tugged the note, but he held on. "I'll hire you on trial for three months." He had to clear his throat before going on, "After that, if the outcome is satisfactory to all, we'll make it a permanent appointment."

He released the note. She took it, tucked it in her reticule, then looked up, met his eyes – and smiled.

Just like that, she scrambled his brains.

That's what it felt like as, still beaming, she rose – and he did, too, driven purely by instinct given none of his faculties were operating.

"Thank you." Her words were heartfelt. Her gaze – those bright hazel eyes – remained locked on his. "I swear you won't regret it. I'll transform the Red Bells into the inn Colyton village deserves."

With a polite nod, she turned and walked to the door.

Although he couldn't remember doing so, he must have tugged the bell pull because Mortimer materialized to see her out.

She left with her head high and a spring in her step, but didn't look back.

For long moments after she'd disappeared, Jonas stood staring at the empty doorway while his mind slowly reassembled.

His first coherent thought was a fervent thanks to the deity that she hadn't smiled at him when she'd first arrived.